In this irresistibly seductive new book, Louisa Burton extends her most provocative invitation yet to the infamous Castle of the Hidden Grotto—a voluptuous sanctuary of pleasure and passion.

Whispers of the Flesh

Hidden in a deep mountain valley in rural France is an ancient castle known only to an exclusive few. Here, four exquisitely beautiful immortals who thrive on carnal energy captivate and ravish their human visitors, fulfilling their darkest fantasies, their most secret hungers.

A chaste young British Jesuit poses as a landscaper to investigate centuries of rumored wickedness at the château, forcing him to confront the long-sublimated desires and urges seething beneath his own pious exterior.... The American daughter of the château's dying administrator can't bear the thought of succeeding her father, since it would mean playing matchmaker to the love of her life. The roots of her dilemma, and its possible solution, hark back to a weekend in 1972 when a group of free-loving hippies descended on the château for a few days of orgiastic revelry, where every convention was broken and nothing was taboo.

Step into the Castle of the Hidden Grotto and lose yourself in a realm of mystery, temptation, and intoxicating sensuality.

ALSO BY LOUISA BURTON

Bound in Moonlight
House of Dark Delights

Book 3 in the Hidden Grotto Series

Whispers
of the
Flesh

Louisa Burton

BANTAM BOOKS

WHISPERS OF THE FLESH
A Bantam Book / October 2008

Published by Bantam Dell
A Division of Random House, Inc.
New York, New York

All rights reserved
Copyright © 2008 by Louisa Burton
Cover design by Jorge Martinez
Cover illustration by Ben Perini

Bantam Books and the rooster colophon are registered trademarks
of Random House, Inc.

Library of Congress Cataloging-in-Publication Data

Burton, Louisa.
Whispers of the flesh / Louisa Burton.
p. cm. — (The Hidden Grotto series ; bk. 3)
ISBN 978-0-553-38530-4 (trade pbk.)
1. Castles—France—Fiction. I. Title.

PS3602.U7698W47 2008
813'.6—dc22
2008013063

Printed in the United States of America
Published simultaneously in Canada

www.bantamdell.com

BVG 10 9 8 7 6 5 4 3 2 1

*For my editor, Shauna Summers, whose insight
added immeasurably to the story you're about to read*

Certain Devils

There is, too, a very general rumor, which many have verified by their own experience, or which trustworthy persons who have heard the experience of others corroborate, that sylvans and fauns, who are commonly called "incubi," had often made wicked assaults upon women, and satisfied their lust upon them; and that certain devils, called Duses by the Gauls, are constantly attempting and effecting this impurity is so generally affirmed, that it were impudent to deny it.

St. Augustine, The City of God, *Book XV, Chapter 23*

Yet Clare's sharp questions must I shun—
Must separate Constance from the nun.
Oh! what a tangled web we weave,
When first we practise to deceive!
A Palmer too!—no wonder why
I felt rebuked beneath his eye . . .

Sir Garvey Scott, Marmion, *Canto VI, Stanza XVII*

One

October 1829

"YOU WANT HIM," Elic murmured into Lili's ear.

Lili, lounging next to him on a damask and gilt chaise in *le Salon Ambre*, lifted her after-dinner brandy to her lips with a silky smile that was answer enough. "Shh . . . He'll hear."

Elic glanced across the candlelit room at the object of their attention, a grave young Englishman with large, watchful eyes. At the moment, he was rhapsodizing in his native tongue about the "rich volcanic soil" of Vallée de la Grotte Cachée while Archer listened raptly and Inigo, ever the peacock in a green and gold brocade waistcoat, his mop of black curls riotously unbound, stifled a yawn.

"I say, Beckett," Elic interjected when their visitor paused to take a breath. "Do you have any French?"

Beckett blinked at Elic, took a puff of his cigar, and said, "I confess, I never read it in school."

"How very curious," Lili said in that velvety, exotically accented voice that still, after all these years, sent a hot shiver of desire humming through Elic. "I thought all gently bred Englishmen knew French—not that I've any objection to conversing in English. It is quite as beautiful a language, in its own way."

"You're fucking him with your eyes," Elic told Lili in the French that had long ago replaced the languages of their birth.

"Can you blame me?" Darius leapt onto her lap, curled up in the crackling nest of her skirts, and yawned, displaying a mouthful of needle-sharp teeth. She glided her fingers through his dusky fur as she smiled at David Beckett.

"Can't quite see the appeal," Elic muttered. It wasn't true, of course. Beckett was a darkly handsome man with a stalwart physique set off to damnable advantage by a well-cut black tailcoat. And there was a certain stillness about him, a sense of strong feelings kept under wraps, that imparted a hint of the mysterious.

"Such lies are beneath you," Lili told Elic as she stroked Darius beneath his chin. "And your jealousy is absurd, my love, considering how many bedmates we've shared over the years. Absurd and surprising. Quite unlike you, really."

Turning away from Elic quite deliberately, she apologized to Beckett, in English, for having conducted that exchange in a language he couldn't understand.

The young man met Lili's eyes for a lightning-quick moment, then lowered his gaze to his brandy, which he swirled in a way that was meant to look thoughtful—though to Elic, it bespoke a deep discomfiture. He actually appeared to be blushing, though it was difficult to tell in the wavering candlelight.

From the moment David Beckett had been introduced to Lili upon his arrival that afternoon at Château de la Grotte Cachée, he had seemed gripped by an uneasy entrancement. It was hardly an unusual reaction among male visitors to the château. Ilutu-Lili, with her lustrous black hair, slumberous eyes, and easy sensuality, had a bewitching effect on men.

She had certainly bewitched Elic; for eighty years he had been caught in her spell. Tonight, with her hair secured by a diamond-crusted comb in a knot of loops and tumbling curls, her shoulders bared by the wide, sloping neckline of her gown—a confection of garnet silk with billowy gigot sleeves and a hand-span waist—she looked the very image of the goddess she truly was.

"What language *did* you study?" Elic asked Beckett.

"I've taken classes in Latin, Greek, Italian, and Hebrew, though of those tongues, the only ones of which I have a true command are Latin and Italian."

"Quite the well-schooled gardener," Elic said.

The taunt earned him a look of surprised amusement from Inigo and scowls from Archer and Lili. Beckett's gaze lit on Lili before returning to Elic, whom he studied for a long, hushed moment.

Shifting his lantern jaw uneasily, Archer said, "I would, er, hardly call our guest a gardener, given the scope of his expertise and the rather ambitious nature of his work."

Bartholomew Archer had just the year before succeeded his father as *administrateur* to Théophile Morel, Seigneur des Ombres, the elderly lord of Grotte Cachée and *gardien* to Elic and his three fellow Follets. Tall and thin as lath, the timorous Brit had yet to grow comfortable in his role as steward of Grotte Cachée; Elic wondered if he ever would.

Archer said, "I should think Mr. Beckett would be more correctly termed, er . . . a horticulturist."

Beckett said, "On the contrary, Mr. Archer, I infer no shame in the title of gardener. Humphrey Repton, who gave me my initial instruction in this field, styled himself a 'landscape gardener.' I am content to be called the same."

"Humphrey Repton trained you?" Archer said. "I'm impressed."

"Never heard of him," said Inigo, who, having a remarkable facility with languages, spoke English with no trace at all of an accent. Of Greek extraction, he had traveled all over the known world before being recruited in A.D. 14 to pose for the bathhouse statues at Grotte Cachée. He'd made his home there ever since.

Archer said, "Repton was famous for designing, or re-designing, the grounds of some of the finest estates in Britain. How came you to apprentice with him, Beckett?"

"I would hardly call it an apprenticeship," Beckett replied. "I was twelve years old at the time. My father had engaged him to devise a plan for improving the park and gardens at the country house he'd just purchased, which had been neglected for decades. This was in the late summer of 1816, two years before Mr. Repton went to his maker. He'd been injured in a carriage accident, so he needed a wheelchair to get around, and I used to push it for him while he sketched panoramic vistas. His aim was to create a natural but picturesque landscape, and he had impeccable instincts. He turned twelve-hundred dreary, over-grown acres into a veritable paradise. Whole areas were excavated and transformed, hundreds of trees were cut and planted, terraces were built, flower gardens installed."

Archer said, "I've seen Repton's work at Blaise Castle—extraordinary."

"How did he manage such rigorous work, being in a wheelchair?" Inigo asked.

"Oh, he didn't actually execute his designs," Beckett replied. "He was more of an advisor, coming up with the plans and leaving it to his clients to arrange for the actual work."

"Mr. Beckett works in much the same manner," Archer told the assembled company. "During his stay with us, he will inspect the grounds surrounding the castle and devise a scheme for improving them. Upon his return to England, he will prepare a book of notes, plans, and pictures in order that we may implement his ideas."

"It is a method I've borrowed from Mr. Repton," Beckett said. "For each client, he created what he called a 'Red Book,' because it was bound in red leather. The book would contain descriptions of what should be done, including detailed illustrations in watercolor depicting the grounds as they then existed, with vellum overlays showing how that particular area would look should his suggestions be implemented. When Mr. Repton discovered my aptitude for drawing and painting, he allowed me to help him with that end of things, and I found it fascinating. For years after that, I read everything I could get my hands on that had to do with botany, floriculture, architecture . . . And I painted landscapes, as Mr. Repton had advised, to help develop my sense of natural aesthetics."

"You made a study of these things at university, I suppose?" Lili asked him as she scratched the purring Darius behind his ears.

"I confess I did not. I say, what an agreeable cat. My mother had one, but it hissed at me whenever I would try to pick it up."

"I am afraid my friend here will do the same," Lili warned. "He might even bite you should you get too close. He hates being touched by strangers."

"What *did* you study?" Elic asked Beckett.

The young man pinned Elic with a brief, trenchant look, as if sizing him up. "It had always been assumed that I would read theology."

Elic hated the way Lili gazed at Beckett, her eyes sparking, her color high. He didn't blame her for her appetites; she could no more ignore them than he could ignore his own. But when the object of that hunger held her in such utter thrall, when there was little doubt just how desperately she ached to possess him, it incited in Elic a primal, almost human covetousness. There was no restraining her when her lust for an exceptionally desirable male—a *gabru* in her extinct Akkadian tongue—ran this hot, no way to keep her from stealing into his bedchamber during the night and ravishing him as he lay immobilized, or partially so, by one of her ancient Babylonian spells.

Were Elic capable of making love to Lili—really making love—he might have some chance of keeping her all to himself. As an *álfr*, he should have been able to bed humans and Follets alike, but a chance dusian mutation had skewed his elfin physiology in the womb. No dusios could ease his constant, seething lust save between the legs of a human female. It was a factor in the blood itself, which would literally recoil, draining from his organ the moment he attempted to penetrate a non-human. No blood, no erection. No erection, no intercourse.

Regardless of how aroused Lili made him, how achingly hard, the moment he tried to enter her, he would wilt. He could pleasure her only with his hands and his mouth, although from time to time he would join her when she took her human quarry, caressing her, kissing her, and whispering his love into her ear as she thrashed for hours atop her groaning, lust-crazed *gabru*.

"Theology, eh?" Lili said. "You would be the second son, then, Mr. Beckett? Destined for the ministry?"

"The fourth son, actually. And, er, it was the priesthood, not the ministry."

"My apologies," she said. "One tends to think of all Englishmen as Anglican. A thoughtless presumption."

"Not at all, quite understandable."

"You seem to have managed to forge your own way despite parental expectations," Inigo observed. "Are they miffed that you didn't join the Church?"

Choosing his words with seeming care, Beckett said, "They are content with the path I've chosen."

"So, Beckett," Elic said. "I cannot help but wonder what your connection to the archbishop might be."

The young man stilled in the act of lifting his snifter to his mouth, his gaze darting toward Elic and then away. He rolled the ash off the tip of his cigar, a Cuban from his own supply with a distinctive aroma that evoked whispers of frankincense and coffee. Elic, blessed and cursed with a bloodhound's sense of smell, could also detect, beneath the whiff of fragrant smoke, the Castile soap with which Beckett had recently bathed, the waxy blacking that glossed his fine shoes, and the fresh sweat with which his face was sheened; curious, since it was a cool evening.

Beckett took so long to compose his thoughts that Archer answered for him.

"As I understand it," the *administrateur* began, "Archbishop Bélanger retained Mr. Beckett's services on the advice of friends in England, so the connection would be professional rather than . . . shall we say, convivial."

It had been at a formal dinner recently hosted by Monseigneur Bélanger for the local personages of note that Archer, who'd attended in Seigneur des Ombres's stead, had made the acquaintance of David Beckett. Intrigued by the young Englishman's proposal for enhancing the archbishop's property, and nostalgic for the verdant and artless gardens of his homeland, Archer had convinced *le seigneur* to invite Beckett to Grotte Cachée.

"When I spoke of a connection to the archbishop," Elic said, "I meant the Archbishop of Canterbury under Henry the Second. It occurred to me that there might be a relation between Thomas Becket and our Catholic gardener of the same name."

"Would that I could claim such an illustrious association," Beckett said.

"How long will we have the pleasure of your company, Mr. Beckett?" Lili asked with a smile that made Elic clench his jaw.

"Less than a week, I'm afraid, so I shall be a very busy man."

Archer said, "I have explained to Mr. Beckett that a sovereign from the East who visits occasionally shall arrive one week from today with his sizable household, and that he will expect to have the château to himself."

What he didn't say was that the "sovereign from the East" was Fadullah the Noble, an Ottoman pasha with an appetite for watching, and that only part of Fadullah's vast household would be accompanying him on this visit—one or two trusted retainers, the most discreet of his servants and eunuchs, and whichever members of his harem he wanted to observe being fucked by other men—specifically, by Elic and Inigo.

"Will six days be enough time for you to come up with a landscaping proposal?" Archer asked his guest.

"It will be if I make efficient use of my time," Beckett said. "Tomorrow afternoon, I shall begin surveying and sketching the grounds, and that will give me a rough idea of the areas that might benefit from a more picturesque approach."

"I can't imagine there's much at Grotte Cachée that wants improvement," Elic said. "You will find little to keep you here, I think."

Lili, clearly put off by his tone, moved away from him in a subtle but stingingly eloquent gesture. She and Darius shared a look. Such petty sniping was out of character for Elic.

Archer said, "It might help to have a bit of guidance on your tour, Mr. Beckett. I've other obligations tomorrow afternoon, but I could show you 'round in the morning."

Shaking his head, Beckett said, "I must go to Clermont-Ferrand in the morning in order to mail a letter."

"Give it to me now, and I shall have someone mail it tomorrow," Archer said.

"It . . . has not been written yet," Beckett said. "I shall write it tonight, and . . . I've other business in town, in any event, things I must buy—more vellum, another sketchbook . . ."

"Very well," Archer said. "I must caution you, though, should you care to explore our cave, as many guests do, not to venture in too far past the bathhouse."

In response to Beckett's look of puzzlement, Archer said, "The Romans who occupied this valley around the time of Christ built a bathhouse on the side of an extinct volcano, which we call Alp Albiorix—its old Gaulish name—so as to take advantage of the cave stream flowing from within. It is quite a lovely little edifice, all of white marble save the back wall, where the entrance to the cave is. It would be prudent, should you decide to have a look in there, to stay within a quarter mile or so of the entrance, where the lamps are. Past that, it becomes a veritable labyrinth. Quite easy to lose one's way, and if you do . . . well. There is no assurance that you will ever be found."

"I shall bear that in mind, Mr. Archer. And now, if you will all forgive me, gentlemen . . . Miss Lili . . ." Beckett stood and bowed in Lili's direction, "I regret that the hour has come when I must retire to my chamber. The letter of which I spoke will be a lengthy one, and all I really want is a good night's sleep."

"May you get your wish, Mr. Beckett," said Lili, her gaze following him as he crossed to the door. "Pleasant dreams."

Two

My Lord Bishop,

This dispatch will serve, I trust, as an account of the progress thus far of my inquiries on behalf of your Lordship and of our superiors in Rome and France. You will be gratified, I think, to know that I am presently ensconced in a guest chamber of Château de la Grotte Cachée, having successfully drawn upon the horticultural expertise I acquired before entering seminary to adopt the guise of a landscape gardener.

This fortnight past I have enjoyed the hospitality of Archbishop Bélanger at his own remarkably beautiful château in the region of Auvergne, where his secretary made me privy to allegations dating back some six centuries of strange happenings in and around Grotte Cachée. Notable amongst these were reputed acts of extraordinary wickedness and lechery committed there by certain individuals whose descriptions and actions would suggest a diabolical nature.

Such accusations have generally been regarded as heated imaginings, and therefore rarely committed to writing save for the most cursory of notations. As a consequence, there exist few pieces of written evidence detailed enough to be of use for our purposes. Per Cardinal Lazzari's instructions, I penned but one copy, translated into Italian, of each of these documents, which I shall dispatch to Rome for His Eminence's inspection on the morrow. First, however, I shall summarize them frankly herein, transcribing verbatim the most condemnatory passages. I do so, I need hardly say, at the express direction of your Lordship, much as it appalls me to relate incidents of such an impure stripe.

The earliest of the written accounts, which is undated but believed to have been recorded in the late 13th century, is a description in Latin by a parish priest of events related to him—not, I hasten to add, under the seal of confession—by a young woman named Fabrisse who had served briefly as a chambermaid at Château de la Grotte Cachée. She gave distraught testimony of having witnessed a libidinous interlude involving four men and a woman engaging in "deplorable acts of sodomy." Particularly distressing to her was the fact that the men were visiting Knights Templar, one of them the Grand Master himself. Fabrisse was deeply disillusioned, having been reared to revere the Templars as upstanding soldiers of Christ.

Following the evening meal, the knights and the woman, a comely, fair-haired resident of the château whom Fabrisse knew to be a wanton despite her aristocratic bearing, amused themselves by playing chess in the great hall.

The priest recorded Fabrisse's account thusly:

"The woman, having been the victor in a match against one of the knights, declared that she could vanquish them all, and that

*should she fail to do so, she would relieve the lust of every man in
the room. The knights looked to their commander, who eagerly
accepted the challenge. The lady won the second and third matches,
but lost the fourth, after which she stripped naked and did as she
had promised with careless good humor.*

*"While all sat about watching, she defiled herself with the first
two men by lifting their robes and committing the sin of coitus
oralis. The third, expressing a desire for coitus analis, placed her on
her elbows and knees and sodomized her.*

*"The last among them to receive her favors was the Grand
Master himself, who instructed her to kneel and relieve him
through oral copulation. Instead, she lay on a table with her legs
opened wide, boldly offering herself as she caressed her breasts and
mons veneris. He mounted her and they fornicated in the
conventional manner."*

*Afterward, according to this account, the woman slipped out into
the night, and as Fabrisse watched, uttered words of enchantment
that turned her into a male. Thus transformed, this "aberration of
nature" proceeded to climb the exterior wall of a tower with naught
but his bare hands and feet, stealing into the bedchamber of a female
visitor to the château, the widow of an English baron. There came a
scream of terror from the widow that greatly alarmed Fabrisse,
however, it was followed in short order by a moan of pleasure.*

*"The lustful groans and cries, both male and female, that
issued from that window for the remainder of the night left little
doubt in Fabrisse's mind as to the activities transpiring there."*

*The priest sent this report to the Bishop of Clermont (under the
Ancien Régime), who transferred it to the Archbishop of Bourges,
who dismissed the matter, having judged the young woman, sight
unseen, to have been bereft of reason. It is worth noting that it had
been, and still is, the long-standing practice of the seigneurs of
Grotte Cachée to make frequent and generous donations of land and
monies to the Church.*

The second of these documents was an age-worn, velvet-bound book titled Una Durata di Piacere, *being an erotic memoir by a Venetian nobleman named Domenico Vitturi, which was privately published under a nom de plume for the author's intimate friends in 1665. Several chapters thereof concern a number of visits to Grotte Cachée by Vitturi and favored courtesans for the express purpose of training them to pleasure men in unorthodox and sinful ways.*

This instruction was carried out most zealously by two men fictitiously named Éric and Isaac, who schooled the courtesans in extraordinarily obscene forms of sexual congress. They were taught to employ various objects, devices, furnishings, and even implements of torture, for the purpose of exciting lust in themselves and their bed partners. They became adept at such debaucheries as sapphotism, le vice anglais, ménage à trois, *the use of bindings, blindfolds, and gags, and other practices of an even more debased nature.*

A notable aspect of these depictions of fornication, many of which Vitturi viewed sub rosa as it were, from a secret hiding place, was the prowess of the two trainers, which strikes one as exceeding the natural abilities of the mortal male. By Vitturi's account, Éric could perform the act of copulation a dozen or more times in brisk succession. Isaac, while possessed of a more conventional, though still remarkable, sexual vigor, boasted a generative organ described as being quite literally "come il penis dello stallion." *Furthermore, one of the courtesans claimed that Isaac possessed* "a tail, slightly pointed ears, and a pair of very small, horn-like protrusions on his head, his hair effectively concealing the latter two peculiarities."

This book was brought to the attention of high personages at the Vatican, who handed the matter over to the Archbishop of Bourges, who declared that Vitturi's reminiscences were simply too fantastical to warrant investigation.

The third document in Archbishop Bélanger's possession was the *letter that prompted this investigation, which was sent this past June from a Mrs. L_____ in New York City to an old friend summering at her family's château in Lyon. (In case this letter should fall into the wrong hands, I shall refrain from using the actual names of the parties involved, as they are prominent in New York and London society.) It was this letter, retrieved by a laundress from a hidden pocket in a skirt belonging to the recipient, which made its way to the Archbishop, who being of a more inquisitive humour than his predecessors, resolved to prove or disprove with finality the existence of diabolical beings at Grotte Cachée.*

Upon greeting her friend with the curious salutation, "From one little red fox to another," Mrs. L_____ proceeds to reminisce about a "slave auction" they had attended at Château de la Grotte Cachée twelve years ago. Having been "sold" to dissolute libertines for one week's sexual servitude, they were locked into collars and cuffs of gilded steel, led about by leashes, and made to engage in activities of the most appalling degradation.

Mrs. L_____, being currently "bound in marital monotony" to a much older gentleman, makes casual reference to alleviating her tedium through sexual affairs with other men. On those rare occasions when her husband comes to her bed, she manages to feign interest in the act by recollecting (in language that I blush to reiterate, doing so only in deference to your Lordship's directive) "that game of blindman's buff during Slave Week, when Sir E_____ took me dogways before the entire company of masters and slaves. As I lie upon the glacial sheets of my marriage bed, with that dusty old goat snorting and twitching atop me, I relive every detail—me stark naked with my face pressed to that scratchy wool rug and my arse in the air, hands clasped dutifully behind my neck, Sir E_____ blindfolded and trying to guess who I was by the feel of my chink. He said he would make me come so as to identify me by my voice, do you remember? I can still feel his fingers on my cherry pit, diddling away while he fucked me silly. I came with such fervor,

I thought my heart would burst, and then he uncunted and I felt volleys of hot spurts all over my back and arse. Heaven! T_____ thinks himself quite the swordsman for making me spend every time. Little does he know it's actually Sir E_____ doing the deed for him."

What most intrigued the archbishop was Mrs. L_____'s description on the next page of *"that curly-haired devil with the lovely smile and towering tallywag."* It is in relation to this man that the lady writes, *"I do not, as you accuse, dear M_____, credit the existence of Satyrs, but I tell you I did espy, in the course of bathhouse disportments, what looked to be a tail—and I was only very slightly tipsy from the opium. Perhaps his mother, whilst in a delicate condition, received a fright from a beast with such a tail. Is it not through such maternal impression that some babes are cursed with birthmarks resembling animals, or even more monstrous disfigurements?"*

The three preceding documents represent the only extensive written accounts of unnatural doings or unclean spirits at Grotte Cachée. There is, however, one additional source of information.

It seems that in August of 1771, a young carpenter by the name of Serges Bourgoin was hired by Lord Henry Archer, the English *administrateur* to the lady who was then mistress of Grotte Cachée, to replace a door and a pair of window shutters. About a week later, as Bourgoin and another carpenter were making repairs at the home of a local physician, the physician's wife overheard him whispering to the other man of the bizarre and ungodly things he'd experienced at Grotte Cachée. She urged him to report these things to their parish priest. When he refused, she did so herself. Given the nature of her allegations, the fact that they were hearsay, Serges Bourgoin's reputation for overindulgence in wine, and the lady's own reputation as a gossip and intermeddler, the priest penned a brief memorandum of the conversation and pursued it no further.

When I was informed that Bourgoin was still alive, I made

arrangements to visit him. At eighty-five, he lives with his daughter in a nearby village, and he still enjoys his drink. Having been told this, I brought him two bottles of one of the finest local wines, from a vineyard in Saint-Pourçain-sur-Sioule, not far from here.

At first, he denied having ever been to Grotte Cachée, but after I explained that I was attempting to confirm or refute the presence of demonic forces there so as to determine whether the castle or its occupants might be in need of exorcism, and that I would share his tale only with trusted ecclesiastical personages, he saw fit to confide in me. I confess, it was helpful to my purposes that he was already somewhat inebriated when I arrived that afternoon.

I took detailed notes while Bourgoin spoke. The substance of what he related to me is this: He had arrived at Grotte Cachée to replace the door and shutters, only to be led by two Swiss Guards up a forested mountainside to a gap in a rocky outcropping. He would never have known it was there, since it was hidden behind a pair of walnut trees so huge and old, they looked to him like "the legs of giant soldiers." From what he overheard of the guards' conversation, he surmised that this was one of several entrances to an extensive cave system.

The opening, although irregular in shape, was fitted out with a door that was old and weathered, its green paint peeling. Next to it was an aperture in the wall of rock to which had been attached a pair of window shutters in a similar condition.

The cave chamber within, he describes as "une petite salle confortable," furnished with a bed, a rug, and bookshelves. Although in appearance a cozy little room, Bourgoin tells me that he felt somewhat muzzy when standing in it, that his skin prickled as it did during a violent lightning storm, although all was calm and quiet. There were more books, he tells me, in a larger chamber adjoining the smaller one, this "secret library" being hidden behind a tapestry. He claims that when he removed a book from its shelf to

*look at it, it was wrenched away from him and shoved back in place
by an unseen hand.*

*Unsettled, he installed the door and shutters as dark clouds
filled the sky. By the time he was finished, a violent thunderstorm
was lashing the valley, forcing him to delay his return home.
Bourgoin spent that night in a room in the castle's servants'
quarters, where his disorientation persisted.*

*When he awakened the next morning, he recalled having been
visited during the night by a black-haired female, a "Démon
féminin," who ravished him in exceptionally sinful ways while he
lay powerless, unable to move his arms and legs. Startled to hear a
male voice, he saw that a tall, fair man was sitting in the corner
with a glass of wine, watching.*

*"He spoke to her as one speaks to a lover," Bourgoin told me,
"but from time to time he would suggest to her things that she
should do to me, depraved things—and I roused to her as I have
never roused to another woman, before or since. He told her to lick
and suck me until I was crazed with lust, and then to 'bind' me. I
discovered what this meant when she buckled a leather band around
the base of my bite. By this means she kept me hard as a pillar of
stone, on the verge of release but unable to achieve it, while she rode
me like a wild creature, moaning with one orgasme after another.
When she removed the band, I exploded, my sperme shooting like a
fountain. She knelt astride my face so that I could pleasure her with
my tongue, which I confess I did eagerly, while the man thrust a
phallus of polished black marble in and out of her chat. This she
then took and pushed into me, rubbing it back and forth inside me
and murmuring soft, filthy things until I shot off again . . ."*

*She—or rather, they—had their way with Bourgoin until close
to dawn. Although the blond man was clearly aroused the entire
time, the "demoness" never touched him intimately, nor did he
attempt to have relations with her.*

Many times over the intervening years, Bourgoin told me, he has tried to convince himself that it had been a dream, but in his heart, he feels it really happened. When I asked whether he had been drinking that night before he retired, he admitted that he had, but he insisted that he wasn't so drunk as to have invented such an experience out of whole cloth.

Bourgoin referred to his nocturnal visitors as "Follets," a French term that encompasses a panoply of Devilkins, Faeries, and Fauns, including the various types of Sexual Demons—which is to say, Incubi and Succubi—that have reputedly been observed here at Grotte Cachée. The latter, who are said to have unnaturally cool flesh, sustain their life force by capturing the vital energy generated through carnal intercourse with humans. For this reason, they are driven and consumed by no higher purpose than the sin of fleshly lust. As St. Augustine observed of them, "Like the gods, they have corporeal immortality, and passions like human beings."

It is not only the occupants of Grotte Cachée whom I will be investigating, but the castle and outbuildings themselves, and of course the cave, to determine whether they are imbued with an aura of evil. Material objects are more susceptible to diabolical infestation than is generally thought, and can only be purified through exorcism.

As to the particulars of my mission—

During my stay with the Archbishop, he issued an invitation to the local gentry to dine with him, as a pretext to throw me together with the present Seigneur des Ombres, Théophile Morel. Le seigneur, being of advanced years and ill health, sent in his stead his administrator, Bartholomew Archer, who is the grandson of the previously mentioned Lord Henry Archer.

I introduced myself to him as "David Beckett"—Beckett being my middle name—rather than David Roussel at the suggestion of Monseigneur's secretary, who informed me that Mr. Archer is known to make inquiries regarding those whom he intends to invite to Grotte Cachée. To be sure, my book is rather obscure, and certainly of interest only to my fellow demonologists, but should Mr. Archer have made the connection between his prospective landscape gardener and the author of Dæmonia, *the jig, as they say, would have been up.*

In any event, the ruse was successful. Mr. Archer left his Grace's dinner party intrigued with the notion of revamping the grounds of Grotte Cachée in accordance with the picturesque ideals in vogue in Britain, and ten days later, today, he sent a barouche to fetch me here. From the moment I entered the château, I became aware of a certain vague light-headedness. I ascribed it to hunger, for it had been some hours since my last meal, but it persisted even after I had dined. If it abates, I shall accredit it to my nervous apprehension at the demands of this covert undertaking.

Upon my arrival here, I requested an audience with Seigneur des Ombres in order to discuss his landscaping preferences—a ploy, of course, to meet him and take his measure, perhaps discover whether he knows of demoniacal activities at Grotte Cachée, and if so, whether he would cooperate with an exorcism or forbid it. Unfortunately, Mr. Archer insists that *le seigneur is too elderly and feeble* to meet with me, and that he, Archer, has *carte blanche* to approve all decisions regarding improvement of the grounds.

The occupants of the château, aside from the staff, Seigneur des Ombres and Mr. Archer (who actually lives with his wife and infant daughter in a house in the woods called la Maison de Forêt), are one female and three males, all young and evidently unrelated. At dinner this evening, I was introduced to the woman and two of the men by first name only: Lili, who hails, I would venture to say, from somewhere in the Ottoman Empire; Elic, who is remarkably tall, and Scandinavian in appearance, with long hair worn clubbed at the nape; and Inigo, who is of Mediterranean or possibly Gypsy stock. The third man, Darius, who was described to me as "a rather dolesome hermit," I have yet to meet.

During our postprandial conversation, I overheard a brief, whispered exchange in French between Lili and Elic. Their words, which concerned myself, had clearly not been intended for my ears. When asked whether I understood French, I replied misleadingly that I had never studied the language in school, which is true. I declined to mention that my father was from France, as were my nanny and nursery governess, and that I had a thorough command of French before I was speaking full sentences in English.

As for the castle itself, it is of a quadrangular configuration around a courtyard, with corner and postern towers, and appears to have been built several centuries ago of dark volcanic rock. It is tucked deep into a heavily wooded valley beneath looming mountains, including an extinct volcano that houses the cave mentioned by Serges Bourgoin, which I am eager to explore despite Mr. Archer's admonition that I not venture too far within.

In his book, Vitturi remarked on the bizarre phantasms one is likely to encounter deep within the cave, which would appear to echo Bourgoin's experience. I should like to determine the veracity of these reports, and to locate the curious little bedchamber described by Serges Bourgoin, if it indeed exists. I should think I stand a better chance of locating its entrance in the interior of the cave rather than the one in the woods through which Bourgoin gained access. Mr. Archer, however, seemed quite adamant that I avoid a thorough investigation of the cave. Were I to remain within it for longer than was deemed appropriate, I would no doubt be escorted out by le seigneur's Swiss Guards and banned from reentering. For this reason, it is wisest, I think, to conduct this particular aspect of my investigation under cover of darkness.

Tonight, after the household has quieted, I shall take a lantern and a compass and explore the cave to as great an extent as practicable—provided I can cross from the castle to the bathhouse, from whence one enters the cave, without being seen, as the moon is quite full tonight.

Given my disinclination to entrust my correspondence to the hands of strangers, this will likely be the last letter I have the chance to post until I return to England to make a full report in person.

> Until then, I remain
> Your Lordship's
> devoted and humble servant,
> David Beckett Roussel

Three

"I'VE RARELY SEEN you as rude as you were this evening," Lili told Elic as they floated side by side in the bathhouse pool, naked beneath the steam-hazed dazzle of moonlight pouring in through the open roof, their hair swirling together like black and gold snakes.

"I've rarely seen you as smitten with one of our guests," he replied, grateful that her ire toward him appeared to be thawing. So vexed had she been by his display of "absurd jealousy" that he'd had the deuce of a time talking her into this midnight swim.

"Wanting to have my way with a man and being smitten with him are two different things, as you are very well aware, *Khababu*. He is a *gabru*, and I sense that he has promise. Why should I not desire him?"

He turned to look at her, a heavenly being floating in the mist, the most exquisite creature he had ever seen. She was his beloved, his *Nyidís*. In the *dönsk tunga* of his early years in

Norvegr, it meant the Goddess of the New Moon, which was what she had been worshipped as in her own motherland of Babylonia some four thousand years ago. Although mankind in its arrogance and narrow-mindedness had long ago ceased believing in the nonhuman races, Lili still wore the gold and lapis lazuli anklet that was the symbol of her divine status. Elic loved her with all his heart, with his very soul. He needed her, he craved her. It was a longing in his skin, utterly consuming. And despite their testiness this evening, he knew that she shared his complete devotion; there was never any doubt of that. Still . . .

"I thought you fancied fair-haired men," he said.

"I fancy *men*." Reaching across the water to take his hand, she added softly, "But most of all, I fancy you."

The very touch of her soft, cool fingers against his engendered a tremble of desire in Elic's loins—a futile response, but his body still stubbornly refused to acknowledge what his mind had accepted long ere this, that he and Lili were doomed to a love that would never be consummated.

Bringing Elic's fingers to her lips, Lili said, "I can't help my needs, Elic, any more than you can help yours. You know this. After all these years, why should it trouble you to know that I want this man? He is just another human to take and use, one of many who've gone before and many more to come."

"Yes, but he's not just one of many, is he, Lili? He's special. You desire him more than you've desired the others." *Most* of the others. From time to time—it didn't happen often, every few years—Lili became enamored of a *gabru* to an extent that made Elic want to throttle the bastard to within an inch of his life. "It isn't just about slaking the hungers of your body," he said. "You are utterly enamored."

"Nonsense. It is simple lust, nothing more."

"I can feel it, Lili." He scooped up a handful of the water on which they floated, letting it slide through his fingers in glimmery, moonlit ribbons. The stream that fed this pool, which gurgled from deep within the adjoining cave, took on a faint, almost electrical resonance as it percolated through fissures in primordial bedrock and solidified lava. On cool autumn nights like this, it ran right around body temperature; on sweltering summer days, a good deal below. In the winter, entering this pool was like slipping into a steaming hot bath. It was also remarkably conductive, transmitting feelings and sensations between bathers, especially lust, in a way that was sometimes subtle and sometimes a potent galvanic charge, depending on the depth of the infused emotion.

That was how Elic knew for sure that Lili's protestation of "simple lust" toward David Beckett was so much dissembling. He felt it in the water that buoyed him, even in the steam rising off its balmy surface to drift away in the cool night air—a frisson of passion flavored with fascination; the thrill of the new, the unknown, the mysterious; a breathless anticipation that had less to do with lust than with discovery, connection, possession. It wasn't just David Beckett's body that Lili longed for, it was something more, and that something made Elic's heart squeeze into a tight little knot in his chest.

"You can't hide your feelings from me, Lili," he said, "not here. You're besotted with him."

"For pity's sake, Elic." She released his hand and looked away, rather petulantly, he thought. "It isn't love, or anything like it. It's . . ."

"I know you're not in love with him. But you *are* infatuated."

She looked for a moment as if she wanted to deny it, but then she just sighed and said, "It is different for me than for you, Elic. For my sex, human or non, desire can be a complicated business. Lust is rarely about simple physical gratification. One can find oneself harboring feelings—even for perfect strangers—that defy all reason. You've experienced this yourself, when you go through The Change and become Elle. More than once, you've found yourself captivated by the *gabrus* you've taken. You've told me as much."

"Only while I'm taking them," he said. "When it's over, I feel nothing."

"Because when it's over, you are once again a male. Yet when you take a human woman, regardless of how desirable she is, how much you've wanted her, how exciting it is to be inside her, your passion always has its limits. It is your body that longs for her, and your body alone."

"If only it were the same for you. I feel sick when I think of you fucking that goddamned gardener. He fancies you, too, you know. He doesn't think it shows, the English never do, but he's mad for you. That's why he can't bring himself to look you in the eye."

Lili stroked Elic's face tenderly, soothingly. "Do not fret so, my love. I'm not really so very different from you. Once I've had this *gabru* and my cravings have been fed, my ardor will diminish—you'll see. My lust will be less tangled up with sentiment. It will be purer then, a simple physical need, as it is meant to be for our kind."

"I want to be with you when you take him—at least tonight." He knew she wouldn't wait to have him; she was far too eager. Not that tonight would be the end of it, of course. By the time Beckett left here, Lili would have enjoyed him in ways his prosaic human brain could never have imagined.

"Of course you may be there, if it will ease your mind," she said.

"I'll put a *liggia spiall* on him," Elic said. "Let him think it was all just a dream. And I want you to use your *mashmashu kasaru*. I don't want him to move a muscle. I'll be damned if I'll watch him putting his hands all over you."

On a weary exhalation, she said, "I hate it when they can't thrust or touch me. It doesn't feel the same."

"*I'll* touch you." Grabbing the pool's marble rim for purchase, Elic rose to his feet in the hip-deep water and leaned down to kiss her as she floated in the moonlit mist. "I know what you like."

Elic closed his hands over her breasts, giving her nipples a sharp little tug that made her moan. He pinched them hard, rolling them back and forth, but slowly, pulling them a little from time to time as they grew stiff. He knew, from his female transmutations, exactly how this felt for her, the stinging pleasure that fell just short of pain, shooting darts of arousal directly to her clit. So sensitive was Lili's succubitic body that she could climax just from having her nipples excited, if it was done properly. He'd made her come merely from caressing certain areas of her body in just the right way; her lips, her ears, her throat, and the cleft of that exquisite derrière were particularly sensitive.

She grabbed fistfuls of his trailing hair, her back arching, the earthy-sweet perfume of her arousal making Elic's cock thicken and rise. He braced one hand under the small of her back to support her while he brushed a finger slowly, lightly, up and down the seam of her sex.

"I know how you hate to be rushed," he said as he slid the finger deeper, stroking the ultrasensitive inner lips very slowly and gently. She moaned deliciously, the water roiling beneath her as she tilted her hips up, up . . .

Elic positioned himself between her outspread legs as he continued the intimate caress. Fully erect now, he steeled himself against his own arousal, for which there would be no relief tonight—he didn't bed the maidservants, and there were no female houseguests at present—and tried to think only of Lili.

He would pleasure her before Beckett did, and he'd make it good for her, he'd make her wait for it, make her scream. The consummate succubus, sexual excitation was like a drug to her; she was addicted to it, ravenous for it, utterly intoxicated in its clutches. She could come twenty or thirty times before she was through with a man, sucking him dry and leaving him deliriously satisfied and utterly wrung out—whereas she, having revived herself with the *gabru*'s carnal excitement, would be flushed with renewed vitality. As with most females, human and Follet alike, her first climax was usually the most powerful. Tonight the first would be his, and a string of others besides; Beckett would get what was left.

"I'll touch you like this while you're on top of him," Elic murmured. "I'll tell him you're really mine and mine alone, heart and soul, and that he's nothing to you but a convenient cock. I'll hold you still with him swelling and twitching inside you while I flutter a fingertip on your clit, bringing you right to the edge and keeping you there while you shake and groan. I'll push a finger up your ass like this."

Lili threw her head back as he demonstrated, squirming the finger around inside her to make her exceedingly aware of it. Suspended on the water as she was, it would feel as if her entire body were supported by that one skewering digit.

"You'll be filled up and quivering and begging me to finish you," Elic said. "He won't be able to take it anymore. He'll scream as he comes, and you'll feel every spurt, every throb, but I still won't let *you* come, not yet." He ceased his ministrations and grabbed her hips to still her. "Not till you're wild with lust and ready to explode."

"Elic, don't tease me," she pleaded, struggling against his grip. "I'm so close."

So was he, painfully close. Ten days had passed since his last opportunity to bed a female visitor to the château. The water lapping against his cock made it throb like a sore tooth.

He was pondering what to do to Lili next—kneel between her legs and fuck her with his tongue?—when a breeze wafted through the bathhouse, carrying with it a medley of scents that made his nostrils flare: musty autumn leaves, ripe juniper berries . . . tobacco with a hint of frankincense . . . Castile soap . . .

Beckett. He was out there somewhere, and coming closer, because the scent was growing stronger.

"Elic . . . oh, God, *please.*" Like Elic, Lili was incapable of achieving climax by her own hand. Most incubi and succubi were entirely at the mercy of others to provide the sexual release on which they thrived.

The Englishman was headed straight for the bathhouse, Elic was sure of it. In half a minute, he would be upon them. He would see them.

He would see them.

"Oh, God . . . Elic, don't leave me this way."

"Of course not." Elic gathered her up and held her close with her back to the arched doorway of the bathhouse, her legs wrapped around his waist. He rocked his hips, sliding his erection against her damp cleft in a sensual rhythm, gritting his teeth against the stimulation. Were Lili a mortal woman, someone he could fuck, he would relish the sensation of being so close to climax, feeling it gathering in his veins, his balls . . . He would ram himself into her and no doubt spend within seconds, given how ready he was. But Lili wasn't a mortal woman, and no matter how close he got, there would be no relief.

"Elic, you mustn't," she breathed, even as she writhed against him, too lust-drunk to resist. "It will only hurt you."

The pain, when he teetered on the edge of an unattainable

climax, could be overwhelming; the longer he'd gone without spending, the more excruciating it was. Already his balls felt as if they were on the verge of splitting open; the shaft felt almost scalded.

Testing the air, Elic guessed that Beckett was close, very close, no more than fifty feet away. "Tell me you're mine," he said softly, peering through the doorway to the gravel path that led to the bathhouse.

"You know I am." She was breathless now, and moving against him with increasing urgency as she gripped his shoulders.

There came into view a figure so well lit by the full moon as to cast a sharp black shadow on the path—Beckett, wearing an open frock coat, boots, and a wide-brimmed hat, an unlit lantern in one hand and a walking stick in the other. He slowed his gait, and then stopped, staring into the bathhouse as Elic pretended not to notice him.

He imagined the scene from the Englishman's perspective—Elic and the enchanting Lili, making love standing up in the moonlit pool, her moans growing frantic as her pleasure crested. Grimacing at his own, nearly unbearable arousal, he thrust harder, faster.

"Oh, yes," she moaned, her entire body undulating in a primal rhythm. "Yes, like that. *Mamitu,* I'm so close. I'm going to come. Oh . . . Oh, God . . ."

"Say it."

"I'm yours," she cried. "I'm yours. I belong to you."

Beckett turned and strode quickly back down the path. Elic smiled to himself.

Lili, still on the verge of climax, grew still, her breath coming in harsh gasps. She'd seen him staring over her shoulder. Before he could distract her, she turned and looked through the doorway, tracking his gaze down the path.

Beckett had already disappeared into the night, or so it appeared to Elic, whose night vision, though excellent by human standards, wasn't remotely as keen as Lili's. Her eyes and brain were structured so as to capture and interpret an unusually wide spectrum of light, not just the narrow range that was visible to humans and most of her fellow Follets. Even Darius, in his feline incarnation, couldn't see as well as she in the dark. And in daylight, her vision was as sharp and far-reaching as that of an eagle.

Elic cursed inwardly when he heard her indrawn breath. Her entire body seemed to stiffen.

Shit.

She whipped her head back around, her eyes black with fury. "You knew he was there, but you didn't tell me. You wanted him to see us, to think we were . . . That's why you . . ." She looked down at their bodies clasped together, then unwrapped her legs from around him and pushed him roughly away.

"Lili—"

She cracked her palm across his face, hard, throwing him off balance. His feet skittered on the floor of the pool. The water closed over his head as he flailed and choked, engulfed in a cauldron of lust, female rage—and shock.

She'd never struck him before, never come close to that kind of anger—not toward Elic, her Beloved, her *Khababu*.

Choking and sputtering, he found his footing and stood, water sluicing off him as he clawed his hair off his face. She was already out of the pool, facing away from him as she reached for the silken *lubushu* she'd tossed onto an iron chair before bathing—the yellow one, his favorite. She'd worn it tonight, he knew, as a gesture of conciliation after the tension between them earlier.

"Lili—"

"You think you've staked your claim," she said unsteadily as she knotted the saronglike garment over her shoulder, "but you deceived me to do it. I should say that claim is now on rather shaky ground."

She stalked off into the night.

Four

LILI AWOKE THE next morning to the dipping of her mattress and the familiar pressure of a hand, Elic's hand, stroking her hip through the blanket as she lay curled up facing away from him. They usually slept together in one of their apartments—but not last night.

"*Shalamu*," he said softly. It was how they always greeted each other, each offering the salutation of the other's homeland. *Shalamu* was the Akkadian equivalent of "Good day," "Goodbye," and "Peace." Her customary response in the ancient tongue of Elic's youth was *kveðja*. Lili couldn't recall when it was that they'd developed this little ritual, but it had become, over time, their own private tradition, a way to connect with each other's far-distant pasts, to remind each other that they weren't alone anymore, that they shared a bond of intimacy and love and trust that was unsullied and absolute.

Until last night.

Tell me you're mine . . . Say it. He'd wanted Beckett to hear her say that, to know that although she might be free with her body, her heart belonged to Elic.

Lili still smoldered with indignation at his subterfuge. It wasn't the fact of being seen naked and in the throes of passion that offended her; she often made love in the company of others—but by her own choice, and with her knowledge.

Elic was waiting for her to respond to his greeting with *kveðja*. "Good morning," she said softly, tonelessly.

His hand left her hip.

Without turning to face him, she said, "How did you get in here, Elic?" She'd locked the door to her apartment on the top floor of the north range upon retiring, something she almost never did.

"I climbed up to a window."

Of course. "You shouldn't have done that. Beckett might have seen you."

"Why didn't you go to him last night?"

She rolled over to face him. He was sitting on the edge of her big bed in his shirtsleeves looking pale and grim, his hair pulling free of the strip of leather tied around it at his nape.

"How do you know I didn't?" she asked.

"I don't smell him on you. I thought you were going to use your *mashmashu* and take him. Don't tell me you've lost your desire for him."

"No." Her passion for the Englishman was like a fever; it made her skin prickle with heat, her heart quiver in her chest. She had wanted to go to him, wanted to whisper her Akkadian incantation and devour him, to slake her terrible hunger. Instead, she'd lain awake half the night envisioning his body laid bare to her eyes, her hands, her mouth, her savage, ungovernable lust.

Many times during the night, she'd tried to sweep such thoughts away, to pacify her mind so that she could sleep, but she couldn't stop imagining David Beckett stripped of that reserve he wore like armor, groaning and shuddering as she coaxed him into one ferocious climax after another. The fever had consumed her, seething through her to pool wet and pulsing between her legs. She'd whimpered in frustration with her breath coming fast, hips straining. How dearly she'd wished, not for the first time, that she had the ability to bring herself to orgasm. Of the few human traits that she envied, that one was foremost.

It had taken a grueling effort of will to keep from stealing into Beckett's chamber and relieving that agony of arousal, as Elic had expected. But she had a different plan altogether for this *gabru*.

"Why don't you just fuck him and get it over with?" Elic asked.

"Is that what you want me to do?"

Grimacing, he said, "Yes, goddammit, if that will get you to stop mooning over the bastard." It was a reflection of what she'd told him last night in the bathhouse. *Once I've had this* gabru, *and my cravings have been fed, my ardor will diminish—you'll see.*

Sitting up with the bedcovers tucked around her, for she did not care to be naked for this conversation, she said, "I have decided not to use the *mashmashu* with the Englishman. It's been some time since I've attempted to seduce a *gabru au naturale*. It takes a bit longer, to be sure, and there can be complications, but the anticipation adds a piquant dimension, and I do so love a challenge."

"What challenge is there in running prey to ground if that prey so clearly wants to be caught?"

"I've been bored. It's a diversion."

"Or perhaps it's just a way to hurt me," he said. "Is that it,

Lili? You want to punish me for last night, so you set about *wooing* this fucking gardener instead of just—"

"I'm not wooing him," she said, "just . . . enticing him, as human women do."

"No incantatory assistance?" he asked skeptically. "None at all?"

She thought about it. "I might expose him to the *magnétisme hallucinatoire* if my unalloyed charms prove insufficient. It would be more entertaining, however, to rely solely on the dance of flirtation and possession."

"Humans cannot perform that dance cold-bloodedly—you know that. You should be discouraging any feelings he may be harboring for you, not nurturing them—and your own, in the bargain. But that's really the point, isn't it? To make me watch the two of you become more and more enamored of each other as you conduct this *dance* of yours, all the while knowing it's my fault you've chosen this route instead of just taking him like you take all the others."

"Elic—"

"What do you want of me, Lili?" he demanded, that vein distending on his flushed forehead as it did whenever he was agitated—or climaxing. "I would take back what I did last night in a heartbeat if I could. You must know how sorry I am. When will you stop giving me the cold shoulder and let things go back to where they were before?"

Lili looked away from his bleak, searing eyes so that she could sort through her thoughts. She could chide him for how long it had taken him to apologize, but what purpose would that serve?

"I know you're sorry," she said softly, "but you did bring this on yourself, and I . . ." Her voice breaking, she said damply, "I'm hurt, Elic. It stung, you deceiving me like that. Of all the people to do that to me . . ." A spasm gripped her throat, choking off the rest of her words.

Elic stroked her arm, saying softly, *"Mins Ástgurdís . . ."*

"Please don't call me that, not now," she said, flinching away from him.

He sighed.

She said, "If you decide to turn the tables on me by transforming into Elle and taking him before I've had the chance to—"

"I won't do that."

"If you do, the cold shoulder will be the least of it."

There came a long moment of awful silence, and then he got up and left—through the door this time.

She scrubbed the scalding tears from her cheeks, drew in a breath, and let it out in a long, shaky exhalation.

Even when Lili yearned for a human man as she yearned for the handsome, quietly intense David Beckett, her beloved Elic always occupied the deep, warm center of her heart. He was the other half of her, her bedrock, her one and only *Khababu*.

He should know that. He should have enough faith in her, in them, to know that her feelings for Beckett, springing as they did from her bodily needs, were trifling compared to her feelings for him.

But he didn't have that faith. He didn't trust her to keep her passion for this *gabru* in perspective. His jealousy had impelled him to stage that tableau of ersatz lovemaking as a demonstration to his imagined rival of his possession of her.

He truly had deceived her. It was the first time he'd ever done anything like that.

It would be the last.

Five

$\mathcal{L}$ILI LEANED AGAINST a massive oak late that afternoon, watching David Beckett, his back to her, drawing in a sketchbook propped on an easel he'd set up facing the château on the West Lawn. She was more than a quarter mile away from him, at the edge of the sprawling woods surrounding the castle, but by concentrating her vision, she could see him as clearly as if he were standing right in front of her.

Upon his return around noon from Clermont-Ferrand, Beckett had changed into the same wide-brimmed hat, brown frock coat, loose nankeen trousers, and scuffed, utilitarian boots that he'd worn during his moonlight stroll the night before. He'd spent most of the afternoon touring the castle and grounds with the sketchbook, in which he'd recorded his observations in the form of notes and quick drawings, with Lili watching from time to time at a discreet distance.

About an hour ago, he'd set up his easel on the carriage drive out front in order to sketch the gatehouse and the drawbridge spanning the last remaining section of dry moat, the other three having been filled in long ago. He'd then moved the easel to its present location so that he could capture the castle's western aspect and the rose garden that had been there when Lili first came to Grotte Cachée in the spring of 1749.

She'd arrived with Sir Francis Dashwood's infamous Hellfire Club, their Black Masses and orgies serving to satisfy her incessant sexual cravings without subjecting her to social stigma and the wrath of the Church. Elic, beautiful golden Elic, had captivated her from the first. Like her, he was a slave to his sexual passions, an enslavement that had doomed them both to an interminable lifetime of physical intimacy with strangers and emotional intimacy with no one. It had taken very little time for them to develop a deep communion of the soul. Communion of the body, true communion, they would experience only in their dreams.

Lili shifted her gaze from Beckett to the distant castle, peering through the double glass door that led from the rose garden into the dining room. She had to squint to penetrate the glare of sunlight on the myriad leaded panes, which painted a stream of radiant little squares on the two-hundred-year-old Savonnerie carpet and the Flemish lace tablecloth swathing the long dining table.

Scanning the shadowy perimeter of the room, she spotted, high up at the edge of the door to *le Salon Ambre*, a pale smudge that had to be a face. She homed in on that face to find that it belonged, unsurprisingly, to Elic, who was evidently spying on her as she spied on Beckett. No doubt he thought himself too well concealed for her to spot him, even with her keen eyesight; were it not for the sweeping brim of her straw sunbonnet, which helped her eyes to focus by shading them, he might have been right. As for his view of her, she was certainly much too far away for him to make out clearly. Attired as she was in a day dress of sea green shot silk, she would be visible to him as a pale speck against the ancient woods at her back.

Fluffing up her skirt, she strode across the lawn toward Beckett. The Englishman, having no doubt heard the whispering of her skirts against the grass as she approached, turned and stared at her. He set down his pencil, removed his hat, and bowed.

She smiled her most engaging smile. "I have been watching you, Mr. Beckett."

He looked as if he were scrabbling for a response.

"The intensity with which you steep yourself in your work fascinates me," she said as she came up to him. "You keep so very still, save for your right hand and the occasional movements of your head. I find it curious that you look at the château more than you look at your drawing."

"Ah. Yes. Well . . ." Clearly rattled by her sudden appearance, he gestured toward the castle and said, "One must scrutinize one's subject if one is to capture the truth of it."

"The truth? It is naught but a building."

"I meant, well . . . not just the outside, but all of it, the entirety of—"

"Oh, my word," she said when she saw the drawing he'd been working on, which was rendered in deft and subtle strokes, the highlights and shading so skillful that the west wall of the château and the garden bordering it seemed almost to rise off the page. "It is really quite wonderful," she said sincerely. "You've a remarkable gift, Mr. Beckett."

"You are too kind, Miss Lili."

She invited him to replace his hat, restating the request more firmly when he demurred, one of those mannerly but pointless gestures inculcated in well-brought-up gentlemen these days.

Resting a gloved hand on his arm, she said, "Please call me

Lili, without the 'Miss.' Such formality only serves to discourage free discourse and intimacy, do you not agree?"

"I . . . well, if you insist." She could feel him tense slightly through his coat sleeve. Of course he said, "You must call me David, then."

"I would like that."

Nodding toward his sketch, she said, "Pray, what fate do you have in store for our venerable old rose garden?"

"Venerable it may be, but it is passé in its formality, and rather tired-looking. I propose instead that the dining room open onto a terrace garden planted with ornamental trees and bushes and, of course, flowers. Not roses, though—they don't quite suit what I have in mind. There would be a colonnade for shade, and appropriate statuary, and a small fountain. Stairs would lead down to a reflecting pool on the lawn, this stretch of which"—he gestured with a sweep of his arm—"will be reshaped in a more pleasing manner, with rolling hillocks, and trees planted in picturesque clusters. Oh, and stone bridges should be built over the streams to facilitate strolls about the grounds."

"It sounds lovely," she said, "and most ambitious, but I must say it saddens me to think of destroying all those beautiful old rosebushes."

"Oh, they won't be destroyed. I've another garden in mind—well, several others—but one of them is to be a small, walled rose garden tucked away in the woods that one can only find if one knows about it. The roses can be transplanted there."

"A secret garden? How tantalizing."

"I shall propose as well that something be done with the castle courtyard," he said. "Aside from the central fountain and a few hedges, it is quite bare. At the very least, I would suggest perennial beds with stone benches, but what I would truly love to see is fruit trees—cherry, perhaps, say two dozen arranged in . . . I'm boring you."

"Not at all," she said earnestly. "It sounds beautiful."

"I say, are you not chilly without a shawl?" he asked. "For all that the sun is shining, it is still a bit cool."

"Not to me. My blood tends to run a bit warmer than most." Taking his hand, she pressed it to her cheek. "You see?"

"Ah. Why, yes." David surprised her, given his reserved manner, by keeping his hand there after she'd taken hers away, his expression one of unaccountably keen interest. "Very warm, indeed." He stroked her cheek as if unaware of what he was doing, only to yank his hand away a moment later, clearly appalled at the liberty he'd taken.

He turned away, saying, "I, er . . . I suppose I'm done for now. The light has shifted. I shall finish up tomorrow."

He lifted the sketchbook, whereupon she took it from his hand, saying "May I?"

"There's really nothing much to—"

"Oh, how lovely," she remarked when she turned to the previous page, on which he'd drawn the entrance to the château. "Such detail. I love how you've captured the shadow of the gatehouse on the drawbridge."

"Thank you," he said as he held his hand out for the book, "but I daresay there is little else in there of interest."

She flipped back through the previous pages, covered with dense paragraphs of penciled notes interspersed with sketches of the landscape and outbuildings—though not of the bathhouse, which he had evidently yet to revisit. The drawings all looked to have been hastily executed except for one—of her.

"Oh," she breathed. It was a portrait of her lounging on that gilt chaise in *le Salon Ambre* the night before—just her, not Elic, who'd been sitting next to her. The black, burnished mass of her hair contrasted sharply with the whiteness of her throat and shoulders, their curves delineated in loose, undeniably sensual strokes. Her own eyes gazed back at her with dark, dreamy interest; her generous lips were parted in a secret smile. That he'd executed such an evocative likeness from memory made it all the more remarkable.

She looked up to find David regarding her pensively. His eyes, shaded by the brim of his hat, were huge and dark; his color was high.

Closing the sketchbook, she set it back on the easel and curled her arm around his. "Walk with me, David. There's something I'd like to show you."

David couldn't help but recall, as Lili guided him, arm in arm, toward the bathhouse, what he'd seen last night as he'd walked up this same path—Lili and Elic, awash in moonlight and completely naked, locked in illicit union. At first, he hadn't realized they were actually copulating, given their upright position.

He wished he could erase the image from his mind. If only he were devoid of fleshly desires, how much easier it would be to remain pure and continent, to keep his mind on higher things without being reminded incessantly of the pleasures he'd foresworn when he entered minor orders. Such pleasures, being reserved exclusively for the marital act, were to be abjured for the remainder of his life on earth. Only a handful of times since adolescence had he resorted to self-gratification, each occasion leaving him deeply ashamed and penitent. When his body betrayed his moral resolve by ejecting its ever-burgeoning cache of seed during a libidinous dream, as it had last night, he felt nearly as much shame as if he'd expelled that seed by his own hand.

The dream had begun with a sense of suffocation as he

awakened, or dreamt he'd awakened. Panic flooded him as he tried to fill his lungs with air, and couldn't. The reason was immediately apparent.

A woman, or a creature that resembled a woman, was sitting astride his chest, grinding against him in a slow, voluptuous rhythm. She was naked, with torrents of glossy black hair, reptilian eyes, and a tail that flared out at the tip before narrowing into a point, like a fleshy arrowhead.

He tried to rise up so as to fling her off, but he found he couldn't move and couldn't speak, although he could breathe again, albeit stertorously. Her tongue, which was long and forked, slithered out from between a pair of needle-sharp fangs. She lifted her full breasts and flicked that snakelike tongue over the nipples until they grew long and stiff and purplish red.

Kneeling over him—she was farther down now, near his hips—she seized her tail and licked the tip, growling with lust as it swelled, a treacly fluid oozing from a little slit on the end. She pressed it to David's own rigidly erect organ, squeezing out a dribble of fluid as she stroked it up and down his length, the lubricious caress wresting a moan from him.

The tail twitched wildly, thickening to several times its original girth. Using her fingers, with their clawlike nails, she spread her labia wide open and pushed the engorged tip into her sex until she couldn't shove it any farther. She aimed David's slickened organ at her nether orifice, rubbing the glans against the puckered little opening while thrusting the tail in and out of her sex.

"I'm yours," she hissed. She pushed him into her, then pressed down slowly, groaning with the effort.

He groaned, too, as he penetrated her, his shaft inching deeper, deeper, into the impossibly snug flesh. It gripped him like a fist gloved in cool satin. The lack of warmth should have repelled him, as should his being forced to perform an act of sodomy, but the pleasure was mounting too swiftly, robbing him of his qualms—of his very thoughts.

"Yours, all yours," she whispered in Lili's voice, her movements growing sharper, more frenetic. "I belong to you, David, and you belong to me. You're *mine* now."

She was kneading her sex with one hand and manipulating the tail with the other, as David thrust faster, deeper . . . for he found that he could move his hips now. He'd been reduced to a rutting beast, straining and grunting in a frenzy of lust.

"Fuck me," she ordered in a hellishly deep, hoarse voice. "Fuck my arse. Fuck it hard, David. Squirt it full."

Loath to submit to this unholy creature, he tried to lie still, to resist his body's urgent quest for release, but it was so hard, agonizingly hard. His ballocks tingled and swelled, his groin growing tight and heavy with seed. He was gasping for air, his heart racing.

Hold back, hold back. Don't let her make you spill. Don't give her that victory.

"Ah, yes," she said as the tail began to pump, pulsating tremors coursing all along its length. She milked it as she rubbed herself, moaning the foulest things David had ever heard as her body convulsed wildly. Hot cream oozed from her sex onto David's lower belly.

"No," he groaned, struggling to stave off the inevitable as the tingling in his ballocks spread down his legs and up his turgid organ to the throbbing tip.

"Yes, David. Now," she rasped, riding him hard, churning her hips. "Shoot your load. Shoot it deep."

His back locked into an arch as the spasms ripped through him, discharging gush after gush of pent-up seed, a screaming deluge of it.

He'd awakened moaning in time with the last few diminishing spurts, lying on his back with his buttocks clenching, clenching . . .

"God's bones," he'd whispered as his lungs strove to stop heaving, his body to stop quaking. Throwing aside the bedcovers, he'd lifted his shirt, muttering "Shit" upon finding his thin linen drawers soaked through with his spendings.

He'd rinsed out his drawers and lain awake the rest of the night, wondering what to make of that dream. In its immediate aftermath, he'd briefly nurtured the notion that it might not have been a dream at all, but a real diabolical visitation. However, even with his mind prone to flights of fancy as it tended to be during nocturnal musings, he'd had to conclude that it had been no actual succubus ravishing him in his sleep, but rather his demon-obsessed mind.

"What do you think of our bathhouse?" inquired Lili from the arched doorway of the edifice, which looked rather like a Roman temple fitted out with wrought-iron furniture and scatterings of jewel-toned pillows.

Its white marble walls had been eroded by time and the elements, but it was still a beautiful structure, the focal point of which was the square, mosaic-floored pool in which he had spied Lili and Elic coupling the night before. The water was glassy-smooth except at the far end, where it rippled as it emerged from a conduit to the underground cave stream; presumably it flowed out through a similar aperture that David couldn't see from where he stood. The open roof, which emblazoned the water with sunlight, was supported by four pillars with a life-size figurative sculpture at the base of each.

David was about to respond that it was a very lovely bathhouse when he realized that the four statues were of couples locked in sexual concourse, each position more indecent than the last. Two depicted acts of intercourse, the other two of oral copulation, the male being the recipient in one case and the female in the other. The male's generative organ was unnaturally large, a thick, veiny column about a foot long. David's scalp tingled when he noticed a tail with a little tuft at the end, ears that came to a slight point, and two stubby horns that were barely visible within the satyr's cap of tightly curled hair.

He had been aroused already, remembering that dream. It didn't help to be in such close proximity to the exotically seductive Lili. The delicate pressure of her arm linked with his, the silken brush of her skirts and huge puff sleeves, and most intoxicating of all, her perfume, which made him think of night-blooming flowers in a Persian garden . . . jasmine, he thought. These things provoked in him a low hum of desire, like the resonance from a tuning fork, that made him keenly aware of every inch of his body—especially of that all too excitable organ between his legs, now stirring heavily beneath his coat as he took in these ribald statues.

Lili said, "The man who built this bathhouse, and the villa that once stood where the castle is now, regarded this valley as a pleasure retreat. Of course, the Romans had a rather sportive view of fleshly matters. It was simply a leisure pursuit to them. I do hope you aren't shocked."

"Of course not," he said, but wanting to mitigate that bit of fiction—for truly, the mouth that belieth killeth the soul—he added, "I suppose I am a bit taken aback, but not *shocked* per se. I have viewed the Pompeian artifacts at the Secret Museum in Naples, so I do realize that artwork portraying satyrs was frequently quite obscene. I will confess, however, that the . . . well, the lifelike size and quality of these statues, and the skill with which they were executed, makes them all the more . . ."

"Titillating?"

Incredulous that he was discussing such matters with a female—and not some trollop, but a lady of obvious breeding and cultivation—he said, "Clearly they were created with titil-

lation in mind. I suppose what truly shocks me is that they remain standing after all this time. I would have thought they'd
have been removed long ere this, on moral grounds."

"You said yourself they're beautifully executed. They're exquisite works of art."

"Art? They are prurient in the extreme."

"Which means they cannot be regarded as art?" she asked.

"To my mind, no."

She smiled at him in a way that made him feel like some
dim-witted Philistine. Would that he'd never followed the conversation down this particular path.

"Is this what you'd wanted to show me?" he asked.

"No, it's something else, another statue even older than
these, one of the most ancient artifacts at Grotte Cachée. It's in
the cave."

David looked toward the slab of dark, moss-draped volcanic rock that formed the back wall of the bathhouse. Slightly
off center in the rock face was a roughly triangular opening
about five feet high. A little bluish bird—a thrush, he
thought—stood sentinel just inside this natural doorway.

She said, "There is a chamber called the *Cella* about a quarter mile in, where the Gauls who once lived here used to worship their gods. They carved a stone effigy with some rather
curious features."

A quarter mile in. Precisely the limit imposed upon him by
Bartholomew Archer. Far be it for her to have invited him to
venture farther than that.

David had yet to set foot in the "Secret Grotto" for which
this valley had been named, and he was eager to do so, but not
with Lili as a guide. He'd meant it when he'd told the archbishop that he would refrain from becoming too familiar with
the residents of Grotte Cachée. Doing so could only muddle his
judgment and call his conclusions into doubt.

It would be particularly unwise to cultivate an attachment to Lili, with whom, if he were honest with himself, he'd been enthralled from the first. And, too, how likely was it that this effigy would be of interest to his investigation, given how keen she was to show it to him? He would be better off exploring the cave on his own, at night, as he'd planned.

"It is a statue of a dusios," she said.

He looked at her sharply. "A *dusios*?"

"Do you know what that is?"

He hesitated for a moment, choosing his words. "I understand it to be a type of demon."

That smile again. "What some call demons, others call gods. A French term for them is Follets. 'Dusios' is a Gaulish name for a type of Follet with the ability to transform himself from male to female."

It was a simplistic description of a complicated being, to which a large section of *Dæmonia* was devoted. *According to the writings of St. Thomas, Vallesius, Maluenda, and others,* he'd written in his introduction to this type of incubus, *Dusii procreate, after a fashion, by assuming a female form so as to fornicate with an exceptional man and secure his seed, after which they revert to the masculine and lie with a woman into whose womb they inject that seed. The offspring of these unions, although the human children of the men whose seed were captured, are reputed to be endowed with extraordinary gifts. Plato, Alexander the Great, and Merlin, among others, are thought to have been conceived through the intervention of a Dusios.*

This is not to say that Dusii only engage in coitus for the purpose of reproduction. They are, like all Incubi, sexually voracious. In a state of almost constant carnal excitation, the Dusios, in his native male form, will copulate with any and every desirable female who puts herself at his disposal, as well as with some who do not, by means of enchantment that causes his victim to sub-

mit willingly to such violation. There is no agreement amongst demonologists as to whether Dusii, or Incubi in general, are in the habit of taking human women by physical force. From my study of the subject, I would suspect that there are some who are and some who are not.

Lili said, "The stone figure in the cave portrays both male and female physical attributes. I had thought you might find it interesting, given your artistic inclinations, but having witnessed your reaction to these satyr statues . . . well, I'm afraid you might be put off by—"

"No, no, not at all," he said quickly. "I . . . I do think I would find it interesting, very much so. I'm sorry if I gave you the wrong impression of me. I daresay I'm a good deal more broad-minded than I let on."

"Well, if you're certain . . ."

"Quite."

The thrush left its post to fly onto the back of a chair near Lili, cheeping furiously in her direction.

"Calm yourself, my friend," she told it in a soothing tone. "We won't go anywhere near your home."

The bird lit off the chair and flew into the cave.

"It lives in there?" he asked.

"Yes, deep inside."

"Do you make a habit of talking to birds?"

With a little smile, she said, "Just that one." Before he could pursue the subject, she turned away from him and began tugging off her long white kid gloves. "I wonder if you wouldn't mind unbuttoning my dress."

$\mathcal{S}ix$

$\mathcal{D}$AVID STARED AT Lili's back, thinking he couldn't have heard her right. Was she asking him to *undress* her?

"It's a new frock, and it will end up filthy if I wear it in there," she said, nodding toward the cave. "Silk is so wretchedly difficult to get clean."

"Do . . . Do you really think it seemly for you to disrobe in the presence of a man whom you barely—"

"This from the gentleman who professes to be broad-minded," she said with a little chuckle. "I assure you I do plan to retain my underpinnings—which, I might add, is more than I had on last night."

Last night. He was ambushed with the image of Lili naked with her legs wrapped around Elic and her head thrown back, gripped in a paroxysm of lust. *"Yes, like that. Oh, God, I'm so close. I'm going to come . . ."*

"Considering what you saw of me then," she said, "your protestations of impropriety strike me as a bit disingenuous."

"I . . . You . . ." *Dear God.* Stammering like some Peeping Tom who'd gotten caught, he said, "I . . . I didn't realize you knew I was . . . That is, I didn't mean to . . ."

"You didn't mean to see what you saw," she said as she turned to face him. "I know that, David, and I'm not trying to embarrass you, truly. I wouldn't have brought it up, but for your objection to unbuttoning me. I shan't press you about it, but neither am I willing to ruin this beautiful dress." Pulling a glove back on, she said, "Let us return to the château, shall we? They'll be serving tea soon."

"Yes, of course, but . . . Perhaps if you told me how to locate the effigy within the cave, I could come back later and—"

"You might have a bit of trouble finding it on your own, even with directions," she said. "It really isn't that important for you to see it, and it would take time away from your work here."

"But . . ." Looking back toward the cave entrance, David thought, *A dusios.* "I must say, you've whetted my curiosity to a very great degree. I, er . . . Perhaps I was, after all, being a bit, well, priggish."

"Not at all. We enjoy a rather bohemian outlook here at Grotte Cachée. Most visitors think us utterly shameless—at least until they get to know us. I should like to get to know *you* a little better, David. You strike me as a man who keeps much of himself hidden. I would find it a most diverting challenge to unearth the real David Beckett."

God help me. He gestured awkwardly for her to turn around so that he could undo her dress.

The buttons that ran like a string of pearls down her back were tiny, round, and covered in the same material as the gown, an iridescent, pale green silk that shifted color with every rustling sway of her skirts. It glimmered bluish one moment, violet the next, imparting an air of illusion and mystique that suited her perfectly—unlike her wide-brimmed sunbonnet with its stovepipe crown, which was charming, to be sure, but a bit too provincial to look quite right on the elegant and alluring Lili.

As if she'd heard that thought and agreed, she untied it and set the bonnet on a chair, along with her gloves. Her hair was scraped up into a simple Apollo knot with the front parted crisply down the center, sans the ringlets that were all the rage at the moment. Most women would have looked rather hard with their hair styled so austerely; Lili looked like a Greek goddess.

It took him some time to pry each button loose from its little loop, a process made all the more arduous by his nervous, fumbling fingers. Gradually the back of the dress parted, revealing a corset of ornately quilted ivory sateen laced with a silken ribbon; the same ribbon connected the front and back with a little bow at the outer edge of each shoulder.

Affecting as casual a tone as he could muster, he said, "I cannot imagine that Elic would take it well, were he to come by and find me undressing you."

After a few seconds of silence, she said, "Are you familiar with the concept of free love, David?"

"I have read the writings of Percy Shelley on the subject."

"What do you think of it?"

"In truth? Not much, I'm afraid."

"Why?"

"I . . . Perhaps we shouldn't discuss this. I do not care to insult you."

"If you intend no insult, none will be inferred."

"I cannot help but believe that indiscriminate coupling reflects poorly upon one's character."

"Ah, but what if one is discriminating?" she asked. He could hear the amusement in her voice.

"It is still a sign of moral weakness. I was brought up to revere the bodily integrity represented by virginity."

"As regards *females*," she said. "I suspect you are a good deal more lenient as regards the transgressions of your own sex."

"Not at all. Continence is as much a virtue for men as for women."

"Don't tell me you're a virgin, David." Her tone implied that such a state of affairs was impossible, even ludicrous.

David paused in his unbuttoning, wishing he'd had the presence of mind to avoid this line of conversation.

She looked at him over her shoulder, her eyes wide with incredulity. "You *are*."

Trying not to let his discomfiture show in his voice, he said, "The union of the sexes is rightly reserved to those joined by the sacrament of marriage."

"You are a pious man, then."

He considered his response as he pushed another button through its loop. "I am regarded as such."

"An intriguingly vague reply. Are you or are you not?"

Oh, how he wanted to be. The counsel of Father Cullen, David's confessor at Stonyhurst, was never far from his thoughts. *"Blind conformity to the laws of the Church ought not to be confused with true devotion, David. You've confessed to taking an excess of pride in your truthfulness, your perfect observance of your vows and of ecclesiastical law. You've done penance for the sin of vainglory, yet it is a sin from which you cannot seem to refrain. A priest should be, first and foremost, a man of faith, not an exemplar of correct behavior—or a slave to it. Sometimes I think you've chosen a religious vocation more to minister to yourself than to minister to others. Think long and hard on this before your ordination, my son."*

"Genuine, unassailable piety," David told Lili carefully, "is something to which I aspire."

"Do you think, if you live your life in a cage of righteousness and rectitude, that you will awaken one morning suddenly aglow with true faith?"

Jolted by her perception, David didn't answer her. Instead, he pried the last two buttons through their loops and said, "That should do it."

She pulled two pillowy pads from the sleeves and tossed them aside, then raised her arms, saying "Would you be so kind?"

He divested her of the dress with unpracticed awkwardness, gathering it up as best he could into a great mass while working the sleeves free.

"You can just lay it on that table." She set about untying a sort of backward apron of starched white lace ruffles affixed over her voluminous petticoats—a bustle, only the second one David had ever seen.

The first was a pink one that his sister Blanche's lady's maid had been laying out on her mistress's bed, along with a ball gown and assorted other underpinnings, as fifteen-year-old David passed by in the hall. There'd been a corset there, too, as well as a chemise and stockings and a great white lather of flounced petticoats. David had gaped at the indelicate display for perhaps three full seconds before Eileen noticed him and shut the door in his face, saying "You'll see your fill of such things soon enough, Master Davey, a handsome youngblood like yourself."

But he hadn't seen his fill. In the decade that had passed since then, he hadn't so much as touched a woman—not in that way. He'd imagined, he'd yearned. More than once, while lying in bed with a rock-hard, weeping cockstand he couldn't will away, he'd been tempted to seek out a woman, any woman, and slake his raging lust in her—but not once had he surrendered to that temptation.

Having laid the dress carefully across the table, David turned to find Lili pulling off the last of several stiffly corded petticoats.

"I . . . thought you were going to leave those on," he said.

"The hems will get grimy—as would my shoes and stockings." Adding the petticoat to the others mounded on a chair, she kicked off her satin slippers and reached under her calf-length chemise to peel off her stockings and garters. Around her left ankle she wore a circlet of hammered gold ornamented with a disc of dark blue stone.

All she had on now was the corset over the chemise, which had a wide, scooped neckline and elbow-length sleeves. The corset nipped in snugly at the waist, flaring out at the bottom to accommodate Lili's hips. It flared at the top a bit, too, pushing at the underside of her bosom to plump her breasts into high, firm globes that strained the filmy linen of her chemise. So fine, indeed, was that linen that David could tell from the way it draped her legs that she wore no drawers or pantaloons.

"David?"

He met Lili's gaze, heat suffusing his cheeks when he realized she'd seen him eyeing her.

"Shall we do it?" she asked in that throaty-soft voice as she approached him.

David stopped breathing for a moment as she curled her hand around his elbow, her flimsily clad breasts nudging his arm. He fancied he could feel their heat through the layers of wool and linen that separated his flesh from hers.

"Here," he said, shrugging out of his coat and offering it to her. "Take this."

"I don't need it."

I do. Improper though it was for him to be coatless in the company of a female, *her* state of undress was by far the more scandalous—and likely to set his blood astir. "Caves tend to be chilly and damp."

"Not this one. Besides, I told you, my body runs warm."

Draping it over her shoulders, he said, "Take it anyway."

The *Cella* reminded David of a chapel, regardless that the people who had once worshipped here were pagans. The entrance was a wide, arched opening rimmed in rainbow-hued stalactites and other formations, quite majestic, really. It was flanked by a pair of lighted iron cresset torches identical to those that lined the cave corridor they had followed to get here. Clearly, Lili had been fibbing when she'd told him he would have trouble finding this location on his own.

The *Cella* was accessible via a natural stone bridge spanning the cave stream, which flowed directly across the entrance. It was a sort of alcove, but a sizable one, with a high, domed ceiling perforated by a shaft to the outside. The shaft evidently served as a chimney for the bronze-lined fire pit beneath it, which did not appear to have been used for some time.

Directly in front of him, looming a good ten feet high on the back wall between a pair of cressets on iron stanchions, stood a massive, crudely carved sculpture of a human-type being with two roundish lumps denoting breasts and a longer one jutting up from the groin that was meant to represent an erect penis. The face was stylized in the extreme—two almond shapes had been etched for eyes, an oval depression for the mouth. The body was thick and ponderous, with shapeless legs and arms, the latter holding aloft a pair of cups. Badly rusted iron torques encircled the wrists, ankles, and neck, the latter having been forged in the shape of a male organ penetrating that of a female.

DUSIVÆSUS had been carved in surprisingly precise Roman letters onto the base of the statue. Scratched over that rather crudely was a string of symbols David would have taken for runes had they been somewhere in Scandinavia rather than France.

"What is the meaning of the inscriptions?" he asked Lili.

"The one on top has been a subject of speculation for centuries," she said. " 'Dusivæsus' means 'Great and Worthy Dusios' in the ancient Gaulish tongue."

"Great and worthy? I realize the Gauls had many gods, but I'd never have guessed they engaged in demon worship."

"They didn't worship this dusios, precisely." She paused; he had the sense that she was choosing her words with care.

So painfully beautiful was she, with the torchlight gilding her hair, her face, the upper slopes of her breasts, that he had to look away for fear that she would catch him ogling her again.

"They did have a god whom they worshipped with especial zeal," she said, "one they venerated above all others and were sworn to protect, an ancient god born of fire who lived deep in this cave."

Returning his gaze to her so as to gauge her reaction, he said, "Listening to you, one would almost think you believe this 'god' really existed."

She lifted those delicate, luminous shoulders. "The world is very old and very mysterious, David. I do not pretend to be privy to its many secrets—nor do I feel the need to ferret them out so as to know the absolute truth of things. My mind and my heart are open to all possibilities, but I am content in the knowledge that there are some things that I am destined never to know."

She was, of course, alluding to David and his painstaking quest for faith.

"Why, then, *is* there a statue of a dusios in this place of worship if they didn't regard dusii as gods?" he asked.

"I understand they erected it to help their druid—that was a sort of high priest . . ."

"Yes, I know."

"It was meant to help him summon a dusios to their village."

"They *invited* a demonic being into their midst?"

"You seem astounded," she said with a bemused little laugh.

"Horrified, actually."

He was. "To lay oneself open to a diabolical creature, one of the Devil's minions . . . That way lies earthly misery and an afterlife of torment in . . . the dark place."

Lili's mouth quirked at his use of the euphemism for Hell, which he had been taught from boyhood never to utter in the presence of a lady. "You are speaking of demonic possession, yes?"

"Possession and influence both. There are said to be demons—not malevolent spirits, but real, flesh-and-blood diabolical beings—who work their evil from without, by tempting their human victims to unholy thoughts and actions." Just as Lili, with her breathtaking beauty and feral sexuality, tempted him. Were she not so warm to the touch, he might be inclined to label her a demoness, so thoroughly had she bewitched him.

"Such demons," he continued, "will exploit a human's vulnerability to evil—his lack of faith, or a secret taint of sin—in order to exercise their diabolical influence."

"An influence that would be impossible, or at least unlikely, if a human were exceptionally pious—or at least exceptionally desirous of piety."

That statement cut close to the bone, as it was clearly intended to do.

"You believe in this?" she asked.

"No doubt you find that laughable."

David had learned not to discuss demons and the like except within the ecclesiastical community. His brothers used to taunt him mercilessly, donning grotesque costumes and leaping upon him in dark places amid hellish cackles and shrieks. Even some of his fellow clerics were openly skeptical about the existence of diabolical entities. He would not be expounding on the subject with Lili had she not broached it herself by showing him this pagan effigy—not that he regretted it. It could prove beneficial to his investigation to establish the attitude of Lili and her fellow Grotte Cachée residents in regard to demons and demonic forces.

"I don't find it at all laughable," she said, so soberly that David was disposed to believe her. "Did I not tell you that my mind is open to all possibilities? It is just that so few hum—people still credit the existence of these types of beings. I can't help but wonder how you came to believe in them."

"It was my nursery governess, Mademoiselle Levesque. She was an elderly spinster who had served my father's family for decades in France."

"Your parents are French?"

Cursing that slip, David said, "Just my father."

"A Frenchman named Beckett?" she said. "I gather he anglicized his name."

David didn't correct her assumption. "Father had a family in France, a wife and children, before he came to England and married my mother. They were arrested during the Reign of Terror—not my father, who was away at the time, but his parents, his wife, and his four children. A band of revolutionaries abducted them from their château, carted them to the town square, and guillotined them all."

"Oh, how awful."

"Mademoiselle Levesque witnessed it all, and described it to me in . . . rather graphic detail—how the freshly severed heads of the victims were lifted by the hair to face the mob, because their brains would remain alive for ten to fifteen seconds. Their eyes could still see the faces twisted in hate, their ears could still hear the taunts and jeers."

"She was your nursery governess, you say? How old were you when she told you this?"

"Five, six . . ."

"What on earth was she thinking, recounting such things to a child of that age?"

"The Terror had traumatized her deeply. She was devoted to my family, had helped to rear my father and his siblings. Two of his three brothers, who were priests, were brought before the Revolutionary Tribunal and condemned to the guillotine. The third was beaten to death by a mob. His only sister was among sixteen Carmelite nuns put to death at the Barrière de Vincennes in the final days of the Terror."

"I know of them," Lili said. "Their martyrdom wasn't in vain. People were outraged, and that outrage helped to bring down Robespierre."

"By the time I knew Mademoiselle, she was . . ." *Half mad.* "She was a melancholic, deeply tormented soul, very much lost in her wretched memories—she talked of little else. My father was the only member of his family to survive the Revolution. He escaped to England, along with Mademoiselle, in the summer of ninety-four. Two years later, he married my mother, who was a good deal younger than he, and started a second family. He told me he'd very nearly become a Carmelite monk instead, but after praying on it, he knew that wasn't the path that God intended for him."

"I am deeply sorry for your family's losses," Lili said, "but I don't quite see what this has to do with demons."

"Mademoiselle Levesque used to tell me that the revolutionary mobs had been acting under diabolical influence. How else to explain such rabid brutality?"

"You are young, David. You have not seen the enragés, *with their wild red eyes and their filthy hair, you have not heard them screaming for the blood of the innocents. The Devil's minions, they crawl into the hearts and minds of the impious and make them commit these* actes d'abomination. *God has a purpose for you,* mon chouchou. *You have a vocation,* oui? *You will hunt the demons down and cast them out, banish them to the fiery pit. This is your destiny, your sacred obligation."*

David said, "My father told me it was true, what Mademoiselle had said about the demons inciting the Terror. He also taught me that honor, duty, and religious devotion would protect me from Satan's influence, and that there was no more worthy calling on earth than the . . ." David bit off the rest, cursing his loose tongue.

"Than the priesthood?" Lili smiled. "You said last night that your parents are content with the path you've chosen. I'm glad of that for your sake. A man should choose a vocation based on what he's passionate about, not afraid of. A life devoted to fear is a sad thing, indeed."

David tried to summon a response to that, but none was forthcoming.

As they were walking away from the *Cella,* David turned to glance behind them at the stretch of corridor that led deeper into the cave. It was black as Hades that way, the cresset torches extending no farther.

Testing the waters, as it were, he said, "I would dearly love to explore a bit more. Is this cave system really complex enough to get lost in?"

"Oh, it's a warren of twisting and turning passages," she

said. "Even I get confused if I wander too far off the main cor-
ridors, and I daresay I know this terrain as well as anyone—except, perhaps, for Darius."

"I have yet to meet this mysterious Darius." David's investigation would be sorely lacking in scope were he to leave here
without having personal contact with each and every inhabi-
tant of Grotte Cachée. "I cannot help but wonder if he really
exists."

"Darius is a solitary soul," she said. "He tends to avoid our
guests. As for the cave, if you really want to go deeper, I suppose
I could guide you, say another half mile or so—providing you
don't tell Archer. There's something rather interesting that you
might enjoy seeing."

"Indeed?" said David, thinking of the curious little bedchamber described to him by Serges Bourgoin. "I should be
very much in your debt."

"You would, at that," she said, smiling as she wrested a cresset from its bracket. "But I believe there is a way you can repay
me."

Seven

ONE WISH, DAVID mused as he stood gazing at what Lili called the Lake of a Thousand Diamonds—which was resplendent, but which was not Bourgoin's *petite salle confortable.*

He had promised to grant her one wish of her choosing—her whimsical notion of how he could "repay the debt" of her having guided him here against the *administrateur*'s wishes. Not once, that he could recall, had he ever reneged on a promise, and he did not intend to do so now. He prayed that what she asked of him wouldn't be something he would have to confess to Father Cullen when he got back to Stonyhurst.

That is, part of him prayed for that. The other part, the part that lived chained up in the shadows, hot and hungry and trembling with need, would gladly say a lifetime of Hail Marys for the chance to cast off those crippling fetters just once.

"What think you, David?" Lili gestured with her cresset toward the shimmering subterranean pool, a crescent-shaped widening of the cave stream, which flowed mostly below-ground.

The pool was tucked into its own glittering grotto, the walls and ceiling of which were encrusted with a dazzling array of crystal formations—flowers, feathers, coral-like nodules . . . Rippling draperies of peachy, translucent stone swooped and swayed at the entrance to this enchanted niche like curtains frozen on a summer breeze. The water itself was a glassy aquamarine that glowed from within, projecting lazy waves of iridescence onto the interior of the grotto, making the crystals sparkle and wink.

It was dizzyingly beautiful—literally. All that dazzling splendor . . . it just looked so unreal, so not of this earth. A rush of vertigo overtook him for a moment, then faded away. The light-headedness he had experienced previously had escalated considerably as they'd ventured deeper and deeper into the cave. His perceptions felt skewed, his thoughts strangely slippery. David couldn't help but recall Domenico Vitturi's account of the delirium and strange apparitions the deeper precincts of this cave could produce. Was he feeling this way because Vitturi had put the suggestion in his mind, or because there really was some supernatural energy emanating from within these walls of rock, this mountain of cooled lava?

"Was it worth the trek?" Lili asked.

"It is one of the most beautiful things I've ever seen," David said. "Astonishing. Where does the light come from?"

Pointing, she said, "If you'll look beneath the surface on that side, you'll see two outlets. They're tunnels that curve upward, opening to the outside and letting the sunlight in. If we want to swim here at night, we sometimes put torches out there, so that their light emanates from below."

"Extraordinary," David said.

"It cannot be properly appreciated when there are other

sources of light." Lili lifted an iron bucket tucked between two of the pinkish stone "curtains" and filled it with water from the pool.

"Wait," David said, walking toward her. "What are you doing? You're not going to—"

The cresset sizzled as she plunged it into the water, hissing the dirty tang of doused embers and engulfing them in darkness—except for the radiant pool behind her.

"Why the devil did you do that?" David asked, hating the strident edge to his voice. "That cresset was our only source of light for the return trip."

"No, it wasn't." Lili shoved the cresset with its iron basket full of sodden pine chunks into a bracket on a floor-to-ceiling natural column. "That's full of more pitch pine," she said, pointing to a kindling box on the floor nearby, on top of which sat a tarnished brass casket about the size of a deck of cards. "And there are Lucifer matches in that match safe."

Thus reassured, David was in a more receptive state of mind to appreciate the sight of Lili backlit by the Lake of a Thousand Diamonds as she shucked off his coat and hung it on a nearby stalagmite. She untied the shoulder ribbons of her corset, reached behind to loosen the lacing, and stepped out of it. Holding his gaze, she walked toward him, her body silhouetted by the lambent glow through her chemise.

David grew instantly hard. *Please, God, don't let her see,* he thought, since he no longer wore that concealing coat.

Lili came to stand before him, so close that he could feel her heat, breathe in the exotic floral warmth of her skin, plummet headlong into those inky eyes.

She reached up and, with a fluid gesture, lifted his hat off his head and spun it away into the darkness. His heart thundered in his ears as she untied his cravat, pulling that off along with his collar.

Unbuttoning the top few buttons of his shirt, she said, so softly that he could barely hear her, "Swim with me."

David undressed down to his shirt and drawers as she waded into the pool. When it was deep enough to swim in, she did so, disappearing around the curve of the crescent for a little while before reappearing. She swam with practiced grace, seemingly unencumbered by her chemise.

She stood, whipping her head back to fling her wet hair off her face. The water rose to just beneath her breasts, to which the chemise clung damply, revealing their lush contours and the shadows of her nipples.

"You're not going to leave your shirt on, are you?" she asked.

"Yes." Even if he was willing to invent some specious excuse, it would be pointless. Lili was a woman experienced in the ways of the flesh. He was quite sure she knew why he wanted to retain the long, concealing garment.

David braced himself for a jolt of cold as he stepped into the water, only to feel a delicious, all-encompassing warmth . . . followed by a thundercrack of lust so profound that it almost brought him to his knees.

"Are you all right, David?" she asked.

"Just a bit . . . Yes," he said. "Yes, I'm fine."

She beckoned him with a provocative smile as old as mankind.

The stone floor of the pool felt pleasantly smooth beneath David's feet as he entered the water, with just enough friction to maintain his footing, and no trace of the sliminess he'd half expected. It sloped downward until he was standing waist deep with a suitable expanse of water, about two yards, separating him from Lili. The watery phosphorescence set her face aglow, as if she were bathed in the very light of heaven.

"Keeping your distance, are you, Mr. Beckett?" she teased. "Is it to protect me from you, or the other way 'round?"

He looked away, a grudging smile tugging at his lips.

She splashed him with water, which so startled him that he gasped with laughter. He reflexively splashed her back. With a squeal of mock outrage, she leapt upon him and dunked him underwater.

He surfaced, his legs tangled in the clinging billows of her chemise, his hand brushing a soft and weighty breast.

He took two stumbling steps backward, skimming the hair off his face.

With a nonchalant smile, she said, "Come," then turned and swam away.

David stood staring after her for a moment—*One wish . . . Swim with me*—and then he swam, too. He followed her around the curve of the crescent to find that the pool narrowed, flowing through a doorlike opening before widening again. Very little light from the main pool penetrated into this secondary lagoon, making it seem as if night had suddenly fallen—a moonless night, but alive with darkly glinting stars, courtesy of the crystalline walls.

The water was deeper here, as David discovered when he found his footing; it came up almost to his neck. It was too deep for Lili to stand, of course. She kept her head above water by holding on to his shoulder with one hand and the side of the pool with the other, and lazily treading her feet.

There was no gradual declination here, the pool walls being roughly vertical. Peering into the darkness, he could see that they were almost completely surrounded by a flat shelf of stone. He squinted at a heap of something, trying to make it out. The shelf, although no more than six or eight feet wide at its broadest point, was furnished with rugs, pillows, and perhaps a dozen fat, unlit candles on the floor and in iron wall sconces.

"We call that *la Galerie des Diamants Noirs*," she said.

"The Gallery of Black Diamonds," he said. "Most appropriate."

She gave him a puzzled look. "I thought you didn't speak French."

Scrambling for a response, he said, "The, er . . . most of the words sound like their counterparts in English—*galerie, diamants* . . ."

"As for 'noir,' I suppose it's been used in enough poetry and so forth . . ."

"Exactly." He cringed inside at this wormy prevarication. Having long ago resolved to be, in the words of the Fifteenth Psalm, "He that walketh uprightly, and worketh righteousness, and speaketh the truth in his heart," David was determined to avoid outright untruths during the course of this investigation. He had realized some lies of omission would be unavoidable; he just hadn't realized how many would pass his lips.

Redirecting the conversation to safer territory, he said, "This is quite a cozy little haven."

His voice sounded both hollow and strangely deep as it echoed off the walls. There was a winded quality to it, too, not because that brief little swim had tired him, of course, but from Lili's closeness, the warmth of her hand on his shoulder, the teasing underwater caress of her chemise as her legs pumped back and forth in a languid rhythm.

"This is one of my favorite places," she said, her own voice taking on a velvety resonance that seemed to vibrate within him, stoking his arousal even as it soothed his nerves.

The strange intoxication that had crept up on him as he'd ventured deeper into the cave took on a different, dreamier quality in this dark little sanctum. There was that lingering surge of lust, yes, but something else as well, a sense of ethereal harmony such as he had never known. It was like being drunk,

but without the mental bedlam, just pure and idyllic content-
ment.

"You seem . . . contemplative," she said.

"I'm not sure that's the right word. In truth, I feel . . . not
quite like myself."

With a knowing smile, she said, "Our guests ofttimes experience a certain confusion of the senses in here. It has to do in
part with the hardened lava that formed this cave system eons
ago. From what I've been told, it is imbued with a special sort
of magnetism. We call it *le magnétisme hallucinatoire.* Some experience a milder form of the same disorientation within the
walls of the castle, and also the stable and carriage house, because they were built of volcanic stone taken from this mountain. This force even affects the water of the cave stream."

"And the other part?"

"Other part?"

"You said the phenomenon was due 'in part' to the hardened lava."

Lifting her hand from his shoulder to stroke his cheek, she
said, "You are a man of many questions, David. This need to get
to the root of everything, to ferret out answers to the unknow-
able . . . it will only lead to misery. As will the demands you
place upon yourself. You are so rigid, so correct. Your expectations of yourself are exacting to the point of cruelty—self-
inflicted, to be sure, but cruel nonetheless."

Her eyes, enormous in the scintillating darkness, were
almond-shaped, heavy-lidded, utterly mesmerizing. David
could not, for the life of him, tear his gaze from hers.

Softly she said, "Have you never wanted to lie with a
woman, David?"

"Of course." To deny that would have been absurd.

"Most young men of your station relieve their urges by

frequenting the local brothels. Were you never tempted to visit them yourself?"

His hesitation must have been telling, because she said, "You did, didn't you? But you paid the women there to pleasure you without actual intercourse—to fellate you, perhaps?"

"No! My God, no," he said, momentarily astounded to hear her speak of such a thing—but of course Lili was no ordinary lady. Some would protest that she was no lady at all, but despite her libertinage, she was far from some common grisette. "I never . . . nothing like that."

"But you *have* been to brothels," she said.

"Just once."

"When?"

David looked away, raking a hand through his wet hair. He could refuse to answer her, but in his pleasantly bleary state of mind, he just couldn't quite see the point.

"My, er, my brother Louis dragged me to one in London shortly before I left for . . . left home for the first time." *"Come on, Davey, don't be such a Nancy boy. Don't you want to exercise the old lob before those Jesuits make a bloody eunuch of you?"*

"What of your reverence for the bodily integrity represented by virginity?" Although Lili was echoing his words, to her credit, her tone was not mocking.

"I had no notion where he was taking me till we were in the place. It was a handsome town house, finely appointed. One would never have known it was . . . that sort of establishment. Louis had poured gin down my throat beforehand—all part of his scheme, of course. I told him he could lead a horse to water, and so forth. He said, 'Fine, let's just watch the show. Perhaps you'll have a change of heart.'"

"Show?"

With that interjection, David became suddenly aware of what he was telling this woman whom he'd met barely twenty-four hours ago. It was the lulling influence upon his mind of the strange forces lurking in the walls around them, the very mountain looming above them. He should have been ashamed to be here like this with Lili, much less recounting this particular experience, but he felt too tranquil for shame.

"Tell me," she said as she stroked his arm. "I won't be shocked. Was it a lewd performance?"

"You know of these things?"

"I've seen them."

His jaw literally dropped.

"Was it just a little tableau in the drawing room," she asked, "or something more elaborate?"

"Well, er . . . more elaborate, I should say." Emboldened by her candor, the nocturnal intimacy of the dark little grotto, the voluptuous embrace of the water, he said, "It was a . . . well, a stage play of sorts, conducted in a double parlor that had been turned into a theater, with chairs and couches facing a little stage that had been furnished like a sitting room. Some of the couches for the audience had curtains 'round them so that . . . well, for privacy if a fellow was sitting with one of the . . . women of the house."

"Did this stage play have a story, or was it just a series of vignettes?"

"No, there was a story. A maidservant and the master of the house . . . well . . ."

"Let me guess," said Lili. "The maid had been disobedient, and the master had to punish her."

"Something like that. It was called 'Taming the Trull—a Master's Revenge.'"

"Tell me about it."

David groaned theatrically. "He . . . he suspected she'd been stealing from him, pilfering small items, so he told his footman to keep an eye on her. The footman spied on her from behind a curtain as she started dusting and polishing her master's sitting room. She dusted for a bit, and then she lay down on a couch and . . . lifted her skirts and . . ."

"Pleasured herself?"

"With the, er . . . handle of the duster." David had never seen the female sexual organ before that evening, nor imagined that women engaged in such behavior. He'd watched with utter fascination . . . and an adamantine erection.

"What did she look like?"

"Bright red hair and an Irish complexion."

"I take it the footman found this little display interesting."

"He, er, rubbed himself as he watched her. He was a brawny fellow, tall and muscular, and he wore very snug breeches, so that one could see . . . well, that he was genuinely aroused."

"It must have been quite a shock to you, in your naïveté, to witness such things," she said.

"I couldn't believe my eyes. I was aghast."

"But you didn't leave."

David sighed.

"What happened next?" Lili asked. "Did she steal something?"

Nodding, David said, "She took a silver wax sealer from the master's writing desk and secreted it . . . inside herself . . ."

"The quim or the arse?" Lili asked, as conversationally as if she were making drawing room small talk.

"The, er, latter. She coated it first with some of the linseed oil she'd been using on the furniture. And then she got up and started polishing the desk with the seal still in her." David heard himself saying these outrageous things with a sense of hypnotic detachment. "The footman came into the room and told her he'd keep mum about what he'd seen if she would give him a French trick. I didn't know at the time what that meant. He took off his coat and opened his breeches, and she got down on her knees. I couldn't believe it when she . . . took him into her mouth."

"Did it excite you?"

"How could it not have?" He was hard as a club just remembering it all . . . and recounting it to the beguiling Lili as she floated so close, her hand light and warm on his shoulder, her legs brushing his from time to time as she treaded water.

"Did he come?" Lili asked.

Come. David had always assumed that this word, with this particular connotation, was one that only men used, or were even aware of. *Fool.*

He shook his head. "The master entered the room with a friend of his, both of them in riding clothes. He was livid when he saw what the help had been up to while he was away. The footman started babbling excuses, but the master would have none of it. He and his friend wrestled the fellow into a hardback chair, tied him up, and shoved a gag in his mouth."

"With his breeches still open and his cock out, I suppose."

"Er, yes. The master demanded of the maid whether she'd stolen anything. She denied it, showing him that her apron pockets were empty, but he didn't believe her, so he ordered her to strip and hand him each piece of clothing to examine. She refused at first, until he threatened to sack her without references, and then she reluctantly undressed down to her stockings and a . . . It wasn't an ordinary corset, because it didn't come up to . . ." He gestured in the vicinity of his upper chest. "It was of black satin with a great deal of boning, very snug about the waist, like a wide, tight girdle. I don't know what to call it."

Lili chuckled. "It's called a girdle. It's for cinching in the waist while leaving the bosom unencumbered. Did she have beautiful breasts?"

"They were . . . very large and white." And, if he wasn't

mistaken, she'd reddened her nipples with the same rouge she'd used on her lips. "The master and his friend stared at her quite openly as she disrobed, the tied-up footman, too, and I could see that all three of them were aroused. She said, 'There, you see? You've found nothing because there was nothing to find.' The master said, 'We'll see about that,' and he ordered her to bend over and hold on to the writing desk, so that her . . . posterior aspect was facing the audience. He made her spread her legs, and then he searched . . . inside her for the seal."

"The arse, or . . . ?"

"No, the, er . . . the other. He felt around with his fingers, shoving them deeper and deeper, the thumb, too, until his entire hand was buried to the wrist. The maid was groaning and struggling and begging him to stop—the friend had to hold her down. She admitted that she'd filched the seal, and told him where it was, but that only earned her a whipping on top of . . . the bit with the hand. He took a riding crop to her bum as he worked the hand around inside her, saying . . . well, some things I would rather not repeat."

"You like it hard and nasty, don't you, you thieving cunt? I've never felt such a wet pussy. Fucking whore. Trollop. Lying little slut. Let's feel that clit—why it's hard as a bullet."

"He bet his friend ten quid that he could make her . . . well, bring her to climax in twenty seconds, and she said he couldn't make her do it if she didn't want to. He pulled the seal out partway and shoved it in and out of her while stroking her very quickly with his fingertips, and she did climax—or pretended to. But Louis told me he was sure she really did, because the master had her stand up and turn 'round then, and she had a sort of mottled flush all over her chest and face. He said that happens to women when they come."

David almost apologized for uttering so vulgar a word as

"come." Absurd, of course; Lili had used that word herself, and "cock" and "quim" and "arse." He really was a prig.

"Some women flush like that," Lili said, "especially the pale ones—but there are even women with my coloring who do."

He wondered whether *she* did, but even in his current, serenely muddled state, he had the presence of mind not to inquire.

"What happened next?" she asked.

David suspected, from the breathiness of her voice and the way her eyes glistened in the dark, that his ribald recounting was affecting her the same way it was affecting him. He supposed the smutty little scenario, however brutal and unsavory, had been designed to titillate, and titillate it did. It was a heady feeling, knowing that he had the power to arouse this exquisite seductress without even touching her.

"The master ordered her to finish up the dusting and polishing just as she was, practically naked. He made her crawl on all fours to get under the furniture, that sort of thing. He and his friend sat on a chaise longue and smoked cigars and fondled themselves as they watched her. The footman was watching her, too. He was moaning through the gag and writhing and thrusting his hips."

"He was still hard?" Lili asked.

"Oh, yes. The master laughed and said it looked as if the footman needed a good dusting, too. He had her brush him with the feather duster—his cock, I mean—very lightly, over and over again, until the poor bloke was bucking and thrashing like a wounded bear. The way the chair was creaking, I was sure it was going to break apart at any moment. It may have been just a stage play, but the sensation was obviously very real. Finally, his body went all rigid, and his eyes rolled up, and he . . . well, he ejaculated."

"Just from being brushed with the duster?" Lili asked. "Are you sure he actually came, and didn't just pretend?"

"It shot halfway across the stage."

"Mm . . ."

"The master stretched out on the chaise then, and took out his cock, and had her sit astride him. He had her like that while his friend got behind her and . . ."

"Buggered her."

David nodded. "He greased himself up with the linseed oil first, but she still gritted her teeth when he pressed into her. It started off fairly slow and controlled, with the men thrusting in the same rhythm and saying filthy things to the maid, but by the end, it was wild, a frenzy of writhing bodies. I believe she came twice. When the men came, they pulled out and did it on her. That was the end of the program. They actually took bows, all four of them."

"Did you have a 'change of heart' then, as Louis had hoped?"

"Well . . . I didn't admit as much, even to myself, but I did let him take me upstairs 'to meet someone,' who of course turned out to be a woman wearing naught but a lace shimmy and a string of pearls. He left me with her and went with one of the other whores."

"Were you willing to let her ply her wares, as it were?"

"By that point, I was beside myself with lust. I would have done anything to assuage it. She said she knew I'd never been with a woman before—Louis had told her—and would I like to see a pussy up close? She didn't wait for me to answer, just lifted her shimmy, propped a foot on a chair, and spread her . . . private parts wide open. She started unbuttoning my breeches, and I begged her to stop. She told me not to be shy, and kept at it. It wasn't shyness, but rather a fear of humiliating myself by coming off in my drawers . . ." He let out a gust of air. "Which was precisely what I did."

"Oh, David," Lili murmured.

"She tried to reassure me, but she couldn't quite contain her giggles, and I was . . ." He shook his head. "Utterly humiliated. I fled the brothel and flagged down a hack." He lifted his shoulders. "And so ended my brush with defloration."

"My poor, virtuous David." Lili stroked his forehead, his cheek. She brushed her thumb over his lower lip, the sensation rawly carnal despite the relative innocence of the gesture. Even in near darkness, her skin had a luster to it that made him think of firelight through a frosty window. She was beyond ravishing; she was the most magnificent creature he had ever beheld.

She said, "You have a beautiful mouth, David. Have you ever been kissed?"

He swallowed, gave an infinitesimal shake of his head.

"Surely you don't think *kissing* should be reserved exclusively for the marital bed," she said.

"No. No, of course not. It's just that . . . I've not actually had many opportunities to . . . be in the company of women."

Lili took his face in both hands, prompting him to put his arms around her so that she wouldn't sink. She cupped the back of his head, coaxing it gently down as she craned upward, her gaze on his mouth.

She whispered against his lips, "You are in the company of a woman now."

Eight

LILI STOPPED BREATHING when her lips met David's. She didn't think she would ever grow blasé about first kisses, the shivery thrill they evoked, that rush of newness, anticipation, sexual promise. But to kiss a man who had never been kissed before, a gravely serious young man harboring deep, untapped passions . . . The sweet, hot pleasure of it made her heart thrum in her chest.

His mouth was soft and hot, unsure. He moaned when she deepened the kiss, sliding the tip of her tongue very lightly along the sensitive flesh inside his upper lip.

His arms tightened, crushing her to him. He pinned her against the wall of the pool, his mouth suddenly greedy and demanding, his erection prodding her belly. Through her breasts, she could feel the pummeling of his heart, like a fist trying to smash through a door.

She moved against him, desperate to ease the terrible lust that held her in its talons. He pressed himself to her, rubbing his cock against her belly, his hectic breathing, and hers, echoing in the little chamber.

She yanked his shirt up and reached between them to untie his drawers. He gasped as her fingers brushed the head of his cock through the thin linen.

"Oh, God." Drawing back, he closed a quaking hand over hers. "Stop. Stop. I can't . . . I can't, Lili. I made a v—" He groaned like an enraged beast, slammed his fist against the stone wall of the pool. "*Goddammit.* I just can't."

He backed away from her, crossing himself as he whispered something, perhaps a mea culpa for the profanity, perhaps a plea for strength.

Lili had a much better view of him than he had of her, thanks to her ability to see in the dark. Her vision at night, or in a place like this, was similar to what a human might see on a cloudless night with a full moon. Colors were washed out, shadows black as pitch, and brighter areas, like faces, almost phosphorescent.

She said, "You're a man, David, with a man's needs. Why must you scourge yourself this way? I don't understand."

"And I can't explain. By my word, if I were free to . . . do this in good conscience, I would. You've cast a spell upon me, Lili. I've never felt such passion, but . . ." He shook his head helplessly. "I'm sorry. This is all my fault. I should never have told you all that, about the brothel and the play . . ."

"It wasn't that which excited my passions," she said. "My blood has been simmering since the moment I met you."

He looked astounded.

"If you are under a spell," she said, "then I am, too, because I am utterly in your thrall. I am weak with desire. If I cannot have you, then at least let me feel your body against mine, your hands upon me . . ." She took his hand and gently pressed it to her sex through the chemise, inciting a spasm of pleasure.

"Please, David, I'm so close, I can't bear it. I shan't ask for more, I promise, but don't deny me this, I beg you."

He shifted his hand just slightly, molding it to the inflamed flesh, feeling its contours, one finger pressing on the seam between the lips.

She pushed against his hand. "Yes . . . David, please . . ."

"I shouldn't," he said in a low, unsteady voice—but he did not withdraw his hand.

"You promised me a wish."

"Just one," he said in a gently chiding voice that held a hint of amusement. "And I did swim with you."

"That wasn't a wish, it was an invitation. This"—she pressed his hand to her more firmly—"is my wish."

He smiled and shook his head. "You are a witch."

"So I've been told."

He studied her in charged silence. Finally he said, "All right."

She sighed in relief.

"But not here." Nodding toward the *galerie,* he said, "There."

Lili hoisted herself up with the aid of David's hands about her waist—not that she needed the help, but men liked to do that sort of thing. David leapt up with masculine grace, wringing out his shirt as he looked around. "Are there matches for the candles?" he asked.

"Yes," she said as she pulled the sodden chemise off and slung it aside, "but I rather fancy the dark." Darkness eased the inhibitions of humans. It was one of the first things she'd learned as a young goddess with an unquenchable appetite for the beautiful *gabrus* who came to pay homage at her temple in Akkad every month when the moon was new.

It was dark, yes, but not so dark that David couldn't see her standing naked before him. He surveyed her with those big, watchful eyes, his chest rising and falling beneath the damply clinging shirt, every muscle sharply delineated. The wet linen clung, as well, to his erection, which rose even taller as he took her in. He noticed the direction of her gaze and pulled his shirt away from his body.

"Lie with me," she said, lowering herself onto a velvety rug heaped with pillows.

He lay on his side facing her, but without touching her. Lili took his hand, kissed his palm, and cupped it over a breast. He squeezed and stroked it, his expression rapt.

They kissed some more, and then Lili moved his hand from her breast to her sex, parting her legs a bit. He trailed his fingers very slowly along the slit, then into it, exploring her slippery inner lips with a curiosity that was both touching and intensely arousing.

She gasped in startled pleasure when a fingertip grazed her clit.

He felt the stiff little bud, saying, "Is . . . is this . . . ?"

"Yes. Oh, God, don't," she said, grabbing his wrist. "It's too sensitive. I don't want to come yet. Here." She guided his hand lower, nudging his middle and index fingers inside her.

He propped himself up on his elbow, his expression one of utter fascination as he felt the damp, hot passage from within.

"Like this," she breathed, pressing against his hand until his fingers were completely sheathed. Their movements, as he investigated her interior contours, made her hips tremble, her back arch.

"It feels amazing," he murmured, lowering his head. His mouth felt hot and hungry against hers. He groaned when her thigh brushed his straining erection.

"I could kiss you, David," she whispered.

"We *are* kissing."

"No, I mean in the French manner, like in the play at the

brothel. You must have wondered how it would feel to have a woman pleasure you with her mouth."

Through a guttural chuckle, he said, "Hundreds of times—thousands. After I saw that play, I could think of little else, especially at night, when my passions are hardest to control. I still lie awake sometimes, imagining the sensation of a tongue . . . lips . . ." He shook his head, his jaw tight.

"Let me—"

"I can't."

"But it wouldn't compromise your chastity, not really."

Ruefully he said, "My chastity was compromised the moment our lips touched. Being with you like this is sinful enough. I do not care to compound that sin by letting you . . ." He sighed.

"I wish I could do that for you, David."

"So do I, believe me."

"Would it be as grievous an offense if you pleasured *me* that way?"

David's gaze shifted to his hand, his fingers still half buried inside her. "I . . . No, I, um . . . I shouldn't think so, but . . ."

"But you would rather not. I under—"

"What? No! No, I . . . I should very much like to. I just . . . I don't really know how."

"There's no right way or wrong way." Stretching out onto her back, she said, "Don't think about what you're doing, just do it."

Lili shivered as he settled between her legs and gently spread her open. The anticipation as he dipped his head was maddening—the hot gusts of his breath, the tickle of his hair on her inner thighs. When she finally felt the first light sweep of his tongue, the pleasure was so acute that she cried out.

"Are you all right?" He tried to raise his head, but she pushed it back down, moaning, "Don't stop. Don't stop."

Clearly relishing the experience, David took his time about it. He probed her gently with his inquisitive tongue, licking the delicate little creases with languid thoroughness, as if to memorize their shape and taste.

Before long, Lili was panting and clutching at the pillows. Untutored, but unerring in his instinct, he gripped one writhing hip as he pushed the two fingers back into her, and then a third, thrusting them slowly as he lightly tongued her clit.

"Yes . . ." Lili grabbed his hair, her head thrown back in rapturous abandon. "Oh, David, yes . . ."

This—the gratification of her incessant, debilitating lust— was Ilutu Lili's greatest joy and her most fundamental need, her very reason for being. To feel the mounting, heart-pounding thrill of an approaching climax was to be carried away into a different realm, one of this earth but not of this earth. It was like feeling the ocean heave beneath her as a wave surged into being, carrying her aloft as it rose higher, higher, and higher still . . .

When the wave crested past the point of no return, she loosed her grip on the earth and let go, floating in weightless expectation as the pleasure built quietly, inexorably . . .

Lili cried out as it crashed around her, shaking her with its force. She moaned with each sharp spasm—or rather, heard herself moan, so transported was she.

She became dimly aware, as her climax ebbed, of David kissing her with aching gentleness on the still-pulsing flesh between her thighs.

"You're beautiful, so beautiful." He glided his tongue over her clit, inciting a lovely little post-orgasmic tremor. Were David under the influence of one of her *mashmashus*, she could keep him mesmerized with lust until she'd spent herself through climax after climax, but such was not the case.

Lili rose onto an elbow to stroke his hair with a trembling hand. "Thank you, David."

Planting another kiss upon her sex, this one punctuated with a feathery little flick of the tongue, he said, "Would you mind if I . . . didn't stop quite yet?"

Lili smiled slowly as she settled back onto the pillows. *I knew you had promise.*

Nine

I SHOULD TURN BACK, David thought after his foot slid for the second time on the deer trail, mud-slicked from yesterday's rain, that he was climbing through the densely forested north face of Alp Albiorix with the aid of a covered lantern and a walking stick. It would be arduous enough to negotiate such rough terrain at midday in good weather, but this misty predawn gloom made it especially perilous—as did the craggy ravine dropping off just to his right, in which a stream burbled about eighty feet below.

He wouldn't be out here, risking life and limb, were he not leaving Grotte Cachée tomorrow. This was his next to last chance to locate the little bedchamber where Serges Bourgoin had a book snatched away from him by an invisible hand—or so he claimed. Bourgoin was a drunk, after all, and the events he recounted had occurred many years before.

Having abandoned any hope of locating the chamber from within the mind-skewing, mazelike cave, for the past five days,

David had risen in the wee hours of the morning to try to find the entrance that Bourgoin had described as being hidden behind a pair of walnut trees that looked like *"les jambes des soldats géants."*

It was grueling work, though, especially today, with this choking fog and treacherous footing. He would prefer to do his exploring in full daylight—surely he wouldn't be the first houseguest to hike up this mountain for sport—but for the time it would steal from his landscaping work. Not only would that raise questions, but David had found himself taking pleasure in that work to a degree that he would not have anticipated.

For the first time, he was in a position to put to practical use the horticultural and artistic disciplines that had consumed his adolescent mind, and he found it immensely gratifying. He frequently got so wrapped up in his plans for Grotte Cachée's gardens and parklands that he had to force himself to put them aside so as to address his primary objective, that of determining whether the valley had been the site of demonic activity for centuries.

During his self-guided excursions through the nearly impenetrable woods that blanketed the valley, David had come upon trees growing in eerily twisted shapes, as well as a stone altar in a clearing in the woods—a freshly mowed clearing—that looked as if it dated back to the ancient Gauls. These things, like the magnetic force in the cave, the satyr statues, and Dusivæsus, while curious, were not necessarily indicative of a demoniacal presence.

David doubted he would be able to contrive an audience with *le seigneur,* and the recluse called Darius remained equally elusive. The other denizens of this place, residents and staff alike, had revealed nothing of import either in response to David's subtle interrogations or during conversations in French on which he eavesdropped while presumably unable to understand a word. From time to time, he revisited the subject of demons with Lili, but thus far, none of their conversations had borne fruit.

His lack of progress was frustrating, as was every second he spent in the company of Lili, whose flirtatious glances and beguiling smiles put his vow of chastity to continual test. He hadn't kissed her since their enchanted interlude in *la Galerie des Diamants Noirs* five days ago, hadn't even touched her except to escort her by the arm on their occasional strolls about the grounds. What transpired between them that afternoon would surely never have occurred but for the unbridling influence of *le magnétisme hallucinatoire*.

David recalled, with a bitter chuckle, what he'd written with such smug assurance to Bishop Sullivan. *It goes without saying that I shall refrain from becoming too familiar with those whom I meet here, so as to avoid jeopardizing the credibility of my conclusions.* Eighteen hours later, he'd had his face between Lili's thighs.

He had resolved, upon coming to his senses afterward, to confess the incident in full to Father Cullen, but hard as he tried, he couldn't bring himself to truly regret it. Nor could he manage to put it out of his mind. Indeed, he relived it every night as he lay in bed aching with unrelieved lust.

Even now, as David picked his way up this blasted mountain one painstaking step after another, he grew half hard remembering the feel and smell and taste of her, the way her sex squeezed his fingers when she came, the way she thrashed and moaned and cried out—especially the first time. She climaxed perhaps a dozen times in all, a veritable riot of pleasure.

It was a pleasure he could have shared. "*Have you never wanted to lie with a woman, David? You must have wondered how it would feel to have a woman pleasure you with her mouth.*" Resisting her entreaties had taken every scrap of moral strength at his disposal, especially given the effect of *le magnétisme*. His satisfaction in having done so, however, gave him little solace, underscored as it was by a self-righteousness that he couldn't seem to banish either by prayer or force of will.

It was a struggle with which David was familiar. "*A priest should be, first and foremost, a man of faith, not an exemplar of correct behavior—or a slave to it.*"

David flinched as something hard struck the crown of his hat and rolled off, landing on the path in front of him. He crouched down, holding his lantern close to the ground, although the sky had paled enough that it served little point.

Lying on a slab of stone half buried in mud was a small green sphere that he recognized as the outer husk of a walnut; several more were scattered nearby. Peering up through the milky haze, he made out a canopy of heavily leafed branches bearing clusters of the ripe nuts.

The tree itself, which grew on the far side of a clearing to the left, was extraordinarily tall, with a massive trunk and gnarled roots that crawled over and around an oblong boulder at its base. A similar tree stood nearby, each of them swathed, from the root-covered boulder to a point about twenty feet up the trunk, in a mantle of woolly green moss.

David smiled as he took in the pair of monumental trees with their boots of moss. "*Les jambes des soldats géants,*" he whispered.

A mesh of underbrush, saplings, and vines between the trees obscured what lay beyond—but David suspected he knew what he would find there. As he crossed the clearing, he noticed a trampled-down path in the spongy grass that bore the imprints of booted feet; it emerged from the woods to the west, disappearing behind the soldiers' legs. This David followed, circling the barrier to find a nearly vertical wall of rock with two openings, one fitted out with shutters, the other with a door; both were painted green.

The window shutters stood open. Through them, David could see a frayed old tapestry hanging on the far wall and the foot of a narrow cast iron bed. Setting down his lantern and walking stick, he approached the window slowly, cursing the dried leaves that crackled underfoot.

A dark-haired man clad in a shirt and trousers, braces dangling, feet bare, lay faceup on the pillow-heaped bed with his head turned toward the wall and a book open on his chest. David read the title upside down: *Jacques le Fataliste* by Denis Diderot.

David knew of this book. It had been condemned by the French government two or three years ago on moral and religious grounds, and all copies of it had been destroyed—except, apparently, the one this fellow had been reading when he fell asleep. On a little table next to the bed stood an unlit oil lamp and a short stack of other books with titles in French, English, Latin, and some other language with an unfamiliar and exotic alphabet.

Was this, at long last, the mysterious Darius? Who else could he be? He lived in a cave, after all; was there a more hermitlike abode? It was an abode David was eager to explore.

He stood there for a minute considering his options. He could come back later in the day, but there was no guarantee that Darius wouldn't still be there, and a very good chance that David's absence from the château and its immediate environs would be noted. From the slow, steady rise and fall of the man's chest, David gathered he was in a deep sleep. As a boy, David had acquired a talent for moving about noiselessly in order to avoid a cuff in the head should he awaken his brother Peter, with whom he shared a room.

David tried the door; it was unlocked, and the knob turned without squeaking. He took off his boots, eased the door open, and passed through it on stockinged feet, grateful to find the stone floor within carpeted with a scruffy old Persian rug; it would help to muffle his footfalls.

By the grayish dawn light, he took stock of the *petite salle confortable* with its walls of rough volcanic stone and its incongruously homey furnishings. In one corner, next to a row of pegs hung with clothing, stood a green-painted cupboard; in another, a large trunk of Oriental design. A leather chair and a little marble table faced a stone fireplace with a chimney that disappeared into a cave shaft.

The chamber's most remarkable feature was a pair of shelves supported between two snarled rootlike formations that emerged from the ceiling and disappeared through the floor. At first, David took them for something akin to stalactites, but on closer examination, they were indeed the roots of ancient trees that had somehow become calcified.

A row of books, one of them a Bible, occupied the top shelf, with various bottles and flasks arranged on the bottom, as well as a crucible, a scale, and a microscope. Braced between a mortar and pestle and a blue and white porcelain leech jar was a book which David pulled out, noting without surprise that it was not wrested from him by an invisible force. The title was stamped in gilt on the cover.

BELL'S
GREAT OPERATIONS
OF SURGERY

PRICE FIVE GUINEAS

He opened the book to the first illustration, a large and skillfully executed color lithograph of a negro man—a cadaver, hopefully—with his head sliced open, the various layers of flesh peeled back to expose the brain. Swallowing down the sting of bile in his throat, he shut the book and returned it to its place.

A volume on the top shelf caught his eye: *Les Liaisons dangereuses* by Pierre Choderlos de Laclos. Sliding it out, he found it to be an older edition than that which Peter had kept hidden under his mattress to read in secret, their father having banned it for depicting the French aristocracy as wicked and decadent. David flipped to the title page, which gave the date of publication as 1782. It was a first printing, and signed by the author, to boot, judging from the inscription inked across the page.

Octobre 1782
Pour Darius, de Votre Ami Dévoué, Pierre

For Darius, eh? David turned to look at the sleeping man, whose robust physique and unlined face would suggest that he was no older than thirty. The book had been signed forty-seven years earlier. Assuming the occupant of the bed was, indeed, the Darius of whom Archer and the others had spoken, he had to be the namesake of the father or grandfather to whom the book had been inscribed.

David padded cautiously over to the tapestry, which he pulled aside. There was, indeed, a cavernous chamber on the other side, its walls lined floor to ceiling with fully stocked bookshelves. Two small shafts to the outside, located near the lofty ceiling, provided just enough light to see by as David stepped into the *bibliothèque secrete* and pulled a book at random from its shelf.

No unseen hand snatched it away. He withdrew several more, from different shelves; nothing. He did feel slightly light-headed, but that was to be expected, given the cave's magnetic charge.

David returned to the bedchamber, exasperated at his failure to get to the root of the various accounts, over the past four centuries, of diabolical occurrences at Grotte Cachée.

Bourgoin's ravishment by a *"Démon féminin,"* real though it had seemed to him the following morning, could very well have been a dream not unlike that which David himself had experienced during his first night here.

The medieval chambermaid who saw a woman turn into a man may, indeed, have been delusional.

Domenico Vitturi's memoir of courtesans being schooled in debauchery by two men of unnatural sexual capacities, one of them evidently a satyr, may simply have been a bawdy tale to amuse his friends.

A satyr was also mentioned in the letter "from one little red fox to another" about the depraved slave auction in which they'd sold themselves to rich libertines. Coincidence? Or was it, perchance, the opium delusion of a young woman surrounded by statues of men with tails and horns and pointed ears?

Would he ever know for sure? To return to England with no clear conclusions for his superiors, no way to advise them as to the need for exorcism of the buildings or inhabitants of Grotte Cachée, was a humiliating prospect. Despite his youth, David had acquired, in ecclesiastical circles at any rate, a reputation as a brilliant demonologist. Had not Cardinal Lazzari himself requested him for this mission after reading *Dæmonia* and pronouncing it "an erudite and persuasive treatment of an increasingly enigmatic subject?"

I cannot fail in this, he thought as he crossed to the door. He mustn't fail.

Were there nonhuman entities here or not? That was the question. It was his responsibility—his mission—to answer it.

He stepped on a hard little ball that pitched him forward as it rolled away with a silvery jingle.

Shit! David stumbled and fell, grabbing automatically at the nearby bed. Landing on the floor with a grunt, he found himself clutching the arm of the sleeping man, now bolting out of bed, his book tumbling to the floor as he flung David halfway across the room.

"Qui est-tu?" demanded Darius, standing over David with an expression of fury. He was tall, with dark, overgrown hair in sleepy disarray, and fierce black eyes. *"Qu'est-ce que tu fais?"*

"E-excusez-moi," David stammered as he sat up, hands raised in a gesture of appeasement. *"Je ne voulais pas—"*

"You," Darius said in a gravelly, just-awakened voice, his vague accent nominally French, but with a trace of something older, almost primeval. "The English gardener."

"Er . . . Yes. Yes. I am, indeed." David grabbed his hat and went to push himself off the floor, pausing as his hand brushed the little ball that had tripped him up. He lifted it, squinting in bewilderment.

It was a walnut, sans husk, the two halves of the shell held together with a network of carefully knotted gold thread. Two threads dangled off it like tails, each one terminating in a tiny silver bell. "What the devil . . . ?"

Darius sat on the bed with a sigh. "It's . . ." He scraped a hand over his jaw with an expression that struck David as almost embarrassed. ". . . something I play with. Inigo made it for me."

David looked from Darius to the walnut, wondering how to

respond to that. Before he could decide, Darius said, "You speak French remarkably well for a man who doesn't speak French, Mr. Beckett."

Shit. David rose slowly to his feet as he dusted off his trousers, thinking *Shit shit shit shit shit.*

Ten

"WHAT ARE YOU doing here?" demanded Darius, appalled to think that a stranger had found the well-hidden entrance to the footpath that led here.

No sooner had he asked the question than he knew the answer. He'd known it on some level since the moment he'd sprung awake, bombarded by this human's needs and desires, his arm buzzing ever so slightly where the bastard had grabbed him.

Are there nonhuman entities here or not? That is the question. It is my responsibility to answer it.

Just as it was now Darius's responsibility—his undeniable compulsion, now that Beckett had touched him—to provide that answer.

Fuck, thought Darius. *Fuck fuck fuck fuck fuck.* The little hairs quivered from his nape right down to his tailbone. Were he in his feline persona right now, his fur would be bristling, his back arched.

"You have me at a disadvantage, sir," said Beckett. "You know who I am, but I don't believe I've had the pleasure of—"

"We've met."

Beckett regarded him with guarded curiosity. "When—"

"Several times. My name, as I suspect you are already aware, is Darius."

"You must forgive me, but I do not recall having made your acquaintance."

With a resigned sigh, Darius said, "I can become invisible when forced into contact with humans. More commonly, I will adopt the guise of a cat, or sometimes a blue rock thrush. You've seen me in both of those incarnations."

Beckett's nonplussed expression turned knowing. "I think Lili has told you that I credit the existence of demons, so you've decided to have a bit of fun at my expense. You're not the first to do so, and I daresay you won't be the last."

"I'm afraid the notion of 'fun' has been quite foreign to me for some time, and in any event, I do not lie."

"At all?"

"Yes, I know," Darius said. "Most people have trouble believing that it's possible to go through life without telling the occasional—"

"No, it's not that. I believe it's *possible*. I mean, *I* don't lie, so—"

"Christ, why the devil not?" Darius would if he could, at least when his survival was at stake.

"I took a vow as a boy," Beckett said.

"It is a rare boy who exhibits such extraordinary righteousness."

"I did it at the behest of my nursery governess, but I was old enough to know what I was doing. Truth is a special virtue. We men are social animals, so each man naturally owes the other whatever is necessary for the preservation of human society. It

amusing yourself at my expense. After all, knowing who I am and why I'm here, why on earth would you freely admit to being a dem—a Follet?"

Darius sighed as he refilled their glasses. "Because, as I have already explained, I am compelled by a physiological force beyond my control to satisfy your desire for the truth about the presence of our kind at Grotte Cachée. As for what I'm going to do about you to make sure you don't go running to your Church superiors with the information I'm being forced to reveal . . ."

Darius scratched his morning stubble as he thought about it. Beckett could not be permitted to leave here with this damning information. This valley had been a haven to him and his fellow Follets for a very long time—a haven they would lose if outsiders were to discover the truth about them.

"Christ, but I wish one of the others was here," Darius muttered into his wineglass. "They know how to deal with humans."

"Others?"

"I am not the only Follet who makes his home at Grotte Cachée. Lili, Elic, and Inigo are—"

"Lili?"

"She is what is commonly referred to as a succubus, although the Babylonians considered her a—"

"That's enough." Beckett stood abruptly, wine sloshing from his glass. "You will leave her name out of this perverse heresy."

Oh, for pity's sake. "For an expert on demons, you certainly are hard to convince."

Not only was Darius obligated to satisfy Beckett's quest for answers about the Follets, he felt an increasingly fervent need to provide them. It always happened this way, with the human's desires gradually insinuating themselves into Darius's mind until he was utterly fixated on satisfying them. In essence, the human's wants and needs became *his* wants and needs, usurping whatever else he cared about at the moment, including his own well-being. This psychic thralldom didn't stop until the desire in question had been fulfilled.

"Demonology is a science, not a superstition," Beckett said. "I need to be persuaded by irrefutable evidence before I accept a claim as fact."

"Why didn't you say so?"

Darius pulled his legs up and crouched on the trunk, arms bent and slightly outstretched. The more similar his position before and after the conversion, the less jolting it would be.

"What are you doing?" Beckett asked.

"Providing irrefutable evidence." Darius closed his eyes, held his breath, and concentrated fiercely. Before his next heartbeat, he was tottering on eight spindly toes, wings fluttering for balance, eyes squeezed shut to block out his dizzyingly panoramic range of vision until he'd attained some equilibrium.

"Jesus."

Darius opened his eyes to find Beckett gaping at him. The glass slipped from his hand, shattering on the table in a spew of blood red that made Darius jump. It was hard to tell for sure, because his avian depth perception was abysmal, but the stunned Englishman appeared to be backing up as he executed the sign of the cross.

Darius walked to the edge of the trunk, nodding his big, ungainly head to keep Beckett's image from jittering wildly. *"Don't leave,"* he called out as Beckett turned and lurched through the door, but of course it emerged as a warbly little chirrup.

With a screech of vexation, Darius pumped his wings and

flew after him. He'd been an idiot to transmute so suddenly, without taking the time to warn this human what he was about to witness. It had been a precipitous decision born of irritation. Darius had wanted to prove his assertions, yes, but in truth, he had also wanted to shock this demonological "scientist" with his smugly wrongheaded convictions. Now that shocked human was fleeing before Darius had figured out how to convince him to keep his newfound knowledge about the Follets from his superiors—assuming that was even possible. If it wasn't . . .

Would that David Beckett could just disappear from the face of the earth; that would take care of things.

The sun had broken over the mountaintops, lightening the fog a bit, although the air still felt thick and damp as Darius scooped it with his wings. He'd expected Beckett to head for the footpath to the west, but he sprinted instead to the deer track along the edge of the stream gorge. It was a precarious little strip of mud and rocks, and he was scrambling down it much too fast on stockinged feet, grabbing tree limbs to keep from slipping.

Beckett pulled up short when Darius swooped down in front of him. He swiped at the bird, clutching at a branch as his feet slid out from under him. The branch was thin, and snapped off in his hand.

Shit! Darius willed himself back into a human before he'd even landed. He hit the ground hard, smashing a knee into a rock and twisting an ankle. He lunged for Beckett, grabbed for his legs, but it was too late.

Beckett screamed as he pitched over the side of the gorge, and then the only sounds were the thuds of his body slamming into rocks and trees. Darius converted back into a thrush and dove to the bottom of the ravine, watching helplessly as Beckett landed faceup beneath a tall pine tree at the edge of the stream.

Settling next to the limp and battered Englishman, Darius resumed his human form, thinking, *Christ, what have I done?*

Beckett's right leg and left arm lay at unnatural angles, as did his bloodied head. He looked toward Darius with a dazed expression that swiftly turned to alarm. At first, Darius assumed he was simply unnerved to find a "demon" hovering over him, but then he realized that Beckett was fighting for air. Every labored breath he managed to drag into his lungs sounded like a death rattle.

Darius hovered his hands over Beckett's chest, moving them in a circular path as his mind probed and searched. He sensed no open wounds, just some contused flesh over the ribs, four of which—no, five—were cracked, two in several places. Thankfully, none had punctured a lung.

Still, something felt wrong inside him, very wrong. Darius skimmed his hands over Beckett's body, deeply dismayed by what he felt—or rather, didn't feel. There was a dull stillness within him, as if his body from the neck down were that of a corpse.

Darius pushed Beckett's right sleeve up and pinched his arm. There was no response. The alarm in Beckett's eyes turned to raw panic. Still straining to breathe, he gritted his teeth as if striving vainly to move his arms and legs.

"Easy." Darius slid his hand very gently under Beckett's nape, barely touching him. His worst suspicions were confirmed. The third and fourth cervical vertebrae were broken, and that section of spinal cord torn. The paralysis from such injuries was always permanent and inoperable; every great surgeon from Imhotep to Charles Bell had acknowledged this. If Darius had to choose between being perpetually incapable of movement or being heaved over the side of a boat with a stone around his neck, he would unhesitatingly choose the latter.

David Beckett would not be in this hellish predicament but

for Darius's poor judgment. It was his doing, and now there was but one humane course of action available to him, although he loathed having to resort to it.

The odds were slim that there was anyone nearby to witness what he was about to do, but just in case, Darius scanned the area thoroughly. Then he drew in a deep, fortifying breath and wrapped his hands around the Englishman's throat.

Eleven

*M*ARY MOTHER OF *grace,* David prayed silently when he realized what this unholy creature was about to do. *Mother of mercy, do thou protect me from the enemy and receive me at the hour of my death.*

David's body may as well have been a hunk of clay, so heavy and lifeless did it feel. Much as he dreaded the prospect of being strangled, had he the wherewithal to speak, he might very well have begged for death rather than spend the remainder of his life as a lumpish thing to be spoon-fed and diapered and hauled about like an infant. His only real regret was that he was going to his Maker without Last Rites. *Forgive me, Father . . .*

David closed his eyes and waited for Darius to tighten his grip and squeeze, putting an end to this grueling struggle for air, but he could barely feel the demon's hands about his neck. Perhaps he was losing sensation there, too. Were that the case, though, would he feel this strange, ticklish heat spreading downward from the base of his skull?

He opened his eyes and saw Darius scowling in concentration as he lightly cradled David's neck, the movements of his fingers barely perceptible. Heat flowed down David's back like a river of lava, sprouting smaller rivulets that sizzled down his arms and legs, into his fingers, his toes, every last part of his body. His flesh started prickling all over, like a foot that had fallen asleep but in a more intense, sparkly-hot way that made him gasp.

That was when he realized he was breathing, *really* breathing, not just struggling to suck air into his lungs.

The prickling peaked and gradually abated, flooding him with a soothing warmth not dissimilar to being immersed in the Lake of a Thousand Diamonds. All too soon, though, the warmth dissipated, to be replaced by pain—just a hint at first, focused mostly in his right leg, left arm, and the side of his head, but it escalated rapidly.

David didn't care; he was grateful for the pain, evincing as it did the return of sensation to his body. He flexed his feet, wriggled his fingers, closed his right hand around a fistful of pine needles, which pricked his palm.

"You . . . you didn't kill me."

"You noticed that, did you?" Darius moved his hands from David's neck to the painful area on the side of his head, which grew warm and ticklish as the flesh there re-formed itself into what it had been before—for it felt as if that was what was happening. It was astounding, miraculous—but no more so than watching a man turn into a bird in the blink of an eye.

Darius pulled a penknife from his pocket and used it to slice the sleeves of David's frock coat and shirt from cuff to shoulder. "You'll want to hold still for this."

Darius began moving his hands over David's grossly distended upper arm, not quite touching it, but generating the now-familiar tingling warmth. His face was bleached of color, and he had a drawn look about him.

David's stomach pitched as he felt the bones moving about and locking together beneath the flesh. Once the broken halves were aligned and merging back together, the pain began to dissipate.

David said, "Whatever you are, Darius, human or non, you are clearly doing the work of God. He has graced you with the power to heal. It is an extraordinary gift."

Darius scowled as he took his penknife to David's right trouser leg. "Try living with this 'gift,' and tell me if it isn't more of a curse." Parting the rent trouser leg, he said, "This one is a bit thornier."

David's lower leg was curved like a bow, with two bloody gashes one above the other; from the bottom one emerged a few inches of jagged white bone.

"Both bones are smashed," Darius explained as he passed his hand over the injury, "the tibia in three main pieces, the fibula in two—and there are a good many bits of bone floating about in there. This is one you really are going to want to keep still for."

David lay motionless, his eyes closed, as he tried to ignore the sensation of dozens of little fragments of bone coming together along with the five larger pieces.

"The dicey bit's over now."

David looked up to find Darius moving his hand back and forth over the two still-gaping wounds, which fused together as he watched, until all that was left were two ragged pink scars amid some redness and swelling.

This is really happening, David thought. *This isn't a dream. This isn't my imagination.*

"With my type of healing," Darius said, "the bodily tissues regenerate with extraordinary speed. By tonight, you'll feel virtually as good as new." He closed his eyes on a long, exhausted sigh, looking for all the world like a man dying of consumption.

"I say, are you quite all right?" asked David, pushing himself to a sitting position, which brought on a wave of dizziness. He managed to scoot himself back and lean against the tree trunk, relying mainly on his two relatively uninjured limbs.

Draping an arm over his forehead, Darius said, "Doing that drains my vital humors. The more severe the injury or illness, the more it depletes me."

"Is that why you consider it a curse?"

"Partly."

David waited for him to continue.

Darius sighed. "Mostly, it's because of things that happened a very long time ago, in my homeland."

"Where was that?" David asked.

"What is now called Petra, in northern Arabia. It was an ancient city sculpted into a mountain of pink rock. The people had their gods and goddesses, various demigods, and my kind—the djinn."

"*Djinn?* As in the *Thousand and One Nights?*"

"The djinn existed long before those stories were first recorded." Darius sat up with a groan of effort, stretching his neck until it popped. "Many in Petra knew that I was a djinni— too many. When it was discovered that I could heal the sick and wounded, I was captured by a Bedouin priest named Raz and held in chains for years."

"How could they have kept you from turning into a bird or a cat, or becoming invisible, and escaping that way?"

"Djinn can be born with any number of different powers, but shape-shifting is among the rarest, and for a long time I had no idea that I could do it. The chains held me. The sick and lame were brought to me, and I was made to cure them or I would be weighed down with stones and thrown into the stream that flowed through Petra—which would have been the end of me."

"You can be killed?"

"Only by drowning, which sets me apart from most Follets, who are only susceptible to fire. The threat worked. The more healing a human requires, the more it depletes me. It wasn't long before I was barely alive myself."

"Obviously you got away."

"A woman came to me," said Darius as he rubbed his fingers, "the widowed daughter of a Persian warrior-chieftain of great renown. Her name was Parmis. She was a learned and well-traveled woman who spoke fluent Aramaic. And she was beautiful, very beautiful, with a laugh . . ." Darius looked beyond their patch of pine-scented shade as if he were gazing back in time.

"She was seeking a respite from her sick headaches," Darius continued, "but before I could heal her, she laid her hand upon my arm. Those who were brought to me were told never to touch me, but I suppose, being a princess, she felt herself above such constraints. As she touched me, I felt her desire. She wanted me, and so I took her—or rather, I let her take me. I was weak, I was in chains, but it was still . . ." He shook his head. "I had forgotten the joy of lying with a woman. It reminded me of all that had been stolen from me. I told Parmis that I wouldn't heal her unless she used her father's influence to free me from my enslavement."

"Weren't you afraid of being drowned for refusing to heal her?" David asked.

"I didn't care anymore. Parmis agreed on the condition that I return with her to her tribe and remain there for as long as she cared to keep me. I consented to this, her father bought me from Raz with a sack of gold, and Parmis took me to her home in the mountains of Persia. It was a large stone house, palatial even by modern standards. The Persian variant of my name was Darayavahush, and this was what she called me— Darayush for short. I couldn't marry Parmis because I wasn't from a kingly Persian family, and she was a respectable widow, so I lived with her in the guise of a high-ranking slave, a sort of librarian. She collected writings from all over the known world, mostly papyrus scrolls and tablets of stone and clay, and I helped her to acquire and translate them. In private, well, my bedchamber was connected to hers by a secret passage. She was . . ." Darius almost smiled. "She was the last woman I have loved."

"Was it known that you were a djinni?"

"God, no. We were very careful about that, after what had happened to me back in Petra. It wasn't easy to assume the role of a human. It rarely is, for any kind of Follet. There are some humans, the gifted ones especially, who sense that we're different, even if they're not quite sure how."

"Gifted?"

"These are people with faculties beyond the usual scope of humankind. We call it the Gift. It is an inborn trait, which both parents must possess in order for the child to inherit it. The only other way is for the mother to have been impregnated by a dusios, like Elic."

"Elic . . . Of course." It would have been Elic, David realized, who had been summoned there by the Dusivæsus effigy.

"You know about dusii?" Darius asked.

"I *am* a demonologist." Albeit, as it turned out, a pitifully ill-informed one.

"Gifted humans tend to have heightened senses. Some have dreams that foretell the future, and many can detect coronas of colored light about the heads or bodies of others, or even listen to their thoughts. They can utilize certain spells if they're taught to do so, but they rarely are. Most of them don't even recognize their abilities, just as I hadn't recognized that I could shape-shift. Sometimes they realize they're different, but they don't know why, and they find it deeply troubling. In the past, those who accepted and nurtured their Gift were revered as seers, soothsayers, oracles, druids . . ."

"Were there gifted people in Parmis's tribe?" David asked.

"Unfortunately, yes. It was they who suspected I wasn't quite human. I worked very hard at passing for one of them. It is a taxing business, hiding one's true nature. Yet at the same time, those nineteen years I spent with Parmis . . . Of the thousands of years I have been alive, they were by far the happiest."

"She sent you away after nineteen years?" David asked.

"Oh, no." Darius looked down, a muscle tight in his jaw. "She became ill—cancer. No sooner did we realize something was wrong than she was bedridden, unable to swallow, in terrible pain. I wanted to heal her, but she said it was too risky, that those who harbored suspicions about me would deduce the truth if she were to arise from her deathbed miraculously cured. I insisted, so she ordered me confined in my chamber by armed guards until she had passed, at which point her home and riches were to become mine. But she must have missed me as much as I missed her, because when she was on the verge of death, she sent for me, not thinking I would try to heal her with her family and retainers at her side. But I cared more for her welfare at that point than for my own, and I tried. She had her guards take me away, screaming and . . . well, it was the last time in my life that I have shed tears. She died soon thereafter, and I was branded a *daeva*, which was a demon that brings disease upon humans. They assumed that Parmis's illness was my doing, and that she'd had me locked away because I'd been trying to steal her soul. They tried to kill me several different ways, but of course none of them worked, so they tied me up, dug a deep hole in a remote place, and buried me in it."

David sat forward, his lingering pain all but forgotten. *"Alive?"*

"To spend eternity trapped in the earth. As they were shoveling in the dirt, I admitted that I could be killed by drowning, and I begged them to do it, but they thought it was some kind of demonic trick, so they filled in the hole and left."

"How . . . how long were you . . . ?"

"Months, perhaps even years. It's hard to say for—"

"Years?"

"There was no way of judging the passing of time. I couldn't see, couldn't hear, couldn't move or breathe. I went a bit mad, imprisoned in my own thoughts. In my sentient moments, I would often think about Parmis. I grieved for her even in that fucking hole. Other times, I entertained fancies about wriggling free of the ropes that bound me and digging my way out, but I was like a worm lodged in the dirt. I used to wish I *was* a worm, so that I could tunnel up to the surface and feel the sun on me, breathe the air. I would imagine it constantly, just to comfort myself, until it began to seem real to me. At one point I thought I'd lost my sanity altogether, because I felt a lurching sensation, and the earth seemed to shift and rumble all around me. When it stopped, I couldn't feel the ropes anymore. It felt as if I were inhabiting a sort of fleshy tube—the body of a worm. I found myself contracting my muscles while taking in dirt through what passed for my mouth, burrowing through the cooler earth toward the warmer. I sensed sunlight through the dirt, and although it repelled me on a physical level, I was thrilled beyond measure. When I finally broke through . . ."

Darius put his head back and closed his eyes, as if reliving the moment. "Ah, to feel the sun on me once again. I couldn't see it, but I could feel myself growing warm. I hadn't been warm for so long. For a while, I just lay there on the ground, stunned and jubilant—but then I realized I was growing stiff, drying out, and that I needed to find shade, fast. I crawled over giant blades of grass and fallen leaves until I found a cool, dark nook where I addressed the question of how to return to my natural form. It took some time and a great deal of fierce concentration, but finally there came a tremendous concussion, and a crack of scalding white light. When I opened my eyes, I was lying facedown beneath a tree, still wearing the clothes I'd been buried in, although they were filthy and threadbare. I was emaciated and parched, and my skin . . ." He shuddered. "But I was alive, and in a man's form once more."

David let out a pent-up breath. "So this was when you learned that you could will yourself into other forms."

"Or no form at all. I traveled west, searching for sanctuary in some part of the world where they'd never heard of the djinn. At length, I found this valley, this cave. I'd lived in a cave back in Petra—there were thousands of them there, carved into the mountain, so I felt right at home here. And I was hopeful that *le magnétisme hallucinatoire,* as we call it now, would help to discourage any human wanderers from venturing too deep within."

"The valley was uninhabited then?" David asked.

Darius nodded. "The Gaulish tribe that settled here didn't arrive till around six hundred B.C. Their druids decreed that I was a god of fire, and that it was their sacred duty and the duty of their descendants to keep me safe—and so they have to this day."

"To this day?" David said. "How . . . ?"

Darius smiled. "Théophile Morel, Seigneur des Ombres, is the descendant of Brantigern Anextlomarus—Brantigern the Protector—a young druid who remained here for my sake when the Romans came. Morel has the Gift, as have all his ancestors, the better to safeguard me—and the other three, who came later."

"And the four of you have managed to live here all this time without the outside world discovering what you truly are?"

"Brantigern's heirs have done their duty well."

"After all you've been through," David said, "I'm surprised you're still willing to heal people."

"I'm not, not really. When I left Persia, I resolved to never heal another soul."

"You healed *me.*"

"You would never have taken that fall if not for my ineptitude. I will admit there have been other times over the centuries when I've been compelled to use my powers of healing, but those occasions are rare. Even when someone I care about is dying . . ." He shook his head gravely. "No matter how agonizing it is to watch, no matter how tempted I am to intervene, if there is any chance that my healing this person will put me at risk of exposure, I won't even consider it—not for a moment."

"Do the other Follets ever ask you to make an exception?" David asked.

"They don't know I can heal. Nor does Archer, nor even Morel."

"You've kept it a secret from those closest to you all these years?"

"I've had no choice," Darius said grimly. "They *would* ask for exceptions, especially Inigo, who makes human friends easily. If they knew, they would beg me to heal just one more person, promising that no one in the outside world would find out, but they would. It's inevitable. And then I would once again find myself subjected to . . . who knows what this time. I can't take that chance."

"Then why on earth are you telling *me* all of . . . Ah. The conduit. You have to satisfy my curiosity about the Follets."

"That, and . . ." Darius shrugged. "You were awake when I healed you. I could hardly have kept it a secret."

"It was a dangerous thing for you to do," David said. "I will be eternally in your debt. Should there ever be some way I can repay you, pray don't hesitate to—"

"There is something."

"Anything."

"Don't ever disclose what happened this morning to another living soul, either here at Grotte Cachée or in the outside world. I mean the healing, of course, not . . . you know, me telling you about the Follets, and your being a demon hunter sent by the Church. I daresay the others have a right to know about that."

"I intend to make a full confession to Lili as soon as I get back to the château."

"But you won't tell anyone else who we really are? Even your superiors who sent you here? I know you don't like to lie, but—"

"Nothing I report will be a lie. But nor will it add up to the truth." David put his hand out for Darius to shake. "You have my solemn word."

Twelve

LILI TURNED THE doorknob of *la Chambre Romaine* about half past midnight that night, pleased to find the door unlocked and the hinges well oiled. She hesitated as she pushed the door open, having expected darkness, not candlelight. David had retired three hours earlier, saying he wanted to get a good night's sleep before the predawn commencement of his journey back to England tomorrow. His trek up Alp Albiorix that morning in search of Darius's *maison dans la caverne* appeared to have tired him out, judging from how stiffly he'd moved when he first returned.

She stepped into the palatial bedchamber, her feet silent on the wine-red carpet, the only sound that of her breath and the silken hush of her *lubushu*—cinnabar tonight, to complement the roseate hues in the room. Her hair was loose, her breasts and throat rubbed with oil of jasmine, her upper arms twined in golden bracelets a thousand years old.

David was fast asleep on the big velvet-curtained bed,

reclining in a semisitting position on a mountain of pillows in shades of maroon, rust, and brick. The bed had been turned down already, exposing sheets of sleek Egyptian cotton.

He wore nothing but his underdrawers. This was the first time Lili had seen him shirtless. His torso was beautifully proportioned, the shoulders not quite as wide as Elic's but nicely squared off, the chest lightly adorned with hair that wasn't at all coarse; in fact, it looked almost downy. On David's lap sat a portable writing desk which he'd been using to compose a letter, judging from the sheet of foolscap on its slanted lid and the quill in his slack right hand.

Lili came around to the side of the bed, slid the quill out of his hand, and put it on the nightstand alongside the ink pot and half-burned candle. She carefully lifted the desk off his lap and set it on the dressing table. The letter was written in a sharply precise hand and signed with his real name, David Beckett Roussel.

17 October 1829
Grotte Cachée, Auvergne, France

My Lord Bishop,
Your Lordship will wonder why I have chosen to convey the results of my mission in writing rather than during a meeting with you upon my return to England, as planned. Suffice it to say there is little to discuss. My investigation has convinced me with absolute certainty that there are no diabolical entities of an evil nature who reside in this place, nor have there ever been. ...

Lili didn't read the rest, not so much out of respect for David's privacy as out of simple disinterest. David would keep the secrets that Darius had been forced to reveal to him that

morning, of that she was quite certain. He had promised Lili as
much, swearing unnecessarily on his Bible. Her initial pique at
his having misled her this past week about his true purpose in
being here had dissipated upon reflection. Had she not deceived him all along as to her very nature? She wasn't even human, for heaven's sake, yet he had accepted her charade with
the equanimity she had grown to find curiously attractive—
for, she knew that, Jesuit or no, his reserve masked a deeply passionate nature.

She sat on the edge of the bed and caressed his face, whispering "David."

He awoke with a quizzical little grunt, blinked, and focused
on her. "Lili." His gaze lit on her hair, her braceleted arms, her
silk-clad breasts, and finally her lips, stained a deep crimson; it
was the first time he had seen her wearing rouge.

He met her eyes again; his throat moved. He knew why she
was there.

"I thought you were going to turn in early," she said.

"I, er . . ." He sat up, rubbing his eyes. "I had some things to
sort through."

"How to tell your bishop about us without lying outright?"
she asked.

"Among other things."

"I've been thinking, too," she said, "about what you told me
when we were in *la Galerie des Diamants Noirs,* that you have
always ached to know how it would feel for a woman to pleasure you with her mouth."

After a moment of stunned silence, he appeared to be grop-
ing for words.

"I know," she said, stroking her fingers through his hair.
"You took a vow of chastity, and I respect your fidelity to it. At
the same time, it strikes me that when you made that vow, you
really had no idea what you would be giving up. For a man to

choose to abstain for the rest of his life from the pleasures of the flesh without having sampled those pleasures . . ." She shook her head. "It doesn't sit well with me."

"But, Lili—"

"*Kasaru*," she whispered, stroking her fingertips lightly across his forehead.

David fell back onto the pillows, his look of bewilderment swiftly turning to panic as he realized he was paralyzed save for a very limited range of motion in his trunk and head; she could have imposed a greater or lesser degree of paralysis, but this level seemed to suit the situation. He moved his mouth, but only weak, straining sounds emerged, the *mashmashu* having rendered him mute as well as immobile.

"It's all right, David." She kissed his forehead, skimmed her hands soothingly over his shoulders and arms. "Relax. Don't fight it."

He frantically shook his head as much as he was able; he could only move it an inch or two either way.

Lili pressed a hand to his chest to feel his wildly hammering heart. The *mashmashu kasaru* could be disconcerting to a *gabru,* but they didn't generally get quite so wrought up so quickly.

"There is nothing wrong with you, David. It's just a spell, very simple and very old. You can't move, but you *can* still feel. You see?" She grazed her fingernails lightly down his chest.

He stilled, his gaze on her hand. She thought she saw a glimmer of relief in his eyes. His body seemed to relax a bit.

"You shan't remain this way," she assured him. "I shall release the spell in due course. But first, I think it only right that you should experience at least one of those pleasures which you have chosen to sacrifice."

He watched her intently as she untied his drawers, his sex stirring beneath the thin white linen.

"I shan't deprive you of your virginity," she said. "I shan't even bring you to climax, if you do not wish it. But I shall give you a taste of that which you should have experienced long ere this."

Lili smiled in anticipation as she opened his drawers. He grew erect without being touched, the skin stretching taut as the shaft thickened and rose, drawing the foreskin back to expose the blood-flushed glans. Her mouth literally watered. She loved a gleaming-hard cockstand pulsing with heat; the very sight of it made her wet. She couldn't wait to taste it.

"The *mashmashu* is for your peace of mind," she told him as she positioned herself, "so that you needn't truly be in violation of your vow. You never asked for this, you are powerless to prevent it. You have no control, and therefore no need for contrition."

His cock had reared up so high that it lay nestled in the thatch of black hair on his lower belly. Leaning down, she gave it a soft kiss, causing it to twitch involuntarily; David sucked in a breath. She licked it with unhurried strokes, delighting in the glide of his hot, silky skin against her tongue. He was quivering already, his breath coming fast.

When a *gabru* was under the influence of this type of *mashmashu,* it intensified sexual stimulation, magnifying his pleasure and giving him one explosive orgasm after another. This was normally an excellent thing, ensuring as it did long nights of abandoned bedsport, but Lili had promised not to make David spend without his leave.

Mindful of that promise, she proceeded slowly, letting him savor the sensations he'd lain awake imagining all these years without allowing those sensations to race out of control. She licked his scrotum, then cradled it in her hand, rubbing behind it with measured strokes as she teased the tip of his cock— flicking it with her tongue, popping it in and out of her mouth.

When she finally closed her crimsoned lips around him and sucked him in hard and deep, a low, grinding moan rose from his chest. David's expression was one of rapture; his chest was pumping like a bellows.

Lili slid him out of her mouth, then back in even deeper than before, sucking it in strong, rhythmic waves from the base up with the head seated firmly in her throat. No human woman could take a man this deep without choking, nor did they have the physiological ability to milk a cock with their palates and tongues; a pity for human males, many of whom had told her it was the most ecstatic sexual experience of their lives. It was, however, an experience that tended to produce a swift and violent ejaculation. In fact, so erotic was the sensation of a man shooting volleys of come down her throat that Lili could easily climax from that alone.

Wanting David's pleasure to last as long as possible, Lili switched tactics, bestowing airy kisses and little licks up and down the shaft. A bead of pre-ejaculate materialized on the tiny slit. Lili rubbed it onto the shaft to slicken it, pumping him lightly with her hand as she took him in her mouth again. He thrust his hips inasmuch as he was able, trying to push deeper into her mouth. She let the tip nudge her throat, then backed off again. He thrust harder, his body quaking.

He was right on the edge. It was time to put an end to this.

"David." Lili had to say his name several times before he seemed to hear her. "David, if I do this any longer, you'll spend. Do you want me to finish you this way?"

He shook his head, forming the word "no" with his mouth.

With a sigh of regret, she retied his drawers over his erection. Sitting up, she stroked his forehead lightly while speaking the words that would lift the *mashmashu*. "*Hadatu.*"

"Bloody hell," he gasped as the feeling flooded back into his arms and legs.

"You are a man of remarkable self-control," she said, lowering her feet to the floor. "I don't know if that's always such a good—"

David seized her, threw her onto the bed, and whipped her *lubushu* up to her waist. He tugged twice at the waist cord of his drawers, then ripped them open and fell upon her. She felt his fingers searching, fumbling, heard him swear under his breath as a sharp thrust slid away from its target, and then a second— but with the third, he pushed in about halfway.

He gasped at the sensation, pausing as if to savor it, then bulled into her with an anguished groan.

He took her with a mindless ferocity, putting his strength into it, his entire body heaving, pounding. She came within seconds, clawing at his back as she bucked beneath him. He shuddered, pushing deep. A shout roared from his lungs as his arms tightened around her, his cock pulsing, pulsing, pulsing . . .

He collapsed onto her, damp and trembling. They lay together catching their breath for a minute, Lili relishing, as always, the singular bliss of lying motionless with a man's spent cock still full and heavy inside her.

She kissed his neck, saying "I thought you didn't want to come."

"Not that way. I wanted to come inside you."

"Why, what an inspired idea," she said through a chuckle.

He growled contentedly, nuzzling her hair.

"I'm sorry, David."

He lifted his head to look down at her, frowning in puzzlement. "Whatever for?"

"Your vow of chastity. I made you—"

"You didn't *make* me do anything, Lili. And I'm not constrained by the vow anymore, or I won't be soon."

"How can that be?"

"I wrote to my bishop, requesting temporary secularization so that I can . . . think things through. If I decide to pursue my ordination, I can return to the seminary and do so. If not, I shall apply to the Holy See for permanent release from my vows."

"Do you think that's what you'll do?" she asked.

"I don't know. Whatever I decide, I know that I shall never regret coming here, meeting you . . . It isn't every man who can say he's been ravished by a Babylonian goddess."

"I beg your pardon, sir, but who ravished whom just now?"

"After being pushed to the limits of his endurance."

"Oh, that was your limit, eh? Too bad. I'd had such high hopes for the rest of the night."

"Witch," he growled, thrusting against her.

"I thought I was a goddess."

He lowered his mouth to hers, saying "I do believe you're both."

Lili climbed the winding stone staircase in the northeast tower early the next morning garbed in her yellow silk *lubushu*, her hair wet from the dip she'd taken in the bathhouse after seeing David off before dawn.

The door to Elic's apartment was a slab of oak so thick and heavy that she had to lean her weight into it to push it open, both she and the door groaning with the effort. She went directly to his bedchamber, finding it dark within because of the closed window shutters, and cool, and very quiet.

Elic lay on his back in the big bed with the bedclothes rucked around his waist, his head angled toward her, his beautiful hair spilling over the pillows like streams of honey. His mouth was slightly open in sleep, as it often was, making him look terribly young despite the sharply carved face, the muscle-packed shoulders.

She unwrapped her *lubushu* and climbed under the covers,

which roused him from his slumber. He opened his eyes, radiant as blue fire in the shadowy room, and gave her a groggy smile as she tucked herself against him. His body felt like an oven against the coolness of the sheets.

"*Kveðja*," she said softly.

Elic gathered her up, kissing her damp hair as their bodies settled into the natural embrace in which they often slept together, wrapped in each other's arms. "*Shalamu, mins Ástgurdís.*"

Satisfaction

Still if some are occasionally begotten from demons, it is not from the seed of such demons, nor from their assumed bodies, but from the seed of men taken for the purpose; as when the demon assumes first the form of a woman, and afterwards of a man; just as they take the seed of other things for other generating purposes, as Augustine says (De Trin. iii), so that the person born is not the child of a demon, but of a man.

St. Thomas Aquinas, Summa Theologia, *Part I, Question 51, Article 3*

AND truth, you say, is all divine;
'Tis truth we live by; let her drench
The shuddering heart like potent wine;
No matter how she wreck or wrench
The gracious instincts from their throne,
Or steep the virgin soul in tears

From Realism *by Arthur Christopher Benson*

One

*I*NIGO WAS PLAYING doctor with a couple of nurses when Isabel Archer came to check her father out of the hospital.

Isabel didn't realize at first what was going on. She did find it odd that the curtains were drawn around the other bed, since her dad had a private room; the only reason there were two beds was because there hadn't been any single rooms available when he was admitted. As she passed the curtained-off alcove, she heard a woman's frenetic breathing and the sound of someone shifting around on the vinyl-covered mattress in a way that seemed anxious, perhaps even pained.

The noise had evidently not disturbed her father, who was sleeping propped up with pillows in the corner recliner, attired for his "breakout from this antiseptic Purgatory" in a pin-striped suit and lemon yellow tie with matching pocket square. Despite the nasal cannula delivering oxygen to his lungs, his breathing was strained. On his lap sat a huge, shabby old book, its spine secured with duct tape, the cover stamped Война и мир in archaic lettering from which the gilt had mostly rubbed off.

It had been last August that he'd confided to Isabel, during a visit to Grotte Cachée from her home in New York City, that he was suffering from aggressive, drug-resistant pulmonary fibrosis. She'd flown back to see him every few weeks since then, watching his salt-and-pepper hair bleach to ash gray, his lean, patrician features turn gaunt. Mindful of his admonition that she "not grieve for me while I'm still alive, thank you very much," Isabel took pains, when she was around him, to act as if nothing were amiss. She'd internalized the act over time, becoming, if not quite accepting of her father's fate, a good deal less anguished. Maybe there was something to all that stiff-upper-lip stuff after all.

The woman behind the curtain let out a tremulous moan. *That's it.* Isabel swept the curtain aside, gaping at a tableau that instantly, and no doubt permanently, seared itself onto her retinas.

Chloe, the nurse's aide whose job it was to assist Emmett Archer's private duty nurse, but who seemed to think she'd been hired as Inigo's personal little anything-goes, living, breathing party doll, was tethered spread-eagled to the bed by four-point medical restraints made of black webbing and Velcro. The skirt of her powder blue nurse frock was pushed up, exposing the lacy tops of her thigh-high stockings and a snatch as hairless as a Barbie doll's, a big, scary syringelike device emerging from within. When she saw Isabel, Chloe yelped, displaying a tongue stud with the ace of spades on it.

"Oops! Sorry," Inigo whispered from beneath his surgical mask as he paused in the act of thrusting the syringe thingy. He had on full operating scrubs, including one of those shower cap deals to contain his headful of wild black corkscrew curls. "Are we making too much noise?" To hear him talk, you'd think he'd been born and bred in his beloved New York City, where he'd kept a *pied-à-terre* for the past hundred sixty years—a home away from home whenever the château began to feel "like being stuck in the fifteenth century."

"*Merde!*" The pretty blond nurse standing next to him, who'd been masturbating him via a side slit of his lab coat, judging from the humungous bulge beneath it, whipped out a hand covered in lube and crossed herself frantically.

"*Ne te fais pas de la bile,*" Inigo told her in a softly reassuring tone. "*Elle pas tattle.*"

"Why the hell *shouldn't* I tattle, if this is what my father's nurses are up to when they're supposed to be taking care of him?"

"It's a hundred percent my fault. Could there be any worse influence in the world than me?" He pulled down the mask so as to display his disarming smile to full effect. "C'mon, Blondie. No harm, no foul. We're just passing the time till they let your dad go."

Isabel just sighed and shook her head, partly because of the nickname—he'd been calling her Blondie since she was a tow-headed toddler—and partly because there really was no point in getting het up over this. For a regular human-type person to "pass the time" by playing kinky sex games in the hospital room of a gravely ill friend would be outrageous. But for a satyr, whose deep-rooted instinct was to squeeze the maximum pleasure out of every second of every day, having half an hour to kill and two frisky nurses at hand meant one thing: time to enact the psychosexual hospital fantasy from hell.

She said, "Look, just do me a favor and . . . wrap things up, okay? Dad's itching to get out of here, and we can't leave without you. I don't drive a stick."

"You got it," he said as she shut the curtain.

She turned to find her father awake and regarding her with that patented ultra-arid smile of his. "You do realize the poor fellow can't help it," he said in his now-thready British accent.

Isabel rolled her eyes as she came to crouch next to his chair, whispering, "*She* can."

"Who?"

"That *Chloe*. She's supposed to be keeping an eye on you while Grace handles your release paperwork. I hate to think what's gonna happen back at the château. She's got the night shift. What if she's off taking a little midnight nookie break when you have your next episode?"

"I'm counting on it. It's no mean feat, trying to shuffle off this mortal coil with people constantly hovering about and butting in."

During her father's latest bout of respiratory distress, the worst yet, he had stubbornly refused to be put on a ventilator. "*If I must turn up my toes, then turn them up I shall, but not in one of those ghastly, exhibitionistic gowns with tubes sprouting from every orifice, and not in an opiated coma.*" Isabel had promised to go along with this on the condition that she be allowed to hire medical personnel to return with him to Château de la Grotte Cachée so that he could be kept as comfortable as possible during the time he had left. A control freak to the end, he had insisted she call a London nursing agency called Savoir Care that had a particularly sterling reputation.

Three days ago, the agency had sent a nurse practitioner named Grace Garvey . . . and Chloe. The two women could not have been more different. Grace was experienced, skilled, and compassionate, while Chloe was an orange-haired whore whose legs had been locked in the open position from the moment she'd made the acquaintance of their "dishy" visitor with the puppy-dog eyes and monumental cock. It turned out she was a wild child from a wealthy and aristocratic London family, which Isabel should have guessed from her Sloane Rangerish twang. Exasperated with her self-centered, shallow lifestyle, her parents had placed a condition on her trust fund before she could access it. She'd been made to attend a nurse's aide training program followed by one year of full-time work, that particular job having been chosen in the hope that it would teach her to think about people other than herself. Having just graduated from the program, this was her very first assignment for Savoir Care, and if Grace had any say in the matter, it would be her last.

"Please, Dad," Isabel begged, "*please, please, please* let me fire that little slut and have them send someone else. Grace wants her gone, too. She's told me so, like a dozen times." Switching to a rough facsimile of Grace's South London/Barbados lilt, Isabel said, " 'She's a spoiled, selfish little slag and a bloody fucking menace to her patients.' "

Chuckling drowsily, Emmett said, "Would you believe me if I told you I like her?"

"No."

"Perhaps she reminds me of your mother."

"Are you fucking serious?"

"*Must* you swear like a cutter, my dear?"

"Again with the 'cutter,' " Isabel groaned. "Tell you what, Dad. You tell me what that word means, finally, like in relation to swearing, and I'll work on the language, okay? But Chloe and Mom? First of all, you and Mom called it quits twenty years ago, so as for you liking her—"

"*She* was the one who filed for divorce," he said raspily. "She may have been impossible to live with, but there were always things about her that were . . . captivating. When I first knew her . . ." He trailed off, gazing out the window with rheumy eyes. "She was one of those girls . . . you know. The girls one finds oneself staring at, thinking about, trying to please, trying to make laugh. She was dazzling, utterly charismatic."

Isabel was speechless. She'd never heard her father talk this way about the woman who had abruptly shucked him off and moved back to her native New York City, taking fifteen-year-old Isabel with her, rather than take up residence at Grotte Cachée when her husband succeeded his father as *administra-teur* to young Adrien Morel, Seigneur des Ombres.

"And Chloe isn't completely dissimilar to your mother," he continued. "There's that bright red hair."

"Mom was *born* with hair that color, which, by the way, is not remotely similar to Chloe's. No one has ever, in the history of the universe, been born with Crayola red hair."

"She has an attitude of joie de vivre," he said.

"You hate joie de vivre. You're always saying people should be less impulsive, exercise more self-control. That girl is juvenile, irresponsible . . . everything you've always hated. Honest to God, Dad, I just don't get it."

"She amuses Inigo, and it's my job to keep the Follets amused."

Keeping them amused: a euphemism for providing humans for them to fuck, without which they would go bonkers or deteriorate to a vegetative state—or in Elic's case possibly even die, despite the Follets' virtual immortality. Isabel knew this despite the secrecy surrounding the Follets because she was Emmett's heir apparent to take over the administration of Grotte Cachée.

The operative word was "apparent," because she had resolved never to step into that role, a fact known to Adrien Morel and the Follets, but kept from her father so as not to worsen his condition through stress. It wasn't so much that she was unwilling to trade in her life in New York City for rural

France; she loved Auvergne, and being a freelance graphic artist had never provided the level of creative satisfaction she'd once hoped it would. It was about Adrien, and what had happened during that late-night swim in the bathhouse last August, the consummation of feelings that had been simmering between them since adolescence.

No one knew about the two of them, not the Follets and certainly not her father, and no one ever would, because nothing could come of it. As the last in a line of psychically gifted seigneurs of Grotte Cachée dating back over two thousand years, Adrien was duty bound to marry a woman with the Gift. It was the only way to ensure gifted offspring to carry on his sacred obligation of safeguarding the Follets. Gifted women being difficult to identify, Isabel's father had yet to locate a wife for *"le seigneur"* despite years of looking. His successor, it was hoped, would have better luck.

Isabel had no intention of being that successor. How could she possibly play matchmaker for the man she'd loved with all her heart from the time she was sixteen years old? Even being in his company was painful, for both of them. For this reason, Adrien stayed in the hunting lodge, where he'd been brought up, whenever she was there, and they seemed to have an unspoken agreement not to visit Emmett at the same time during his hospitalizations. In fact, although she'd been at Grotte Cachée for almost a week now, they'd had but a few brief, excruciatingly cordial phone conversations.

"Seeing to the needs of the Follets will be your responsibility soon," Emmett said, pausing to cough into a handkerchief. "Perhaps you and I can sit down and discuss the transition with *le seigneur* before you head back home. When do you suppose that will be?"

"Oh, um . . . Actually, I don't have any firm plans."

"I thought you said you had a deadline looming."

"Yeah, but I don't want to leave until you're back at the château, and I'm sure you're . . . that everything's . . ."

"You'll be called if and when there's any need for your presence," he said. "In the meantime, I've got Grace and Chl— well, I've got Grace."

"See, even you admit Chloe's a freakin' waste of DNA."

"Go home, for heaven's sake."

"Here's your hat, what's your hurry?"

Giving her *that look,* he said, "You know perfectly well how gratifying it is to have you at my side, but not if it's a deathwatch, especially given that you've responsibilities of your own to tend to. Book a flight home, Isabel. Do it tonight. Promise me."

"Look, just let me get you settled, and then we'll talk about it."

His sigh devolved into a deep cough. "Fine. Meanwhile let's meet with *le seigneur* sometime soon, get you briefed on what to expect when you take over the helm as *administrateur.* By the way, you do realize you should be advising your clients that you won't be in the graphic design business for much longer, and you certainly don't want to be taking on any new jobs."

"Um . . ."

"Here we go, then," announced Grace Garvey as she strode briskly into the room pushing a wheelchair. Grace was a slender, toasty-brown beauty whose baby dreads with their bleached tips provided just the right funky counterpoint to her officious white tunic and stethoscope. "I've negotiated your ransom, Mr. Archer. Time to flee your captors' clutches."

"And not a moment too soon," Isabel said.

Looking out the front passenger window of Inigo's hulking Peugeot SUV as he drove up to the front of the château, Isabel spied Adrien standing at an open window of his gate-tower study smoking one of his Sobranie Black Russians. Lili and Elic had been after him to quit, which he'd promised to do "when things settle down and I haven't got so much on my mind." Meaning when Emmett was gone and he'd managed to scare up a new *administrateur,* who in turn had managed to scare him up a gifted wife.

Adrien's brown hair had the kind of unruly waves that made it seem as if a comb had never touched it, whereas his ubiquitous button-down shirts with their tidily rolled-up sleeves always managed to look freshly pressed even at the end of a long day. He met Isabel's gaze with those big, soulful eyes as the car came to a stop in front of the gatehouse, held it for a moment, then nodded in greeting. He didn't smile, exactly, but his expression softened a bit. Isabel nodded back, then looked away, taking a deep breath.

Every moment she spent in Adrien's presence, she had to pretend her heart wasn't twisting in her chest. She tended to speak to him as little as possible. She even avoided looking at him more than necessary, for fear of what he'd see in her eyes, the raw yearning that felt as if it would be with her until the end of her days.

The two guards on duty—Mike, the American, and Luc, the Frenchman, both uniformed in black polo shirts and black chinos—emerged from the gatehouse and crossed the drawbridge that spanned the dry moat. Mike was wheeling the cushy, way-too-complicated electronic wheelchair that Adrien had insisted on buying after Emmett's first collapse last October. Until then, her father had managed to keep his illness a secret from everyone but Adrien, who had known, from Emmett's darkening aura, that something was very wrong.

"Do you need me?" Chloe asked Grace.

"Nah, we're set," replied Grace, helping the just-awakened Emmett out of the car as Mike positioned the wheelchair and set its brake. "Why don't you rest up for your shift tonight?"

Chloe asked Inigo if she could "nap" in his apartment.

"Sure, if I can nap with you." Inigo tossed his car keys to Luc and set off with her toward the southwest tower.

Grace and Isabel exchanged a baleful look of the type they'd been sharing a lot lately.

"I don't want to hear it," Emmett said. "Hit the gas, Michael."

Mike transported him to his second-floor apartment by means of a nineteenth-century rope-pulley elevator, then returned to the gatehouse. In Emmett's oak-paneled sitting room, the leather couch had been taken out and replaced with a hospital bed that he refused to get in, saying he would be permanently horizontal soon enough. And, too, he wanted access to his balcony overlooking the castle's central courtyard, where the cherry trees were abloom in frothy pink blossoms.

When Grace asked him if he wouldn't be more comfortable in sweats, he told her he didn't own any.

"Pajamas, then?" she asked.

He scowled at her. "At two o'clock in the afternoon?"

"Don't know what I was thinking."

She did manage to talk him out of his suit coat and tie, but the wingtips stayed on, and he kept that big, duct-taped tome—an early Russian edition of *War and Peace*—firmly planted on his lap. Isabel suspected that it was a sort of security blanket, a comforting reminder that although his body had betrayed him, he still had his mind.

Emmett sat back in his chair, eyes closed, his breathing labored. Grace filled a glass and stirred in a spoonful of "Thick-N" powder from a big red can. Within half a minute, the water was the consistency of a milk shake; Emmett would choke on it otherwise. Soon, Grace said, he wouldn't be able to swallow anything, even his pills.

"Snack time," Grace told Emmett, tipping three pills from their vials and handing them to him.

Emmett put one of the pills in his mouth and took a careful sip of his thickened water. He squeezed his eyes shut as his throat spasmed, but he got the pill down.

Grace said, "I do wish you'd let me give you these meds by IV."

"No IV," he said in a weary, we've-been-over-this tone. "No tubes, no wires, no beastly little beeps and blinking lights." Something out on the open balcony seemed to catch his eye as he raised another pill to his mouth. "Darius! Good to see you, old man. Paying the obligatory sickroom visit, are you?"

Grace and Isabel turned to see a small, bluish bird, a rock thrush, sitting on the little iron café table as if quietly observing the goings-on in Emmett Archer's sitting room—as he no doubt was, for this was the most reclusive of Grotte Cachée's permanent residents, the shape-shifting djinni Darius.

Darius cheeped. Isabel smiled at him; he bobbed his head. Of course she wasn't going to greet him out loud in front of Grace. She was surprised her father had done so, meds or no meds.

A movement in a tower window diagonally across the courtyard caught Isabel's eye. It was the southwest tower, in which Inigo had his apartment, and in fact, it was Inigo she noticed first, standing with his back to her in the same *Big Lebowski*–style bowling shirt he'd had on earlier, kicking off his jeans. A pair of hands—Chloe's, of course—reached around to knead his perfect ass with blue-tipped fingers. It wasn't just perfect, it was a work of art, one of nature's great masterpieces. Every time Isabel looked at the bathhouse statues, for which he'd posed, she thought, *No man has a butt that perfect,* a tight little package of muscle. But the thing was, whoever sculpted those statues was either an ass man or a damned brilliant sculptor, or both, because the marble representation of Inigo's ass and the real thing were identical in every respect—except, of course, for the tail, which he had removed as soon as they came out with chloroform in the mid-nineteenth century.

Inigo pushed Chloe to her knees and held the shirt up around his waist while guiding her head with the other hand. The Perfect Ass flexed and released, flexed and released . . .

It took Isabel about a nanosecond to grow wet. She hadn't slept with a man, hadn't wanted to, since Adrien last August; she'd even gone off the pill. Between ten months of celibacy and the fact that it was midmonth, she was a veritable tinderbox, arousal-wise. Even so, that little doctor-nurse scenario back at the hospital hadn't done much for her; she'd always found sexual playacting a little too goofy to really get off on. But a magnificent male ass thrusting and churning while one of the world's most spectacular cocks got sucked . . . That was a different matter entirely.

"Isabel?"

She turned to find her father and Grace, neither of whom were in a position to see what she was looking at, thank God, regarding her quizzically.

"Woolgathering, my dear?" her father asked.

No, I was getting turned on by watching Chloe blow Inigo instead of paying attention to my terminally ill father. Oh, yeah. She was definitely going to Hell.

"I was telling your father he seems a bit tired. Time to get some high-test into you, Mr. Archer," Grace said as she uncoiled the tubing from the oxygen concentrator in the corner.

"God, how I loathe this bloody thing," Emmett grumbled as she looped the cannula over his ears.

Grinning at the vulgar language—he never used to say "bloody," at least not in front of her—Isabel said, "Dad, must you swear like a cutter?"

There came a chuckle from behind her. She turned to find Adrien Morel standing in the doorway.

"Isabel," he said with a little duck of the head.

"Adrien."

They shook hands and smiled their carefully opaque smiles. *Showtime.*

Adrien filled Emmett in on Inigo's proposal to turn the chapel withdrawing room into a screening room while Isabel, who had ended up seated with a view of the courtyard, tried to resist the urge to steal glances at the ongoing X-rated shenanigans in the tower across the way. It was a futile effort, though, like trying to turn away from an Internet porn site you'd stumbled across by accident when you were really horny and it was really good porn.

Under normal circumstances, she would have been consumed with shame to be engaging in such frank voyeurism, but nothing at Château de la Grotte Cachée was what you'd call "normal," especially when it came to sex. And after all, if Inigo and Chloe hadn't been more than happy to be seen, they would hardly be doing it in front of a window that was so clearly visible. She smiled when she saw that Darius was watching them, too.

When Inigo had enjoyed enough of Chloe's mouth for the time being, he stood her up and pulled off her nursie dress, beneath which she wore the lace-topped thigh-highs, a sparkly navel ring, and a sheer, flesh-colored push-up bra. She was unusually stacked for such a petite woman, and the bra made her large, economy-size jugs look like a pair of cantaloupes with hard red nipples. No undies, of course. He bent her over with her hands on the window ledge, and then *he* dropped to his knees and performed a little doggie-style cunnilingus—pretty skillfully, judging from her histrionics.

She came three times by Isabel's count, and then Inigo stood. She held her hands behind her, wrists together, saying something to him over her shoulder, ending with "Please?"; Isabel could read her lips.

With an obliging smile and a little shrug, Inigo stepped away from the window, returning a moment later with a length of wide red ribbon. Positioning her with the windowsill supporting her just under her breasts so that she was looking down into the courtyard, he lashed her hands behind her, then yanked her head back by the hair and leaned over to whisper something in her ear. His snarly expression was a shock to Isabel, who'd never seen him in any mood other than one of mellow good humor. Of course, he was just putting on a show to please Chloe, but it was a good enough act to send shivers down Isabel's spine, making her think he must have been into it on some level. Of course, if there was any way to make sex even sexier, a satyr would be into it, wouldn't he?

Chloe nodded, saying "Yes, sir. Yes, sir."

Inigo disappeared again and brought back a little plastic bottle, which he flipped open, squeezing a stream of fluid onto his colossal cock. He rubbed it up and down the shaft with firm, masturbatory strokes. Squeezing some of the lube onto his fingers, he pushed them inside Chloe, taking his time as he slid them around, saying things Isabel couldn't hear, of course, but that made the little redhead squirm and nod. "Yes, sir."

When he'd judged her to be suitably lubed up, he pressed one hand on the small of her back while he used the other hand to push his gleaming wet cock into her pussy.

Chloe tensed, wincing. This wasn't the first time they'd fucked, of course, but he was very huge and very hard, and there was no amount of lube that was going to make him an easy fit for the average woman. He gave it another slow push, pausing when she flinched. Another push, and another, and he was still only halfway in.

He gave her ass a hard slap; it looked like she yelped. He spanked her about a dozen more times, saying things between each smack that Isabel couldn't decipher except for "dirty girl," which he said several times. That seemed to help. She arched her back like a kitten getting petted, and even started cocking her hips up to take him deeper. Smiling, he sank it home.

Inigo unhooked her bra and tossed it aside, leaving her heavy breasts hanging free. He tugged on her nipples as he fucked her with deep, even strokes. Before long, she was thrashing with such abandon that he had to grab her hips just so he could keep thrusting. Isabel was pretty sure she came at least one more time. Inigo's movements grew erratic, and then he hunched over Chloe, his face darkening. His eyes closed. His mouth opened.

A phone trilled, making Isabel jump in her chair. She pressed a hand to her skittering heart, whispering "Jesus."

Adrien dug his cell phone out of the front pocket of his khakis. "*Allô. Oui*, Mike," he said in that deep, roughly soft voice, a lion's purr with a French accent. "*Escortez-les à l'appartement de Monsieur Archer.* Hm? That's right. They're expected."

"*Who's* expected?" Emmett asked. His breathing was still strained despite the meds, hence the steadily increasing dosages.

Adrien caught Isabel's eye and gave her a look that said the floor was hers, which was only fair, since this was essentially her doing.

Here goes. "Um, look, Dad, I know you said no visitors, but—"

"Oh, *bloody* hell," he growled.

"Dad." Kneeling next to him, she put her hand on his arm—an unusually physical gesture for the two of them—and said, "It's Hitch. I told him you didn't want any visitors, but he insisted, wouldn't take no for an answer. He was online booking the trip from Chicago even as we spoke. He said he was gonna bring his new wife and stepson, since you hadn't been able to go to the wedding last spring, and I remembered you saying you wished you'd had the chance to meet them."

"And you didn't tell me this because . . . ?"

"*We* didn't tell you," Adrien said evenly, "because we knew how you would carry on if you thought there was still time to cancel the visit."

"Dad, it's not just anybody," Isabel said, "it's Hitch. My God, he saved your life. Now he wants to see you. Don't you think you kinda owe him?"

"He saved your life?" Grace asked.

Emmett sighed, nodded.

"It was during a heli-skiing trip about three years ago," Isabel said.

Grace said, "A what trip?"

"Heli-skiing—it's where you spend a week or two on a mountain, and every day a helicopter takes you from the base camp to a different place to ski."

"You did this just three years ago?" Grace asked Emmett.

"I haven't always been a pathetic invalid," he said.

Isabel said, "He's always been into that whole 'sound mind in a sound body' thing—right, Dad? Remember that RAF exercise routine you used to make me do before school when I was little?"

Adrien said, "The first thing Emmett did when he succeeded his father as *administrateur* was to turn the upper hall into a gymnasium. I didn't see the point at the time, but now, of course, I use it every day."

Grace brightened. "There's a gym here?"

"Yes, indeed," Adrien said. "Cardio machines, Nautilus, free weights—even a sauna. You are more than welcome to use it. It's in the west range over the dining room."

"So, anyway," Isabel said, "Hitch lives in Chicago—he's American—so he and Dad would get together a couple of times a year for these macho, testing-the-limits type expeditions. You know, white-water rafting in India, climbing K2, skiing every double black diamond slope in the Canadian Rockies . . . Three years ago, they booked this heli-skiing excursion on Makalu, which is one of the tallest mountains in the world. It's in the Himalayas, near Everest. One morning, Hitch gets up before dawn, straps on his snowshoes, and sets out on a little prebreakfast solo hike. About ten minutes later, an avalanche comes roaring down the mountain and totally demolishes the base camp—with Dad and their Sherpa guide still asleep in their tents."

"I woke up with the rumbling, actually," Emmett said dryly. "Had just enough time to unzip my sleeping bag before it slammed into me."

"Blimey," Grace murmured.

"Everything's just *gone* in, like, a minute," Isabel said. "Hitch knows my dad and the guide have to be buried under the snow downstream of where the camp had been. If they'd been skiing at the time, they would have been wearing these beeper thingies—"

"Transceivers," Emmett said.

"Right. You know, so you can be located if you're buried in the snow—but of course they didn't have them on, 'cause they were sleeping. So Hitch has to take his best guess as to where they might be, but luckily he's got this walking stick—"

"Trekking pole," her father corrected.

"Fine, a trekking pole, and the thing telescopes to, like six feet, and he probes the snow with it and finds my dad. And on his backpack, he's got this little . . . it's like a shovel for avalanches."

"Avalanche shovel," Emmett said with a snarky smile.

"So he digs my dad out of the snow, then finds the Sherpa and digs *him* out. Dad owes Hitch his life, and he hasn't even seen him since that trip, 'cause he got sick and stopped traveling after that."

"Hitch didn't come here to visit?" Grace asked.

"Dad wouldn't let him. God forbid his closest friend in the world, the man he's always said was like a brother to him, should see him when he's not in tip-top form. He's like family, Dad, and family should be with you at a time like this."

"She's right, pal," said Robert Hitchens from the doorway.

The peevishness faded from her father's expression as he took in the old friend he hadn't seen in three years. Hitch, a retired commercial airline pilot who was exactly her father's age, had the kind of rangy, sandy-haired, sun-gilded good looks that turned the heads of much younger women. In fact, the pretty honey-blonde standing next to him—his new bride, a lawyer named Karen—looked about half his age; but given her college-age son, looming behind her, she was probably at least forty.

Hitch's smile didn't falter for a moment as he greeted Emmett with a handshake and a shoulder pat, despite the shock he must have felt at seeing his surrogate brother and fellow adventurer reduced in such short order to a feeble old man. He shook Adrien's hand and gave Isabel a big hug, as always, and then everyone got sort of haphazardly introduced to everyone else.

"Were you named after the Henry James character?" Karen asked Isabel.

"Ah, a *brainy* beauty," praised Emmett. "Looks as if you've caught yourself a live one, Hitch. Can't imagine what she was thinking, throwing in her lot with the likes of you."

Turning to his wife, Hitch said, "I *told* you he was a pain in the ass."

Emmett glanced at his watch, a gesture not lost on Adrien, who ordered up a heavily laden tea tray.

"I saw Lili and Elic downstairs," Hitch said. "I swear they look exactly like they did the last time I was here, which was thirty-something years ago. What is it, something in the water?"

"That's the theory, actually," said Adrien, offering the standard, if misleading, reply to that observation. "Auvergne is known for its therapeutic mineral spas. Some visitors to Grotte Cachée have theorized that our cave spring is unusually high in the types of substances that promote longevity."

Hitch said, "I'm surprised you haven't become a mecca for the people who are into that kind of thing."

"Oh, we are very covetous of our privacy," Adrien said.

Jason, Hitch's stepson, said, "Is that why your guard confiscated our cameras and cell phones?"

Adrien nodded. "He'll give them back when you leave. If people started taking photographs of our little valley, others would soon find out about us, and we would be overrun with trespassers looking to rejuvenate themselves in our bathhouse pool."

"A fountain of youth," Karen said incredulously. "Didn't that pipe dream die with Ponce de León?"

"It's not necessarily a pipe dream," replied Jason, a bulky, bespectacled young man in a Northwestern sweatshirt and baggy jeans who had a kind of a geeky bear thing going on. With his almost-blond hair and his height, he could have been the natural son of Hitch, who'd never actually fathered any children himself; Katie, his daughter with his first wife, had been adopted from Korea. Twelve years ago Katie moved to New York to study theater at NYU, where Isabel was a senior. The two only children became fast friends, almost like sisters. Katie was a working actor now, with regular roles on the various *Law & Order*s, the soaps, and off-Broadway.

Jason said, "Studies have indicated that certain enzymes, amino acids, and hormones actually do have anti-aging properties. They retard the aging process either by encouraging cells to continue dividing after they should have died, or by preventing them from releasing the free radicals that cause oxidative stress. Who's to say there aren't minerals or other components in the water here—or elsewhere in the environment of this valley—that have that effect?"

"My son the know-it-all," Karen said with a smile of pride and affection. "He's one of those brainiacs who doesn't sleep. Stays up till the wee hours of the morning, gets three or four hours of sleep, max, then he's good to go. He's majoring in biological sciences, and then he plans to get his Ph.D. in . . . What is it? Molecular biochemistry . . . ?"

"Biochemistry, molecular biology, and cell biology," he said.

Emmett said, "University of Chicago, isn't it, Justin?"

"It's Northwestern, actually. And, um . . . it's Jason."

"Of course it is," said Emmett, looking abashed. "My memory . . . This blasted disease, you know. The lack of oxygen to the brain."

"Well, and those don't help," said Isabel, nodding toward the vials on the desk behind Jason and Hitch.

As Adrien expounded on the importance of keeping Grotte Cachée's theoretical healing qualities a secret from the outside world, Jason quietly scooped up the three vials and scanned their labels, ignoring his mother's stern shake of the head. He found one of the vials particularly interesting, judging from his scowl of absorption as he read the label.

Hitch, sitting next to him, leaned close and mouthed, "What?"

Jason held the vial so that his stepfather could see the label. Isabel was probably the only person in the room, aside from Hitch, who heard Jason whisper, "Diamorphine."

Hitch shrugged, as if to say *So?*

"It's heroin."

Hitch sat back and fixed his gaze on Grace, who noticed after a few moments and met his eyes. He cocked his head toward the door, Universal Sign Language for *Let's talk outside.*

She nodded and stood.

"Excuse us," Hitch said as he ushered her out into the hall. "We'll just be a minute."

Isabel got up and slipped out the door behind them. Hitch gestured for her to close it, which she did, and then he turned to Grace. "You're giving him heroin? It's not even legal."

"Hitch—" Isabel began, but Grace held up an I'll-take-care-of-this hand.

"Diamorphine can be prescribed in the UK," Grace said.

"Is he in that much pain?"

"No. He's uncomfortable, certainly, but—"

"Then why *heroin*? He hates feeling drugged. He's never even smoked pot, not once. He likes to be sharp."

"He also likes to be breathing," Grace said in the calm, even voice of a woman accustomed to explaining things to her patients' loved ones. "He's not taking it for pain, Mr. Hitchens, he's taking it to help his lungs do their job without seizing up. And it's actually not the diamorphine affecting his memory, it's the lorazepam. He takes it for the anxiety caused by the shortness of breath, but unfortunately it is an amnesiac. As for the grogginess, some of that really is the disease, like he said. He's got too little oxygen in his system and too much carbon dioxide, and that tends to make people sleepy and disoriented. Eventually, he may even slip into a coma."

"Oh, God," Isabel said. Hitch patted her back. "How, um . . . how long before . . . ?"

"Without extraordinary measures," Grace said, "it could be any day now."

"Any day?"

"He's putting on a good front because he's such a self-contained bloke," Grace said, "but his last bout of respiratory distress was very severe. The next one will probably be his last. I'm sorry, Isabel."

With tears squeezing her throat, Isabel said, "Don't let him know."

"He knows," Hitch said.

Isabel looked to Grace, who was eyeing Hitch curiously, as if wondering how he came by such prescience—but anyone who'd been through what he had in Vietnam would have acquired more than a passing acquaintance with death.

"I think he does know," Grace said. "I think he senses it."

"But . . . then why would he have told me to go home?" Isabel asked. "He said I should fly back to New York, that I'd be called if . . . if . . ."

"Many people don't seem to want their family members hovering 'round as they . . . depart," Grace said, "especially people like your father who are used to presenting a certain image and being in control."

The door to her father's apartment opened and Jason poked his head out. "Everything okay?"

"Peachy." Isabel put on her best bearing-up-well mask and followed Grace and Hitch back into the sitting room.

"You've been holding out on me," Karen chided her husband as he took his seat. "How come you never told me Emmett's ex-wife knew Princess Di?"

Hitch gave her a reproving little smile. "Been cross-examining him, have you, counselor?"

"Not at all," Emmett said. "We've simply been getting to know each other. How *do* you bear him?" he asked Karen.

"I love you, hon, but I really don't get you sometimes," Karen told Hitch. "Your best buddy's ex was friends with one of the most famous women of the twentieth century, and you never think to mention it?"

"Just"—Hitch shrugged—"never came up." He glanced at Emmett, then away, looking ill at ease. Isabel had always suspected that there was never much love lost between the new age, goddess-worshipping Madeleine Lamb and her ex-husband's straight-arrow best friend. Even before the divorce, Hitch hardly ever visited them at the London town house in which Isabel spent her early years.

"Don't be too hard on him, Karen," Isabel said. "I mean, Mom and Di weren't even really friends, exactly. Mom read Di's palm, interpreted her aura, did the Tarot card thing . . . She was a kind of clairvoyant to the rich and famous. Still is, but she moved back to New York when she divorced Dad, so now it's trust fund babies, rock stars, actors . . . American royalty."

Isabel's lifelong embarrassment over having a charlatan for a mother had dissipated with the recent revelation by her father that his ex actually was the "druidess" she claimed to be; she had the Gift. Not that it was properly channeled and mastered—far from it—but underneath all the cliché bullshit fortune-teller trappings were genuine extrasensory abilities.

"She's American, then?" Karen asked Emmett. "How did you meet? Unless I really am prying, and then you should just tell me to take a—"

"Not at all," Emmett said, to Isabel's surprise; he normally disdained personal questions from people he didn't know well. "Maddy and I met in London in the summer of nineteen seventy-two."

Isabel said, "A dinner party at a friend's house, right, Dad?"

He nodded, his fingertips absently rubbing the duct-taped spine of the book still sitting like some mangy but beloved old pet on his lap. "The Turners."

"Dad was in the RAF," Isabel said, "a flight lieutenant."

"Yeah?" Jason sat up straighter, suddenly interested. "Did you fly fighter jets?"

"Fighter-bombers." Emmett coughed sharply. "Not that they did much fighting *or* bombing—which I suppose is a good thing."

"Back in the seventies, he was teaching flight school at the Brize Norton RAF base, not far from London," Isabel said. "Which was what he was doing when he met Mom, who had long red hair and wore love beads and was this total hippie goddess, and here he's Mr. Uptight, Super-straight Spit-and-polish—"

"*Lieutenant* Uptight, Super-straight Spit-and-polish," he corrected with mock umbrage.

"Mom was studying at the Wimbledon College of Art," Isabel said as she plucked a cucumber sandwich from the tea tray. "Dad went totally ga-ga over her, which I still don't quite get, but she didn't seem to know he was alive, so he organized this hippie love-in here at Grotte Cachée."

Karen said, "You're joking."

"She isn't joking," Emmett said hoarsely, "but neither is she correct. It was not a 'love-in,' it was a weekend house party, which was not even, strictly speak—" He pressed his handkerchief over his mouth as he coughed, his whole body shaking.

Grace said, "Mr. Archer, maybe you shouldn't be trying to—"

"Which was not," Emmett continued, "strictly speaking, even my idea. My father, who was *administrateur* at the time, was setting out on holiday with my mother—three weeks in Australia and New Zealand. Since I had leave coming, he asked me to stay at the château and be of whatever assistance I could to Seigneur des Ombres."

"Adrien's father," Isabel clarified. "Julien Morel."

"He told me I should feel free to invite a guest or two for a few days," said Emmett. "So I asked Hitch and Maddy—two Yanks who had never been to France. And I thought Hitch could use a bit of R and R. Maddy asked if she could bring a couple of friends along. Unfortunately, I said yes."

"You two knew each other then?" asked Grace, looking from Emmett to Hitch.

Emmett nodded as he coughed into his handkerchief, so Isabel answered for him. "Hitch was a fighter pilot, too, and a guest flying instructor at Brize Norton when Dad was teaching there. Before that, he'd spent two years as a prisoner of war in Hanoi."

"Oh. Wow." Grace regarded Hitch with interest, and maybe a smidge of awe. "But wait. I thought the POWs weren't released till the U.S. withdrew from Vietnam in 'seventy-three, so how could you have been in London in 'seventy-two?"

"Time off for good behavior," Hitch drawled into his teacup.

The dismissive quip didn't surprise Isabel in the least. One of the reasons Hitch and her father had always gotten along so well was that they both tended to hold their cards close to the vest.

"The Geneva Convention required the North Vietnamese to release their seriously ill and injured prisoners," Karen explained, "so in 'sixty-nine, they finally caved to international pressure and freed some of the men they'd starved and tortured half to death.

Hitch was one of them. He wasn't ready to return to his old life in the States, though, so Uncle Sam lent him to the Brits for a couple of years."

"I always wondered about that," said Jason as he snagged three butter cookies off the tray. "I mean, if I'd been through that kind of hell, all I'd want to do is go home and chill."

It was something Isabel had always wondered about, too. She'd asked her father about it when she was nine or ten, and he'd replied curtly that it was none of her affair.

Karen and Hitch exchanged a glance, she looking a bit sheepish for having broached the subject. The moment dragged on about a second and a half too long, so Isabel said, "The POWs who were released weren't allowed to talk about their treatment till the rest of them were home, which had to put a lot of pressure on them when they were with their friends and family."

Which was true enough, though unlikely to be the reason for Hitch's self-imposed exile after his repatriation.

Karen smiled at Isabel the way you smile at someone when what you really want to do is wink.

When Jason, ruminating on this as he chewed and swallowed, opened his mouth to pursue the subject, Isabel decided to yank the conversation back to its original path. "The reason Dad's always regretted letting my mom bring along a couple of friends is that it wasn't just a couple, it was, like twenty or thirty. Plus Dad and Hitch. It was like *Dazed and Confused* meets *Full Metal Jacket*."

"There were fifteen at the most," Emmett said. "But it seemed like fifty."

"The owner of the place," Jason said, "Julien Morel, he didn't have a problem with all these strangers descending on his home?"

"No, he was used to that sort of thing," Emmett said. "I did apologize to him for the lack of advance warning. He was very gracious, said they seemed like just the type to provide some much-needed diversion for the Follets."

"Who were the Follets?" Karen asked.

Isabel stilled with another cucumber sandwich halfway to her mouth. Her father winced. He wouldn't have mentioned the Follets but for his bleariness of late; he'd never been the careless sort.

Isabel said, "The Follets were staying here." She didn't volunteer that they had, in fact, been staying here for thousands of years.

Emmett said, "It was a long and . . . interesting weekend."

"To say the least," Hitch said quietly.

Two

July 1972

I SMELLED IT AS I climbed the southwest tower to Inigo's apartment, that miasma of weed and incense that had been hovering around this place like a psychotropic fog for the past couple of days. The thump-thump-thump from his celebrated and much-envied quadraphonic stereo system reverberated in the winding stone stairwell, Mick Jagger howling about being on a losing streak, but he tries, and he tries, and he tries, and he tries . . .

Yeah, buddy. Right there with you.

The first thing I noticed through the open door on the second-floor landing was Inigo sitting on the electric orange shag carpet at the far end of the room with a topless chick whose abundant breasts he was painting in psychedelic swirls of red, yellow, and green. All around him were heaped pillows and bean bag chairs draped with long-haired bodies decked out in beads and scarves, tie-dye, flowing skirts, halter tops, dashikis, and of course the ubiquitous bell-bottomed jeans, the wider and more threadbare, the better.

"Hitch! My man!" Inigo yelled over the music. With his long mane of wild black curls, his vintage top hat, pink-tinted granny glasses, multipatched hip-hugger jeans, and striped vest—sans shirt—he looked like he could have stepped off the cover of *Sgt. Pepper's*.

Some of the others greeted me with smiles and waves. One guy proffered a hash pipe, which I declined as always. In the taxonomy of hippies, these were the Blissed-Out Flower Child variety, as opposed to, at the other extreme, their Molotov-hurling Pseudo-Revolutionary second cousins. As such, they'd been thankfully accepting, or at least tolerant, of Emmett and me despite the uniforms hanging in our closets at home. Most of them, that is. There were a handful who gave us the hairy eyeball, like we were baby-killing storm troopers instead of lieutenants in our nations' respective Air Forces, but I'd gotten used to that since returning from my little vacation in the exotic Hanoi Hilton; it didn't really faze me anymore.

"About time you checked out my pad," Inigo said as he raised his omnipresent tequila bottle to his mouth; most everybody else looked to be drinking beer, from all the bottles scattered around. "What do you think?"

"Cool place," I said, though what I really thought was that my eyeballs just might short out from visual overload.

Bolts of afternoon sunlight glittered in the musty haze, illuminating stone walls and a raftered ceiling almost completely wallpapered in posters, most of them advertising rock concerts or denouncing the war. In each corner of the room loomed a fridge-size speaker draped in batik-printed Indian throws and swaths of fishnet. Bathing the room in a cool, otherworldly radiance was the ambient light from an immense built-in aquarium, the biggest I'd ever seen. Must have held three hundred gallons, easy.

Some of the room's occupants were just staring, transfixed, at the particolored fish dancing and flirting in the tank. Two guys were sucking from a gurgling hookah. There were couples making out, one of them basically dry-humping in rhythm with the music: *I can't get no, oh no no no . . .* Thing was, they could have had privacy if they'd wanted; it was a big fucking castle. Not exactly a shy bunch.

Through a beaded curtain I saw a little alcove furnished with a couch on which a couple lay facedown, the guy on top, both of them with their jeans pushed down around their thighs. I recognized the guy. It was an Irishman named John Fitzgerald Kennedy—a kick-ass name, but they all called him Val because of his uncanny resemblance to the tall, inky-haired, angelically handsome Prince Valiant of comic strip fame. The girl beneath him clutched the couch cushion as he pushed hard and slow, pushing, pushing . . .

He's fucking her in the ass, I thought. But then she turned her head, and I saw it wasn't a girl at all.

Jesus Christ. I turned away with a sense of dull shock. Two guys making it—that was one thing I never thought I'd see with my own eyes.

In the middle of the room, a petite blonde with a daisy painted on one cheek and a peace symbol on the other lay faceup on a long coffee table, taking her turn having her chakras healed by their resident snake-oil salesman, who also happened to be the Grand Vizier of the Hairy Eyeball Fraternity.

"Starbuck," as he'd dubbed himself, was a Brit with long, well-brushed golden hair, a dark beard, and phosphor blue eyes. In his white Indian shirt, he looked like Presbyterian Jesus.

My ears tuned out the music to hear what he was telling the

girl as he rested one hand on the crotch of her super-short denim cutoffs, the other on top of her head. "The second chakra is called the Svadhishthana, and yours is badly blocked—I can tell by the imperfections in its aura."

He moved the hand he was copping a feel with in a slow caress, his eyes closed, his expression one of deep concentration. Like all the other girls here, the little blonde was manifestly, and exquisitely, braless; the best fashion trend of my lifetime. Her peasant blouse was so sheer that I could make out not just the contours of her breasts, but her nipples, rose-petal pink. They grew erect as the chakra-fondling Starbuck did his thing. Damn hard to keep from gaping.

Damn hard.

Starbuck said, "It's critical that something be done about this, Willow. This is the chakra that governs your inner child, your creativity . . . your sexuality. I need to unblock it so that it can take its place as part of the spiritual whole made up of your past and present incarnations . . ."

Apparently, I wasn't the only one whose bullshit alarm was going off, because the gorgeous redhead sitting on the floor nearby gave him a dubious glance—ironic, inasmuch as she was in the process of interpreting a crosslike arrangement of Tarot cards laid out in front of her.

Madeleine Lamb was her name, and she was actually the reason for this weekend of orgiastic hippie revelry.

Emmett Archer, my best friend and the custodian of my sanity, had invited Madeleine and me to Grotte Cachée, ostensibly because he found it bizarre and unacceptable that two Americans who'd spent the past couple of years in London should have never crossed the Channel. In fact, the real reason he asked me was that I was perennially wound up and he thought I could use four days of chilling out in a remote French château. The reason he invited Madeleine was because he'd fallen hard for her during a dinner party in London a couple of weeks ago, and wanted an excuse to spend some time with her.

"*You know Botticelli's Venus?*" Emmett had asked me on the way here.

"*You mean Venus on the Half Shell?*" I said.

"*She looks just like that, long, rippling red hair, the same kind of face, just ethereally beautiful. But her body is different, tall and lithe, like Jean Shrimpton. You'll see when you meet her. And she's a terrific artist, smart, funny . . . She's just amazing. I've never met a girl like her.*"

In the two-plus years I'd been palling around with Emmett—in between training jet jockeys for the RAF—I'd never seen him lose it like that over a girl, especially not a hippie artist type. Handsome and dryly charming, he dated—and scored—on a regular basis, although unlike some guys, he never volunteered the details. But while he'd liked all those women, and regarded a few of them as "choice birds," he'd never gotten ga-ga over anyone—until now.

The joke was on him, though, because the girl of his dreams had brought along this freak show entourage, half of them fellow art students and the other half old friends of hers from New York who were spending their summer vacations crashing in her London flat. They called themselves the Merry Gangsters, like Ken Kesey's Merry Pranksters, only a little less witty and a lot less original. The bad news for Emmett had come when Madeleine introduced one of the art students as her "old man."

Starbuck.

"This is The Chariot." Madeleine turned the card so it could be seen by the friend she was doing the reading for, a black chick with luscious curves, a super-sweet baby face, and a colossal Afro, one of the Americans.

"What's it supposed to signify?" asked the guy sitting with them, a Dutch art student named Pieter who looked a hell of a lot like Robert Redford, only with shaggy hair and wire-rimmed glasses.

Pieter was Madeleine's Backup Boyfriend. You know, the guy who hangs around a chick who's already taken, ready to move in if and when she goes back on the market. I liked him. He was smart and friendly, and he wasn't being a pain in the ass with Madeleine, just staying close, politely waiting his turn.

"It's a warlike card, or at least that's the way it feels to me right now," Madeleine said as she held it between her palms. "I see someone taking up the role of the warrior. I think someone close to you may have joined the Army. Your . . . brother? Do you have a brother, Diane?"

Diane gaped at her. "Ron. He . . . he just enlisted Thursday. He called to tell me, and I chewed him a new one, 'cause they're just gonna send him to 'Nam. I haven't told anyone. How could you know that?"

Madeleine smiled enigmatically as she shrugged her delicate shoulders.

"Is he gonna be okay?" Diane asked.

Madeleine held her friend's gaze for a long moment, her expression fading to neutral. She carefully replaced the card in its spot in the arrangement, saying "It's in the hands of fate" without looking up.

I needed to pay rent on the pot of coffee I'd emptied that morning, so I asked someone where the head was, and he pointed to a spiral staircase leading up. Climbing it, I found myself in a kind of anteroom with a big, lavish bathroom off to one side. Straight ahead was an arched doorway through which I could see a naked girl reclining against a stack of pillows on a king-sized bed. Four fully dressed people were painting her body by the sunlight streaming in through the windows, augmented by scores and scores of candles lining every surface in the room.

The human canvas was Lili, one of the four who lived in this castle-turned-carnival, and one of the two men sitting across from each other painting her upper body was Elic, whom I took to be her boyfriend. Lili was beautiful, sensual, a fox of the highest magnitude. If she was my girl, no way in hell would I let another guy even shake her hand, much less stroke a paintbrush over her naked breasts. Elic had to be out of his fucking mind.

The other guy, holding a big wooden palette laid out with blobs and smears of paint, his paint-spattered jeans held up with red suspenders, was one of the art students, Doobie. His girlfriend, Anna, a delicate, black-haired, black-garbed little thing who danced with the Royal Ballet, was on the other side next to Elic, working on Lili's abdomen. A blond, tanned, well-stacked Amazon named Josepha, or Jo for short—also an art student, judging from the snug Wimbledon College T-shirt she wore with her Army fatigue pants—did the same from the opposite side.

Jo must have seen me, because she caught my eye and smiled. She opened her mouth, but I ducked into the john before she could say anything.

I took my leak and was heading for the stairwell when Elic called out over the music thudding up from downstairs, "Hitch!"

I sighed as I turned around to stand in the doorway. "Hey, man."

"The girls are wondering if you'd like to join in. Jo says you look like the artistic type."

"Not even a little bit," I said, shoving my hands in my front jeans pockets.

Lili raised herself up on her elbows to look at me. "Come on, Hitch. We can use the help, and you don't have to be Leonardo. Doobie already sketched out the design, so it'll be like coloring in a coloring book."

It was all I could do to maintain eye contact and not just stare at those luscious breasts, between which had been painted a black band about two inches wide. "Um . . ."

Giving me one of her breath-stealing smiles, she said, "Please?"

Damn, she was hard to resist. *What the hell,* I thought. "Yeah, okay," I said. "Sure."

As I entered the room, I saw that Lili was lying not directly on the tie-dyed bedspread, but on a paint-stained canvas drop cloth. Between her parted legs sat an open, battered toolbox with DOOBIE Magic Markered on the outside that held jars of brushes in water, mangled tubes of acrylic paint, and various other art supplies.

Lili wasn't being painted with the usual random designs I'd been seeing on people's faces and bodies that weekend, but rather with the image of a guitar, a detailed outline of which had, indeed, been painted onto her in thin sepia brushstrokes, and was now about halfway filled in with color. The black band between her breasts, which I could now see had frets and strings painted on it, was the guitar's neck, ending just under her chin. The hourglass shape of the soundboard, rimmed in a narrow checkered pattern, had been positioned to echo Lili's womanly contours, the top edge bisecting her breasts just above the nipples. It was obviously intended to give the effect, when painted in, of a low-cut strapless bodice. The guitar dipped in at her narrow waist, then flared out again with her hips so that the bottom cut across her upper thighs. The sound hole encircling her navel was ringed in the same pattern as the guitar itself and decorated inside with an astonishingly intricate, lacy design. The outline of the bridge, positioned across the upper fringe of her pubic hair, was unusually wide, with a flowery curlicue at either end spiraling up over her hip bones.

"What do you think?" Doobie asked in a stoned-out, lord-of-the-manner drawl. "I'm gonna photograph her for my master's project, which is about using human beings as canvases to make living art."

"Pretty fucking heavy, no?" Jo said.

I agreed that it was fucking heavy. "Shouldn't you be painting it by yourself if it's your project?" I asked Doobie.

"Hey, man, even Picasso has assistants."

Yeah, 'cause he's pushing a hundred, I thought, but I just said, "That's a cool-looking guitar."

"It's a baroque guitar," said Jo as she painted an impressively realistic golden-brown wood grain over Lili's stomach. Her British-inflected English bore just the faintest Germanic undertone. "That one." She nodded toward an instrument propped on a stand in the corner of the stone-walled room. It was the oddest guitar I'd ever seen, narrow, ornately carved, and inlaid precisely like the one being painted on Lili.

Hanging nearby was a large, age-crackled painting of a dark-haired young man in a Renaissance-style white shirt playing a guitar that was identical to the one on the stand. It was a dramatic, richly hued work of strong contrasts: ebony shadows, luminous saffron highlights. It almost felt as if the light source for the painting was the bank of candles on the table underneath it.

"Wow," I said.

"That's an actual Caravaggio, can you fucking believe it?" Doobie said.

"No kidding." I wasn't much for art history, but I'd heard the name spoken in the same breath as "Rubens" and "Vermeer." I asked them what the painting was doing there. "Shouldn't it be in some museum somewhere?"

"It's always been here," Elic said. "It was painted in sixteen oh-seven, when Caravaggio was hiding out here. He'd killed a man in a fight in Rome, and our *gardien*—that is, our *seigneur* at the time—offered him refuge for a few months in return for painting this portrait."

Studying the subject of the painting—the thick black curls, laughing eyes, and boyish grin, I said, "He looks like Inigo."

After a brief pause, Elic said, "You're not the first person to mention that."

"Is he an ancestor of Inigo's?" I asked. "Is that why he has the painting? And the guitar? Or is it a reproduction?"

"No," Elic said. "No, it's the same guitar."

"Hitch, are you going to paint me or not?" Lili asked with mock petulance.

I turned to find her giving me *that smile* again. Jo took a paintbrush from the jar and held it out to me handle first, patting the bed next to her.

They assigned me the responsibility of painting the curlicued bridge black. I approached the task tentatively, not because it was particularly challenging from an artistic point of view; I really was just coloring inside the lines. This was the first time I'd been this close to a naked woman's groin since the time I let that Saigon bar girl lure me back to her hovel, only to feel so lousy at the prospect of cheating on Lucinda that I shoved a handful of bills at her and split without even doing the deed.

"Use long, firm strokes," Jo told me. "She won't come out as well if you pussy around like that."

Whether intentional or not, her suggestive wording made Doobie snort with laughter.

"He's doing just fine," Lili said. "I like how it's coming out."

She wasn't looking down at me, as I'd expected, but at the ceiling. I followed her gaze and saw that the entire thing was mirrored. Taking in the bird's-eye reflection of Lili, stretched out like some sacrificial goddess, naked but for the paint with which she was being adorned—and, I saw now, a gold ankle bracelet—made the situation seem even more erotically charged than it already was.

As I watched in the mirror, Elic leaned down and kissed her, casually stroking her left breast. I looked away and dipped my brush in the paint, marveling, as I had this entire weekend, at how uninhibited these people were. It was off the wall . . . and tantalizing. From the corner of my eye, I could see that both men had obvious erections under their jeans, which they were making no attempt to hide.

I lowered my gaze as Elic whispered something into Lili's ear. She nodded, smiling into his eyes. "Please do."

He asked Anna if she might like to take a little break from painting the guitar. "You know that op-art poster downstairs on the ceiling? The one with the black and white lines that look like they're moving? Why don't I paint that on you?"

Anna was very pretty, with features that suggested a hint of the Orient in her DNA. She was somewhat reserved compared to the general run of Gangsters, but in a good way; not the type to run her mouth just for the hell of it. She agreed to Elic's proposal with a nod and a quiet "Okay." Scooting back against the headboard, he sat the petite ballet dancer astride his lap and began decorating her face and neck with undulating stripes.

Pointing with her brush to the neat patch of pubic hair that interrupted the bridge I was painting, Jo said, "Bummer about the shrubbery, huh? Kind of ruins the effect."

Lifting her head to take a look, Lili said, "Hitch should just shave it off."

That directive was greeted with incredulous laughter from everyone except Elic and me. *Say what?* I thought.

"Oh, man," Doobie said through excited laughter that was damn close to a giggle. "Now, *that* is a bitchin' idea."

Elic smiled at Lili, as if to say *How clever of you.*

"Are you fucking with us?" Jo asked Lili. "You really want him to . . . ?"

Lili settled back down with a shrug. "It will grow back."

"Yeah, and it'll itch like a motherfucker," Jo said.

"It's for *art*," Doobie snapped at her, "so shut the fuck up." Turning to me, he said, "Do it, man."

"You really want me to?" I asked Lili.

"Please."

What the hell, I thought. *In for a penny, in for a pound.*

"Inigo's shaving stuff should be in the bathroom," Elic told me as he went back to painting wavering black and white stripes on Anna's throat and upper chest. "He won't mind. Oh, and you can use that bowl with the candles floating in it for water."

I opened Inigo's medicine cabinet looking for a can of shaving cream, only to find a badger brush and shaving mug, like my dad used to use. The brush had a yellowed ivory handle, and the mug looked like something out of an antiques shop, with worn edges and a hairline crack. The black and gold decoration, which was meant to resemble one of those ancient Greek urns, featured three or four satyrs—the kind with normal legs, not hooves—grabbing at one another's tall, pointy erections.

My search for something to shave with turned up not the safety razor I'd been looking for, but a folding straight razor with a mother-of-pearl-handle. Not what I would have expected from a dude who seemed to be up on all the latest trends.

I tested the razor's long blade on my thumb and found it

incredibly sharp. Nevertheless, there was a leather strop hanging on the wall, so I gave it a few swipes the way I'd seen it done on TV and in the movies; probably did more harm than good.

I wasn't snooping, honest, but I couldn't help noticing a row of small bottles on the top shelf of the medicine chest: mineral oil, coconut oil, olive oil, almond oil, and something called "Kama Sutra massage lotion." Lined up next to these were a tube of K-Y Jelly, a tub of Vaseline, another of cocoa butter, and—here's where I did a double-take—four cans of pie filling: chocolate, cherry, lemon, and pumpkin.

The man's got a sweet tooth, I thought with a grin. I filled the bowl with hot water, snagged some towels and washcloths, and returned to the bedroom to find Jo hovering over Lili's snatch with a pair of scissors.

"I've cut the hair close to the skin," she said. "It'll make it easier to shave."

"Does anybody here have any experience with straight razors?" I asked. "I'm afraid I'm gonna hurt her."

"Hold the blade steady at about a twenty- to thirty-degree angle and go with the direction of the hair," Elic said. Having covered Anna with serpentine stripes from her forehead to the neckline of her long-sleeved black leotard, which fit her like skin, he proceeded to extend the pattern by continuing the white lines onto the leotard itself. He'd painted her hands, too, except for the palms, and her lower body was garbed in tights and a wrap skirt, both black. When he was done, she really would look like living art.

"Don't worry about cutting me," Lili told me. "You'd be amazed how fast I heal."

Reaching for the razor, Doobie said, "I'll do it if you won't."

"Thanks, but I think I'd rather have Hitch." Lili gave me that smile again. "Fighter pilots know how to keep a steady hand under pressure."

Taking Jo's place between Lili's spread legs, I saw that her hips had been propped up on a pillow to provide maximum access to the operative area. With any other woman, the pose might have looked awkward and sleazy, but with Lili's graceful nonchalance, she put me in mind of an odalisque in a painting.

I tucked a towel under her and stroked her with a warm washcloth, which made her sigh with pleasure. *I can't believe I'm doing this*, I thought as I lathered up the brush and started dabbing it on what remained of Lili's sweet little muff. A shame to be shaving it off, the hair being the same dramatic blue-black as that on her head, and almost as silky.

I felt a little queasy as I started in with the actual shaving. To take a six-inch, ultra-sharp steel blade to a woman's most delicate, intimate, vulnerable region . . . *Your hand damn well better be steady*, I told myself as I angled the razor and took my first cautious stroke.

"That's perfect," Elic said, "but you need to sort of pull the flesh as you're shaving it."

"Here, I'll do it," said Jo, who unhesitatingly reached over to press Lili's outer labia taut. I tried to imagine a guy touching another guy's cock so nonchalantly, but with the exception of gay guys—and apparently ancient Greek satyrs—I just couldn't see it.

"Mm, it feels lovely," Lili murmured, her eyes drifting shut, a beatific smile on her face. "It's the most delicious scraping sensation. I may have to have someone do this to me every morning."

The more I shaved, the more intrigued I became with the feminine anatomy being gradually revealed. I'd slept with my share of women before Lucinda, but I'd never seen one without hair down there except for paintings and statues, and they never showed anything, even the slit. Knowing what lay beneath female pubic hair was one thing. Seeing that mysterious terrain up close and naked was altogether different.

I heard Anna's breath quicken. Looking up as I rinsed the razor, I noticed Elic's hand grazing her breast repeatedly as he painted a spiral around it.

"Sorry," he whispered, but he didn't change the angle of his hand to avoid stealing second base, and he could have.

The little dancer glanced over at her boyfriend, her eyes strikingly blue against the face paint, but Doobie was too mesmerized by the denuding of Lili's pussy to care about what was transpiring on the other side of the bed.

Anna held Elic's gaze for a moment, smiled. "That's all right."

"You know what would be cool?" Turning his paintbrush around, Elic used the tip to trace circles around both of her breasts. "If we were to cut away the leotard, just here and here, I could paint the pattern right onto your bare skin, but no one would realize it was just paint. They'd think it was the leotard. It would be a little secret that no one would know about but us."

Again Anna looked toward Doobie, who was actually paying attention this time. He opened his mouth to speak, his brow furrowed, whereupon Lili reached over to stroke his thigh. "It's for the sake of art, too, no?"

With a fleeting glance at his denim-clad boner, which Lili's arm just happened to be rubbing against, he said, "Um . . . Okay. Sure, why not? It'll be a gas."

Jo handed the scissors to Elic, who painstakingly snipped away the two circles, revealing a pair of creamy champagne-cup breasts, the only visible flesh on her entire body. The effect was shockingly erotic—as was the sight of Lili's now-hairless vulva. The pristine smoothness of it, like soft little pillows on either side of the cleft. Seeing it so boldly exposed struck me as both pure and obscene at the same time. Made me wish it was socially acceptable for women to shave there if they were so inclined.

My handiwork reaped praise all around as I wiped off the remnants of shaving soap and patted the area with a towel.

"Far fucking out," murmured Doobie as he stared in unblinking fascination.

"It's perfect," decreed Jo. "So much better. It'll look amazing once it's all painted."

As I resumed the task of painting the bridge across Lili's now-smooth pubic mound, I noticed Elic lifting Anna's right breast by the nipple—although it was hardly necessary, given how small and firm she was—while he painted a white spiral over the black paint he'd already applied. I saw his finger and thumb tighten, rolling the nipple back and forth a bit before he released it. It was rigid now, and rawly pink against all that black and white paint.

Elic took hold of the other nipple and looked at her; she met his eyes directly, not exactly smiling, but not looking remotely troubled by what he was doing. He toyed with the nipple as he painted that breast, rubbing it, flicking it with his thumb . . .

There came an almost imperceptible movement as she pressed herself against him. He set down his brush, closed his hands around her hips, and rocked them slowly.

Lili reached over to untie Anna's skirt as Doobie, Jo, and I continued to paint her. She was also absently fondling Doobie through his jeans, which may have been why he didn't seem too het up about his op-arted girlfriend in the cut-out leotard grinding against another guy. He must have figured he'd be getting some himself before long, unless Lili was a world-class cock-tease, and she didn't exactly seem the type.

There came a minute of silence from downstairs as the albums were switched out, and then Jimmy Cliff started singing "You Can Get It If You Really Want."

"I love reggae," Lili said as she pulled away Anna's skirt. "It's so inspiring, but so sexy, too, with those rhythms. Every time I hear it, I get wet."

"I know what you mean," Anna said.

"Mm, nice," Elic murmured as he felt her dampness through the leotard and tights. "But you girls don't have a monopoly on wet." He unbuttoned his jeans, whereupon his erection, unencumbered by anything as prosaic as underwear, sprang up so hard it almost looked like it was vibrating. Taking Anna's hand, he ran her fingers over the tip of his cock, which was oozing pre-come. "See?"

She glanced in Doobie's direction again. The fact that he was enjoying a little heavy petting from Lili while staring with lurid fascination at her antics with Elic seemed to embolden her. When Elic released her hand, she not only continued to stroke him, but leaned over to give him a long, pull-out-the-stops kiss while she did so.

Tugging at the crotch of her leotard, Elic said, "Damn, I wish this was the kind that snaps."

"I'll take it off," she said, pulling the leotard down off one shoulder.

"Stop that." Jo slapped her hand. "The whole op-art effect will be ruined. Here." She handed Elic the scissors. "Problem solved."

"Do you mind?" Elic asked Anna. "I'll buy you a new—"

"Do it," said Doobie, who seemed to have gotten that pesky jealousy thing under control.

Anna rose onto her knees to give Elic better access. Pulling the crotch of the leotard away from her body so as not to nick her, Elic cut a front-to-back slit, then did the same with her tights. The stretchy material pulled open, framing her pussy with its black pubic hair and glistening pink gash. She steadied herself with her hands on his shoulders as he gripped her by the waist to position her.

When his first attempt at penetration missed the mark, Lili sat up and reached between them. Taking hold of Elic's cock, she tilted it toward Anna's pussy, which she opened with the fingers of her other hand. "Wow, you really are wet. Okay, ease down. That's it," she said as Anna lowered herself, sighing in unison with Elic.

He stroked Lili's hair as she lay back on the pillows. Taking his hand, she pressed it to her lips, the two of them exchanging a tender smile that kind of threw me for a loop, given that his cock was, at the moment, embedded to the hilt in another woman. But then, nothing in this place made any sense, especially when it came to sex.

As Elic started fucking Anna, his long fingers almost spanning her waist as he set a leisurely pace, it struck me that he'd been right when he said no one would know that it was just paint, not the leotard, concealing Anna's breasts. Black and white from head to toe, with the exception of her nipples and palms, she could have been some weird, sex-starved alien from another planet, or an android programmed for exceptional sexual performance. And exceptional it was.

Still waters run deep, I thought as I watched the soft-spoken ballerina go at it, her entire, lithe little body undulating with every thrust, the op-art stripes swaying and pulsing. It was exquisitely beautiful on the one hand, incredibly hot on the other, and damned near hypnotic.

"Hey, guys?" Lili said.

Doobie, Jo, and I wrested our gazes from Anna to find Lili smiling at us.

Indicating the nearly finished baroque guitar painted onto her, she said, "Are we going to finish this? 'Cause if not, I'll just go run a bath and—"

Doobie wouldn't hear of leaving it undone. I completed the bridge, then started helping Jo with the soundboard, painting the golden brown background while she added the wood grain over it. Doobie concentrated on finishing up the last remaining section of the checkered border, which cut across Lili's breasts.

My job was simple and pretty quick. It wasn't long before everything was filled in except for that triangle of glaringly bare flesh between her thighs. I'd never been shy around women, but there was something about painting a virtual stranger's naked snatch that felt just a little too goddamned intimate.

Jo waved a hand in front of my face and snapped her fingers. "You worried it's gonna bite? Come on, man. I can't do my bit till you do yours."

I dipped my brush in the paint and charged ahead, stroking it as gently as I could over each outer labium to the accompaniment of Anna's increasingly urgent moans, each coinciding with the grunt of a bedspring.

"Don't ignore the slit." Jo handed me a small sable watercolor brush like the one she was using, saying it was "better for detail work."

This is just too unreal. I glanced at Lili, who was holding Elic's hand as he banged Anna. He had his other hand cupped around the ballerina's tight little ass while he sucked on a nipple, his eyes closed, low moans rising from his throat.

Lili moaned softly, which was when I noticed that Doobie was painting one of her nipples, using a stiff little brush and taking his time about it. His gaze, however, was almost exclusively on Elic and Anna.

"Move aside," Jo told me, nudging me with a shoulder. "I'll do it."

I held my ground. "You've got a bossy streak, you know that?"

"Some guys don't mind," she said with a suggestive smile.

And those who did probably put up with it for the chance

to get their hands on those tits. Jo was gorgeous, a walking wet dream, in a master race kind of way. *I wouldn't kick her out of the sack . . .* I started thinking, before I remembered that yeah, I would.

Elic and Anna came pretty much simultaneously, it seemed like. Shortly thereafter, Anna started to rise off of Elic, but he pulled her back down, saying "Bored with me so soon? You'll hurt my feelings."

They started in again, Elic giving it to her just as enthusiastically as the first time, without so much as taking a breather. Damndest thing I ever saw.

As Jo finished up the wood graining, I dipped the brush in the paint and slid it along one side of the cleft. Lili let out a kittenish growl and parted her legs wider.

Oh, man.

"Get all the visible flesh," Jo said.

Problem with that was, the more I painted, the more flesh became visible. Lili's sex lips were swelling, the juncture between gradually widening to expose not just more of the outer labia, but the inner ones, as well.

"I, um, I guess this is where I call it quits," I said as I rinsed my brush in the jar of clean water.

Lili arched her hips in a frankly carnal way, making a little mew of dismay. "Don't stop."

Rinsing out her own brush, Jo said, "You wouldn't want to leave her unfinished, would you?"

I said, "Do you think it's a good idea to apply paint to . . . you know, such sensitive flesh?"

"No." She put the business end of the brush in her mouth, closed her lips around it, and pulled it out, shaping it into a perfect point.

Then she lowered it to Lili's pussy and brushed it over the flesh in question, coaxing a deliciously carnal moan from her.

Jo took my brush out of my hand, reshaped the point with her mouth, and handed it back. "Two hands are better than one."

It was the first time in a long time that I'd set about pleasuring a woman, and the first time ever that I'd done it with such a clever little tool. It was really perfect for the job, soft, but with a snappy resilience, and that nice, precise point was ideal for gliding in and out of the slick little furrows, petting and teasing the clit . . . Jo would attend to one area while I did the other. Lili writhed and panted as Elic, still fucking Anna, reached over to caress her breast. She came four times, and pretty hard, from what I could tell.

"God, that made me hot, watching that," Doobie said huskily.

"It made *me* hungry," Lili replied.

He looked puzzled until she unzipped him, and then the lightbulb went off. She pulled out his cock and had him kneel over her face with both hands gripping the headboard. Hooking her fingers around two belt loops of his jeans, she pulled him toward her. He let out a deep, long, ragged groan. "Holy *fuck*," he gasped when she pushed him back, only to groan again as she tugged him back into her mouth.

He hadn't been on this ride for very long when Elic and Anna shared another window-rattling orgasm, which apparently was the last straw for Doobie.

"Oh, God, I'm coming," he moaned as he thrust hard and fast into Lili's mouth, the headboard creak-creak-creaking. Reaching down to grab his cock, he said, "You . . . you want me to . . . ?"

She gripped his ass with both hands, holding him right where he was. He came with a long, strangled groan.

By the time he pulled out and zipped himself back up, Elic

and Anna were at it *again,* which didn't seem remotely possible, but there it was.

Jo said my name. I turned to find her long, Teutonic body sprawled at the foot of the bed, one hand down her unbuttoned fatigue pants, the other under her T-shirt, squeezing one of those glorious breasts. She smiled at me the way a lioness smiles when she's lying in the grass testing the air for something raw and warm with which to slake her terrible hunger.

She said, "Did you kill people when you were in the Army?"

Lili said, "Jo, don't ask him—"

"It was the Air Force," I said.

"Did you?" Jo asked, still caressing herself.

I thought about all the bombs that dropped from the F-4 Phantom I piloted before it was shot down over North Vietnam. "Yes."

She sat up and threw me to the bed, straddling me with iron-band thighs as she closed her mouth over mine. Her tongue was . . . *strong.* Damn, she was strong all over. It was all I could do to haul her off of me, saying "Look, Jo, I—"

"God, you're hot." She grabbed my crotch, expecting me to be hard, I guess, because she said, "Don't tell me you're gay."

"What? No," I said, yanking her hand away.

"So, what? I don't turn you on?"

Yeah, right. The carbon-based life-form didn't exist that was immune to Fräulein Josepha's robust if slightly rapacious brand of sexuality. "It's just that I have to be someplace," I lied.

"Me, too. I have to be underneath you as soon as possible."

"Jo, that's really not gonna work."

"On top, then. I love it on top."

Well, knock me over with a feather. I looked toward our bedmates to see if they were enjoying the show, but they were making their own performance art, Lili getting it doggie style from

Doobie while she kissed Elic, who had yet to disengage from his black-and-white ballerina.

"You can't just get me this horny, then not let me come," Jo said, doing her damndest to wrestle me horizontal.

"Fair enough." I muscled her onto her back, whereupon she popped open the snap of my jeans and yanked at my zipper. "Will you just stop trying to rape me for one fucking second?" I said.

"Make me."

I grabbed Jo's T-shirt and whipped it up, but not off, pinioning her arms over her head and effectively blindfolding her in the bargain. God, those blue-ribbon tits! Her pants, I pulled down to immobilize her legs. With her hobbled this way, I was able to pin her to the bed, spread her knees, and go down on her.

She tried to free herself for a few seconds before she felt my mouth on her pussy and realized what was going on. She struggled a little as I started eating her out, not because she wanted me to stop, but because she still wanted to fuck me. But then she had a three-alarm orgasm, and another one close on its heels, which proved to be a pretty effective sedative.

I snuck out while she was lying there limp and purring, still with her T-shirt up over her face and her pants around her ankles, and ducked into the john. I splashed water on my face with unsteady hands and smoked a cigarette, listening to the music from downstairs, Jimmy Cliff singing "Sitting Here in Limbo." The perfect sound track for my life.

"Don't tell me you're gay . . . I don't turn you on?"

"Limbo" yielded to a reprise of "You Can Get It If You Really Want." An admirable sentiment, but not all problems fix themselves if you "try and try." Some are just gonna hang in there for the duration, man, and there's nothing you can do but set the throttle to low and hold a straight and steady course.

The Jimmy Cliff album ended as I was coming back down the stairs.

Ah. Blessed silence. It wouldn't last, though. I liked music as much as the next guy, but it seemed like nobody could go through life anymore without a sound track. I blamed it on the movies.

"Who's got the sleeve for *The Harder They Come*?" asked Inigo, lifting an album off the turntable as I descended the spiral staircase. "It was right here."

"Over here," said a guy in two braids who was holding the album cover at an angle and shaking it to winnow the seeds and stems out of a handful of pot. "Hold on just one sec."

"Don't bogart that sleeve," snorted Starbuck. He'd finished healing Willow's chakras, and was now placing something invisible on her tongue, as if miming communion.

He noticed me staring and nodded toward a little open metal tin on the coffee table, which held a cluster of infinitesimally tiny, clear squares. "Windowpane," he said. *"Acid,"* he added when I still looked confused. "Even you G.I. Joes must have heard of LSD."

"Take a hit, Hitch," said Willow in an airily drowsy voice that suggested her state of consciousness was plenty altered already. "It melts in your mouth, not in your . . . Wait a minute. It melts in your hand, not . . ." She frowned as she tried to puzzle it out.

"Melts in your mind, not in your hand." Proffering the little tin, Starbuck said, "You *should* take a hit. It'll open up your head."

"I'm not sure there's anything in there that should be getting out," I said.

"Let your demons out, man. Let them do their thing. What's the worst that can happen?"

"A complete nervous breakdown?" I said.

"They can actually be very liberating." Gesturing with the

tin, he said, "You should try it, man. Maybe make you loosen up a little, get you to grow that Ken doll haircut out, throw a little bleach in with those jeans next time you wash them."

Turning my back on the arrogant little shit so as to resist the impulse to tell him what he could do with his life lessons, I asked Inigo if he'd seen Emmett, whom I'd lost track of that morning. "Doesn't look like he's here," I said, "unless he's in some other room."

"Nah, man, this isn't his scene. Wish I could help you, but I haven't seen him since yesterday."

One of the bong smokers, his lungs filled with a fresh toke, croaked, "I think I saw him talking to that Morel guy out in the courtyard." *That Morel guy* being their host, Julien Morel, Seigneur des Ombres.

"Where will I find Morel?" I asked.

"I'd check his study," Inigo said.

"Where's that?"

"I know," offered Madeleine as she sprang to her feet. "I saw him heading up there a little while ago. I'll show you the way."

"Yeah, I bet you will," sneered Starbuck. "Watch out, Soldier Boy. Those redheads leave scratch marks. Or could it be Morel she's got the hots for? *Les femmes,* zey just love zee French accent, *non*?"

I opened my mouth to invite Starbuck to expound on his theory outside, but Madeleine grabbed my arm, whispering "He's not worth the scraped knuckles."

Inigo caught my eye, flicked a dismissive glance in Starbuck's direction, and waved his bottle toward the door, effectively seconding her advice. "Oh, hey—we're gonna light a bonfire later tonight out by the bathhouse. You and Emmett should check it out."

"Ooh, a date," Starbuck taunted. "You and Emmett have a little thing going on, Hitchens?"

It was a junior-high-level reference to the fact that Emmett and I, who were older and straighter than most of these kids, had been hanging out with each other more than with the rest of them that weekend—except for Emmett's long talk with Madeleine in the Beckett Garden yesterday, after which he'd told me he was in love with her.

"You and Emmett going steady?" Starbuck asked me. "Did you pin him, or did he pin you?"

As his pals hooted in laughter, Madeleine looked at Starbuck and said, "You can be a real asshole, Bernie."

"*Bernie?*" said Inigo, laughing like hell. "Are you shitting me?"

"Bernard Marion Pease the Third," she said, "and no, I am not shitting you."

"Fucking cunt," snarled Starbuck, a mottled reddish stain crawling up his throat.

"Uncool, man," Inigo said. "You want to talk that shit, you talk it somewhere else."

"Are you fucking *serious*?" Starbuck said.

"You don't talk to a woman that way in my place."

"What about women's lib?" Starbuck said.

"What about I liberate your teeth from your mouth?" I asked.

Inigo cocked his head toward the door. "Time to boogie, Bernie."

Three

"I FELL IN LOVE with your mother in this garden," Emmett Archer said as he lingered over lunch in the Beckett Garden the next day with Jason and Grace.

Not that Emmett had eaten what you'd call "lunch." Darius, perched on a crossbeam of the colonnade that shaded the lushly planted terrace, had seen the *administrateur* consume perhaps three spoonfuls of milk toast pressed upon him by his nurse. Nevertheless, he was having what Grace termed "a good day." Were he not, he would hardly have asked to be brought down here—no easy task, what with the oxygen concentrator and all—to enjoy the spring sunshine in this, his favorite garden.

"You must have fallen hard and fast." Isabel, sitting across from her father at the linen-draped table with a sketchbook and a mechanical artist's pen, was working on a drawing of him with the garden and reflecting pool in the background, and beyond that, the bucolic parkland that surrounded the château. "You dated Mom for what, like, two months before you tied the knot. Your most impulsive act ever," she told him with a grin.

"Was she pregnant?" Jason said. He was dressed as he'd been the day before, in baggy jeans and a baggy flannel shirt over a baggy T-shirt, this one sporting an image of a double helix.

"Oh, no, you did not just ask that," Grace said, sounding more New York than London.

Glancing up from her drawing to give Jason a *look*, Isabel said, "She wasn't pregnant."

Archer smiled. "Of course she was."

Isabel gaped at her father.

"You were born seven months later," her father said.

"I was premature. I was conceived on your honeymoon. I weighed four pounds, two ounces."

"You were eight pounds even." He gave her a rueful smile. "Your mother insisted on the preemie story. I'm sorry, my dear. It never sat well with me, lying to you."

Jason, his chair tipped back, hands behind his head, looked back and forth between father and daughter as if he were watching one of those American reality shows.

"Mr. Archer," Grace said, "are you going to take that pill or just sit there fiddling with it all afternoon?"

"Wait a minute," Isabel said. "So I was conceived during the love-in?"

"The *house party*?" Archer said pointedly, only to lapse into a coughing fit. "No, Maddy brought a boyfriend, worse luck. It wasn't until we were back in London again that we started seeing each other."

Isabel said, "You must have seen an awful lot of each other pretty fast, if she was two months' pregnant when you got married, um . . . *two months later.*"

"It took me a few days to work up my courage to call her, once I got back to London. I couldn't believe it when she not only agreed to go out with me, but seemed *enthusiastic* about it. But she was rather . . . mercurial, you know. A free spirit."

"Mr. Archer, do take that pill," Grace said. "I know it's hard, but—"

"Yes, yes, yes," he said in an irritated tone. Darius heard him take a scratchy breath, as if steeling himself. "Bottoms up."

"There you go," Grace said. "And the next one?"

"Ah, look who's here," Archer said, smiling toward the door to the dining room. "Come sit with us, my dear."

Lili stepped into the garden wearing a plum-colored *lubushu*, her gleaming raven hair in a single braid down her back, those almond eyes flashing. Jason looked away from her, took a sip of his wine, and looked back, trying—it seemed to Darius—to keep from leering.

"Why, thank you," Lili said as Jason rose and pulled out a chair next to his. "You're . . . Jordan, right?"

"Jason. Jason MacKenna."

Lili asked Jason where his parents were, and he said they were hiking up Alp Albiorix.

"I'm surprised to find you all still sitting here," Lili said. "Weren't you served lunch around noon? What have you been talking about to keep you so engrossed?"

"Isabel just found out she's a love child," Jason said.

"What I don't understand," Isabel told her father, "is why Mom was such a priss about letting people know. I mean, she was a *hippie*, for cryin' out loud. They were all about sleeping around."

"She's got a point," Jason said. "Love the one you're with? All that free love stuff that came out of the sexual revolution . . ."

Lili, sitting next to him, touched his arm and said, "The concept of free love goes back much further than that, I assure you."

He looked down at her hand on his arm.

She smiled at him as one would smile at a very large but very tame St. Bernard. Jason MacKenna was no *gabru,* not by Ilutu Lili's standards. If she did choose to take him, as she did many of their male guests, it would be because she had hungers to satisfy, not because she found him particularly attractive.

"Maddy was a hippie, yes," Archer said, "but from one of the most venerable old families in New York, descended from the original Dutch settlers."

"From whom she'd been rebelling since she could walk," Isabel countered.

"But whom she still loved and wanted to please," her father said. "And sexual revolution or no, there was still a stigma back then about being an unwed mother. She was quite anxious to disguise the fact that she was in the family way when we tied the knot."

"How times change," Grace said. "Today, she probably wouldn't think twice about it."

"She might not even have bothered marrying you," Isabel said, "at least not right away. It's just not an issue anymore."

"Well . . ." he said. "Not as *much* of an issue, perhaps, but still . . . I mean, *you* wouldn't have a baby out of wedlock, would you?"

"Actually, I've been thinking about it a lot lately, and I think I would. In the plane on the way here, I was sitting next to this woman a few years older than me who had her baby with her—*so* adorable. I mean, I could feel my ovaries screaming *Do it! What are you waiting for?* Turned out the mother was single with no marital prospects and the biological clock had been ticking down, so she finally realized it was do or die. She went for artificial insemination, but it didn't work until she had all these other really grueling and expensive fertility procedures, 'cause she'd waited so long. I told myself that wasn't gonna be me. I've decided to try and scare me up some high-quality spermatozoa."

"Ah, romance," Jason deadpanned.

Her father said, "Isabel, a woman like you shouldn't have to resort to such measures to start a family. You're beautiful, intelligent . . . You've had some serious boyfriends. Hasn't there been at least one you would have considered marrying?"

Isabel looked away. Darius couldn't help but think back to that Christmas visit when she and Adrien were both teenagers. Their mutual attraction had been obvious—to him, if to no one else, thanks to the way humans tended to dismiss him from their minds when he was just a gray cat curled up in the corner. After all these years, was it possible that she was still carrying a torch for him?

She said, "I'm thirty-five, Dad. I can't just keep hoping that someday my white knight will ride up, slip a ring on my finger, and get me with child."

"I'm in the same boat as Isabel," Grace said. "Single and destined to stay that way, but what I wouldn't give to have a baby, if it weren't so bloody difficult to arrange. I'm thirty-nine and living in very contented sin with someone who can't get me pregnant—so what's a girl to do?"

"He's sterile?" Jason asked.

"*She* had a hysterectomy eight years ago, and obviously she wouldn't have been able to do the deed in any event. Laura and I are dying to have a child, and we've thought about artificial insemination from one of those sperm banks, but it just strikes us both as so . . . I don't know. A complete stranger's DNA . . ."

"You can stipulate someone who has similar attributes to your girlfriend," Isabel said.

"Yeah, I know. We actually went and looked at the list of blond-haired, blue-eyed, whip-smart donors, but the chilly anonymity of it . . . We ended up leaving empty-handed, or rather, empty . . . well, you get the idea."

"Have you considered the turkey baster route?" Jason asked.

"Oh, sure, there've been some men of our acquaintance over the past few years who've fit the bill, you know? Laura and I have proposed it to seven of them, but no dice. Straight or gay, men feel threatened by the idea of fathering a child on a woman they're not involved with. They just won't go for it. Usually it's 'cause they're worried that someday they're gonna have responsibilities shoved down their throat that they didn't count on. If I were straight, I might just pick a likely bloke and jump him, that's how desperate I am."

"What prompted this whole 'love child' line of conversation, anyway?" Lili asked.

"Dad was saying he fell in love with my mom right here in the Beckett Garden," Isabel said.

"Why would a garden in France be named after an Englishman?" asked Jason.

Lili smiled. "If you're referring to the Archbishop of Canterbury, I'm afraid you're mistaken, although it's a common assumption. This garden was actually named after David Beckett Roussel."

"I recognize that name," said Jason, who looked as if he were trying to place it.

"Dav— Roussel was one of the foremost British landscape architects of the nineteenth century," Lili said, "along with Capability Brown and Humphrey Repton. It was he who designed this garden and the other major gardens here. He renovated the courtyard and restructured most of the open land around the château. We still have his notebook of drawings and plans. It belongs to Emmett, passed down from his great-great-great-grandfather, Bartholemew Archer. You should take a look at it, Isabel, seeing as you're an artist. It's in the library."

"Oh, yes, do," said Archer, his voice sounding very raw now. "It's really very beautiful. I've also got several books that he published and some others that were published about him. You'll find them in the section of the library that houses the *administrateur*'s books, rather than *le seigneur*'s."

"Where might that be?" she asked. "That is one huge freakin' library."

Darius fluttered down, circled the table to get Isabel's attention, then flew through the dining room door and waited for her on the back of a chair.

"Whoa," Jason said. "That rock finch just totally flew into the house. And I just said 'totally.' How totally embarrassing."

He pushed his chair back, but Isabel waved him down as she rose from the table, taking her wineglass with her. "I'll find it and shoo it out."

As she entered the dining room, she said softly, "Lead the way."

Darius guided her through the castle and up the winding stone stairwell in the southeast tower, which opened onto the library's long, Persian-carpeted, cozily furnished upper gallery. He flew past the book-lined nooks along the outside wall to the large alcove at the very end, settling onto the mantel of the fireplace, its empty hearth shielded from view by a summer screen. To either side of it was an enormous leaded glass window, the left-hand one illuminating a writing desk dating back to the sixteenth century. The only other furniture was a pair of massive old green velvet couches facing each other across a slab of polished black marble scattered with books and magazines, the latter mostly British and American.

"These are my father's books?" Isabel asked as she entered the alcove, looking around curiously. It wasn't surprising that she didn't know this, having avoided Grotte Cachée until her father's illness. She scanned the books, swiftly homing in on the *R* shelves.

Darius fluttered up off the mantel and onto the writing desk. Stretching his neck, his beak tapped a couple of times on a windowpane and turned to look at Isabel, but she was too absorbed in scrutinizing book spines to notice.

He pecked harder and more persistently.

"What . . . Oh, you want out?" she asked.

Duh.

Setting her wineglass on the desk, she cracked open the window. He nodded his goodbye and flew out over the castle's front lawn, interrupted by the gravel drive leading to the drawbridge and gatehouse. Cradled by a balmy breeze, he let it propel him around the perimeter of the castle as he considered how to amuse himself now. He could resume his human form and do some reading, he supposed, but he hated to surrender his wings on such a glorious day.

He thought about those little brown wall lizards that lived in the rock garden and were just now coming out of hibernation. On a sunny afternoon like this, there were bound to be three or four lazing around catching some rays. Of course, they'd scurry the moment they saw him, but it wouldn't be any fun if they didn't.

As he flew around the western range, he saw a flash of movement in a second-story window. One thing about a 300-degree range of vision—there wasn't much that escaped your notice. The window was one of six along the west wall of the sprawling chamber that had originally been the *salle haute*—a private upper hall for the exclusive use of the *gardien*. It was one of the largest rooms in the castle, with views of the West Lawn on one side and the courtyard on the other.

In 1987, when Emmett became *administrateur* following

the death of his father and Adrien Morel's parents in the crash of the Morels' private plane, Adrien gave him permission to turn the little-used *salle* into a gym. It had been improved upon over the years until it rivaled the poshest health clubs in Paris and London. The sauna with its attached, ultra-luxurious steam shower were added a few years ago at Inigo's request.

Lighting onto the windowsill, Darius saw that the movement had been the opening of a door. He watched as Inigo led Chloe into the big, mirrored room by a chain attached to a steel collar around her neck.

She was dressed in a tightly laced red vinyl waist cincher accessorized with matching opera-length gloves, black fishnets, red stiletto heels, and a red ball gag. In her hands were a roll of black bondage tape and a bottle of lube; Inigo never went anywhere without his lube.

The satyr himself wore nothing but snug, black leather trousers and heavy boots, both well broken in. The trousers, which he'd had specially tailored for him some years ago in Florence, featured a pouchlike fall front secured with three brass zippers, two on the sides and one connecting it to the waistband. The purpose of the fall was both to accommodate his outsized satyric genitalia and to provide maximum access to same while keeping his pants from falling down around his ankles. With his butch attire, hard-cut torso, ruby earring, and the faded *In Vino Veritas* tattoo on his left pec, he looked like every submissive's fantasy dom.

Inigo clipped her leash to the Roman chair, fetched one of his fucking machines from what he called "the toy closet," and clamped it to the barbell rack at one end of a sharply angled decline bench. The machine was a custom-made accessory for this particular bench, built to Inigo's precise specifications. He'd dubbed it the "Personal Trainer."

Chloe stared with eyes like silver dollars as he attached a

steel dildo covered with little knobs to the machine's piston rod, which he adjusted at an upward angle parallel to the bench and just slightly above it. He fine-tuned the length and angle of the rod, plugged in the machine, and thumbed a button on its remote control. The rod glided back and forth with smooth, even strokes, its well-oiled, precision-crafted motor almost noiseless. He pushed another button to make it speed up, another to make the dildo undulate in a circular motion, and another to make it vibrate.

"Get it?" he asked Chloe.

She nodded with gusto.

Chalk up another satisfied customer for the ever-accommodating Inigo.

A minute or two of watching this sort of thing could pass for idle curiosity; any more, and you were a Peeping Tom.

Darius flew off in search of wall lizards.

Inigo retracted the piston, unclipped Chloe's leash, and had her lie faceup on the bench with her head at the higher end, where a bench presser's knees would normally be, and her hips at the lower. He lifted her legs and taped them to opposite ends of the rack, so that they were forced wide apart. Her hands he pulled over her head and behind her, taping them to the bench's foot braces, to which he also clipped her neck chain. He took a moment to admire what the position did to her exposed breasts, and then he dribbled lube onto the steel dildo, coating it thoroughly.

He lubricated two fingers and shoved them into her rectum, making her arch off the bench as she sucked in her breath through the gag.

"You've been wanting it up the ass," he said in his best bad-ass growl as he slid the fingers in and out. "Filthy little whores like you always want it up the ass. Look, your clit's getting hard already." He rubbed the little knot of flesh, making her hips jerk upward.

Man, this girl was as good as it got—as long as stimulating conversation wasn't high on your list of priorities. She wasn't the kind of girl you found yourself thinking about when you were away from her. Inigo didn't want to impress her or make her laugh, or any of that shit. Put it this way: If Salma Hayek—with that body, that face, that brainy earthiness—were a great big three-flavor hot fudge sundae with nuts and sprinkles and whipped cream and a cherry on top, Chloe was a store-brand ice cream bar. You wouldn't turn it down on a warm day, but all things considered, it lacked the luscious depth that distinguished a truly first-class dessert.

But Chloe had one thing going for her that a lot of women didn't, and that was her attitude toward sex, which she viewed purely as a form of entertainment. If there was any way to amp up the experience, make it a little dirtier, a little crazier, she was down with it, and then some. With a chick like this, the wild thing was guaranteed to be *Wild*.

Wiping his hands off on a gym towel, Inigo used the remote to make the steel phallus advance very slowly toward its intended goal. She gasped when it nudged her body.

"It's not gonna stop," Inigo said, "so you better make sure it goes where it's supposed to."

She squirmed around a bit until the tip of the dildo breached her anus, pressing the little aperture open. It gradually plowed into her body, the little knobs making her tremble as they popped in.

Inigo halted its progress when about six inches were buried inside her. She made a little mewing sound and shook her head; she wanted more.

"Greedy little slut." He smiled as he pressed another button. The dildo moved back and forth at a leisurely pace. "Faster?"

She nodded.

Of course. *Faster, harder.* It was practically her mantra.

He pushed a button. It speeded up, but evidently it still wasn't enough for her. She looked at the remote with pleading eyes. He shrugged and made it go faster. She wanted yet more, but he said, "All in good time."

She moaned and writhed like a chick in a porno, only in Chloe's case, Inigo had no doubt whatsoever as to her sincerity. He straddled the bench over her shoulders and unzipped his trouser fall, freeing a cock that felt like a column of steel-reinforced concrete. Because of the bench's incline, Chloe's face was at the same level as said organ, at which she gazed hungrily.

He removed the ball gag. "Lick your lips," he said, then he grabbed her head and pushed himself into her mouth.

Chloe fellated him like a woman who was literally starving for the taste of cock and balls, feasting on them with practiced zeal as he thrust faster, faster.

"Oh, yeah," he whispered as it started, that pre-orgasmic thrill of tension that seemed to radiate between his cock and his tail—or what used to be his tail. The spot where it had been removed was still acutely sensitive, especially when he was aroused. During sex, it almost felt as if someone were pressing the tip of an electric vibrator right there, the pleasure buzzing up his spine, down his legs, all along his cock.

Inigo's legs started quivering, his heart thumping like an Aerosmith bass vibe at a hundred-forty decibels. *Here it comes.* "You want it in your mouth or on your tits?"

"Tits," she said, arching her back to thrust them out.

He stepped back, squeezing out spurt after spurt while she thanked him and begged for more.

He zipped up, cleaned her off, and went to turn off the Personal Trainer, but she said, "No, don't! Please, sir, leave it on."

"I thought you might be getting sore, but whatever."

"Lick me."

"What?"

"Lick my pussy. Please, sir. Suck my clit. Stick your tongue in my—"

Inigo jammed the ball gag back in her mouth. In keeping with character, he should have refused to do her bidding, but her bare-naked pussy, all desperately pink and swollen, was just too appetizing to resist.

Crouching next to her, he said, "For a sub, you sure like to get your way."

"Hey, man, it's me," Inigo murmured into his cell phone as he stood at an open window of the gym, slugging back a rejuvenating dose of tequila while Chloe, still strapped to the bench, luxuriated in her subjugation. The other Follets generally spoke French with each other, but he preferred English, which had been the semi-official language of Grotte Cachée ever since the first British *administrateur,* Lord Henry Archer, started inviting certain of his countrymen and their American colonists as houseguests.

"Hey, what's up?" Elic said.

"So, listen, bro," Inigo whispered as he glanced over his shoulder at the subject of this covert phone call. "I've got Chloe up here in the gym, and I've been doing my damnedest to keep up, but man, I am telling you, she is inde-fuckin'-fatigable. Which is awesome, except the old heroic dimensions"—he gave his crotch a gingerly pat—"need a little power nap between workouts. Which is where you come in, my friend. Where art thou right now, brother?" Inigo took a healthy swallow from the bottle.

"At your place with Lili, watching a movie." They usually watched their DVDs in Inigo's apartment because of his sixty-inch TV.

"What movie?"

Elic sighed. "*Casino Royale.*"

"Wait, haven't you seen that movie, like, three or four times already?"

"Lili can't get enough of the blond James Bond. That scene where he walks out of the ocean is like porn to her. So, what's up, man?"

"When's the last time you got some? Coupla weeks ago when those Cirque du Soleil chicks were here, right?"

"That's right."

"Your balls must be throbbing like a motherfucker by now." Another swig of tequila.

"You could say that."

"Why don't you come on over to the gym and help me out with the Energizer hottie? The tits are real, man, and she's got the Dyson vacuum of pussies—never loses suction. And need I tell you she is premoistened for your convenience? I'm not talking sloppy seconds here. I've been money-shotting ever since I realized I was gonna have to call you in for backup." With another glance over his shoulder, he grinned and dropped his voice down a notch, "I've got her wrapped up like a birthday present, bro, you gotta come check this out."

"Hold on." His voice so muffled it was almost inaudible, Elic said, in French, "Lili, you know that little redhead of Inigo's? He wants to share her with me, and you know I can use it. You can finish the movie without me, right?" A brief pause, and then he said, "Sure, man, I'll be right up."

"Oh, but listen, bro, you gotta be a real prick with this one, or she'll get all pouty and shit. Call her a dirty little slut. She loves that."

"I'm on it." *Click.*

Elic *must* have been chafing at the bit, because he was there about two minutes later, with that locked-and-loaded glint in his eye that meant Chloe was really in for it.

Chloe, still strapped to the bench but with the steel dildo unmoving inside her, looked startled to see him. But then she took him in—six and a half feet of golden-haired, well-muscled male with a rock-solid bulge in his jeans—and despite the ball gag, she almost seemed to be smiling.

Elic whipped his black T-shirt off over his head and tossed it aside. "I hear you're a dirty little whore who likes it rough," he said in his deep, vaguely European-accented voice as he stalked toward her.

Chloe stared at him yearningly until he started unwrapping the tape from her hands, and then she shook her head frantically.

Inigo, leaning against the windowsill as he lit a cigarette, said, "Hey, don't do that, bro. She likes that shit, I told you."

"I'm with the program." Pulling her arms down straight, Elic taped her wrists to the merry widow so that her hands rested on her upper thighs. He stepped over the foot of the bench, which was narrow enough and low enough to the ground that he could kneel between her splayed legs. "Open your cunt," he said as he unzipped his fly.

She parted her labia.

He pushed into her, burying himself in one smooth thrust. His head fell back, the air rushing from his lungs. After more than a few days of abstinence, Elic was always on a hair trigger, and it had been two weeks.

"What did I tell you?" Inigo said as he lifted the tequila bottle to his mouth. "Like a vacuum cleaner, no?"

"Stop that," Elic said, slapping Chloe's hip as she started thrusting wildly. "Be still."

"I've only let her come once since I strapped her to that thing," Inigo said. "She's a little tense."

"How does this work again?" said Elic, indicating the Personal Trainer.

"I'll do it," Inigo said as he pulled the remote from his pocket. "She likes it fast."

"It's for me, not her. Make it do this," he said, demonstrating a rotating motion with his finger. "Yes," he breathed as the device started churning inside Chloe, massaging his cock in a steady rhythm as it did so.

"Don't move," he told Chloe, gripping her hips as she started squirming again.

Elic didn't thrust, didn't move a muscle, but within seconds, his breath was shuddering, his face flushing. A vein bulged on his forehead. His body grew rigid, except for his hips, which trembled as he let out a long, low groan. The climax went on for some time, as they generally did with him, and then he slumped over, panting. "Stop that thing."

Inigo aimed the remote and pushed a button. "You laugh at me every time I have one of these built, but you've got to admit, they can add a certain *je ne sais quoi, non*?"

"*Oui.* You got any lube?"

"You kidding?" Inigo stubbed out his cigarette and brought the bottle over. Watching Elic take his turn had roused the old rolling pin from its slumber; Inigo adjusted it through its leather pouch to give it some stretching room.

Elic took the lube and dripped a little onto Chloe's vulva, making her squirm. "Don't move," he ordered. "Just your hands. Make yourself come."

Inigo caught Elic's eye and mouthed a prompt.

"You filthy slut," Elic added.

She began eagerly masturbating with her taped-down hands, both orifices still stuffed full.

Inigo took back the lube, drizzled some onto Chloe's breasts, and rubbed it all over them, squeezing, stroking, teasing the nipples . . . His cock felt like a length of steel pipe that had been forced into a too-small leather sack.

Chloe moaned helplessly.

"I said *don't move.*" Elic held her hips down as they started moving.

She whined in frustration through the gag, but managed to hold still until the orgasm hit, and then she convulsed as if zapped by an electric prod, the gag muffling her groans. Elic closed his eyes, his ass contracted, clearly relishing the sensation.

He gave her a moment to catch her breath, then said, "Again," as he set about fucking her with long, slow strokes.

"You mind a little company, bro?" Inigo asked as Chloe went back to fingering her greased-up pussy.

"Be my guest."

Inigo straddled her, unzipped his pants, squeezed her slickened breasts together, and rammed his cock between them. "You like this?" he asked Chloe. "You like getting it from two guys at once with a dildo up your ass? You like getting your tits fucked? Course you do, 'cause you're a dirty, nasty little slitch."

"Slitch?" Elic said breathlessly.

"Slut and bitch," Inigo rasped. "Slitch."

Chloe nodded as if to say *You haven't heard that?*

The three of them came at roughly the same time amid a chorus of groans, Inigo ejaculating onto Chloe's throat and upper chest. As Elic withdrew his cock, dripping with his extra-thick semen, she twitched her hips as if begging to have it back.

"You're not sore?" he asked.

She shook her head.

"All right, then," he said as he stroked his erection back to life.

"Told you, man," Inigo said as he reached for his tequila. "Inde-fuckin-fatiguable."

Adrien Morel stood outside Emmett's library alcove with that day's *Le Monde* and a cup of coffee, watching Isabel, sitting on a sofa with her back to him, leaning over a book in her lap.

She hadn't heard him approach, the carpet having muffled his footsteps. He told himself he should turn and walk away before she realized he was there. Her emotions were getting enough of a workout right now, what with her father's condition; she didn't need him injecting himself into the mix.

He'd just about decided that he really should leave when a cloud drifted somewhere far overhead, and a bolt of sunlight streamed through the window and touched her hair, and he found himself utterly transfixed.

Isabel's hair, looped with a covered rubber band into a prettily disheveled pseudochignon, had darkened only slightly from the cool platinum it had been as an adolescent. Adrien recalled having been captivated by it during that Christmas break she'd spent at Grotte Cachée when she was sixteen and he not quite eighteen. He used to catch himself gazing at it during those long hours they'd spent sitting around talking and listening to music, marveling at its pale, silken sheen.

Once she caught him staring and blushed, but he still couldn't look away, so struck was he by the contrast, at her hairline, of her scalding pink skin against the silver-blond roots of her hair.

Isabel turned a page of her book, whispered, "Holy shit," then gave her cheek a little slap. "Fucking potty mouth."

Adrien chuckled.

She turned and looked at him over her shoulder, stared for a second. "How long have you been standing there?"

"Not long. I just came up here to read the paper, then I'll be heading back to the lodge to finish scanning some scrolls for *L'histoire*." The *Histoire Secrète de Grotte Cachée* was a project Adrien had launched some time ago, an attempt to take the written accounts of his ancestors and combine them into one comprehensive, multivolume document for the benefit of future *gardiens* and *administrateurs*.

Apologize for the intrusion and leave, he told himself. "What are you reading?" he asked, coming close enough to look over her shoulder.

She closed and held up the book, which was about twelve inches square and bound in age-softened black leather with the initials D.B.R. tooled on the front.

"Ah, the Beckett notebook. It's been a long time since I've looked at that. May I?" He gestured toward the couch.

"Sure," she said, holding the volume to her chest. "Of course."

She was wearing big, dangly, primitive silver earrings that should have looked all wrong with her sleeveless white blouse and tan shorts, but instead looked just perfect. Her skin was like cream except for rosy-gold sun stains across the bridge of her nose, the upper ridges of her cheekbones, and her shoulders. Would those spots feel hot to the touch, he wondered, if he were so foolish as to reach out and stroke them?

As he sat—careful to maintain his distance from her—Adrien noticed the stack of books on the table: three biographies of Beckett, one published in the nineteenth century, two in the twentieth; a modern, limited edition set of his four books about landscape design in a slipcase, although they had the first editions as well; and an original edition—there had only been one—of the obscure but intriguing *Dæmonia*.

"Making a study of David Beckett, are we?" Adrien asked as he set down his coffee cup and newspaper.

"Why do you call him by his middle name?" Isabel asked. "And that terrace garden is called the Beckett Garden. Shouldn't it be the Roussel Garden?"

"Beckett is the name he went by when he came here in eighteen twenty-nine," Adrien said. "He was posing as a, well what we now call a landscape architect in English, and he had a genuine love for that field of work, but he was actually a Jesuit demon hunter who'd been sent by the Church."

"Ah, I'd wondered what that book about demons was doing mixed in with all these books about gardening."

"That one," Adrien said, nodding toward the Beckett notebook still pressed protectively to Isabel's chest, "has got to be the rarest and most valuable book in your father's collection."

Lowering the book to her lap, Isabel opened it almost reverently. "When I was a little girl," she said, "we had an encyclopedia that had anatomy illustrations with transparent overlays showing, like, the bones over the organs and the muscles over the bones. I used to spend hours looking at those pictures, flipping the overlays back and forth. This book reminds me of that. The paintings are amazing—so detailed, but so vigorous and colorful. And I can't stop looking at the little maps, you know, the garden plans, and comparing them to how those gardens look now. The whole thing just blows me away."

Adrien said, "What was it that provoked that heartfelt 'holy shit'?"

"Let me find it again." Isabel leafed through the book slowly, so as not to damage the brittle old pages. The front section was composed of notes and fastidiously inked plans showing layouts of Beckett's proposed gardens and parklands. Following that were twelve watercolor illustrations of different vantage points around the château and grounds as they had existed in 1829. Tipped in over each illustration was a painting on translucent vellum showing how that particular view would look after its suggested overhaul.

Isabel stopped at one of these before-and-after illustrations and handed him the book, saying "The difference is unbelievable. It doesn't look like the same space at all." He caught a whiff of her perfume, the same scent she'd worn last August— earthy, complex, not sweet, but deeply feminine all the same.

"Ah, the courtyard." Adrien lifted the overlay very carefully, cringing at its muted crackle. The painting beneath was an overhead view—from the northwest tower, he would guess— of the castle's central court as it had looked before its Beckett-inspired overhaul. The fountain, with its sculpture of a couple making love beneath a stream of water from a jug held by a servant girl, was the same, but it was otherwise bare except for a perimeter of box hedges.

He lowered the overlay and smoothed it down, marveling at the transformation. It was one of Beckett's more symmetrical designs, with a walkway of volcanic paving stones spanning the length of the courtyard from the gatehouse to the great hall's majestic doorway in the north range. In the middle of the courtyard, this central aisle was interrupted by the fountain, which it circled. Branching off from this circle were smaller paths laid out in a knotlike pattern, *un hommage* to the decorative style of Grotte Cachée's Gaulish forebears. In the grassy spaces between the knots stood twenty-four cherry trees, depicted in full bloom. Stone benches were situated here and there along the paths and on either side of the fountain.

"The courtyard is one of the most beautiful places I've ever been," Isabel said. "Seriously, it's one of my favorite places in the world. And this picture—I mean, it could have been painted this afternoon. It still looks exactly like this after, what—a hundred and eighty years?"

"Especially with the cherry trees being in bloom," Adrien said.

She said, "I assume Roussel—or Beckett, or whatever you want to call him—came back to supervise the execution of his designs."

Shaking his head as he handed back the book, Adrien said, "Your ancestor, Bartholemew Archer, saw Beckett's plans through to completion—all of them, down to the last detail. Beckett himself never came back to Grotte Cachée. About a year after he returned to England, he married the daughter of one of his landscaping clients, Wilhemina Rhodes, and fathered quite a brood of children."

Smiling, Isabel said, "One of his books is dedicated to 'My darling Mina.' Not all of the plans were implemented, though."

"Yes, they were," Adrien said. "The landscaping, the courtyard, the hunting lodge, the Beckett Garden, the rock garden . . ."

"But not *this* garden." She turned to the plan toward the front of the book for the walled garden labeled *Sub Rosa* in Beckett's distinctive, angular hand. "I've never seen this one."

"That's because it was never meant to be seen. In former times, if private matters were to be discussed, a rose would be hung overhead so that everyone would know that the meeting was 'under the rose,' or confidential."

"Are you saying this is, like, a *secret* garden?"

Nodding, he said, "It's hidden deep in the woods to the north, about halfway between here and the lodge."

"Seriously?" She looked back down at the precisely inked layout in the book, her eyes glittering.

Her excitement was contagious. "Would you like to see it?" he asked.

"*Hell,* yeah," she said, springing to her feet. "I mean, *heck,* yeah. But I feel guilty keeping you from your work. You could, um, give me directions, and I could just—"

"You'd never find it on your own, and it's not an imposition. I'll enjoy it." Adrien stood and started to hold out his hand, then withdrew it, hoping she hadn't noticed.

"This is unbelievable," Isabel said as Adrien led her through the gate in the stone wall enclosing the secret garden, the wall itself so thick with foliage and vines that it was almost indistinguishable from the surrounding forest.

He took her on a tour of the garden: the koi pool with its scattering of lily pads, the fanciful corner turrets, the statues and birdbaths nestled among tangles of fragrant roses . . .

"How come you never showed me this when I was here that Christmas?" she asked. "We skied all through these woods."

"No way to get here on skis," he said. "There are no paths leading here."

"Right . . . So then, how do they get lawn mowers in here to cut the grass?"

"It's done with scythes," he said.

"Seriously." Isabel kicked off her sandals and walked around a bit with an expression of childlike wonder, as if trying to determine whether scythe-cut grass felt different underfoot than mower-cut grass.

Sitting on the stone lip of the pool, she said, "Those are some big freakin' carp. And the water's so clear."

"It's well filtered."

Dipping her hand in, she said, "Oh, it feels awesome. I thought it'd be cold, but it's just right." She trailed her fingers back and forth through the water, a speculative gleam in her eyes. With an impish grin, she said, "You think these fish would mind a little company?"

"What, you want to swim?"

"It's not big enough to swim in, but a little dip to cool off?"

She stood up and began undoing the buttons of her blouse. "I don't know about you, but I'm really feeling the heat after that hike through the woods."

He imagined the two of them in the water together, naked and alone in this remote, sunny little oasis in the midst of an ancient forest. It made him think about the bathhouse last August, and the hunger that had flared between them with such pure, sweet, violent force. It had been the most powerful lovemaking he'd ever experienced, an explosion of passion . . .

Followed by stinging regret.

Her smile faded as he stood there in idiotic, conflicted silence. God, how he wanted her. It might not be wise, but since when had reason not been at odds with desire?

She looked down and started rebuttoning her blouse.

He started toward her. "Isabel . . ."

"Nah, dumb idea." She turned and headed toward the entrance to the garden, still buttoning. "Anyway, I should really be getting back. It's almost teatime. Dad will expect me."

"No, wait. We can . . ." *Merde.* "We, um, we can walk back together. You won't know the way."

"I paid attention, and you've got work to do. Catch you later," she said as she strode through the gate.

"Isabel," he said.

She didn't turn around.

He didn't follow her.

Four

"THANKS FOR KNEECAPPING ol' Bernie in there," I told Madeleine as she guided me out into the courtyard. "You should have let me take him outside, though. Might have relaxed me a little to punch his lights out."

"He would have peed his pants if you'd called him out," she said. "You do realize he had no clue you were heading in that direction."

"You think?"

"I know." She stopped walking and faced me, shielding her eyes from the sun with her hand. "Please tell me those cigarettes in your back pocket are American."

I produced my Marlboros and shook out two.

"There *is* a God," she said.

I touched a match to her cigarette, which crackled as it ignited. With her absurdly high platform sandals, she was as tall as I was.

She inhaled with an expression of bliss. "It would have been shorter to take you to the gate tower through the corridor inside, but I wanted a smoke, and I don't like to smoke in other people's houses."

"Me, neither."

She sat on a stone bench in the shade of a cherry tree, crossed her long legs, put her head back, closed her eyes, and savored her little taste of tar and nicotine from the good ol' U.S. of A. I leaned against the tree trunk to light my own cigarette.

I could see what Emmett meant about the Botticelli thing, especially the hair, which was a hot n' spicy ginger. She had a classic redhead's complexion, skim milk with freckles spattered just about everywhere, even on her eyelids. Her eyelashes were long and coppery.

She glowed.

Madeleine's style of dress was hippie chic without that fresh-from-the-dustbin look that distinguished her friends' attire. From how she'd dressed that weekend, I guessed she shopped in boutiques rather than thrift shops. Today, for example, she was wearing a long, slinky blue dress with dramatically flared sleeves. It had a bodice that laced up in front, exposing a good three-inch-wide gap of flesh all the way down to her waist. On a woman who was really stacked, it might have looked like she was selling it by the hour, but Madeleine's breasts were small, with no cleavage to interrupt that smooth white band of skin. Her nipples pushed hard against the slick material of the dress.

Without opening her eyes, she blew out a stream of smoke and said, "Bernie's a little boy. Just a rich, coddled little boy who has no idea what grown-up men are all about."

"You two break up?"

She nodded. "Last night."

I thought about Emmett, hoping he'd materialize soon so he could snap her up before Pieter beat him to it.

208 · Louisa Burton

She slitted her eyes open and looked at me. "Most people would ask why."

He took a puff. "None of my business."

She looked away to tap her ash on the ground, didn't look back. "I walked in on him fucking Mindy Black last night in our room, on our bed. He wasn't even that flustered. He said, 'I've been meaning to talk to you about this whole establishment monogamy thing,' without even . . . I mean, while he was still inside her. I closed the door, and I could hear them starting right up again, the bedsprings squeaking, you know. And I heard them laughing." That last sentence kind of crumbled apart wetly.

I pushed away from the tree. "You okay?"

She took a drag on her cigarette and looked at me, pink splotches on her cheeks, her eyes a little too shiny. "So I went to Pete McCormack's room and fucked him."

"Oh."

"He's from back home. He's pre-med at Columbia. He's gonna fucking *do* something with his life. He's gonna be a *man*."

"Mm."

"I mean, not that I want a relationship with him, or anything like that, but you know what I mean."

"Sure." *Not really.*

She looked away again and took another drag. "He thought he could keep me from getting pregnant by"—she mimed quotation marks with her fingers—"realigning my chakras."

"Star— uh, Bernie?"

She nodded. "So he wouldn't have to use a rubber. He doesn't like rubbers, he doesn't like diaphragms. Interferes with spontaneity, he says. Spoiled little shit. He wants me to— *wanted* me to go on the pill, but it makes me fat, so that's not gonna happen, and I hear it hurts like hell to get an IUD. And I *will* not do it without birth control. Never have, never will. Even last night, the pissed-off rebound sex with Pete, he grabbed a Trojan off the nightstand, I didn't even have to ask. I mean, I know they're only eighty-five percent effective, but I'm guessing that's about eighty-five percent *more* effective than that chakra shit."

"I'm guessing you're guessing right." Was I really having this conversation with this woman I'd just met three days ago and barely even spoken to until ten minutes ago?

She looked at me. "Were you really a POW?"

"No, I just made that up to get over with girls."

"Was it awful?"

I shrugged as I drew on my cigarette. "Beautiful downtown Hanoi. What's not to like?"

Awful. What did that mean to a girl like this? A broken nail? A pretentious asshole of a boyfriend? Because of the gag order imposed on the released prisoners, even Emmett didn't know the half of it—the black box, the leg irons, the dysentery . . . I hadn't wanted to leave before the other guys, but given that I was delirious and emaciated, with unset fractures from that marathon, disastrous ass-kicking and two dislocated shoulders from the "Vietnamese rope trick"—punishments for a misbegotten escape attempt—I was given zero say in the matter. Three months in the hospital, and I was good as new—or at least, I could fake it pretty well if you didn't know the full story.

Madeleine looked at me as if she were trying to read my thoughts, and maybe she did, because she said, "Do you have a girlfriend, Hitch?"

In my mind's eye, I saw Lucinda's last letter to me, written in her tidy, straight up-and-down handwriting on the pale green writing paper with the ferns around the margins.

Dear Rob,

*You're wrong. We can make this work. You love me, you've told
me so countless times. And you know how I feel about you. I think
I've made that pretty clear in my letters, and of course in person
before you went to London. If we really do love each other, that's all
that matters, not whether the marriage will be "real" by some
screwed-up standard that means nothing to me and should mean
nothing to you. I've spent so many months writing to you, begging
you not to break off the engagement, waiting for you to come to your
senses. I can't keep doing this forever. At a certain point, I just start
feeling . . . I don't know, pathetic and clingy, I guess.*

*God, what did they do to you in that prison? I know the
outcome, but I don't know how it happened. Obviously it was a
nightmare, the whole experience. I know you can't talk about it, but
I wish I knew. Maybe then I'd be able to figure out how to get
through to you.*

*In the meantime, this is it, Rob. I'm going to do what you've
been asking me to do. I'm going to stop writing. But I'm not going
to stop loving you, ever. And I'm not going to stop praying that
you'll see the light and come back to me.*

All my love forever,
Lucinda

"No," I said. "No girlfriend."

"You didn't hear his message?" asked Julien Morel as he
came out from behind the gigantic desk in his study, a sun-
drenched room hung with paintings and medieval tapestries.

"What message?" I asked.

Crossing to his stereo to turn down the Miles Davis album
he was playing, Morel said, "Emmett, he called your room and
left a message on your . . . How do you say it? *Répondeur.*"

"Answering machine," Madeleine said. Each luxuriously appointed bedroom in the château was equipped with a wooden-cased device that I'd taken for a reel-to-reel tape player, until I saw the name PHONE•MATE on it and noticed that it was, indeed, connected to the telephone.

"*Ah*," Morel smiled at her. "*Parlez-vous français?*"

"*J'ai étudié le français à l'école.*" She gave him a shyly sweet smile that made me think, *Oh, man, maybe ol' Bernie was right. Maybe* les femmes *really did love zee French accent.*

It wasn't just the accent. Morel was charming and aristocratic, and a good-looking guy despite, or maybe even because of, his prematurely gray hair.

"In my house," Morel said, "there is a problem with, er . . . *l'électricité.* This morning, I leave to come here, and is fine, but then Élise—Madame Morel, my wife—she calls to say it stopped working. Is very old, the wires and the fuse box. I know nothing of such things, but Emmett tell me he knows a little, and will try to fix, or get someone else to fix."

I told him I hadn't been back to my room since early that morning, so I didn't get the message. Meanwhile, I was thinking *Great, now what'll I do all day? Play solitaire and drink myself into a coma?*

"Élise, she is nervous to be without the lights when the sun go down," Morel said. "Our house, is in the woods, and get very dark. And *l'électricité* is needed for the stove and the hot water. If it is just she and I, is not such a problem. We come here. But there is Adrien, our son. He is *un bébé*, eight months old. We do not like him here with . . . the guests."

"Can't say as I blame you," I said.

"What are you typing?" Madeleine asked, looking at the IBM Selectric on his desk, which he'd been pecking away at when they came in.

"*Correspondance,*" he said. "This and that."

"I could give you a hand with it," she offered. "I type fifty words a minute."

"Oh, no," he said. "You have your friends . . ."

"They've started to bore me. Seriously, I can type your letters as you dictate them. You'll be amazed at how fast it'll go, and then maybe you can help me with my French."

There came a little grunt that drew their attention to a nearby windowsill on which a gray cat was lounging in the sun, watching them with a languid feline smile.

"Well, who are you?" asked Madeleine, reaching out to pet it.

Morel grabbed her arm as the animal shot to its feet, hissing furiously.

"Jesus!" She would have fallen over as she stumbled back, thanks to those ridiculous shoes, had Morel not maintained his grip on her arm.

"He is very unhappy to be touched," the Frenchman said.

"God, he scared the hell out of me," Madeleine said. "Feel how hard my heart's pounding." She took his hand and pressed it to the bare flesh between her breasts.

He met her gaze.

"Your hand is so warm," she said. "You don't have a fever, do you?" With her free hand, she stroked his forehead, and smiled. "Just one of those hot-blooded Frenchmen, huh?"

Taking that as my cue, I excused myself, leaving Julien Morel to decide for himself whether to take the enticing redhead up on her offer—and wondering if it was such a good idea for Emmett to pounce, after all.

Five

SHOWTIME, ISABEL THOUGHT as she approached the darkened hunting lodge on slippered feet around eleven that night. She was shivering like crazy, not only because she'd just followed an interminable dirt road through the woods on a cool night wearing nothing but her thin cotton travel robe and flip-flops, but because she was *out of her freakin' mind* to be doing this.

It was dark as hell, there being just a sliver of moon hidden behind a suffocating layer of clouds that had been hovering up there waiting to burst into rain since around dinnertime. The illumination from her flashlight jittered as it played over the statue of Diana, goddess of the hunt, that was the centerpiece of the lodge's front garden, before-and-after watercolors of which were included in David Beckett Roussel's extraordinary book of plans. Diana smiled down on Isabel from her pedestal as if to say "Turn back now, honey, before you make a complete ass of yourself."

The lodge itself had been built in the sixteenth century of the same dusky volcanic rock from which the castle and most of the outbuildings were constructed. It was a beautiful edifice, stately but welcoming both inside and out, the most perfect house she'd ever seen.

No guts, no glory, Isabel thought as she turned the knob of the front door.

The door was unlocked, of course. This wasn't New York. She eased it open and stepped into the entrance hall, only to find that the house wasn't completely dark after all, nor completely silent. There was light coming from the rear, where she knew the so-called hunting hall to be because of all the hours she and Adrien had spent there that long-ago Christmas vacation, as well as barely audible music.

Damn. She had hoped to find him asleep upstairs, so that when she stole into his bed and woke him with soft kisses, he would be groggy and malleable.

Fighting the urge to turn back, she switched off her flashlight and padded silently toward the back of the house, the music growing louder as she approached the hunting hall. It was a nimble-fingered piano piece called "I Got It Bad (And That Ain't Good)"—*how perfect is that*—from an Oscar Peterson album she and Adrien used to play a lot that Christmas. *Night Train* was one of the hundreds of jazz LPs, some of them dating back to the 1920s, that his late father had spent his life collecting. While Julien Morel was alive, Adrien had been big on rockers like Springsteen and Bob Seger; he didn't get jazz, didn't care to. After the plane crash that claimed the lives of his parents and Isabel's grandfather, thrusting Adrien into the role of *gardien,* he bought a state-of-the-art turntable with a record changer and set about playing every single album, one after the other. He developed a love of cool jazz that rubbed off on

Isabel that Christmas and never left her. Her own CD collection covered most of the living room wall in her apartment.

Whether from the damp chill in the air or her nerves, or both, Isabel trembled like a rabbit as she stood in the wide, arched entrance to the hunting hall. It was a cavernous, high-ceilinged, dark-timbered room with plastered walls and a massive stone fireplace, in which low flames twitched and sputtered. Against the back wall, lined with leaded glass windows, was a long, slablike table that had come from the refectory of some medieval monastery. A scanner, laptop, printer, and three desk lamps stood on the table amid a sea of books, papers, and parchment scrolls. There was also a record player, the old kind; he was playing the same vinyl album they used to listen to together.

Adrien, standing with his back to her in a dressing gown and pajama bottoms, lifted a bottle of wine from the table and took a swallow right out of it, which surprised and amused Isabel. He'd always seemed like the type who would not only use a wineglass when he was drinking alone, he would use exactly the *right* glass.

From the defined musculature of his shoulders and back through the thin fabric of his robe, she could tell that he wasn't wearing anything else on top. She loved the shape of his shoulders; she always had, even when he was a lanky adolescent. The low drone of arousal she had felt all evening at the prospect of making love to Adrien again morphed into liquid-hot lust within seconds; God bless hormones.

He set the bottle down and lifted a scroll, pulling it open so he could read it.

"Adrien," she said.

He turned and stared at her, the scroll popping shut.

She swallowed hard, thinking back to that night in the

bathhouse last August, when their long-sublimated feelings had erupted in frenzied lovemaking—which he'd immediately regretted. It had been an excruciating reminder of the way he'd suddenly distanced himself from her after their first chaste kiss as teenagers, initiated by her. She knew now that he had put her aside at the encouragement of Darius for the good of the Follets, whom he was duty bound to spend his life protecting—just as he was duty bound to produce gifted offspring with a gifted wife. He was being responsible and dedicated, sacrificing his personal happiness for the greater good. Still, rejection was rejection; it hurt regardless of the reason.

That pain had been echoed, on a smaller scale, this afternoon in the Sub Rosa garden, after she'd impulsively invited him for a dip in the koi pool. His hesitation had spooked her into bolting instead of staying and giving it the old college try. Upon reflection this afternoon, she realized she'd squandered a golden opportunity.

Adrien's gaze shifted from her eyes to a point just slightly above her head, and back again. Her aura would be like a banner to him, broadcasting blatantly sexual vibes. He looked as if he were about to say something, then thought better of it.

She said, "Please don't tell me it was a mistake for me to come here."

Adrien looked down at the scroll in his hand, a palpable reminder of his sacred obligation to devote his life *dibu e debu*—to the gods and goddesses. He raised his gaze to her, his grim expression saying it all.

Isabel stood there for another few seconds, trying to think of something to say that didn't sound totally lame, or desperate, or sappy, heat sizzling up her throat and face. "Shit," she whispered.

She turned and made her way to the front door as quickly as

she could without actually running, her throat clutching. *Asshole. You fucking asshole.*

She opened the door. It slammed shut with concussive force.

Adrien spun her around by her shoulders, crushed her to the door, and kissed her, hard.

The flashlight dropped from her hand, clattering onto the tiled floor. He yanked at the sash of her robe, whipping it open. His hands were everywhere on her, hot and reckless.

She felt him tugging at his own clothes, and then he lifted her against the door and wrapped her legs around him. His initial thrust was shallow, an exploratory probe. On finding her already wet, he lunged into her. She clutched him to her, meeting his grinding thrusts as the pleasure shuddered through her, stealing her breath, squeezing her heart . . .

She came hard, bucking against him. He rammed into her as if he were trying to batter down the door, and suddenly he stilled, groaning low in his throat, his fingers digging painfully into her hips, his cock jerking inside her. She felt the semen shooting against the mouth of her womb in gradually diminishing jets, and smiled.

Adrien's knees seemed to give out as his orgasm waned. He slumped to the floor still connected to Isabel, both of them with their arms still tight around each other.

"*Mon dieu*," he whispered. He kissed her through a breathless chuckle, his mouth tasting like wine.

They uncoupled awkwardly and straightened their clothes. He stood, raised Isabel to her feet, and kissed her again.

"You're shaking," he said, chafing her arms. "Come into the hunting hall. I'll stoke the fire. I'll pour us some cognac, and we can talk. It's been a long time since we just talked together, comfortably. Our thoughts used to be so in sync, remember? That Christmas?"

She nodded.

He stroked a tendril of hair off her face. "And then you can come upstairs and sleep with me."

She looked up into those big, molten chocolate eyes and felt her stomach twist with guilt. He wasn't fretting, as he had that other time in the bathhouse, about not using protection. She had told him then that she was on the pill. He undoubtedly assumed she still was.

"Men feel threatened by the idea of fathering a child on a woman they're not involved with. They just won't go for it."

"I don't know, Adrien. Maybe . . . maybe we shouldn't, you know. Encourage something between us that—"

"There already is something between us," he said gently. "I've spent the past ten months trying to deny it, trying to put you out of my mind. It's pointless. It will always be there."

She looked down and closed her eyes, stinging with tears.

"Isabel." He stroked her face, lifted her chin. "We don't have a future, but we can have tonight. We can sleep together and make love again—properly this time, in my bed, taking our time about it. And in the morning, I'll make you breakfast."

"You cook?"

"I cook very well. I'll brew us a big pot of strong coffee, and I'll squeeze you some orange juice and make you some crêpes with berries. Or if you prefer cheeses, we can have that, and I'll get a fresh baguette and some croissants."

"Adrien . . ." Isabel hadn't planned on this, on him trying to hang on to her for a while longer. If anything, she'd assumed he would exhibit the same postcoital misgivings as last time. That would have made this easier—much easier.

"Twelve hours, Isabel. At"—he squinted at his watch in the semidarkness—"eleven forty-five tomorrow morning, we'll go back to how it's been. And that will be the end of it. We'll lift our chins and carry on, as your father would say. In the meantime, we can have our twelve hours, twelve hours where it will be just us, and we won't talk about . . . afterward. We won't think about it. We'll just be together and be happy."

She sighed.

"Come on, it's raining," he said, and she could hear that it was. "Stay. Just till noon tomorrow."

"You're stealing an extra fifteen minutes," she said.

He smiled. "Can you blame me?"

She stayed.

He lowered the needle on another LP, of Stan Getz and the Oscar Peterson Trio, and they sat curled up together under a cashmere blanket on an old velvet sofa in front of the fire, sipping cognac and talking about things Isabel hadn't ever talked about to anyone, because no one else would understand them, no one else would really care, no one else was the other half of her.

They shared lazy kisses in the glow of the fire to one of their favorite songs, "I'm Glad There Is You" . . . Two lovers caught in amber for one isolated moment in time, a moment they would have to keep and hold, preserving it in their hearts for an eternity, because it was all they would ever have of each other.

She undressed him under the blanket, touching and exploring, memorizing the topography of muscle and bone, the smell of his scalp, the way his hips tightened when she stroked his erection, pressing, pleading . . .

He pulled off her robe and made slow, dreamy love to her with his hands and his mouth, until by the time he entered her, she felt as if her entire body were one quivering, breathless nerve. He took his time, stoking her pleasure as he'd stoked the fire, bringing her right to the point of combustion, then backing off, again and again and again, the muscles of his chest and shoulders and arms flexing as he reared over her, his gaze growing more and more unfocused . . .

It's perfect. That was her only coherent thought as she basked in sensual delirium, her heart thudding so hard in her ears that she could barely hear their pants and moans. *It's perfect because it's Adrien. He's the man I was meant to make love to, the only one.*

She came first, he close on her heels, his groans sounding almost anguished as he clung to her, his back hunched, his body hard. They held each other, gasping for breath, as the record ended, the needle scritch-scritch-scritching around the played-out album.

"I thought we were supposed to make love properly this time," she said, "in your bed."

He chuckled; she felt it deep in her womb. "I'm getting around to it."

They took a warm bath together, then went to bed and held each other and whispered and kissed and made sweet, drowsy love, and sailed off to sleep in each other's arms.

He sailed off to sleep. Isabel lay awake until his breathing was deep and heavy and regular. At two o'clock, she carefully extracted herself from his embrace, got out of bed, put her robe and slippers back on, found her flashlight, and stole out into the night.

While Isabel was walking back to the château in the rain, sobbing, Elle and Lili were standing over Jason MacKenna's empty and tidily made up bed.

"I was afraid of this," Elle said. "Didn't his mother say he's a night owl? I've gone through The Change for nothing."

It was never easy. The softening of her muscles and the compression of her bones was always accompanied by pain, and there was the temporary but harrowing sense of having the breath squeezed out of her as her rib cage tightened around her lungs. Worst of all was the awful nausea—what she called the Change Sickness—as her physiology morphed from male to female. Her thought processes remained much the same—she was still Elic, after all—but those feelings that were governed by body chemistry, such as sexual arousal, were now those of a female.

"Just because he's not in his bed doesn't mean we can't find him and tap his seed," Lili said.

"Are you sure Isabel would want this?" Elle asked.

"She said, 'I've decided to try and scare me up some high-quality spermatozoa.' I should think Jason's would fit the . . . Hmm . . ." Lili was staring through the window behind Elle. "Those lights aren't usually kept on at night, are they?"

"What lights?" Tracking Lili's gaze across the courtyard, Elle saw that the gymnasium windows were brightly lit. "No, they aren't, but somehow Jason doesn't quite strike me as the workout type. It's probably Karen or Hitch."

A figure crossed the gym, almost as tall as Hitch, but much broader, carrying a barbell.

Elle and Lili looked at each other and smiled.

"*Now* where is he?" Lili asked as they scanned the empty gym.

Elle pointed to a T-shirt and a pair of shorts on the floor by the sauna. The view through its glass door wasn't helpful—all she could see of the sauna's interior was the other glass door on the back wall leading to the adjacent steam shower—but where else could he be?

"Feel like getting hot?" Elle asked.

"When am I not eager for a little rise in temperature?" said Lili as she untied her *lubushu*.

Jason, lying naked on a towel on the higher of the two wooden benches against the sauna's left-hand wall, bolted upright when Elle and Lili, also naked, entered the little wood-paneled oven of a room. Hastily wrapping the towel around himself, he said, "Oh, hey, sorry. I, uh, I wasn't expecting anybody else at this hour, so, um . . ."

"No need to apologize," Lili said as she laid a pair towels on the bottom bench, one on either side of his feet. "And please don't cover yourself on our account. A sauna can only be properly enjoyed *sans vêtements, non*?"

"Oh, yeah, definitely," he said, but he made no move to uncover himself, probably because of his physical reaction to their presence.

Lili smiled up at him through those thick black lashes as she seated herself by his left leg, her eyes glinting with sexual interest that wasn't feigned—for Jason MacKenna *sans vêtements* was a revelation. The body that had looked thick under sweatshirts and baggy jeans turned out to be composed mostly of muscle, with just a modest layer of what Inigo liked to call "comfortable upholstery." He was a big man, but in a good way, with a sturdy jaw, beefy arms, and shoulders like a prize stud bull. Without glasses to obscure his eyes, Elle could see that they were green—not hazel, but a remarkably vivid green—set off by dramatically arched blond brows.

Lili slid Elle an amused little look that said, *I know you didn't think I'd view him as a* gabru, *but now I do, and you'll just have to deal with it.* Whether in her male or female persona, Elle didn't think she would ever get used to Lili making love to exceptionally desirable men. On the other hand, Jason's unexpected hunkdom would make the collection of his seed a much more diverting enterprise than it otherwise would have been. Lili wasn't alone in finding him suddenly very hot. His scent, enhanced by the heat of the sauna—shea butter soap, Johnson's baby shampoo, a little hair pomade, and lots of aroused male—excited her intensely.

"Do you mind?" Elle asked Jason as she dipped the ladle in the wooden bucket next to the heater.

"Oh. Um, no. No, of course not."

She poured a stream of water onto the hot rocks atop the heater. It evaporated instantly, steam billowing into the sultry air.

Jason was clearly trying not to stare at Elle as she came to sit on the bench, on the other side of his legs from Lili. Elle smiled inwardly, knowing what this young man saw when he looked at her: a six-foot, blue-eyed blonde with a spectacular centerfold body. Spectacular and naked, as was the exotic Lili, with her sheaf of glossy black hair, her drowsily seductive eyes, her golden skin. She was as narrow-waisted as Elle, her breasts not quite as large, but round and high, with nipples the color of wine. In keeping with current fashion, Lili had her pubic hair waxed into a sleek black strip. Elle's was more or less *au naturel,* just neatly trimmed, since anything she did to it when she was a woman would remain that way when she turned back into a man.

"Elle," Lili said, "this is the one I was telling you about, the genius with the wonderful hands."

"You kidding?" he said, holding his hands out in front of him. "They're freakin' pot roasts."

"No, they are *merveilleuse,* so *masculine.*" Lili tended to dial up the French when she was seducing Americans. Twisting around on the bench, her breasts brushing his leg, she took his jumbo-sized left hand in hers and caressed it. He bunched the towel in front of him.

Still holding his hand, Lili said, "Jason, this is my friend Elle. She's been wanting to meet you."

Elle turned and shook hands with Jason. She held on to his hand, grazing the big palm with her thumb; he drew in a breath. "Oh, you're right, Lili. I can feel the strength in it."

Jason looked back and forth between them as they stroked his hands, the wheels turning behind those crème de menthe eyes.

"Are these yours?" Lili asked, lifting the wire-rimmed glasses sitting on the bench next to her. Wincing, she dropped them and blew on her fingers.

"That's why I'm not wearing them," he said.

With a mischievous smile, Elle leaned closer to Lili and stage-whispered, "He can't see us. We can do whatever we want."

"My vision's actually not that . . ." Jason trailed off as Lili touched her mouth to Elle's.

They kissed with genuine passion, a delicate caress of their lips and tongues, their bodies pressed against Jason's legs. Elle cupped Lili's right breast, tugging the nipple erect as Lili fondled Elle's already damp sex. It was a singular pleasure to be touched so intimately by Lili, a pleasure they reserved for when Elle—or Elic—would be taking a human, since that was the only way a dusios could climax. Unless it was foreplay for intercourse, that kind of direct sexual excitation could be frustrating to the point of pain.

The heat of the sauna penetrated Elle's body, making her skin prickle with perspiration and heightening the stimulation of Lili's deft fingers. Her pussy felt sizzling hot, the flesh there ultrasensitized. Lili's skin grew slick to the touch, Elle's hand gliding over it as if it were oiled. Elle stroked a fingertip along the cleft between Lili's legs, which drew a soft moan from her.

Jason said, "Um, do you girls want me to get lost, or . . . ?"

"No, of course not," Lili said in her throatiest bedroom voice, smiling into his eyes as she stroked his leg. "After all, you were here first."

"Then, deal me in." Jason levered himself down onto the bench between Elle and Lili with a self-assurance that Elle found surprising and sexy. He put his arms around both women, who immediately transferred their attention to him, kissing him as they writhed against his big, slippery-hot body.

"Have you ever done this before?" Lili asked him as she ran her fingers lightly up his rigidly erect cock.

"A threesome? Yeah, twice, but those girls didn't hold a candle to you two."

Elle and Lili looked at each other and then at him. They had speculated that the brainy bear was a virgin. Elle had even been prepared to use a *liggia spiall* on him if he proved resistant to seduction, so that he would not only submit willingly but remember it all as a dream. Clearly, no such measure would be needed.

"Coed dorms," he said. "Greatest educational advance of the twentieth century. Listen, I've got some Trojans in my room. I can be there and back in—"

"We don't need them," Elle said. "It's taken care of."

"Um . . . Yeah, but . . ."

"Up to and including the clean bills of health," Lili added. "So just relax and go with it." Elle knew that Jason's stock had just risen even higher in Lili's eyes. A true *gabru* had brains as well as brawn.

Great.

Jason lifted Lili as if she were weightless and sat her astride his lap, facing away from him. "Here, you can lick us both this way," he told Elle. With one arm, he tucked Lili up against him so that his cock was just south of her pussy; with the other, he played with her breasts.

As Elle dropped to her knees on the smooth wooden floor, Lili gave her a wide-eyed smile of delight that said, *Boy, did we underestimate this one.*

Elle pleasured both Lili and Jason with her mouth while stroking her own clit to maintain the intensity of her arousal. When she took him, she should be ready to come, and come well, at the same moment he did. A dusian *transfert de sperme* worked best when all parties involved—the dusios, the harvested male, and the female recipient—experienced powerful, extended orgasms. On the male's part, this produced an especially copious discharge. On the female's, it caused the cervix to spasm, increasing the likelihood of semen being drawn up into the womb.

"Pinch her nipples hard, rolling them a little," Elle told Jason as she finger-fucked Lili. "She likes that."

Lili bucked and cried out as she came. Jason lifted her up a bit, aiming his cock between her legs, but before he could enter her, she rose off him, saying, "Much as I would love to keep you all to myself, *chéri*, it is Elle's turn, *non*?"

Elle went to take Lili's place on Jason's lap, but he had a different idea. He grabbed one of the wedge-shaped wooden backrests, set it flat on the upper bench, and had her lie down on it with her hips on the high end, canting them up. Draping her legs over his thick shoulders, he buried his face between them and proceeded to do things with his tongue that had her moaning and clutching at his hair in short order.

He shoved a thick, long, deliciously calloused finger inside her, located her G-spot in about a second—of course he would, with his knowledge of physiology—and started massaging it in just the right firm, rhythmic way. Lili kissed her, whispering "Let me know when it gets to be too much, *Khababu*."

Elle nodded, clinging to Lili as the pleasure rocketed higher, higher . . . At its breathless, heart-pounding peak, when a mortal woman would be convulsing in orgasm, Elle remained suspended in carnal rapture . . . until she began to sense the inevitable metamorphosis of unrelieved pleasure into pain.

"Now, Lili . . . Oh, make him stop . . ."

"She wants *this* now, *chéri*," Lili told him, reaching between his legs. "She wants it deep and hard. She wants to come with her pussy stretched around this big, beautiful, hard cock."

"God, you girls are *great*." He mounted Elle with one foot braced on the lower bench, guided his cock into her, gripped her shoulders for purchase, and snapped his hips.

He groaned as he filled her, and then with each sharp thrust, droplets flew off his hair. With his size and ferocious energy, it was like being ravished by a sweaty, rutting beast.

Lili, kneeling on the lower bench, reached around Jason to cradle his balls while rubbing the root of his penis just above them. It was what she often did when she helped Elle in extracting a *gabru*'s seed, not to enhance his pleasure—although it certainly did, judging from his groans—but in order to monitor how close he was to orgasm.

When Lili felt his scrotum draw up tight and full, she caught Elle's eye as if to say *Now*, while brushing a fingertip very lightly and rapidly near her clit. She knew just what she was doing, of course. Elle came explosively, as did Jason, who growled, "*Fuck. Oh, fuck*. Oh. Oh. Oh, shit. Fuck. Oh. Oh. Oh . . ."

He sucked in great lungfuls of air as the pulsing of his cock gradually slowed and then stopped. "Holy shit," he gasped through an exhausted chuckle.

They washed up together in the adjacent oversized steam shower. Built to Inigo's specifications—of course—it had walls of amber-colored Venetian marble studded with two dozen massage jets that were adjustable in intensity from "slow pulse" to "acupuncture." There were four wide rain showerheads in the ceiling, a steam generator, two handheld showers, dimmable lights, stereo speakers, and a telephone, all of it controlled by a digital panel that looked as if it belonged on a space station. Built-in seats of different shapes and sizes facilitated sex play, as did the various handholds and trapeze rings.

After about twenty minutes of soaping each other up beneath a steaming rain shower, with Elle and Lili paying special attention to each other's hard-to-reach places, the two women sat Jason on a corner bench with strategically placed jets and went down on him. They were going to finish him that way—in fact, they were having a friendly argument about whose mouth he would shoot into—but the young man had a different idea.

He stood Lili up facing the wall, lifted her a few inches off the floor with a massage jet thrumming directly between her legs, and had her grab a pair of handles near the ceiling. He pushed his cock deep inside her from behind and just stood there unmoving except for an occasional hard squeeze of his ass. Elle kissed them both, tongued his ear, suckled Lili's nipples, fingered his ass . . . Lili climaxed over and over. Jason roared when his orgasm came.

"Damn," he panted afterward, pushing his hair off his face with a shaky hand as he leaned against the wall for support. "You two are gonna ruin me for other girls."

"We tend to have that effect," Elle said.

$\mathcal{S}_{ix}$

$\mathcal{N}$AKED AND HALF-NAKED hippie chicks danced and cavorted around a roaring bonfire in front of the bathhouse around dusk, breasts and faces polished with sweat, gypsy skirts whirling, streams of hair switching this way and that as they spun and laughed and passed their joints around. A few of the guys were dancing, too, beers in hand, as somebody slapped out a drunken rhythm on the lid of the cooler chest.

I was watching not from within their midst, but from the rear of the bathhouse, where I sat against the rock wall near the cave entrance with my own beer bottle, empty for the past half hour, observing the goings-on like an anthropologist studying the ritual of some primitive tribe.

The ceremonial consumption of these intoxicants induces a trancelike euphoria and diminished inhibitions. In this state of intoxication, the clan performs the sacred fertility rite, a period of ecstatic dancing followed by indiscriminate mating.

Said mating had already commenced, judging from the English-accented whispers of the couple lying under an afghan in a far corner of the pillow-strewn bathhouse. They probably didn't think I could hear them, but I'd always had good ears.

"Lizzy, please, baby, let me put it in. An inch, that's all. I just want to feel it inside you."

"No way. I told you, I love George."

"And I love Elaine, but they're both in London. I'm here. Love the one you're with, baby."

"Nigel . . ."

"Come on, Liz, I'm begging you here. My balls are so blue, it's killing me."

"We should never have started this. I should never have let you kiss me."

"Please, baby. I'll make you come like you never—"

"Don't touch me there."

"Your knickers are soaked through. You want it as much as I do. Come on, Lizzy. One inch, that's all. I promise. It's not shagging if it's just an inch. I just want to stick the head in and feel your pussy hugging it, all warm and cozy, and then I'll pull out."

"Yeah, right," Lizzy said, but her next breath emerged as a soft moan.

"You like when I do that?" Nigel asked. "Right there? Mm, I can feel your clit right through your knickers."

She gasped. "Oh, God. Oh . . ."

They kissed for a while, her breath coming faster and faster; his, too. I lit a cigarette, acting like I had no idea what was going on over there, knowing I shouldn't be listening in, but doing it anyway for the vicarious stimulation—purely mental, of course. If Old Sparky had any voltage left, I would have been sitting there with a boner. Or I wouldn't have been sitting there at all. I'd be off somewhere with one of those bonfire chicks, balling my brains out.

Actually, I wouldn't have even been at Grotte Cachée. I would have been back in Chicago with Lucinda, making love or whispering in the dark, or curled up with my face in her hair. She had the silkiest hair I'd ever touched, and it had a pronounced, sweetly herbal scent from the shampoo she used. It was a popular shampoo with a strong fragrance, so I'd catch a whiff from time to time when I was walking down the street or whatever. Every time, it made my heart beat so hard my chest would hurt.

"Lift your bum a bit so I can get these off you," Nigel whispered.

"Just . . . Just so you can touch me, right? You're not gonna . . ."

"Not if you don't want me to."

I saw movement beneath the afghan, heard the rustle of feathers in the pillows they were lying on, then him saying "Oh, God, Lizzie, you feel so good. How's this? You like being touched like this, nice and slow?"

She nodded, breathing raggedly. After a minute or so of kissing and petting, both of them breathless now, she said, "Wh-What are you—?"

"It's just my finger. Oh, man, you're so wet. God, Liz, you're so fucking sexy. I'm so hot for you. I swear, I'm gonna explode."

There came the metallic grating of a zipper.

"Nigel—"

"I just want to show you what you've done to me. Here, give me your hand."

"I don't think—"

"Feel that? It's aching for you, baby. It wants to be inside you. Feel how hard it is."

"Mm . . . Yeah, but—"

"Just one inch," he pleaded. "Just the tip." She must have shaken her head, because he said, "Let me rub it against you, then, slide it along the slit. No harm in that, is there?"

"Um . . ."

"Like this." More shifting around, him getting on top of her with his hair hanging down. "Open your legs. It's all right, you'll see. Am I heavy?"

"No."

"Ah," he said gruffly, the pillows rustling in a slow rhythm now. "Oh, yeah. How's that feel? Good?"

"Yeah," she breathed.

I homed in on a distant figure beyond the bonfire. It was Madeleine, strolling out of the darkness on the path from the château, a beer bottle in her hand. She was wearing the same sleek blue dress she'd had on earlier, but she'd ditched the platforms. This was the first I'd seen of her since leaving Morel's office that afternoon. Emmett still hadn't returned, so I'd been flying solo for the past six or seven hours.

I waved to catch Madeleine's attention, then raised my empty beer bottle and turned it upside down with a plaintive expression. She veered off toward the bonfire to snag another beer from the guys manning the cooler chest.

"Are you close?" Nigel whispered. "Are you gonna come?"

She nodded, her breaths coming in whimpery little pants.

Stilling, he said, "I want to feel it. I want to feel your pussy squeezing my cock when you come."

"Don't stop now. Oh, God, Nigel . . ."

"Let me put it in, Lizzy, just an inch, just so—"

"Yes, all right, do it. Just . . . *Oh*," she moaned.

"God, but you feel incredible," he growled. "Oh, fuck . . ."

"Don't stop moving," she implored. "Please, I'm so close."

"If I move, I'll go in deeper, and I don't know if you want me to—"

"Oh, God, just do it. Just fuck me. Just— *Yes,*" she said as he began thrusting in earnest. "Oh, God, harder. *Harder.* Oh . . . oh . . ."

I chuckled. *Well played, Nigel, old man.*

I grabbed a pillow and set it next to me as Madeleine circled the pool with that leggy, feline walk of hers, her half-empty beer dangling from one hand, my full one from the other. She turned and lowered herself onto the pillow in one fluid motion, holding my beer out of my reach when I went to take it. "Trade you for another smoke."

"Deal."

As I lit Madeleine's cigarette, I could see by the trembling glow from my match that her eyes were a little puffy. "You been crying?" I asked.

"Hours ago, but I've got the kind of face that shows it for, like, days."

"Morel?"

A cloud of smoke emerged on her sigh. In a broad imitation of *le seigneur*'s accent, she said, " 'You are very beautiful, but, how you say, not quite beautiful enough.' "

"He didn't say that." I took a swig of the beer; it was bitingly cold.

Madeleine drew on her cigarette, squinting at the heaving afghan in the dark corner. "Looks like Nigel finally wore Lizzy down."

"He could give lessons. What did Morel really say?"

"He said he was in love with his wife."

"Well, you've got to respect that."

"Of course you'd say that. You're an old soul, very mature, very into duty and honor."

"How would you know? You've just met me."

"Well, you *are* in the Army, but—"

"Air Force."

"But that's not why I know that about you. It's your aura."

I groaned. "You realize you sound just like Bernie."

"Bernie doesn't know shit about auras *or* chakras. He's picked up a few phrases and now he uses them to get laid. Me, I've always been able to see auras, and over time, I've learned to interpret them. Yours tells me several things. It tells me you're wounded. It tells me you have secrets."

I studied her eyes, trying to figure out if she was bullshitting me, or if she was for real.

She stroked my face. And then she kissed me, or tried to. She touched her lips to mine.

I backed away.

"Okay, *why?*" she demanded, her voice quavering. "What's the matter with me?"

"There's nothing the matter with you, Madeleine. You *are* beautiful. You're really sexy. I don't know, I guess maybe you're just not my type." I winced inside at how lame that sounded.

She looked incredulous, as well she might have. Madeleine Lamb, with her Botticelli hair and her come-hither attitude, was every man's type.

"What *is* your type?" she asked.

Lucinda's face materialized in my mind's eye: brown hair, brown eyes, standard nose, standard mouth . . . But put it all together with that smile of hers, that silly laugh, that warm, bottomless gaze, and it absolutely undid me.

I must have hesitated too long. Madeleine said, "Go to hell," and walked away.

Seven

"YOU REALLY THINK I need to use the *liggia spiall* on her?" Elle asked as she and Lili stood in the hall outside Isabel's room later that night, both of them in silk robes with their wet hair in ponytails. "Why don't we just explain that I've harvested the 'high-quality spermatozoa' she's looking for, and that all I have to do is transfer it to her, and she can have a child who's not only genetically superior, but gifted, to boot?"

When Elle reversed The Change and became Elic again, the semen he'd captured from Jason would end up in his seminal vesicles in an enhanced form. This *zeru*, as Lili called it, having become infused with certain psychic qualities, would ensure that any child born to the worthy female, or *arkhutu*, who received it, would have the Gift. The only other way to produce a gifted child was through the union of two gifted parents.

With a slightly impatient sigh, Lili said, "Problem is, there's only one way for a dusios to transfer *zeru* to an *arkhutu*, and that is through sexual intercourse. You know how human women feel about sex, Elle. It always becomes so dreadfully complicated. Do you really expect Isabel to just lie back and spread her legs for you?"

"But if she wants a baby that badly—"

"She does," Lili said, "and that's why you need to do this discreetly, without giving her the opportunity to freak out over it. And you have to do it now, because chances are you won't have another opportunity. Once Emmett is gone . . ." She shook her head, her eyes glazing over with moisture.

Elle took Lili in her arms, kissed her forehead. "I know. I know, *mins Ástgurdís.*" It was never easy, watching a beloved human depart his mortal form.

"Once he's gone," Lili said, "and it will be soon, we both know that, it's quite possible we'll never see Isabel again."

Although Emmett still assumed that Isabel intended to succeed him as *administrateur,* she had made it clear to Adrien and the rest of them that she had no intention of doing so, thus bringing the curtain down on her family's two and a half centuries of devoted service to the *gardiens* of Grotte Cachée.

In contemplating her motives, one couldn't help but conclude that there was bad blood between Isabel and Adrien. Until her father's illness, she hadn't visited Grotte Cachée for nineteen years. She'd been a frequent guest since then, of course, but she and Adrien always seemed a bit standoffish with each other. The fact that he stayed in the hunting lodge during her visits suggested that it was he, not she, who was at the source of their "cold war."

For whatever reason, Adrien didn't like her, but out of respect for her father, he had kept that dislike to himself. Nor had he confided as much to Elic, although the two of them had developed a close friendship over the past couple of decades. Of all the *gardiens* that Grotte Cachée had seen during the 2,061 years in which Elic had been living there, Adrien was the most compatible with him in terms of temperament and interests. They often hung out in the library together in the afternoons, reading and shooting the breeze. But whenever Isabel's name came up, Adrien somehow always got around to changing the subject. Lili was undoubtedly right in thinking that Isabel would never visit Grotte Cachée after her father was gone; why should she?

"Do it tonight, my love," Lili said. "She'll thank you later."

"So you think I should tell her . . . after?"

"Only if she becomes pregnant, and we should know that within a day or two. *Le seigneur* will see it in her aura—he'll tell us. Since she doesn't have a boyfriend right now, she'll be wondering how it happened, no?"

With a sigh of capitulation, Elle crouched on the floor facing away from Lili, who hated to watch this, closed her eyes, and whispered the "return ticket" incantation. Her stomach churned as organs shifted and bones and muscles enlarged; bile rose in her throat, and she was overtaken by violent trembling. The first dozen or so times she'd done this, as a youth, she'd vomited. She'd trained herself to master the Change Sickness by breathing deeply and steadily, but it was still an utterly wretched feeling.

Her skin stretched to fit the larger, more solid body, except for the breasts, which tightened up. The strangest sensation— but the most comforting—was that of her genital organs rearranging themselves into their male counterparts, especially the expansion of her nerve-packed clit into the heavy, less sensitive but far more familiar penis.

Elic rose slowly to his feet, holding on to the wall for support as he reacquainted himself with the altered center of gravity and the extra height. He reached through the opening of his robe to feel his cock and balls. As usual, he was already half erect from the internal pressure of his burgeoning cache of seminal fluid, both Jason's and his own. He would be even hornier than usual until he emptied his poor, swollen vesicles, which could only happen through ejaculation in a human female.

"They're still there," Lili said with a chuckle. "They're always still there, always the same size and shape, yet every time, the first thing you do is check to make sure you've gotten them back safe and sound."

"If you were male," he said as he massaged and rotated his shoulders, "you would understand."

Elic cracked open the door to *la Salle de Pré*, a romantic Victorian-style bower with dark gothic furniture and wallpaper scattered with wild pansies, Queen Anne's lace, and meadow sage, to find both bedside lamps turned on. It amused Elic that this particular guest room—a suite, actually, with a sitting room and bathroom—was where a self-styled "dazzling urbanite" like Isabel chose to stay when she was at Grotte Cachée.

"Déjà vu," said Elic as they stood over the high four-post bed with its lacy white canopy and crocheted bedspread, which had clearly not been slept in that evening. "Doesn't anyone sleep any—"

The door to the bathroom opened and Isabel walked out wrapped in a towel, scrubbing her wet hair with another one. It hung over her face, so she didn't realize Elic and Lili were there until he said her name.

She screamed and dropped the towel, backing up frantically. Her damp, crazily tousled hair made her panic look almost cartoonish.

"Shh, Isabel. Shh." Elic seized her wrists and closed a hand over her mouth, hoping she hadn't awakened anyone.

There came a muffled exclamation from behind his hand that sounded like *"What the fuck?"*

"It's all right, Isabel," Lili assured her in a soothing tone. "It's just us."

Isabel relaxed a bit as she looked back and forth between them, but her expression was one of utter bewilderment. Lili gave Elic a pointed look, as if to say *What are you waiting for?*

Removing his hand from Isabel's mouth, Elic touched her forehead and whispered the Old Norse words that would render her compliant and turn her memory of this night into a dream. *"Láta, liggia."*

"What's that?" Isabel asked. "What are you saying? What does that mean?"

Elic and Lili exchanged a look. The *liggia spiall* should have made her instantly tranquil, unquestioning, malleable. It always worked on the first try.

Always.

"Is that a spell?" Isabel asked. "Oh, my God, tell me that's not one of your sex spells."

Gripping her upper arm, Elic pressed a hand to her forehead and tried a different but similar *spiall*. *"Hlýðni . . ."*

She wrenched away from him and backed up into the bathroom, hands raised as if to ward off his Follet sorcery. "You have got to be kidding," she said, gaping at them. "I mean, you have *got* to be fucking kidding me."

He took a step toward her, saying "Isabel—"

"Get the fuck away from me," she said, grabbing a can of hairspray off the vanity and aiming it at him. "I'll use this. I'll spray it right in your eyes."

"Isabel, have you been crying?" Lili asked.

Elic took a closer look at Isabel, seeing the swollen eyes and shiny red nose. "She *has* been crying."

"No I haven't," Isabel said, but he could hear it in her voice now, that telltale damp nasality.

"Is it your father?" Lili asked.

"No, it's . . . it's nothing."

Lili said, "It's Adrien Morel, isn't it?"

Isabel looked at her sharply.

"You shouldn't be letting him get to you like this," said Lili, rubbing Isabel's arm, "especially given what you're going through with your father right now. Human beings are complicated. Sometimes there's just no telling why they do what they do or feel what they feel. He probably thinks he has some reason for not liking you, but—"

"Wait. What?"

"We know," Elic said. "We can see how he acts with you, how he avoids you."

"Right," Isabel said with a bitter little chuckle. "Of course. Listen, I haven't been crying 'cause Adrien doesn't like me."

"Then what's the matter?" Elic asked.

"What's the *matter*?" Isabel repeated. "As in, what's the matter with *me*?"

"Well . . ."

"*I'm* not the one trying to use fucking hoo-doo voodoo to get in the pants of someone you have *absolutely* no business messing around with that way," she said, an edge of hysteria in voice. "Geez Louise, what's *wrong* with you people? Oh, wait. You're not people. *That's* what's wrong with you. You're X-rated elves and fairies—sorry, *gods and goddesses*—who have to get your rocks off twenty-four-seven or you shrivel up and die, but never fear, you get your fuckmates delivered hot and fresh right to your door, and you don't even have to fucking *date,* which isn't remotely fucking fair. You just hole up here fucking and sucking, sucking and fucking. The fucking Freak Family Robinson."

She slammed the can of hairspray down, her whole face red now, not just her eyes and nose.

"Not fairies," Elic said.

"What?" Isabel said.

"None of us is a fairy. Fairies aren't even that into sex."

"Well, the rusalki," Lili said.

"The rusalki aren't really fairies," Elic said. "They're more like psychopathic, sex-crazed water nymphs."

"What are nymphs but fairies?" Lili asked.

"Can I *please* get out of this bathroom?" Isabel said.

"Sorry," Elic said when he realized he and Lili had been blocking the door.

They stepped aside so that Isabel could stalk into her bedroom, her palms pressed to her forehead. "I cannot *fucking* believe you were trying to *fuck* me."

"Your father's right," Elic said. "You really do swear like a cutter."

"I'm trying to do better," Isabel said as she sank wearily into an ornately carved throne chair, "but my God, when you step out of the shower and find a couple of supernatural sex hounds lying in wait for you . . ."

"I understand how you feel," Lili told her, "but you should know that we didn't come here for prurient motives."

"Oh, like you have any other kind."

"We came here to make you pregnant," Elic said.

Isabel cocked her head, narrowing her eyes at him.

Shooting Elic that look that said he was being his usual goonlike masculine self, Lili explained their scheme to extract Jason MacKenna's superior DNA and use it to impregnate Isabel with a gifted child.

"You were trying to make me *pregnant*?" Isabel said.

"That's what I *said*," replied Elic, who sometimes just didn't get this whole female beating-about-the-bush thing.

Isabel shook her head, smiling as if at some private joke. "Um . . . hate to tell you, guys, but your timing could not possibly have been any worse."

"It doesn't matter where you are in your cycle," Lili said. "The *zeru* tweaks your hormones and triggers the release of an egg, so your chances of conceiving are actually excellent."

"She's about to ovulate anyway," Elic said.

"Wait—how do you know that?" Isabel asked.

He tapped his nose. "Pheromones."

"Okay, *eeeuw*. So you were just gonna pull the old abracadabra and do the deed while I was in some kind of trance or whatever? I know you guys mean well, but frankly, I'm really glad the spell didn't work. Are some people, like, immune to that shit? That *stuff*," she corrected. "I really am trying."

Lili said, "You don't know what it means when a Follet's enchantment doesn't work on a human?"

Isabel shrugged. "Dad has filled me in on some of this stuff, and I've read the first volume of Adrien's *Secret History*, but that was just about Brantigern Anextlo— what's-his-name, and the Gallic Wars and all that. Why? What does it mean?"

It meant that Isabel was gifted. She might not realize it, but it was indisputable. The only humans who were resistant to enchantment by a Follet were those with the Gift.

Lili looked to Elic as if to say *What do we tell her?* Isabel must know, having read Volume I of the *Histoire Secrète de Grotte Cachée,* in which Brantigern himself tackled this particular issue, that it took two gifted parents, not just one, to produce a gifted child. Isabel's mother had the Gift, but Emmett did not. Elic knew this with absolute assurance, having demonstrated some spells on him at his request when he first took over the administration of Grotte Cachée.

If they were to reveal Isabel's giftedness to her, she would know that Emmett Archer, whom she had grown up calling

"Dad," and whom she was in the process of losing, wasn't actually her father.

"Some humans are not susceptible to our incantations," Lili said, her little shrug suggesting that the reason for this was a mystery, when it was anything but. "You, er, probably shouldn't mention this—our trying to put a spell on you, and so forth— to your father. He might find it . . . disconcerting."

"He's going through enough," Isabel said. "He doesn't need to know about this."

Elic said, "You know, even though we can't use the *liggia spiall* on you, I can still give you a baby, if you really want one."

"A *gifted* baby," Lili added.

"Um, yeah, well, when I said your timing was bad, I didn't really mean . . . Well, it's not about my cycle. This just isn't the right time. Tell you what. If I reach the point where I'm, like, staring menopause in the face and I still haven't managed to get one in the oven, I'll take you up on the offer."

"A rain check," Elic said. "You got it."

As he and Lili were walking back down the hall after taking their leave of Isabel, Elic said, "Do you think Emmett knows?"

Shaking her head, Lili said, "Not from the way he was talking about Madeleine at lunch today. He was talking about that weekend in 'seventy-two when she came here with those friends of hers—you remember."

Elic smiled. "Inigo's bed. We painted that guitar on you, and there were a couple of art students, that little ballerina . . . Oh, and Hitch. Of course I remember."

"Well, apparently Madeleine and Emmett started seeing each other right after they got back to London, and Isabel was born nine months later. He called Madeleine a 'free spirit,' implying that they started sleeping together pretty much immediately. Two months later, she told him she was pregnant and they were married."

244 • Louisa Burton

"Except the baby wasn't his. Do you suppose she ever told him the truth?" Elic asked.

"It didn't sound that way. She wouldn't be the only woman who ever pulled that one on an unsuspecting, besotted boyfriend."

"Thank God I'm not human. Way too much melodrama and not enough screwing. Speaking of which . . ." Elic cupped his aching balls with an expression of mock agony.

"On to Plan B," Lili said.

"Okay, Elic, let me get this straight," said Grace Garvey, sitting up in bed in a white "wifebeater" tank, her stubby little bleached dreadlocks pulled back by a stretchy headband. "You're offering to impregnate me with blond, blue-eyed, smart-ass DNA to match Laura's so that we can have the half Barbadian, half Aryan, café au lait lambkin of our dreams and live happily ever after."

"Well, green-eyed," said Elic, picturing Jason.

"But you have blue eyes," Grace said.

"I keep telling him they're blue." Lili, sitting next to Elic at the foot of Grace's bed, shot him a look. "He keeps insisting they're sea green."

"I don't see a turkey baster sticking out of the pocket of that robe," Grace told Elic.

"Ah. Yes, well . . . I'm afraid it won't really work that way."

"Meaning . . . ?"

"I can't, you know"—he gestured vaguely in the area of his crotch—"in an inanimate object."

In response to Grace's skeptically cocked eyebrow, Lili said, "No, it's true. He can't even come from oral sex, or if I . . ." She stroked her fist back and forth. "He's all about the vagina."

Not that he'd go the turkey baster route even if he could.

Grace's scrubbed-clean, just-awakened face had the quirky prettiness of a couture fashion model. She had just the right amount of muscle shaping her arms, and perfect little breasts that he couldn't wait to taste.

Grace nodded to Lili. "And *you're* here because . . .?"

"Oh. Well . . . We thought perhaps because you're, you know, not really that into men . . ."

With a little laugh, Grace said, "*There's* an understatement. You thought I'd be more into it with you here to, er . . . rev up the old libido, eh?"

Lili gave Grace her most deliciously seductive smile. "Something like that."

Grace, although a prime *arkhutu*—smart, beautiful, and maternal—wasn't remotely the sure thing, in terms of seduction, that Jason had been. In cases where a human's cooperation in the *transfert de sperme* wasn't a given, Elic would usually resort to his *liggia spiall*—unless the use of enchantment was likely to create more problems than it solved. In Grace's case, she would be utterly flummoxed upon finding herself pregnant, given that she didn't even sleep with men. Far from being thrilled, she might conclude, based upon her "dream" of having had sex with Elic, that she'd been the victim of a date rape drug, in which case she was likely to terminate the pregnancy. She might even report the incident to the authorities, which could be disastrous for him. That left seduction as Elic's only practical option, with Lili there to sweeten the deal, as it were.

"I thought you two were an item," Grace said.

"We're not exclusive," Lili responded.

"And you're what—bi?"

"More or less." Actually, discounting Elle, Lili wasn't that interested in making love to other women—unless she knew it would excite Elic or her *gabru* du jour, in which case she approached it with cheerful enthusiasm. Elic, when he was Elle, found both men and women intensely arousing. In his primary male persona, it was strictly women, since that was the only way he could climax. Inigo preferred women, "but my cock isn't always so particular," and Darius would absorb the desires of any human who touched him.

"Yeah, well, not only is this whole thing just a wee bit mad," Grace said, "I'm afraid it's the wrong time of the month for me to conceive. I won't be ovulating till . . ." She did some swift fingertip calculating. ". . . the twenty-second at the earliest."

"That's five days from now," Lili said. "Sperm can stay alive that long."

Grace said, "Yeah, but the longer the interval between sex and ovulation, the less likely it is that any sperm will actually fertilize the egg."

Elic groaned inwardly. He had to pick a *nurse*.

Lili said, "From what you were telling us at lunch today about how hard it is to find a man who's interested in fathering a child—the right kind of man, anyway—I should think you'd want to take Elic up on his offer and see what happens."

Grace cast him a speculative look.

"Have you ever made love to a man?" he asked.

"Oh, sure," she said, "when I was young and stupid and didn't realize the reason I liked girls was 'cause I liked girls. Last time was a good fifteen years ago."

"So it's almost like you're a virgin," Lili said. "Elic is wonderful with virgins."

"I promise it will be good for you," he said.

"It doesn't have to be good," she said. "All I care about is getting your little swimmers where they belong."

"So, you'll do it?" Lili said.

"With *him*," Grace said. "You've got to go."

"Oh."

"It's Laura," Grace explained. "If I come home and tell her I bonked a tall, blond Viking in the hopes of having a baby with some resemblance to her, well, it might give her pause, but she'll be okay with it—more than okay if I actually end up pregnant. But if I tell her you were there, keeping the furnace stoked . . ." She appraised Lili with a wistfully lustful expression. "Well, that would be cheating with another woman, and we don't do that. And we don't lie to each other, either, so I'm afraid it's not to be, but don't think I don't appreciate the offer."

After Lili had kissed Elic goodbye and left, he rose and said, "Would you like me to turn off the light?"

"Yes. No." She thought about it, holding the blanket in front of her chest. "Yes."

He turned it off, slipped his robe to the floor, and climbed under the covers. Without touching her yet, so as to let her get used to his presence next to her, he said, "I know you don't care about it being good for you—you probably don't even want it to be good for you—but with your knowledge of reproductive physiology, I'm sure you're aware that conception is more likely if the woman climaxes at about the same time as the man."

Her response was a long sigh.

"And of course," he continued, lightly stroking her arm, "it will facilitate penetration if you're wet."

He heard her swallow.

He let his hand graze the side of her breast through her tank top. She drew in a breath, but didn't move away from him.

"You won't be sorry," he murmured as he caressed her breast, lightly thumbing the nipple.

Through a low chuckle as she turned toward him, she said, "I'm beginning to get that idea."

Eight

"$\mathcal{I}$S IT TRUE you can deep throat a guy, like in the movie? Doobie told me you—*Oh*. Oh, God. Oh, my God, Lili. Fuck, yeah. Take it all. Suck it deep . . ." It was a guttural whisper from somewhere in the heaps of bodies surrounding me, maybe twenty, thirty feet away, but I heard it like it was breathed right into my ear.

About an hour had passed since Madeleine got pissed and cut out. Having tired of the bonfire, most of the Gangsters had retreated into the bathhouse, where they lit candles and sticks of incense, Pieter playing a guitar and Diane a recorder while the others lay around on pillows toking up and drinking and getting frisky.

I still sat slumped against the rock wall, smoking cigarettes and tapping the ashes into my empty beer bottle as I waited for Emmett to come back. I didn't talk to anybody, just sat there taking in the scene, watching the candles glint like stars amid a dark, slowly roiling kaleidoscope of batik and tie-dye, hair and arms and legs . . .

Tap . . . tap . . . tap . . .

It felt almost as if time itself had been dialed down to a slower speed. Every time I raised or lowered my cigarette, the red-hot tip drew a line of fluorescence that hovered in the darkness for a second before fading away. I wasn't remotely drunk; I'd had, like, two beers in as many hours. I started wondering if maybe I was getting off on all the pot smoke in the air, 'cause my thoughts were getting pretty damn slippery, except I'd smoked pot a couple of times, and it didn't feel anything like this.

I decided it had just been a long, strange day at the tail end of a long, strange weekend. I was tired and bored, but too paralyzed by ennui to get up and make my way out of here and back to the château. The way I was feeling, I'd just end up tripping over everybody, anyway.

As summer evenings go, it was fairly cool, which may have been why there was just one couple in the pool, Elic and a voluptuous chick wearing a leather thong as a headband. She appeared to be sitting on the submerged bench. He was kneeling between her legs, the two of them holding each other close, hardly moving. She had on a white bikini, or at least the top of it, so I wouldn't have known what was going on if I hadn't heard her whispering, in a shuddery pre-orgasmic way, "That's it . . . that's it. Keep it slow, just like that. Grind against my clit. Yeah . . . oh, yeah, oh God . . ."

Her whisper was just one of many reverberating off the marble walls, filling my skull with a hubbub of conversations and low moans, the sucking of joints and cigarettes and cocks, the fleshy kiss of lips, skin rubbing against skin, grunts, endearments, entreaties . . .

"Slow down. Let's come at the same time." It was the whispered, breathless voice of Inigo, who'd been messing around with a pretty little thing named Maria. "All three of us."

I took a closer look and saw that someone else had, indeed, joined them under their ubiquitous Indian throw. It was dark even with the candles, but I recognized the third person by his superblack hair and his height as Prince Valiant. The three of them lay snugged up together on their sides, moving to the same laid-back cadence. With two guys and a girl, you'd expect the girl to be the meat of the sandwich, but it was Inigo in the middle, screwing Maria face-to-face with Val tucked up behind him.

No fucking way, I thought, but through the thin throw, I could see Val's ass pumping in a slow, undeniably carnal rhythm as he reached around Inigo to squeeze and caress Maria's ass. "So, are ye bisexual, then?" he asked Inigo in a husky, slightly strained brogue.

Inigo shook his head. "Hedonist. I like girls, but man, I gotta tell you, having a big, thick cock inside you when you've got your own big, thick cock inside a nice tight, sweet pussy . . . I'm telling you, it doesn't get much better."

All righty, then. I lifted the beer bottle to my mouth, forgetting that it was empty but for ashes and butts, and *Whoooaaa* . . . When I lowered it, I wasn't just seeing double, but triple, quadruple, quintuple, and on and on, a whole waterfall of shimmery green bottles.

What the fuck?

Okay, so it wasn't the beer and it wasn't a contact high. I'd smoked opium in 'Nam once, and it wasn't like that, either. No mellowness, no somnolent bliss. Quite the opposite, in fact. I was starting to feel seriously fucked up.

So, if it wasn't a drug . . .

"Hitch, did you hear me?" a woman said softly.

I looked and saw Jo, my eager-beaver playmate from that afternoon's body-painting session, cuddling under an afghan nearby with Willow. Only, they were doing more than cuddling, as I discovered when Jo lifted the afghan and said, "Join us."

Jo had her Wimbledon College T-shirt tugged up above her breasts, her fatigue pants bunched around one ankle. Willow still had on the see-through peasant blouse she'd been wearing when Bernie read her chakras earlier, but she was naked from the waist down. The two girls were locked together with their legs entwined, rubbing their pussies together.

"We need a nice, hard cock to play with," whispered Willow as she thrust her hips, leaving ghostly shadows.

Oh, shit.

"Please, Hitch?" Jo implored, eyeing me seductively as she plucked one of her friend's hard little nipples through the diaphanous blouse. "I won't be bossy, I promise. We're both so wet already, you won't have to do anything but put it in us—first one, then the other. We'll come in seconds, I guarantee you."

"And then give you a nice long massage," Willow purred, "your back and then your front—a very thorough massage. We'll use our tongues."

"We'll lick you slowly and softly," Jo said, "no sucking, no matter how hard you beg us, just licking, till you're so crazy from it that you just grab one of us and shove it in our mouth and spew like a fucking geyser."

Yeah, good luck with that.

This was every man's dream, two scorching blondes begging for it, talking dirty, raring to go, and there I sat with my limp dick and my galloping dementia, and they were staring at me, their smiles turning perplexed, disappointed.

"Something wrong?" Jo asked.

Only that I was a fucking eunuch in the middle of a nervous breakdown, trying to figure out how to turn down two sex bombs who wanted to fuck and suck my brains out.

Jo and Willow looked at each other.

"You stoned?" Willow asked.

If only. I shook my head before realizing that would have been the perfect excuse, being too stoned to function, if only I'd had the presence of mind to grab at it. "Um . . ."

I lifted my beer bottle to buy a few seconds, groaned at the cascade of iridescent green afterimages, and put it down, and one of the girls whispered, "Fucked up," and the other one said, "I didn't see him smoke anything," and I thought, *They know.* They know I'm not just stoned or drunk, they know I'm fucked in the head.

Tap tap tap . . .

They know. They all knew, not just the girls, 'cause they weren't the only ones staring now. They all saw me there, cowering against the wall, afraid to get up and pick my way through this minefield of writhing, glowing bodies to get out of here, 'cause I didn't think I could manage that, not in the state of mind I was, not with all their grinning faces looking at me like they knew I was crazy, but they had *no idea* how fucking crazy I really was.

". . . scorched . . ."

". . . Vietnam. That's how they get."

All the whispers, no matter how far away, I heard them all, an atonal chorus of hisses and snickers and mutters, and of course the tapping, growing louder and louder . . .

Tap tap tap tap tap . . .

It was like being back in that fucking black box, crouching there in the dark with my fists pressed to my ears, trying desperately to block it all out.

Just breathe, I told myself. *Don't think, just breathe.*

"There it is! Catch it!"

Four guys ran into the bathhouse amid screams and shrieks of laughter, stumbling over the people lying there, leaving jerky streams of afterimages in their wake, chasing a cat, that gray cat from before, as it darted this way and that, skirting bodies.

"I got it!" someone yelled. "Wait. What the fuck?"

"Where is it? Where'd it go?"

"Hey, check it out, it's John Wayne Hitchens." It was Bernie, gesturing toward me with his beer bottle.

Shit. Driven by primal instinct, I rose to my feet without even thinking about it, 'cause thinking wasn't exactly on the agenda, and stepped in front of the cave entrance so there wasn't a wall at my back. My arms were at my sides, hands ready, brain not remotely ready, short-circuited wires in there, twitching and crackling.

Not a good time for this. Not a good fucking time at all.

"Having a good time?" Bernie asked, fixing those sly eyes on me as he took a slug out of his beer bottle. "Having a good fucking time, are we? You look a bit peaked, actually. Doesn't he look peaked?"

His friends agreed that I looked peaked.

I knew I should say something so I didn't look like some kind of zombie just standing there staring at them.

"Cat got your tongue?" Bernie asked. "What are you staring at? You look like a fucking zombie."

"What?" I said.

"I said you look like a zombie."

"But I was just thinking that."

Bernie and his friends erupted in laughter, weird hysterical laughter, their lips drawn back to show their teeth, barking like hyenas in the night, toying with their prey.

"Keep on truckin' there, Hitchens," said Bernie as he turned and led his slobbering pack out of the bathhouse.

"Happy trails," one of them called out, and they screamed with laughter as the night swallowed them up.

I was standing now. That was something. But the prospect

of negotiating my way to the door of the bathhouse through all those bodies, all those eyes now staring directly at me . . .

Not my imagination. They were really staring, just staring like I was something in a zoo.

"You all right, man?" The voice sounded funny. An accent. Pieter.

Man? I sure as hell didn't feel like much of a man, standing there like an idiot in the middle of an orgy, for God's sake, with no way to take part even if I wanted to, thanks to the extra-special attention my captors had paid to Sparky and the boys during that savage post-escape beating. Clubs, boots, that iron rod . . .

"Hitch?" A woman's voice. "Are you—"

I turned and bolted into the cave, ducking through the opening and running right into someone who was sitting there. I stumbled and fell, hearing him grunt as I slammed a knee into his chest, me kicking his legs as I went down.

"Sorry," I said as I sat up on the floor of packed earth. "I didn't see you . . ."

I still didn't see him. There was no one there, although I swore I could hear footsteps retreating into the cave.

Oh, shit. I was gone. I'd completely and totally lost it.

Nine

B Y MORNING, THE rain had ceased and the sky had cleared. Adrien awoke to find his bedroom ablaze with sunshine. He rolled over carefully, so as not to awaken Isabel, but her side of the bed was empty.

He donned his dressing gown and slippers and checked the bathroom. She wasn't there, nor did she answer when he called her name down the hall.

He went downstairs, thinking she might have decided to make *him* breakfast. The kitchen was empty, as was the rest of the ground floor. He even checked the gardens surrounding the lodge, although he didn't expect to find her out there; it was sunny, but chilly.

She was gone. She'd gotten up during the night and left. Slipped away without even saying goodbye. Of course, she hadn't been too keen on sleeping there in the first place, ostensibly because it would only draw them closer together. It was all right to have sex, but not to share a bed and enjoy breakfast together in the morning. So much for their twelve stolen hours, their crêpes and berries and orange juice and big pot of strong coffee.

Adrien returned to the kitchen and set about making his usual small pot of coffee for himself. He put some water on to boil, ground up a handful of beans, got his press pot out of the cabinet over the vintage enameled stove, and hurled it at the opposite wall, where it cracked in a burst of glass shards.

"*Zut!*" Adrien kicked the stove, smashing his three smallest toes into its corner. He could feel the little bones splinter and crumple within the slipper-clad foot.

He dropped to the floor, bellowing "*Merde! Zut! Merde!*"

For a minute, he lay on his back grinding fists into his forehead as if that would help to stifle the pain in his foot. "*Crétin,*" he growled. "*Imbécile.*

He sat up, wincing as he pulled off the slipper, already snug from the swelling on the right side of his foot. By grabbing on to the stove, he managed to haul himself to his feet. Gritting his teeth, he limped over to the phone, snatched it from its cradle, and punched the button for the gatehouse.

"*Bonjour, mon seigneur.*" It was Mike. "*Puis-je vous aider?*"

"*Pouvez-vous me conduire à l'hôpital?*" Adrien said. "I broke my damn foot."

It wasn't until the sun had set the following night that Adrien made it back to the château.

He hobbled into the courtyard on his booted black walking cast, over which he wore a pair of blue jeans with the side seam of the right leg split from knee to ankle. Not wanting to ruin any of his good trousers, he'd dug the ratty, twenty-year-old jeans out of an attic trunk, along with the wrinkled and threadbare Rolling Stones T-shirt and denim jacket he'd put on simply because they'd been underneath the jeans.

On coming back to the hunting lodge from the hospital yesterday afternoon, he'd turned off his cell phone, unplugged the landline, and lain down for a fourteen-hour nap. For the past thirty-six hours, he hadn't shaved, combed his hair, or consumed much more than a half bottle of Grey Goose, a hunk of Saint-Nectaire, and a desiccated old baguette. Nor had he bathed, although he did brush his teeth and splash some water on his face before heading over here to check on Emmett.

The *administrateur*'s aura had dimmed considerably over the past few days. It was irresponsible and shamefully self-indulgent of Adrien to have stayed away so long. Three fractured metatarsals and an aching heart were really rather trifling in the greater scheme of things.

The courtyard was swathed in shadow, its only illumination being the light from a scattering of windows, so when Adrien noticed a faint radiance on the balcony of Emmett's apartment, he stopped and stared up at it. It was an aura, the aura of a woman reclining on a chaise longue facing away from him. He couldn't see anything of her but an afghan with the shape of a pair of legs under it, but the corona of light shimmering around her was unusually vivid.

What struck him wasn't just its silvery color, which was a definitive indicator of pregnancy, but the tiny sparks sputtering within ribbons of light that undulated slowly, like aurorae borealis. The aurorae meant that the child within her womb was a male.

The sparks meant he was gifted.

Adrien didn't have his watch on, but it seemed to him that Inigo's little redheaded playmate, Chloe, should have started her overnight shift by now. It would appear that Elic had taken a turn with her after "tapping" some *gabru,* though why he would have chosen to transfer precious *zeru* to Chloe, when there were far more worthy women available . . .

Something fell from the chaise onto the floor of the balcony—a book. The notion of Chloe turning pages in anything more challenging than *Cosmopolitan* was so unlikely that Adrien realized, with considerable relief, that the lucky *arkhutu* must be Grace Garvey. But then a hand reached down to lift the book, the hand of someone with very fair skin.

Isabel.

Adrien stared, dumbfounded, at the scintillating aura. Isabel was pregnant. With a gifted child. A son.

But *she* wasn't gifted, which meant there was only one way for her to have conceived this child.

"*Je n'y crois pas,*" he whispered.

Adrien entered the castle through the door in the middle of the east range and prowled around until he located Elic in the billiards room. The dusios was standing at the massive, Victorian-era pool table, his back to the door, watching Lili set up a shot while Tony Bennett sang "It Had to Be You" over the speakers built into the walls. Inigo sat in the corner, one hand raising his ubiquitous tequila bottle to his mouth, the other thumb-texting a rapid-fire message on his cell phone.

Looking up as Adrien stalked gimpily into the room, Inigo said in English—he loved English—"Hey, Morel, heard about the foot. Holy shit, look at you. Is it Casual Friday, or what?"

Elic, turning to check out Adrien's atypically grubby attire, smiled and said, "Hey, I remember that T-shirt. You used to wear it when—"

"I just saw Isabel," Adrien said.

He must have looked and sounded as *furieux* as he felt, because Elic paused in the act of chalking his cue, his expression wary and also a little surprised—as well he might. Not only was it incumbent upon a *gardien* to address the Follets in his care with the utmost deference, but Adrien had no closer friend at Grotte Cachée than Elic, regardless that he was a god and Adrien a mere druid.

Lili and Inigo glanced at each other as Inigo rose from his chair.

Elic said, "Adrien, I'm sorry if I'm supposed to know what you're talking about, but—"

"Why *her*?" Adrien asked as he advanced on Elic, wishing he wasn't hampered by the goddamned cast. "What the fuck were you thinking?"

Inigo snorted. "Dude. Mr. Clean said 'fuck.' "

"I think he's talking about the night before last," Lili told Elic softly.

"What on earth possessed you to choose Isabel?" Adrien demanded.

In a pacifying tone, as if he were trying to calm a temperamental child, Elic said, "Look, I realize she's the *administrateur*'s daughter, which under normal circumstances would put her off limits, but it's not like she's going to be taking over from him. And you may not know this, but she's been talking about how much she wants a child, so I thought why n—"

"Whose seed was it?" Adrien asked.

"Jason's, but it's no big deal," Elic said. "Nothing came of it."

"Elic, I just *saw* her," Adrien said, his voice rising unsteadily as he took another step forward. "She's pregnant with a gifted son."

"She *is*?" Elic said, his feigned bewilderment only fueling Adrien's ire.

"Awesome!" Inigo said. "Blondie gets knocked up, Elic gets him a little *arhkutu* action . . . Where's the downside?" he asked Adrien.

"How about me having to know that I wasn't the only man to sleep with her that night?" Adrien said.

After a moment of stunned silence, Inigo said, "Seriously? You and Blondie? That is so totally—"

"Inigo." Lili caught his eye and shook her head.

"But . . . you don't even like her," Elic said.

"I *love* her. If I could have given her a gifted child, don't you think I would have asked her to marry me years ago?"

"So you and Isabel . . ." Elic stared at Adrien a moment, then started chuckling.

"What's so fucking funny?" Adrien asked.

"And now she's carrying a gifted child, and of course it can't be yours, 'cause she's just a civilian." Elic shook his head, still laughing.

"Okay, shut the fuck up," Adrien said, but Elic's hilarity was apparently unquenchable.

So Adrien hauled back and punched him in the face.

Elic spun around, cracking his head on the pool table's side rail of inlaid rosewood as he fell to the floor.

"Holy *shit*!" exclaimed Inigo through a burst of laughter as he darted around the table, along with Lili, to come to Elic's aid. Elic appeared to be unconscious, but being a Follet, he'd be good as new within a few minutes, without even a headache to remind him that the druid charged with seeing to his welfare had just laid him out.

Adrien limped away to the ground-floor balcony off the library, where he smoked a Black Russian. He lit a second cigarette off the first, and smoked that. And then he climbed the stairwell in the southeast tower and walked down the hall to Emmett's apartment.

Not wanting to disturb Emmett in case he wasn't awake, Adrien didn't knock, but rather eased the door open and stepped inside as quietly as he could, given the cast. The room was dim, the only light source being a small lamp on the desk that held the *administrateur*'s medications and various medical paraphernalia. Through the open French door that let out onto the balcony, Adrien could see the bottom end of the chaise and Isabel's blanketed feet.

Emmett was, indeed, asleep in the hospital bed that had replaced his leather couch, dragging in slow, rattly breaths through his nasal cannula. Given how skilled Emmett was at keeping up appearances, it came as a shock to see him like this, bedridden with his hair all askew, a sallow film of skin clinging to the too-sharp bones of his face and hands. With most people, unless some special circumstance had boosted the energy they were emitting, as with Isabel's gifted pregnancy, it took a bit of concentration to get a clear vision of their aura. The healthier the individual, the less effort it took. Only through an intense mental strain did Emmett's darkly moribund aura become visible, an indication that death was imminent.

I will miss you, old friend.

In one bony, spotted hand, Emmett clutched a wadded-up handkerchief. Between his bed and the wall stood a hospital-style swing-out table laid out with a plastic cup and pitcher, the thickening powder, and Emmett's beloved Russian edition of *War and Peace*. The magazine rack on the floor next to his bed was stuffed with an ever-burgeoning cache of periodicals that appeared to have gone unread for weeks: *The Economist, Air Enthusiast, Ski, Vanity Fair, Ski & Board, The New Yorker, Country Life . . .*

Something moved under the bed. Darius was curled up under there on a bunched-up towel, yawning. He blinked his slitted eyes at Adrien, who raised his hand in greeting. Darius nodded, adjusted his position, and went back to sleep.

Adrien crossed to the balcony door. Isabel wasn't reading the book—it was actually too dark for that—but rather holding it to her chest as she gazed bleakly at nothing.

He said her name—whispered it, actually, so as not to disturb Emmett's sleep.

She turned and looked at him, her aura fluttering orangey-pink for a moment. "Adrien."

He held a finger to his lips and pointed toward Emmett.

She nodded, saying softly "If we keep our voices down, I don't think he'll hear us."

"Where's Chloe?" he asked as he stepped onto the balcony. "Taking a break?"

Isabel rolled her eyes. "She didn't show up when it was time for her shift to start, so Grace went to her room and found her sleeping off the day's copulatory antics. Grace dragged her out of bed and told her to shower and dress and get her butt over here pronto. Meanwhile, I'm holding down the fort."

"Chloe should have been sent packing the first day."

"Tell that to Dad. I'll never understand how a man who's so big on duty and responsibility can tolerate such an ass—idiot."

"How's he doing?" Adrien asked, knowing the answer to that, but wanting to find out if Isabel was still in denial about how much time her father had left.

She shook her head, started to say something, cleared her throat. "It won't be long. Only two days ago, he seemed to be doing so well. He was in such good spirits, hanging out with us in the Beckett Garden, talking and everything. But maybe he overdid it. He hasn't eaten a thing for the past two days, and he won't drink water except to take his pills, which he can barely choke down anymore. Yesterday he had trouble sitting up, and today he didn't even get out of bed. And you know how he hates being in that damn . . ." She sighed. ". . . in that darned hospital bed."

"I know. I'm so sorry, Isabel. But at least he seems fairly comfortable."

"It won't stay that way. I wish to God he'd let Grace put in an IV for diamorphine so he doesn't have to suffer at the end. He's such a control freak. He hates the idea of being in an opiated stupor, but *I* hate the idea of him struggling for air, which is what's going to start happening pretty soon. I can see it starting already."

"I'll talk to him."

"I'd appreciate that. He respects you so much." Taking him in thoughtfully, from his bed head to his cast, she said, "What happened?"

He said, "I broke three metatarsals kicking the stove yesterday morning."

She met his eyes, looked down and shook her head. "I'm sorry. About, you know . . . leaving like that. I tried to call you. Did you get my voice mails?"

"I've had the phone unplugged." Indicating the chaise, which was the only seating on the balcony aside from the chairs tucked under the café table, he said, "May I?"

"Oh. Of course." She pulled in her legs to make room for him.

He took a seat. "What is that you're reading?"

She smiled and showed him the cover; it was the Beckett notebook. "I can't put it down. It just blows me away."

"There are little excited yellow streaks in your aura," he said. "It's really beautiful."

She looked dubious. "My aura's violet, right? Yellow and purple are opposites on the color wheel. I've always thought they looked really gross together."

"It's not violet right now." Rubbing her foot through the afghan, he said, "Do you remember, in the *L'histoire Secrète,* when Brantigern's wife had a silvery aura?"

"Sure, after she became pregnant."

"Your aura is silver, Isabel."

She held his gaze unblinkingly.

He smiled.

She sat up straight. "Are you . . . are you saying . . . ?"

He nodded.

"Oh, my God." She covered her grin with her hand, her eyes enormous. "Oh, my God, really?"

"You're going to have a son."

"Are you serious? Oh, my God. That's . . . that's . . ."

He took her hand. "Marry me, Isabel."

She stared at him.

"I love you," he said. "I've never felt this way about anyone else, and I know I never will. We can live in the hunting lodge. I know you like it there. We'll find another *administrateur*, or you can take over, whatever you like. We can have as many or as few children as you—"

"Adrien, I . . . I love you, too. I've loved you since I was sixteen years old, but I can't marry you. God, how I wish I could, but—"

"You can."

"You need to marry a woman with the Gift so you can have a gifted child to succeed you as *gardien*."

"The child you're carrying is gifted, Isabel."

She shook her head, her brow furrowed. "That's not possible."

"I can see it very clearly in your aura," he said. "There are little sparks, like stars in a swirly, silvery fog. Your son has the Gift."

"But doesn't it take two gifted parents to have a gifted child? Obviously, *you're* gifted, but I'm—"

"It's not my child."

She looked bewildered, perhaps even a little offended. "Of course it is."

Taking her shoulders, he said, "I'll explain, but I want you to know that, as far as I'm concerned, this is a blessing in disguise. I get to marry you *and* have a child who can carry on the guardianship of the Follets. And I *will* consider him my child. It doesn't matter that he doesn't have Morel blood. None of that matters."

"Of course he has Morel blood. There's been nobody else, Adrien, not since last August. I wouldn't lie about—"

"I don't think you're lying. You just don't remember, because he must have used his *liggia spiall* on you, but—"

"*Liggia spiall?*" Isabel looked as if a lightbulb were switching on in her brain. She smiled slowly. "Oh. Of course. You think this is Elic's child."

"Well, Jason's DNA, but Elic's . . . Wait. You know?"

Laughing, she took his face in her hands and kissed him. "Wow, your beard is scratchy."

"Isabel, did Elic—"

"He tried. He came to my room with Lili. He did his hocus pocus, but it didn't work."

"What do you mean, it didn't work?"

She shrugged. "It didn't work. He touched my forehead and said . . . whatever it was he said, but it had no effect. He tried another spell, but that didn't work, either."

"At all?"

"Yeah, they thought it was weird, too. I asked them what it meant, but they just said some people are immune to their enchantment."

"*Mon dieu,*" he whispered, and then he started laughing. He grabbed her and kissed her, hard.

"Okay," she said breathlessly when they drew apart. "Mind bringing me up to speed?"

"The only people who are immune to the spells cast by Follets are those who are gifted," he said.

She shook her head, looking baffled. "I'm not gifted."

"Most gifted people don't realize it," he said. "Sometimes they even think they're going nuts. Have you ever noticed a little shimmer of light around someone's head, or had a dream that came true? Perhaps when you were going through puberty? That's often when giftedness comes to the fore."

She shook her head. "Well, I did used to fool around with a Ouija board with my girlfriends, like during slumber parties, and the what-do-you-call-it, the pointer thingie, seemed like it was moving on its own. I thought my friends were making it move, but when I did it alone, it still moved and answered questions. I thought it was my subconscious, but some of the things it said would happen really did happen, like me getting my first kiss in the toy department of Harrod's, which is pretty freakin' specific. And my parents getting divorced, and me moving to New York, and the name of the school I ended up at . . ."

"You have the Gift," Adrien said excitedly.

"But how . . . ? I mean, my mom has it, but Dad doesn't. Or maybe he does, and he just doesn't realize it?"

Adrien shook his head. "He's susceptible to enchantment. He's definitely not gifted."

"Then . . ." She looked toward the door to Emmett's sitting room. "Oh, my God. He's not . . . He's not really my . . . ?"

Adrien scratched his prickly chin and sighed.

Isabel ruminated on this for a minute. "Wow," she murmured, shaking her head. "Wow. Do you . . . You don't suppose he knows, do you?"

"I doubt it."

She groaned and lowered her head into her hands. He took her in his arms and held her.

"I want to tell him I'm pregnant," she said, "and that we're . . . You know, about us. I think that'll make him happy. But don't let it slip that the baby's gifted, 'cause then he'll put two and two together, and the one thing he doesn't need right now is bad news."

From within the sitting room came a dusty chuckle. "I'll be turning up my toes in fairly short order," Emmett said in a voice like the scraping of sandpaper. "Any news beats that."

Isabel mouthed, *Fuck*.

Adrien rose, handed her up from the chaise, and gestured her into the sitting room ahead of him.

"How much did you hear?" she asked her father as she took a seat next to his bed.

"Enough to confirm . . ." He paused to suck in a few strained breaths. ". . . my suspicions. Sit me up, would you?"

Adrien raised the head of the bed and rearranged Emmett's pillow.

Isabel said, "You suspected you weren't my . . . that someone else . . . ?"

He nodded.

"Why?" she asked. "Because of how Mom pounced on you when you got back to London after that weekend here?"

"That, and . . ." Emmett pressed the handkerchief to his mouth as his harsh breaths devolved into a coughing fit.

Adrien said, "This is too much of a strain for you. We should—"

"Blond hair . . ." he said. "Recessive gene, don't you know."

"Oh, yeah," she said. "I did wonder about that during the genetics part of Bio one-oh-one. Mom's red hair is a mutation, but her parents were fair, so she had fair-haired genes. So if she'd been married to a blond guy, this"—she indicated her corn silk hair—"would have made sense, but your hair is so dark, it's almost black."

"My tuition dollars at work," Emmett said.

"So, then, who . . . ?" Isabel shook her head, saying "It doesn't matter. I don't c—"

"He had the Gift, whoever he was," Emmett said, pausing to catch his breath. "And blond genes."

"So you were pretty sure I wasn't really your child," Isabel said, "and you just let her pretend . . . ?"

Regarding her with bemusement, Emmett said, "Of course you're my child—my only child. She never—" He coughed stridently. "Maddy, she never wanted more children after you. I'm so grateful for you. You've been the daughter of my heart. And now, you're to be a mother, eh?"

"And a wife," Adrien said, "as soon as it can be arranged."

Isabel asked whether blood tests were needed in France, or if they could get married right away. Adrien knew what she was getting at. Emmett had just a few days left, if that, and she wanted him to see them married.

Resting a hand on her shoulder, Adrien said, "I would marry you tomorrow if I could, but here in France, blood tests are the least of it. There's a mountain of paperwork to complete, and then we must wait at least thirty days after the posting of *les bans* before the wedding can take place."

"Oh." Isabel glanced away.

The reason for her dismay wasn't lost on Emmett. "The important thing," he told her, his voice nearly inaudible now, "is that I know you two will be together, and that you're giving me a grandson. You can't imagine . . ." He coughed into his handkerchief again. "You can't imagine what joy that brings me." His gaze fell on the Beckett notebook on her lap. "I *thought* you'd like that."

"I love it," she said. "It's brilliant—beautiful."

"Keep it," he said.

"What? No, I can't. It . . . it's far too valuable, too . . ."

"Take it—please. I want it to belong to someone who appreciates it."

Isabel looked down, nodded. A tear fell onto the book. She brushed it off, then wiped the spot dry with the hem of her shirt. "Thank you, Daddy." She let out a watery little laugh of embarrassment, shaking her head as if to say *Silly me, calling him that.*

And then she burst into tears.

"Isabel . . ." Adrien snatched a handful of tissues out of the box on the desk and handed them to her, rubbing her back. "*Mon coeur . . .*"

"I'm sorry, Dad," she choked out. "I'm sorry. I know you asked me not to c-cry around you, but—"

"Come here," said Emmett, holding his arms out.

She stared at him for about half a second, as if stunned that her undemonstrative father should make such a gesture, and then she rose and threw herself into his arms, sobbing.

"It's all right," he said, patting her back, his own eyes shimmering. "Shh, it's all right."

Adrien, thinking to step out into the hall so as to give them some privacy, was crossing to the door when it slammed open.

"Hi, guys," Chloe chirped as she sashayed into the room in her nurse's aide uniform, equipped for her shift with an armload of periodicals, a manicure kit, and her iPod. "Sorry about sleeping in. I've been bloody knackered lately. How are we feeling tonight, Emmett?"

"A bit knackered myself, actually," he said hoarsely as Isabel turned away to wipe her face. "Don't mean to be rude, but I wouldn't mind closing my eyes for a bit."

"Of course," said Adrien, who suspected that Emmett was having a hard time controlling his emotions, and didn't want to be seen shedding tears. He held the door open for Isabel, but she asked him to wait for a moment while she took Chloe out into the hall for a little chat.

Adrien, whose hearing was extraordinary even without the Gaulish spell he sometimes employed for that purpose, had no trouble listening in through the closed door. Isabel was telling Chloe not to call her father by his first name. "I know Grace has told you to call him Mr. Archer. Do it. He doesn't like inappropriate familiarity. And keep a close eye on him. Phone my room if there's any change. And don't you dare leave his side for a second. If you need a break, I'll take over. I don't mind being awakened . . ."

"Eavesdropping, *mon seigneur*?" Emmett asked with a grin. "Shame on you, putting your noble gifts to such an ignoble use. Isabel's reading the riot act to Florence Nightingale, I take it."

Upon inheriting the seigneury of Grotte Cachée as a teenager, Adrien had tried to get his new *administrateur* to call him by his first name, but Emmett had refused. Employing the correct form of address for one's superior, he'd argued, whether in the military or in one's professional life, was both a mark of respect and a way to avoid confusion about one's powers and duties.

"Your daughter is concerned about you," Adrien said as he came to stand by Emmett's bedside. "She wants to make sure you're properly cared for."

"I do hope she realizes there's nothing anyone can do at this point to forestall the inevitable."

"There are things that can be done to make you more comfortable," Adrien said. "I think it's a good idea to let Grace put in an intravenous line so that you can receive—"

"I will not depart this earth as a comatose *thing* hooked up to tubes and wires, with no say at all over my treatment, what drugs I'm given, what's done to me . . ." Emmett shook his head, taking gasping breaths with a strained expression.

"You would choose suffering over a peaceful departure simply to remain in control?" Adrien asked. "Emmett, please just consider it—for Isabel's sake if not for your own."

"I'm sor—" Emmett coughed weakly. "I'm sorry she's worrying. No need for it . . ." He closed his eyes, his lungs straining.

"Well . . . just think about what I've said, and remember you can always change your mind. We can talk again in the morning."

As Adrien turned to leave, Emmett said, *"Mon seigneur."*

"Yes?"

"Promise me you'll take good care of her."

Adrien extended his hand. Emmett took it.

"You have my word," Adrien said.

"You want me to put your bed down so you can sleep?" Chloe asked Emmett a few minutes later, a hopeful note in her voice. Without him to deal with, she could sit and read her fashion magazines and tabloids to her heart's content, perhaps even take a little snooze herself on the balcony chaise, as she was wont to do. She was lazy, dim-witted, and utterly indifferent to her professional responsibilities.

Lady Luck had been shining on him when the agency sent her.

"Actually, I was thinking I might read for a bit first. Would you mind?" he asked, gesturing for her to swing the table with his shabby old copy of *Voyna i mir* over his lap.

She did so, a hint of irritation souring that painstakingly made-up face, and switched on the bedside lamp.

"Oh, I almost forgot," he said, actually grateful for once that his voice was so feeble and short-winded. It would help to disguise this bald-faced lie. "Inigo was looking for you."

That got her attention. "He was? When?"

"About an hour ago. He wants you to take a break and meet him at the bath—" A barrage of coughs racked him, leaving him gulping air. "Bathhouse. Something about getting you in the pool and teaching you a new stroke. He wanted you to meet him there at . . . er, what time do you have?"

She checked her watch. "Ten till nine."

"In ten minutes, then."

Her smile of anticipation was short-lived. "I'm not supposed to take a break unless your daughter's here to watch over you, and it's a bit soon for me to be fetching her."

He rolled his eyes theatrically. "God, but I'm sick of being constantly surrounded, poked at, fussed over like an infant. What I wouldn't give for an hour to myself."

"Really?"

"All I want . . ." More bloody coughing. ". . . is to read for a few minutes, then lay my head down and fall asleep without being stared at. Go." He waved her away. "I'll be fine, I promise you. I shall relish the solitude."

She bit her lip with a contemplative expression, as if she were a bad actress whose stage direction read something like *Chloe thinks it over.* The playacting meant he had her; her "hesitation" was just for show. He'd expected a bit more of the real thing before she agreed to ditch her terminally ill charge for another shagging session with their friendly neighborhood satyr—not that he wasn't relieved to be spared the effort of talking her into it. Still . . .

Grace had hit the nail on the head when she'd called Chloe "a spoiled, selfish, little slag and a bloody fucking menace to her patients."

Chloe spent about fifteen more seconds feigning qualms about abandoning her post, and then she all but sprinted out the door.

His gaze on the massive old tome in front of him, Emmett tried to draw in a steadying breath, only to have his lungs expel it in a ragged coughing fit; they'd had enough, and were closing up shop. Brushing a fingertip along the edges of the pages, Emmett located the spot where they had been sealed together with a solution of white glue and water. He opened the book, revealing the rectangular compartment he'd excised out of the glued-together page block using the drafting knife and metal ruler he'd bought for the purpose back when he could still drive himself into town.

In the bottom of this secret compartment were three handwritten letters on folded notepaper, three matching envelopes, and his favorite Mont Blanc fountain pen. Mounded atop the letters, like M&Ms in a candy dish, were scores of multicolored pills.

For some time now, Emmett had been collecting the sedatives and powerful narcotics with which he'd been dosed—some of them, anyway, as many as he could manage to squirrel away without being seen. It had been easier before the superattentive Grace came into his life, but he still managed to filch a few pills every day. He'd gotten adept at pretending to pop one into his mouth, only to palm it or tuck it into his handkerchief during a feigned—or real—coughing fit. Lowering his hand, he would then slip the pill into the book on his lap—deliberately chosen to be of no interest to anyone else, lest someone be tempted to peek inside. Once people started hovering over him on a continual basis, he'd learned how to casually distract them while performing this sleight of hand.

He actually had continued taking the medication meant to stimulate his appetite, for all the good it did. He had no desire to eat; in fact, the thought of food actually repelled him. All part of nature's plan to shut down a used-up body as quickly and efficiently as possible—a system both sensible and compassionate, to Emmett's way of thinking, and one that had inspired his present course of action. Although he'd never been a proponent of euthanasia and still wasn't—it had always struck him as quite the slippery slope—if one was faced with the prospect of a lingering and unpleasant demise, while still having the wherewithal to speed things along, all that really remained was to straighten one's spine and do what had to be done.

The key to such a strategy was the part about having the

wherewithal. Emmett could feel exactly what was happening to his body. By this time tomorrow, he would quite possibly be in an agony of oxygen deprivation, gasping for air and unable to swallow—either that, or begging for the drugged stupor to which he'd promised himself he would never resort.

Some time ago, he'd realized there was a third alternative, and whereas he was gratified to be able to pull it off, it saddened him that Isabel had to be here at Grotte Cachée when it happened. He wished to God she'd listened to him and gone home after he was released from the hospital, but she hadn't, and now he had no choice but to proceed.

Don't think about it, he told himself. *You've had plenty of time for that. Just do it.*

He filled his cup with water and stirred in a spoonful of Thick-N. While he was waiting for it to work, he pulled out the three letters. After skimming each one to make sure there was nothing more he cared to add, Emmett slid them into their envelopes, sealed them, and addressed them respectively to Isabel, Adrien Morel, and the Follets as a group. He lined them up on the table, capped the Mont Blanc, then uncapped it and turned Isabel's envelope over. On the back, he wrote: *"Cutter": 16th–19th c. slang for a cutthroat or cutpurse. A foul-mouthed ruffian.*

Emmett reread that and smiled. He thought about it for a moment, then added:

"You have got to be kidding."

Emmett, his heart kicking, turned to find Darius, clad in jeans and an old Henley sweater, standing at the head of his bed. He'd forgotten about the ghostly gray cat who'd taken to lurking about these past few days.

"My *God*, man," Emmett gasped. "Are you trying to kill me?"

"Would that have been a problem?"

It felt good to laugh, although it sounded more like a tubercular wheeze, and engendered another bout of coughing.

"Didn't I once hear you and your daughter arguing about those things?" Darius asked, pointing to the freshly inked smiley face. "What did she call them?"

"Emoticons."

"You said they were infiltrating written language like a fungus, and that they were . . . How did you put it? 'Causing the inevitable decay of true linguistic expression.' Whereas she maintained that they were like little emotional snapshots that could sometimes convey certain pure, simple human feelings better than words."

"Perhaps," Emmett said, "she did, after all, have a point."

"You've been quietly industrious of late." Darius reached for the hollowed-out book with its particolored stash of pills.

Emmett instinctively shoved it out of his reach and, in doing so, knocked it onto the floor. "*Shit!*" he yelled as the pills scattered over the rug between the bed and the wall. He leaned over the side railing, straining to reach them.

"Easy." Darius grabbed Emmett by the shoulders and sat him upright.

"No, you don't understand."

"You think not?" Darius circled the bed, scooped up the pills, and replaced them in the secret compartment of the book. He closed it as he stood, but he did not return it to the table.

"Darius . . . old friend," Emmett said, his voice all the raspier from the exertion and yelling. "I don't have time for arguments and explanations. There's no telling how long Chloe will wait for Inigo before she gives up and comes back. If you truly understand why I'm doing this—"

"I do," said the djinni. "Better than you think."

"Then give me those pills. The white ones are lorazepam and the colored ones are diamorphine. Together, they should do the trick, but if I can't swallow them all, or if . . . if they don't quite do the job, finish it—I beg you. A pillow over the face, anything . . ."

"Is this really what you want?" Darius asked quietly.

With a caustic little laugh, Emmett said, "I *want* to live to be a hundred, but these scarred-up old lungs of mine have other plans."

Darius studied Emmett for a long, thoughtful moment. He crossed to the door, book in hand.

"No, don't," Emmett said as Darius reached for the doorknob. "Don't leave."

Darius held a finger to his lips as he eased the door open. He looked down the hall in either direction, shut the door, and locked it; then he shut the balcony door as well. Returning to the side of Emmett's bed, he opened the book, picked out a few of the white pills, and handed them over.

"Thank you—oh, God, thank you." *Just do it.* Emmett put the pills in his mouth and took a careful sip of the thickened water. His throat contracted as he tried to swallow.

"Easy," Darius said, making a stroking motion with his hand about an inch from Emmett's throat, which began to feel warm and relaxed. "Don't tense up. Don't worry about it. They'll go down."

They did—with surprising ease. Darius handed Emmett another few lorazepams, and he swallowed them, as well.

The cup slipped from his hand. Darius caught it and set it on the table, moving as if in slow motion. Emmett felt suddenly smashed, and little wonder, considering how much of the sedative he'd just dumped into a completely empty stomach.

"No," Emmett said thickly as Darius closed the book and set it on the desk. "Gimme the res' before I'm too sleepy. Thas' not enough to kill me."

"But it's enough to make sure you don't remember any of this tomorrow," Darius said as he held his hands over Emmett's chest.

"Oh, God," Hitch said when Grace called him the next morning to ask him to come up to Emmett's apartment. "Is he . . . Is this it?"

There came a pause, then a little chuckle. "No, nothing like that. He's actually having a rather good start to the day—remarkably good, considering how he was yesterday. He just wants to see you."

"Thank God," Hitch said. He knew the end was coming, and when it did, he'd man up and deal with it, but he wasn't anywhere near ready to say goodbye to his closest friend in the world.

Grace was stripping the sheets off the hospital bed when he arrived at Emmett's apartment a few minutes later. She greeted him with a cheerful "Morning, Hitch," then cocked her head toward the balcony and mouthed, *Check it out.*

Emmett was stretched out on the chaise longue, looking terribly Savile Row in a striped shirt and pink tie as he turned the pages of a magazine, the morning sun glinting off his polished wingtips. You'd never guess there was anything wrong were it not for the nasal cannula connected to the machine next to him.

Hitch shook his head, grinning. Wasn't it just like Emmett to rally like this at the end. He always was one for "stiffening one's back when the situation is most dire."

"Hitch, old man," Emmett called out as he took off his reading glasses, his voice surprisingly strong, if still a bit raw. "I've got a pot of American-style coffee out here with your name on it."

"So I take it you've been faking being sick just to get a little attention," Hitch said as he stepped onto the balcony, squinting against the vibrant sunshine. For Emmett to have as good a day as this with death so near was a blessing. Best to take a cue from him and just enjoy what might be their last visit together, without thinking about what tomorrow or the day after might bring.

Gesturing with his magazine toward the open, curtained French door, Emmett said, "Would you mind closing that?"

No sooner had Hitch done so than Emmett pulled off the cannula and draped it over the oxygen machine.

"Wait," Hitch said. "Should you be doing that? Don't you need the oxygen?"

"I really don't feel the need for it this morning. I don't have that cotton-wool feeling in my lungs. And I'm bloody sick of it, I can tell you—but of course Grace goes into a tizzy when I try to take it off." Smiling at Hitch's expression of concern, he said, "It's right here if I start turning blue. In the meantime, do help yourself to the coffee. I had it brought up just for you. And have a slice of bread with some of that fruit paste. It's an Auvergnat specialty, and delicious, but the bread is actually quite good all by itself. They bake it in a wood-fired oven—that's why it has that crust. I guarantee it's the best you've ever had. I just wolfed down half the loaf myself."

Hitch declined the bread, having just eaten his fill of smoked trout and blueberry tarts in the dining room. He pulled a chair out from the linen-draped table and poured himself a cup of coffee. "So, you look to be in fine fettle this morning."

"'Fine fettle?'" Emmett said. "Does anyone still say that?"

"I just did. Seriously, your color's good, you're in a great mood, you're eating like a horse. Maybe there really is something in the water."

"Of course there is," Emmett said nonchalantly. "Not that it's quite as simple as 'something in the water,' but this place . . ." He took a contemplative sip of tea. "There are complex electromagnetic forces at work that can bring about rather curious phenomena from time to time."

Could that explain what had happened to Hitch in that cave thirty-six years ago? Had it been a "curious phenomenon" brought about by "complex electromagnetic forces"? He wasn't exactly buying it, but neither could he dismiss it wholesale, given the lack of any other explanation.

"What is that you're reading?" Hitch grinned when Emmett held up the magazine, the cover of which featured a spectacular photograph of Mont Blanc in the setting—or was it rising?— sun. "*Ski & Board*? Itching to get back on the slopes, are you?"

"I woke up with skiing on the brain. Dreamt about our little heli-skiing adventure in the Himalayas last night."

"About the avalanche, you mean?"

Emmett nodded. "Lorazepam tends to give me lucid dreams, and I'd taken . . . a bit more than usual. It was actually a rather entertaining experience, incredibly vivid, felt absolutely real."

Hitch shuddered, recalling the horror of watching a mountain's worth of snow roar down on Emmett and Nawang as they slept in their tents. "An incredibly vivid nightmare, entertaining?"

"It should have been a nightmare, but it turned into one of those dreams that helps you sort through things that have been on your mind. You know, when your subconscious takes the seemingly random bits and pieces and fits them together in ways that wouldn't necessarily have occurred to you during your waking hours."

"I can't imagine what was going on in your subconscious to make you revisit something like that."

"I did revisit it, exactly as it really happened, but just a little . . . I want to say in slow motion, but that's not quite right. It happened calmly, almost peacefully—waking to that rolling thunder, with the tent vibrating, knowing what was happening, knowing there was no way to avoid it, but trying anyway, yelling for Nawang to wake up as I unzipped my bag, reminding myself of all those things they teach you about surviving avalanches—keep your mouth closed, try to swim up through the snow. I did those things, but with no hint of fear, just a sense of . . . alert curiosity, as if I were looking forward to the novel experience of being buried alive."

"Uh-huh. Remind me never to take lorazepam."

"I remember thinking, as I was being trundled down the mountain, 'What a jolly good turn of events. I get to relax and enjoy the ride this time, knowing that no harm will come to either of us, because Hitch will come along and save us. He'll know exactly where to dig.' "

Raising his cup, Hitch said, "All hail telescoping trekking poles."

"Yes, the trekking pole." Emmett frowned at the mountain on the cover of the magazine, absently tracing its craggy contours with a fingertip. "The bit I keep running over in my mind is after you've dug me out, and I'm so grateful to see the sun and breathe the air, but I'm gasping and shaking, and I collapse on the snow as you sprint over to where Nawang ended up, and dig him out." Looking up at Hitch, Emmett said, "You didn't use the pole to locate Nawang, you just picked a spot, stuck the shovel in, and started digging."

Hitch set his coffee cup down. "So the dream *wasn't* exactly like it really happened."

"Yes, it was," Emmett said quietly, evenly. "I will admit to being pretty out of it afterward. I barely remember the ambulance and the hospital. I was just grateful to be alive. So the details sort of . . . got lost in the shuffle, I suppose. Until last night."

"It was a dream, Emmett."

"No, I remember now. The dream made me remember. You didn't use your pole to find Nawang. You'd tossed it aside. It was right next to me while I was lying there trying to catch my breath. How did you know where to dig, Hitch?"

After all this time, Hitch had stopped expecting the question to come up. There was no explaining what had really happened on that mountain that morning, even to himself, except that forty-two years ago, he'd arrived in Vietnam a pretty normal guy, and two years later, he left with the old Stark Raving Radar tapping away in his skull. He didn't have an explanation, but he did have an answer. He'd thought it up while he was frantically assembling his avalanche shovel, picturing Emmett under three feet of snow.

"I saw you," he said in a matter-of-fact tone, just like he'd rehearsed it in his mind. "I saw where you ended up."

"How could that be? I mean, we were swept down by a bloody avalanche, and a huge one at that, half a mile long and a hundred yards wide at the base."

While Hitch was plumbing his mind for a response to a question he himself had no answer for, Emmett said, "I've been putting two and two together, and I think I know why you found us so easily. I think you have something we call 'the Gift.' "

"We?"

Emmett sipped his tea, and when he spoke, Hitch had the impression he was choosing his words carefully. "The subject

of giftedness is something in which *le seigneur* and I take a particular interest. What is meant by 'the Gift' is what you might
call psychic powers."

"You believe in that?"

"You don't? You're the one who's gifted."

"Uh, yeah, well . . ."

"Haven't you ever noticed anything unusual about yourself? A heightened sense, like hearing, or—"

"Hearing?"

"When did you first notice it?" Sick or no, the man was as
animated as Hitch had ever seen him.

"Emmett . . ." Hitch raised his hands as if to ward off this
unaccountable attack of new age woo-woo from the formerly
rational Emmett Archer, especially since he'd decided to aim it
at this particular subject.

Or maybe it wasn't so unaccountable. "*He's got too little oxygen in his system and too much carbon dioxide,*" Grace had said.

"Emmett . . ." Hitch shook his head. "Pal, we should really
talk about something else, 'cause—"

"When?"

Hitch picked up his coffee cup, set it down. "Hanoi, all
right? But it wasn't psychic anything, it was stress, mental
trauma. From being stuck all alone in that fucking little box. I
started imagining things—and hearing things."

"What things?"

On a sigh, Hitch said, "Tapping."

"Tapping?"

"You know, like on the walls between the cells, the black
boxes."

"But that was how the prisoners communicated. Isn't that
what you said? They never got to see or talk to one another, so
someone developed a tap code and taught it to someone else . . ."

"Right," Hitch said, "and there were two guys tapping to me, one on either side, and I tapped back, but . . . I didn't need the tapping. Or I thought I didn't need it, 'cause I started thinking . . ."

He rubbed his neck, thinking *Here goes four decades of managing to keep this shit under wraps.* But Emmett really was like a brother to him. And he really was dying. And he really wanted to know.

"I started thinking I could hear them, you know, those two other guys? Talking to themselves, moving around . . . Right through the walls, and they were pretty thick, let me tell you. But when I tried to talk to them, they couldn't hear me even when I yelled at the top of my lungs. And I could hear other guys in other cells beyond those two, more and more every day, all of them after a while. I could hear everything they did, and of course all the tapping. They were constantly tapping, it never fucking stopped. It was like being in a roomful of type-writers going rat-a-tat-tat, rat-a-tat-tat, all at the same time, just layers and layers of it."

"My God," Emmett said quietly. "What a bloody nightmare."

"It drove me insane. Or rather, I was already insane, and that's why I heard all that shit, and listening to it made me even more unhinged. A vicious circle of Crazy. And it didn't go away when I left Hanoi. I was still hearing things I wasn't supposed to hear, and whenever I did, there was always the tapping, too. That never went away."

"And of course you assumed it was a delusion. What else would you think?"

"Aural hallucinations, that's what my shrink called them."

"You saw a psychologist?" Emmett asked.

"A psychiatrist—in the hospital, when I was recovering. He was a good guy, too, smart, perceptive—I really liked him. He said the best thing was to try and . . . well, basically, keep myself firmly connected with the real world, the better to block out the unreal. He taught me to focus on the here and now by

284 • Louisa Burton

concentrating on my breathing. It's worked pretty well, for the most part."

"Look, Hitch, I know you respected that shrink, and I'm sure he was a good one, but believe me when I tell you that we here at Grotte Cachée are far more knowledgeable than he about this phenomenon. The black box didn't make you crazy. It sounds to me as if it forced your mind inward and brought your giftedness to the fore."

"Emmett . . ."

Sitting forward, Emmett said, "Think back to when you were in the black box, and you heard all those sounds, the tapping . . . Close your eyes and go back there. Relive it in your mind and try to remember whether it felt real to you, or like something your mind could have conjured up."

"*Relive* it?" On a bitter laugh, Hitch said, "I've spent four decades trying to block it out."

"Humor me," Emmett said. "I'm supposed to be on the verge of croaking."

Supposed to be? "Pretty cheesy tactic, pal."

But effective. Hitch closed his eyes and concentrated. It took an arduous mental effort to force himself back into that black-painted, windowless little tomb of a cell, but eventually he was there, hunkered down on the floor with his hands over his ears, hearing all the rest of them, the other guys locked up alone in their own black boxes, shuffling around in there, slurping up that rancid cabbage slop, shifting their chains . . .

"Hitch?"

. . . moaning, snoring, singing hymns and drinking songs, whispering prayers, muttering in their sleep . . . A fucking cacophony, and always, tangled under and through and over all the rest of it like snarls of typewriter ribbons, there was the tapping, great thrumming, prattling, incessant fucking torrents of it . . . *Tap tap tap tap tap.*

"Hitch—was it real?"

Tap tap tap tap tap tap tap tap tap . . .

"Was it—"

"*Yes.*" Hitch opened his eyes, took his hands off his ears. "Yes, goddammit, yes, it was real, it was fucking real, it was . . ." He bolted to his feet, turned and walked to the far end of the balcony, gripping the railing to make his hands stop shaking.

"I don't suppose you've ever had a precognitive dream," Emmett said.

Hitch shook his head. "Well, sometimes I would dream about, like, minor little stuff, like flights being canceled, or Katie getting another ear infection."

"Precognition is precognition," Emmett said, "no matter how mundane."

"I did—" His throat snagged. "I, um, I did dream that Lucinda had a heart attack. It was the night of our thirtieth wedding anniversary. And of course, two days later . . ."

His voice was quavering. *God, get a grip, Hitchens.* He sucked in a deep breath, let it out slowly.

He heard Emmett's chaise longue creak, heard his footsteps approaching from behind. To his absolute shock, because they never touched—not homophobia, just the kind of guys they were—Emmett patted him on the shoulder as he came to stand next to him at the railing.

"It's been six years," Hitch said in a thick, unsteady voice that should have embarrassed him but, strangely enough, didn't. "You'd think I'd have gotten over it by now."

"She was your soul mate," Emmett said. "So far as I can tell, you two appeared to have a preposterously happy marriage."

He nodded. "Except . . . Well, there were those early years, when she couldn't get pregnant—lots of tears then, I can tell you. But after we adopted Katie, it all changed. We really were preposterously happy."

"I must admit, I was a bit worried about you after you lost her."

"Yeah. Took me a while to come to grips."

"But you did. You lifted your chin and carried on. And now there's Karen. Two soul mates in one lifetime. Most men don't even get one."

Hitch thought about the fifteen years Emmett and Madeleine were together. They were pretty good years in an opposites-attract kind of way—until he inherited the *adminis-trateurship* of Grotte Cachée and she decided to pass on moving to a volcanic valley in the middle of Nowhere, France. In no time, she was back in New York with Isabel and married to an old boyfriend, Douglas Tilney, who'd gone from being a male model in his twenties to one of the biggest broadcasting tycoons in the world.

There'd been no one for Emmett after that, at least no one meaningful. Had he been lonely? He wouldn't be the type to bring it up in conversation.

Wait a minute. "Emmett, what the hell are you doing on your feet?"

"Standing."

"Aren't you supposed to be staying off your feet?"

"It's not so much that I'm supposed to. I simply haven't had much choice in the matter. As for auras?"

"What?" Hitch said, thrown by the non sequitur.

"Do you ever see halos of light around—"

"Oh. Auras." He rolled his eyes and leaned his elbows on the railing. "Guilty as charged. I mean, I don't see them all the time. Rarely, in fact."

"Because you've closed your mind off to them."

"I guess. But sometimes they ambush me."

Like when he was smoking with Madeleine in the courtyard that day after she'd done the number on Bernie and before they'd gone to see Morel. There was just the faintest blue glow all around her—almost the same blue as that dress.

And then there were the thoughts and memories that sometimes drifted into his mind from elsewhere—other people's thoughts, other people's memories . . .

"Jesus," Hitch whispered as it hit him. It had been real, all of it. All those years of thinking the insanity inside him was just lurking there in the dark corners of his psyche, waiting to wreak havoc with his mind unless he kept his guard up . . .

"Jesus."

"Hitch . . . Isabel has the Gift."

"Really?" Hitch turned to look at Emmett, but his friend, his hands braced on the railing, didn't avert his gaze from the courtyard.

Emmett gave a little cough, the first during this entire conversation; he really *was* having a good day. "One of the things we know about giftedness is that one is almost never born with it unless both parents are gifted."

"Then you and Madeleine are both . . . ?"

Still staring out into the courtyard, Emmett said, "Madeleine has the Gift. I do not."

It took a moment for the implications to start sorting themselves out. Hitch realized he was standing there with his mouth hanging open, but he couldn't seem to close it.

"I'd always suspected that Isabel was fathered by another man." Finally, Emmett straightened up and turned to look Hitch in the eye.

There came the muffled trill of a phone from somewhere on the other side of the courtyard. It started to ring again, but somebody picked up.

Emmett smiled. "I'm actually quite gratified to know that it was you. Your DNA is no doubt top drawer."

Hitch was reeling like he'd just gotten a liter of bourbon

pumped directly into his veins. "Isabel . . . ? She's my . . ." He slumped against the railing, pummeled by warring emotions, not the least being gratitude that Emmett—good old, unflappable, stiff-upper-lip Emmett—was making this easy on him.

Easier than he deserved.

Hitch said, "You have a right to be pissed off, you know."

"That would be so banal."

"Emmett . . . Oh, God. Listen, I want you to know why it happened, me and . . ." He couldn't even say her name. "And . . . and why I didn't tell you about it at the—"

"There's no need," Emmett said. "It was a long time ago, and I assume it happened that weekend, before Maddie and I were even involved. As Inigo says, 'No harm, no foul,' eh?"

"No, you deserve to know," Hitch said, "if only because I kept it a secret from you all these years."

Soberly Emmett said, "We all have our secrets, friend. There are things I've never told you about Grotte Cachée, about Elic and Lili and—"

"Emmett." Hitch pulled a chair out from the table for Emmett and another one for himself. "Will you please just sit down and listen?"

Ten

I SPRINTED THROUGH THE cave, along a sort of corridor that would have been black as hell if they hadn't installed electric lights, one every hundred feet or so.

About a quarter mile in, I came to something that made me stop and stare. Through a wide opening rimmed in ornate cave formations was a domed chamber on the back wall of which stood a huge, crude sculpture of a . . . Well, it had breasts, but male genitals, too. He/she wore rings of iron around the neck, ankles, and wrists, and was holding aloft a pair of cups. The androgynous figure—some kind of fertility symbol, probably—stood on a platform on which had been carved the word DUSIVÆSUS, with something indecipherable scratched over it.

A fertility symbol. Perfect. Was it real, or just more evidence that I was completely deranged?

I entered the chamber over a little bridge spanning the cave stream that flowed across its entrance, went up to the statue, and touched it. It felt rough. It felt real.

I sat on the base of the statue, leaning on my elbows while my heart slowed, wondering how a man could just crack like this all of a sudden, with no warning. Well, that was stupid. There'd been years of warning. Nothing happened in a vacuum.

I stretched out on the stone platform, closed my eyes, and watched a kaleidoscope of incredibly vivid images play out in my mind. Puffs of smoke on the ground far below my Phantom, exploding in another world, *puff puff puff* . . . fingers tapping on black-painted walls, *tap tap tap* . . . Dancing top hats singing about trying to make some girl, but they're on a losing streak, come back next week . . . Lucinda laughing her silly laugh behind a veil of patchouli-scented smoke . . . demons dancing around a bonfire . . .

I could actually feel the heat of the bonfire, that was how vivid the hallucination was. It stung my face, my scalp, filled my skull . . . And as I watched the naked girls silhouetted against the flames, twirling and laughing and beckoning to me, it pooled in my groin, pooled deep, so deep I actually started getting a little hard.

Me, hard?

I opened my eyes to find a man crouching over me, one hand hovering over my head, the other over my crotch.

"What the *fuck*?" I leapt up off the platform, heart slamming.

He was gone. There was no one there. There never had been.

"Oh, Jesus." I sank down onto the platform, my head in my hands, shaking. "Oh, fuck." I *was* crazy. There was no doubt about it now. Proof positive.

I shook my head, clawing through my hair. What now? A mental institution? Would I ever be normal again, or was this it?

"Hitch."

I looked up to find Madeleine crossing the little bridge, looking like an angel wearing a corona of sapphire light. Her hair seemed to radiate, it was so fantastically red; her skin glowed, too, with the luster of white marble.

"Listen to me," she said, crouching in front of me to take both of my hands in hers. "They told me what they did, Bernie and his cronies. They put a hit of windowpane in your beer, the one they gave me to bring to you."

"Windowpane? LSD? Are you kidding?" I slumped back against the statue, reeling with relief.

"Listen, I know you're feeling pretty funky," she said. "They told me you seemed kind of out of it, but it's just the acid. You're tripping. It'll be over in a few hours, and I'll stay with you till you're feeling okay again. Just remember it's only a drug. The things you're thinking and seeing aren't real. You're not crazy."

"No, I'm crazy, all right," I said with a grim little chuckle. "But at least I'm not crazy with a capital K."

Sitting next to me on the platform, she said, "You're not crazy at all, Hitch."

"There's an Air Force shrink who might disagree with you."

"What? You're kidding."

"No, I spent some time in the hospital after I got back from Hanoi, and it wasn't just my body that was messed up. I was kind of a basket case." *Tap tap tap tap tap.*

"But you seem so normal. Almost too normal. Even now, I'd never know you were tripping your teeth out."

"You should have seen me a few minutes ago. I think it's you being here, saying all the right things. I do have my demons, just like Bernie said, but most of the time, I can keep them under lock and key and act like nothing is wrong."

"We all have those demons. We're all putting on an act of one sort or another."

She stroked my back, and I remembered that day in eighth grade when she came home early from school with cramps from her period; it was *her* memory, not mine, but I remembered it all the same. She went up to her room, and as she was passing by her parents' bedroom door, she saw him hanging there, her dad, the one person in the world who really loved and understood her . . . She saw his twisted neck, his blackened face. Her head hit the floor, and that was the last thing she could recall for some time.

She said, "I think you really are an old soul, Hitch. I think that's why you're getting it together like this. It's because you have a deep well of wisdom to draw upon."

She leaned over and kissed my cheek.

I took her face in my hands and kissed her on the mouth, a long, deep kiss, thinking a woman's lips had never felt like this, so amazingly hot and soft, but of course I was tripping, but still . . .

A feeling uncoiled in my groin, a heaviness, a heat . . .

I kissed her harder, my heart hammering, thinking *This isn't possible.* But it was happening. I was getting hard. Was it the acid making it happen? Would it still be possible when the drug wore off?

It didn't matter. Permanent or temporary, it was a miracle as far as I was concerned.

I unlaced the front of Madeleine's dress and caressed her breasts. She unzipped me, freed my cock—a full-on, ironclad hard-on, my first in over three years.

I laughed through my groan of ecstasy as she stroked me.

"What's so funny?" she asked as she reached under her dress to pull her panties off.

"Nothing, I'm just . . . I don't know. Happy."

"Well, let's make you even happier."

She straddled my lap and positioned herself.

"Go slow," I said, gripping her hips. "I want to feel everything."

The thrill of penetration was even more acute than when I lost my virginity, not just because of my altered state, but because of my gratitude at being able to experience this again. As a horny nineteen-year-old, I'd assumed I would have a lifetime of sex ahead of me.

I savored every bit of it—her gasping breaths, her slippery heat. The sensation as she rode me, my cock sliding in and out of her, was heart-stopping. It was as if every nerve in my body were clustered in that one organ, quivering faster and faster as our thrusts grew sharp and frantic . . .

She came right before I did, her internal spasms igniting my own orgasm. I went off like a payload of cluster bombs, yelling till I was hoarse.

As we were holding each other, letting our hearts and lungs resume their normal rhythm, me still inside her, she said, "Oh, my God, we didn't use anything. I never do that."

"Lost in the moment," I said, but she looked sincerely anxious, and little wonder. Slipups like this impacted the woman a hell of a lot more than the man. Turning her chin so that she was looking me in the eye, I said, "I actually still believe in doing the right thing. If anything happens, it's your call. If you decide to have the baby, you'll have my support, my money, whatever you need. You'll have a wedding ring, too, if you want it—promise."

"Wow, you really are Mr. Honor and Duty. Good thing you don't have a girlfriend."

I pictured Lucinda in my mind, hoping to God I didn't have to follow through on that promise.

"Oh, my God," she said, fixing me with a keen gaze. "You do have a girlfriend."

I wasn't sure how to answer that. How about *Yeah, if she'll take me back after I tried my damnedest to burn her off?*

She kissed me. "You're a good man, Hitch. There aren't too many of them left out there."

As we were tidying ourselves up, I said, "Listen, um, one thing. Don't tell Emmett about this, okay?"

"Why would I tell him?" she asked as she shimmied into her panties.

"I mean, I don't want him to find out. You know he's got a thing for you, right?"

"Yeah, I kind of guessed that. He's sweet."

Sweet. Emmett, you poor bastard.

I said, "He's crazy about you. I mean, head over heels. I need you to promise, Madeleine. I mean, *really* promise that you'll never let it slip."

I held out my hand.

She looked at it as if she'd never been offered a handshake before, and maybe she hadn't. It didn't seem like the kind of thing her crowd would be into.

She took my hand and met my gaze squarely. "I promise."

Who did we encounter as we ducked out of the cave but Bernie and his minions standing right in front of us, passing a joint around, with everybody else still lazing around in bacchanalian euphoria.

Madeleine and I must not have tidied up as well as we'd thought, because he took one look at us and said, "Spreading them for the baby killer now, Maddy? I guess drippy little snatches like yours can't afford to be too particular."

I walked up to Bernie with my hand fisted, and slammed it into his face. His posse watched like a trio of baby birds as he hit the ground in front of them. He lay still for a second, and then he stirred, a whiny little whimper issuing from his bloodied nose.

I looked at his friends.

They stepped back in unison, as if they'd rehearsed the move.

Most everybody else in the bathhouse stood up and applauded. Some actually offered me a sharp salute.

"You see?" Madeleine said. "I told you he has no idea what grown-up men are about. He didn't see that coming."

"I knew that when I did it. I guess I should feel bad about that." I smiled at her. "But I don't."

It was past midnight before Emmett's car pulled up in front of the château. The library had a sort of terrace that looked out onto the front drive, so I sat there while I waited for him to return. The effects of the drug were much diminished, which I wouldn't have expected so soon from what Madeleine had told me, but I wasn't questioning it.

To tell Emmett, or not to tell him, that was the question I pondered as I sat there, smoking and thinking. Having secured Madeleine's promise of silence gave me the option to go either way. I didn't like to lie, and I most definitely didn't like to lie to a close friend who'd taken me under his wing and kept me from becoming a gibbering lunatic these past two years.

But telling him . . . I rehearsed it in my mind. *Emmett, I've got something to tell you. You know the girl you're wild for, the*

*one you can't stop talking about? The one you just told me yester-
day you've fallen in love with? Well, funny thing . . .*

It would be like sticking a knife in his chest and twisting it,
not something you wanted to do to a friend.

Of course, I could simply not bring it up, but that was tan-
tamount to lying. It'd be like that time when I was a kid and
my bully of an older cousin wanted night crawlers to fish with.
He's turning over stones in my yard and not having any luck at
all, and I could have rolled aside that fallen log over by the
back fence and shown him about a million of them. But I
didn't.

Emmett looked weary when he got out of his car and
handed the keys to the guard, his T-shirt rumpled, jeans
grimy—an unusual state of affairs for the crisply pleated flight
lieutenant. I waved to him, and in a few minutes, he joined me
on the terrace carrying a bottle of cognac and two snifters.

"Cheers." We clinked glasses. The cognac was warm and
nutty and felt pleasantly hot sliding down my throat.

"Sorry to have abandoned you," he said. "I had no idea it
would take so long to get the electricity sorted out over there. I
had to call in these people, but they made a complete hash of it,
so I called this other guy who didn't even show up. I don't want
to talk about it any more than you want to hear it. So, how did
you fare among the lotus-eaters?"

"I knocked Bernie Pease unconscious."

"Who?" Emmett asked as he lit a Dunhill.

"Starbuck."

"Well done." He raised his glass.

"With any luck, I broke his nose and it'll heal ugly."

"Anything else happen while I was gone?" he asked. "Not to
come off like some pathetic, lovesick prat, but did Madeleine
ask about me?"

I took a long swallow of cognac, and then another one, staring out into the night.

"Well, did she or—"

"No." I shook my head, still not looking at him. " 'Fraid not. Sorry, pal." It was the truth.

If you didn't look under the log.

August of This Year

"WHERE THE HECK *is* he?" demanded Isabel, her veil wrapped around her left arm while the other cradled a trailing bouquet of Auvergnat wildflowers. "What time is it? Shouldn't he be here by now?"

Her father held his watch close to his face, squinting. The gatehouse, from which they were to enter the courtyard when the processional began, was unlit, and the last of the twilight was rapidly waning; night fell fast in Grotte Cachée Valley.

"Perhaps there was traffic," Emmett said.

"*Traffic?* There's no freakin' traffic in Auvergne." She heard the shrillness in her voice, but at this point, she was beyond trying to come off as the cool and collected bride. "Where could he be?"

Pulling a cell phone from inside his elegantly tailored tuxedo coat, Emmett said, "I'll see if I can get a signal. These blasted mountains. Meanwhile, do calm down, my dear. *They're* relaxed," he said, nodding toward the courtyard, "and they've been waiting as long as you have."

"Yeah, but it's not their show."

While her father punched out the number, Isabel went to lurk in the shadows of the gatehouse's interior entrance, where she had a view of the castle courtyard. Even wrought up as she was, she had to smile at the effect of two dozen cherry trees twinkling with innumerable tiny white lights. It was breathtaking, a resplendent fairyland with the perfect background music—cool jazz, of course. Inigo, who had eagerly volunteered to be "Tunemeister," stood at a rented professional DJ table spinning the LPs that she and Adrien had chosen for the prewedding cocktail party and the ceremony itself—mostly jazz, with some jazzy rock and reggae thrown in to mix things up a little. Two gorgeous young things were hanging all over the hunky satyr, whose interpretation of black tie included a vintage knee-length frock coat and top hat, both of which he'd owned for over a century.

At the far end of the courtyard, in front of the imposing entrance to the great hall—even now being readied for the dinner reception—stood an arch fashioned of thousands of white roses lit from within. Facing it were white-draped chairs arranged in rows beneath the trees, most of them occupied by guests who did appear, as her father had said, to be taking the delay in stride.

Not all chose to wait in their seats, though. Some strolled about the courtyard enjoying their drinks and hors d'oeuvres, and there were quite a few clustered around the arch. Among the latter was the youngish mayor of a nearby medieval village, a longtime friend of Adrien's who'd been recruited to officiate. Elic, who was to serve as best man—and who looked even more godlike than usual all tuxed up—stood hand in hand with Lili, wearing a *lubushu* of gold-shot midnight blue silk and earrings that probably should have been sitting in a museum case somewhere. Even Darius was there, in his human form no less, standing somewhat apart from the rest to avoid being touched.

There were a handful of American friends and relatives, including Katie Hitchens, Isabel's de facto sister and maid of honor, and her fiancé. The most striking among them, given her coppery hair and her height—unnecessarily boosted with a pair of crystal-studded Blahnik stilettos—was Isabel's mother.

Madeleine Lamb Tilney took a sip of her martini—"ice-cold Cîroc in a pre-chilled glass with a drop of Lillet and four capers, please"—as she turned to look toward the gatehouse with a frown, proving that not all the guests were as blasé about the delay as Emmett would have it. She saw Isabel and made a *what's-the-holdup* face.

Isabel gave an exasperated shrug.

Her expression morphing into one of maternal concern, Madeleine snatched another martini off the tray of a passing waiter—anybody's guess who it had been intended for—and started up the courtyard's central aisle toward the gatehouse. She paused for a moment at the aisle seat occupied by her husband, leaning over to whisper something to him as she gestured toward Isabel.

He turned and looked in Isabel's direction, giving her a reassuring thumbs-up, which she acknowledged with a blown kiss. Doug Tilney was one of those men you would never recognize from his youthful photographs, like those in his old modeling portfolio, which held a place of honor on the living room coffee table of their Trump Tower duplex. The bitchin' bod that had once captivated the heart, or at least the hormones, of his socialite wife had been transmuted by steady exposure to Sardi's, Le Cirque, and gravity into its fat-suit doppelgänger. Too many San Tropez suntans had wreaked their dermatological havoc, and the hair was history. Doug was a great guy, and he treated Madeleine like a queen—as if she would have it any other way—but his sexual appeal had long since gone from pretty-boy to power-as-an-aphrodisiac.

Heads turned as Madeleine continued up the aisle toward Isabel, the skirt of her Naoki Takizawa evening dress billowing with each long stride, her gait so fluid that neither martini was at risk of losing a drop. When forced to reveal her age, Madeleine routinely subtracted a decade. Nevertheless, people had been known to say, "You're forty-six? You don't look a day over forty," to which she invariably replied, "Healthy living." Karen Hitchens's youthful appearance was from healthy living. Madeleine Tilney's owed more to a healthy bank account, which paid for the personal trainers, the posh spas and salons, and the occasional judicious nip or tuck.

Not that Isabel begrudged her mother these indulgences. For every dollar she spent "in the shop," as she put it, she spent hundreds, maybe thousands, on her charities. And, too, she'd been as good a mom as one could hope for. Aside from the occasional mother-daughter contretemps during her adolescence, usually over Madeleine's *so embarrassing* Tarot cards and crystal balls, they had enjoyed a relationship that was the envy of Isabel's friends.

That closeness was what had inspired Isabel to accept her mother's offer of her own wedding gown, a 1972 empire-waisted Christos confection of satin, Belgian lace, and seed pearls with dramatic Camelot sleeves. The only alteration it had required was five inches off the hem.

Madeleine thrust the purloined martini at Isabel as she entered the gatehouse. "The standard dose for a jittery bride is one of these half an hour before the ceremony, and another for every half hour it's delayed."

"And what's the standard dose for the bride's fetus?" Isabel asked.

"Oh!" She almost did spill it then, yanking it back. "God, that's right."

"I'll take it." Emmett plucked the glass from his ex-wife's

302 · Louisa Burton

hand as he flipped the phone shut, slipping it back into his jacket.

With Adrien's help, Isabel had gotten to where she could make out the occasional aura, if the emotion or condition that generated it was strong enough. Her mother's aura, especially visible in these dark surroundings, had been its usual sapphire when she joined them. Now, as she turned her attention to the husband she'd cut loose a little over two decades ago, it turned reddish with orange tips, like a low flame—a sure sign of intense attraction.

And why not? You didn't have to have an Electra complex to see that Dad was looking pretty babe-a-licious of late. Following what the doctors called his *"rétablissement miraculeux"* two months ago, he'd resumed his former life as if he'd never been sidelined by a presumably terminal illness, up to and including his daily runs and workouts. The only change was his hair, which had turned a gleaming silver that, ironically enough, made him look even more aristocratically handsome than before.

Raising his glass, Emmett said, "To our beautiful daughter."

Madeleine held his gaze as she touched her glass to his, her eyes awfully shiny all of a sudden. Isabel was pretty sure it was because of how "saintly" Emmett had been—that was how her mother had put it—when it all came out about her tricking him into marrying her to legitimize his best friend's baby.

"He could have raked me over the coals," she'd told Isabel, *"and I would have deserved it, but he didn't. He actually thanked me for what I did, because if I hadn't, he wouldn't have had you."* And then she had sobbed so long and so hard that her face was red and swollen for two days.

"So, did you get through to him?" Isabel asked her father.

"I did. *Bloody* good martini," he said, taking another sip. For some reason, he had taken to swearing a bit more than before his illness, while Isabel had scrubbed her mouth pretty much squeaky clean.

"So, where is he?" Madeleine asked.

"Less than a minute away."

"Oh, thank God," Isabel said.

Emmett said, "Not only was there that six-hour flight delay, but the alternator on the rental car gave out around the same time as their phone reception. They just turned onto the drive, though, and he got dressed in the car on the way, so there shouldn't be any further delays once he gets here. Maddie, if you could ask everyone to take their places . . . Oh, and if you wouldn't mind telling Inigo that I'll be cueing the processional in about five minutes . . . It's a hand signal. He knows what to look for."

Smiling, Madeleine said, "Still a pain-in-the-ass control freak, I see."

"Yes," he said.

Madeleine hesitated a moment, and then she put her arms around him and kissed him on the cheek and whispered something in his ear that made him smile. "Me, too," he said quietly, stroking her hair as she drew away.

"Here," said Madeleine, handing her drink to Emmett so that she could fluff Isabel's veil and position her bouquet. "I love you," she murmured as she kissed her daughter's forehead, a damp rustiness in her voice.

Madeleine turned to leave, spun back around to snatch her martini out of Emmett's hand, then glided back down the aisle to the rose arch, where she proceeded to relay Emmett's instructions.

Gravel crunched as a black Peugeot pulled up in front of the gatehouse. Hitch scrambled out of the backseat straightening his tux and saying "Sorry! God, what a day we've had. I'm so sorry to have made everybody wait. Sorry! Sorry!"

Emmett said, "All will be forgiven if you let me do something about that bow tie of yours. Looks *almost* as pathetic as my own first attempt at tying one. It was the same day I learned to tie my shoes, but I had more luck with them."

"First things first," Hitch said as he wrapped his arms around Isabel and gave her a good, long hug. "Listen, honey, I hope it didn't come off as presumptuous, me suggesting music for the processional. If you decided to go with something else, I really don't—"

"No, your idea rocks. It's perfect."

Karen and Jason offered hurried greetings while Emmett brought Hitch's bow tie up to his exacting standards, and then mother and son made their way to their seats.

The music, Miles Davis's "Stella by Starlight," faded into silence. There were some low murmurs from the guests, then nothing. It was that air of hushed expectation that did it. Suddenly, the magnitude of what she was about to do came washing over Isabel in a vertiginous wave.

Her father stroked her cheek, a gesture that, however small, would have stunned her a few months ago. "You okay?" he asked quietly.

His touch had grounded her. She smiled. "I'm fine."

She turned toward the courtyard, her gaze homing in on the members of the wedding party standing in their assigned places beneath and to either side of the rose arch: Katie, who despite being maid of honor, had chosen to wait by the arch rather than walk down the aisle solo, the mayor, Elic . . .

And Adrien. He looked almost impossibly handsome in his evening clothes, poised and grown-up as always, but there was something about him, a hint of nervous excitement.

She fixed her gaze, concentrating the way he'd taught her, and presently his aura came into view, almost as if she'd turned up the dimmer switch. The "root" of the glow, as Isabel thought of it, was his usual blue-green, but for the most part, it was pink, the kind of pink that signified one thing: LOVE.

Isabel caught Adrien's eye as she caught his, his gaze shifting from above her as if he'd been checking out her aura, too. If he had, she knew it would have been just as pink as his.

Holding his gaze, she bit her lip and widened her eyes. *Do you believe we're doing this?*

His smile was warm, reassuring. He nodded, as if he'd actually heard her unspoken question.

Who knows? Maybe he had.

Her father raised his hand, his signal to fire up the processional. Inigo lowered the needle on the album he'd cued up. He must have cranked up the volume, because when Jimmy Cliff started singing, "You Can Get It if You Really Want," they probably heard it all the way in Clermont-Ferrand.

Her dad took one arm.

Hitch took the other.

Showtime.

ABOUT THE AUTHOR

Louisa Burton, a lifelong devotee of Victorian erotica, mythology, and history, lives in upstate New York. Visit her website, www.louisaburton.com.

If you loved

Whispers of the Flesh,

Don't miss the next
novel in the Hidden Grotto series,

In the Garden
of Sin

by *Louisa Burton*

*Coming from Bantam Books
in summer 2009*